(bought 2004)

The
MAKING
of JUNE

ANNIE WARD

The
MAKING
of JUNE

G.P. Putnam's Sons
New York

This is a work of fiction. Names, characters, places, and incidents either are the product of the author's imagination or are used fictitiously, and any resemblance to actual persons, living or dead, business establishments, events, or locales is entirely coincidental.

While the author has made every effort to provide accurate Internet addresses at the time of publication, neither the publisher nor the author assumes any responsibility for errors, or for changes that occur after publication.

G. P. Putnam's Sons
Publishers Since 1838
a member of
Penguin Putnam Inc.
375 Hudson Street
New York, NY 10014

The excerpt from *London Fields* by Martin Amis is used by permission of Sterling Lord Literistic, Inc.

Library of Congress Cataloging-in-Publication Data

Ward, Annie Nigh, date.
The making of June / by Annie Nigh Ward.
p. cm.
ISBN 0-399-14890-6
1. Americans—Bulgaria—Fiction. 2. Separated women—Fiction.
3. Bulgaria—Fiction.   I. Title.
PS3623.A73 M35   2002   2001048847
813'.6—dc21

Printed in the United States of America
1   3   5   7   9   10   8   6   4   2

This book is printed on acid-free paper. ∞

BOOK DESIGN BY JUDITH STAGNITTO ABBATE / ABBATE DESIGN

To my family,
for their unwavering love and encouragement

And to another family:
the incredible and crazy cast of characters
skulking around the Balkans in the past decade, who found each
other in magical Sofia. You know who you are, you know who
else was there, and we all remember just how it was.

AMERICA is beyond power: she acts as in a dream, as a face of God. America thought she was awake, brightly awake, but in reality she was sleeping, and deep dreaming: and she was all by herself. She wanted to be good, to be better—special. We all do. When you go insane, what happens? Wanting to be good and right: can this do it? Can love do it? Too much love, and all the wrong kind. Love unreturned, tantrum love, collapsing into hurt feelings. Feelings ripped and torn. Inconsolable America, cruelly stung, breathing deeply, and not coming out to play. Marriageably she slept, and dreamt, and thought she was awake.

MARTIN AMIS, *London Fields*

PART ONE

"The End of June"

[APRIL 1997]

1

Subject: Greek Island Getaway?
Date: Tue, 8 April 1997 20:07:17 -0800
From: James McKinnon <McKinnonJ@smnet.com>
To: June <jcarver@sof.cit>

Comrade June: Agent McKinnon accepts his mission, and will
follow your orders exactly. I will meet you at the ferry in
Athens with one bottle Jim Beam, one liter diet Coke, one
pack Marlboro Lights and a bag of 69 cent Taco Bell tacos.
As requested, I will be clad in nothing but an American flag
Speedo (are you *sure* about that one?) and will be carrying a
month's worth of *Variety* to ease your information deficit.

Seriously . . . email with more Santorini details. I can't
believe I'm going to see you. I am stunned at the prospect
of sharing a bottle of wine with you, looking at your face
in front of me rather than in my photos after so long. I
hope this means you have forgiven me for what I've done to
your life. I'm still sorry, but I'm not sorry too. This is
everything I've hoped for all these years. You're still my
best friend.

Love,

James

*A*T FIRST SHE WAS an adulteress only in her mind. The occasional forbidden fantasy, a momentary walk on the wild side of late-night cable when no one was around. Adulteress. It seemed such a beautiful word for a bad woman. Maybe it was profane to find beauty in those whispered vowels. If she said it slowly, the sounds passed provocatively between her lips, like the hiss of a snake. *Adulteresssss.*

Snakes and sin. Well, they do go together, she thought. In the biblical sense, certainly, although June didn't subscribe to that black-and-white, good-and-bad view much anymore. Did she really live up to the trashy-novel image of a whore? No money had changed hands. No fishnet stockings had been slowly rolled down to reveal crotchless panties, and no synthetic fabrics, battery-operated devices, or small animals had been employed. If there was one word to describe her, it must have been adulteress. Something sophisticated and historical and worthy of literature such as *Les liaisons dangereuse.* Ordinary wanton women were born that way. Adulteresses were created by Shakespearean actors with Southern accents and bedroom eyes, or foreign tycoons who whispered, "Zaharche, let me be your slave."

June walked down Boulevard Levski and wiped her nose with a tissue. I won't cry. I won't cry even though I have a few good reasons to let it go. I'm not going to be a weepy girl anymore. Instead I'm going to be a drunk girl, a sarcastic girl, a horny girl, a rambling girl. I'll be worse than a country-western song. I'll be dangerous or just in danger. I'll wear black to weddings and lie out in the sun without protection.

She would be the lady in red even though she was dressed in drab. Now that things had come to this, she couldn't believe that she and Ethan had ever joked about it. "I may be married but I'm not dead," is what they always said, each with an indulgent smile at the other. They had been beyond envy, between worlds, better than fidelity. "Fools," she said out loud. "We were fools."

TEN O'CLOCK ON a Thursday night and the streets were full. Men with wrinkled faces and stooped shoulders hawked rings of hard bread and rolled-up newspapers filled with sunflower seeds. Booksellers lined the sidewalks with foldout tables piled with Bulgarian translations of Jackie Collins and

John Grisham. Sweet corn dipped in salt water was sold from plastic tubs and metal cauldrons, and skinny women stood picking it from their teeth with long, painted nails. Exotic kids, really gorgeous despite poor dentistry and lank hair, stood around joking and drinking plastic cups of cola and orange Fanta, and chain-smoking Marlboro Reds. Techno music was everywhere, coming from the many black-market music booths selling pirated West European dance mixes. The street was like a party. A sad party thrown in the weary Balkans, attended by exquisite-looking people, their inherent glow dimmed by the grayness of faded hand-me-down clothes.

June bought some wine at a street kiosk and stopped walking when she reached the long plaza in front of the National Palace of Culture. The modern black glass building was built to be one of the glories of Sofia. At one time, Chavdar had told June, the Palace had been splendid. For years now though, there had been a water shortage, and the fountain in front was dry. The exposed pipes were brown with caked rust. A Mafia dispute had resulted in a bombing inside the underground disco, and there had never been enough money to make repairs. Exposed metal beams and wiring were still visible from the blast.

On the roof there was a terrace bar with an incredible view of the city, as far as the Sheraton Sofia, the Church of Sveta Nedelya, and the Banya Bashi Mosque. Beyond those landmarks was the northern range of Balkan Mountains, which stretched west into Macedonia, then north into Serbia, until finally meandering back into Romania. They made a beautiful backdrop to the low-lying city, but since the bombing, the riots, and the recent period of hyperinflation, no one was willing to pay with either their lives or their life savings just to sip lukewarm Zagorka beer with a view of the crumbling city. The terrace bar was now empty, and the bored waitress smoked cigarettes and ashed over the heads of those strolling below.

June walked past the lighted gambling games and outdoor cafes with their broken plastic chairs and loud music, to where the sidewalks and benches were dark but not deserted. Under a distant streetlight a boy did tricks on his bicycle, circling a woman dressed in a baggy sweater, skirt, and thick hiking socks, who danced alone in the middle of the walkway. While he did wheelies, she twirled with her eyes closed, moving like a crippled and blind ballerina.

June took all of this in as she pulled a corkscrew from her purse. A corkscrew in a pocketbook. Red wine in a picnic cup instead of crystal goblets.

With the first sip, she imagined her mother's disapproving "tsk tsk" and slight Southern accent: "June honey, with every drink you have, you're subtracting a month from your life and a year from your beauty."

JUNE DRAINED HER CUP of wine. The time to make the call was approaching. With this call June would end the game. It had gone on long enough.

Maybe at first she had been an adulteress only in her thoughts. In the end, however, she had fulfilled the physical requirement necessary to earn the title in truth. Little Jimmy McKinnon, the family friend from Texas. Despite numerous preadolescent slumber parties in which they had said whispered good-nights from twin beds, bathed in the glow of the *Endless Summer* palm-tree night-light that June refused to sleep without until she was eleven, the two had never ever even kissed. When Jimmy (now James, and now six-foot-two with brown eyes, brown hair, cowboy boots, and dimples) moved to Los Angeles to join the Los Feliz theater, they had become even closer—but never *that* close. Not until one night when Ethan had been in Cape Town seven weeks. One night when June hadn't received an e-mail or phone call for nine days, and when the flu, loneliness, and thoughts of Ethan's first serious girlfriend, a South African blond volleyball player named Ellie, were making the wait for him to return unbearable.

James had brought over some videos, a bag of Taco Bell soft tacos, and a bottle of whiskey to put in tea to soothe her throat. He'd propped up the pillow behind her back and told her she looked cute despite the red nose and rings under her eyes. "I know you're sick, but why are you crying, darlin'?"

"I'm worried about Ethan. Cape Town is dangerous. He said he'd call over the weekend. A week ago."

James hugged her. For a long time. He rubbed her back and got her another hot toddy. He had one himself. The rental-movie was a romance.

It didn't matter. There were no excuses. June knew that. She'd told Ethan everything. Standing on a Turkish carpet in a hotel room that stunk of sewage, she had admitted that single, fleeting betrayal to her husband. She'd apologized, pleaded, explained, and prayed, but to no avail. He'd left her, and for someone he'd already had his eye on. Oh, to hell with it! To hell, to hell to hell! It was a chant she might have actually enjoyed back in her silly cheerleading days.

Now the phone call she would make would take her away from the city where her husband lived with another woman, and would reunite her with her best friend who should have remained a friend—the only person who might make her feel better. Soon June would no longer be an adulteress, but a divorcée. Another exotic word. Rather nice, really, she told herself. The stuff of schoolboy fantasies. Single, all sexed up, and old enough to wear leopard print panties and look at least a little bit like Mrs. Robinson.

How did it happen? she asked herself. Had she not been ready for marriage? Claire had just killed herself, and life seemed short and joyless anyway. At twenty-two June had thought she was old enough to promise never to touch another. To promise to be true to Ethan. To be independent and supportive when he went away for months at a time to do research for his book. To be understanding even when he could not be found at the library, where he had promised he would be and where she'd had him paged from the fetal position on the floor of their apartment, the night her appendix burst. Even when he seemed as far away as Hong Kong though he was right there in the living room engrossed in CNN BizAsia, telling her to "shhhhh"—she'd thought, *I can make this work.*

When he'd asked her to leave her job and family to accompany him to a Third World Balkan post-Communist country where her pets and friends disappeared as systematically as new wars ignited—where her world was constructed out of concrete blocks, and no one would look her in the eye—she had said, "I will."

JUNE LOOKED DOWN and more than half the bottle of wine was gone. The park was a dark blur, swimming in the glow from falsely festive strings of lights hanging from trees above plastic tables at outdoor cafes. *How did it happen?* She had no answer. It just had.

A TEENAGE BOY and girl sat down next to June on the bench. They both had greasy hair and slightly slanted eyes with long dark lashes. Their skin was perfect and the girl wore no makeup. They lit cigarettes and glanced at June. It was the older Balkan people who looked worn out. These kids just looked gorgeous and poor.

June knew they had no money for schoolbooks or new shoes, much less an evening drink. She held out the wine bottle toward them. "Iskate li malko?"

The boy wordlessly took the bottle and swigged, and then the girl took her turn. In return, they offered June a cheap Bulgarian cigarette, which she accepted. "Thanks. I will tonight actually, even though I quit. Just one, because I'm celebrating. I'm celebrating because I'm going to Greece. I'm going away to sunny Greece and I'm going to buy a spaghetti-strap sundress and walk around with a rose clenched between my teeth."

The boy nodded and the girl crossed her legs impatiently. She wore a very short skirt and platform shoes.

"A festive dress. Short and swishy, like I wore back when I was in college. Before I got married."

— The boy glanced at the girl and raised an eyebrow.

"Back then I used to have a better figure. More meat on my bones. I was a teen beauty queen! Seriously, no joke. There was a time when I had, as Claire put it—a cute caboose." She laughed, her first real laugh in a long time. "That's right. Not small, mind you. Not bony. My friend James—he said it was an ass with attitude."

The boy smiled and his girlfriend gave him a dirty look. "One hundred dollars for sex," she said suddenly. It sounded like she'd said it before.

"What?"

"This husband around here? He waiting for you? You tell him one hundred dollars."

June was momentarily shocked into silence. "How come kids like you never speak any English when I'm asking directions?"

"Foreigners don't pay for directions. They pay for sex," said the boy.

"Oh," June said, cocking her head to one side and thinking about it. "That makes sense, I guess. A hundred dollars, though? That's kind of steep, isn't it? I mean, I may be a foreigner and everything, but I've lived here a year, and that's, like, more than a normal person's monthly salary."

"Okay, fifty." The girl stood up.

"Hold on," June said. "However delightful the prospect of putting my hepatitis A vaccination to use might be, I have to decline. I was just curious about the price. My husband, or my ex . . . well, actually my soon to be ex . . . Anyway, Ethan is a Locke-Fields scholar here writing a book on the transformation from Socialism to a market economy and I just thought he might be interested in your display of . . . well, I guess he would call it unbridled Capitalism."

"How long you have this husband?" asked the boy.

"Had. Past tense of the verb." June looked away. "Sorry. That's my language lessons talking."

The middle-aged woman in the baggy sweater and hiking socks was still dancing her ridiculous dance, singing to herself. They all watched in silence, smoking, the boy blowing rings.

Suddenly June reached out and touched the boy's hand. "Are you two in love?"

"K'vo?" The girl looked over with a questioning scowl.

"You know how to say 'one hundred dollars for sex' but not how to answer 'are you in love?' Come on. Love is very important. *Very* important."

"You want to tell us the difference between sex and love?"

"No. You'll find out. We all do."

"Then what?"

"Nothing. I just wish the people in this country would start wearing some brighter colors. It's so goddamn depressing here." Then June turned away from the kids so they couldn't see her eyes. The boy stood up and joined the girl, and they left June alone on the bench, smoking her cigarette and getting the rolling paper wet with the fingers she used to wipe away her tears.

Later, June lay in her bed and stared at the ceiling. She'd had too much to drink, and was floating. She flung her arms out to the sides of the bed, and the comforter became the magic carpet of her childhood imagination. It could take her anywhere, like the one in Grandmother Penny's attic, and like the one she and Ethan had bought on their trip to Turkey.

They'd had a horrible hotel room because they hadn't called ahead for reservations. June had tried to make the best of it. She bought flowers and lit candles so they could keep the lights off and not see the dirt on the sheets. Ethan burnt incense to take away the smell of the hole-in-the-floor toilet. They wanted to cover the floor with a carpet and then take it home with them as a keepsake.

Ethan, as the son of a diplomat, had played in the dirt of nearly every continent in his youth. He spoke French and Spanish fluently and could get by in a number of other languages. He had spoken enough Turkish to haggle with a merchant at the Grand Bazaar, and when he and June returned to the hotel room in Sultanamhet, Ethan unrolled their new carpet on the floor. He told June to sit down on the kilim of a hundred colors and close her eyes. "Remember you told me when you were a little girl, your Grandmother Penny would take you and Lilly for magic carpet rides in the attic?"

"And that during the ride she'd drink an entire bottle of sherry and hide from my grandfather when he tried to get her to come down."

"Yes, that too. Well, now we're going to play by the same rules. I'm going to take you on a magic carpet ride and describe to you everything that I see below us, but if you open your eyes the spell will be broken and we'll just be back in this crappy hole-in-the-wall hotel. And we definitely don't want that, do we?"

"We most certainly do not."

"Now, tell me where you want to go. Anywhere you want, my special girl. Money's no object, the sky is the limit. And don't say I never pamper you."

June's smile disappeared from her face.

"June? Your travel agent awaits your answer. Ah-ah! Don't break the spell!"

If she answered truthfully, she would have said, Back to Los Angeles, back to the Ikea futon in the Santa Monica apartment where James had said, "Sssh, sshhh, it's okay, darlin'," before that first and fatal kiss. Go back and take it away. Make it not happen. Erase it.

JUNE STARTED AWAKE and was, for a moment, surprised to find herself alone in the bed she used to share with Ethan, in their apartment in Sofia. Then she remembered. Just a few hours earlier James had said yes, tomorrow he would buy his ticket to Greece. Her husband was on the far side of the city just before the Turkish slums, on a narrow foldout cot with an inch-thin mattress, peacefully asleep in the arms of a twenty-two-year-old Bulgarian maid named Nevena.

I did it, June thought, realizing her eyes were open. I broke the spell.

2

Subject: WooHoo, Spring!
Date: Wed, 9 April 1997 14:36:19 -0800
From: <DD@netcal.com>
To: June Carver <jcarver@sof.cit>

Hey girl, it seems like you've been gone forever. Someone's
got a birthday coming up! How's it feel to be almost thirty
in the Third World? So, did you get to see the Oscars?
Didn't Madonna look awful? She needs more cardio and less
weight training. I'm still going to aerobic funk and I love
it. It really helps me to release my energy in such a positive way. Ever since the Vernal Equinox, it's been like sum-
mertime here, with the exception of the "areas of morning
low clouds and fog along the coast—otherwise mostly sunny."
Los Angeles!!☺

Anyway, I was inspired to buy a great new roller-blading
outfit. Blue and green shorts with big white flowers on the
matching sports bra. Write me back and tell me what's up
with Ethan and "the other woman." I'm so sorry, baby. Come
home and we'll eat sushi and go dancing and you'll feel
better.

Miss and love you, Dee

*T*O *ETHAN'S EYES* it was another beautiful morning in Sofia. The sky was clear, the winter had just turned into spring, and the view from Nevena's balcony was spectacular. By some strange twist of fate, the cramped one-room apartment in the center of the city had a balcony that faced south, and the buildings in that direction rose in such a harmonious way that you could see through the hanging laundry and television antennas to the peak of Vitosha Planina.

Ethan's shaggy blond hair glinted in the morning light. He took a sip of the Turkish coffee that Nevena had prepared for him. Vitosha was turning green in the unseasonably hot onset of spring, and behind it the sky was blue. He thought of the previous Saturday, when he and Nevena had gone hiking up to the peak. They'd taken the gondola from the bottom of the mountain halfway up to the ski lodge. The slope of the mountain was dotted with people from the city. Families picnicked, teenage girls lay out in bikinis that would have been forbidden by the moral watchdogs of the Communist regime, and children gathered wildflowers, raspberries, and strawberries.

He and Nevena had walked far beyond the picnic grounds. They traversed the mountainside and climbed to where the trees stopped growing. Where the oxygen grew thin, there was only sparse grass, strange bright flowers, and huge boulders. Nevena spread out a blanket. Her straight coffee-colored hair blew slightly in the breeze, and Ethan couldn't take his eyes off her coltish legs as she bent over to dig through the picnic supplies, wearing only shorts and a T-shirt.

Ethan had given Nevena money to buy things for a picnic, and she had provisions for a decadent afternoon lunch. They ate everything in her satchel: tomato and cucumber salad with white Bulgarian cheese, fresh-baked bread, spicy lukanka sausage, Black Sea caviar, plums and figs. When the food was gone, Ethan put his hand on Nevena's olive-skinned stomach and kissed her, tasting the salt she put on everything she ate. They made love on the blanket, rolling over onto the peeled fig skins, falling into shadows as the unstable clouds moved across the sky above.

ETHAN TURNED HIS back on the view of the mountain. Leaning against the balcony railing, he watched as Nevena folded the bed back into a sofa and started dressing for work. She wore street clothes to Roxanne's house, where she would change into her housecleaning dress. She sat on the couch and her hair fell over her face as she slipped on her shoes. Her dark eyes were sad, inconsolably sad. The set of her jaw and the slump of her shoulders conveyed pessimism. In these ways she was the quintessential Bulgarian, and it was his current mission to study Bulgarians, their economy, their politics and beliefs. Recently, though, he had forgotten his project and cared about nothing but discovering everything about Nevena, reading her like a book and memorizing her childhood stories as if they were history lessons. She was melancholy, intelligent but humble, sometimes passive and reliant. She was not stunning. Her body was thin, her hair was fine, and her face was somber and unglamorous. You couldn't say that she possessed anything resembling classic beauty, but Nevena's eyes were emotive, her lips were softly red, and the three small moles that dotted her face gave her a childish charm, like freckles. She had small hands and a soft voice, and at night she slept with her head on Ethan's shoulder and her hand over his heart.

Nevena walked toward him. "Ethan, I don't want to go," she said, slipping her arms around his waist and laying her head against his chest.

"Has Roxanne been giving you problems?"

Roxanne was June's friend, the first friend June had made after moving to Sofia. She was a writer, an American, and rich. She'd lived all over the world and her reason for settling in Sofia for the past five years had more to do with the city's central location between her two favorite lovers, one Greek, one Turkish, than anything else.

"She has stopped giving me bad looks. Ethan, you know what I want."

Ethan kissed Nevena's ear and rubbed the small of her back. "I've told you not to think about June. In your world she doesn't exist."

"You are my world. I'm afraid she will take you back from me," Nevena answered in her heavily accented English. She'd studied the language on her own since childhood, and after cleaning the homes of Brits and Americans for six years, she could speak almost fluently. Ethan found her mistakes adorable. "I wish she would go back to America."

"She'll go soon. I'm sure of it."

"Good," she said. Nevena kissed him deeply, then grabbed her purse and left, throwing one last come-hither look over her shoulder before closing the door.

Ethan enjoyed the silent aftermath of her theatrical exit for a few minutes, until he reached the grounds in the bottom of his coffee. Humming, he rinsed out his cup in the bathroom sink. Nevena had no kitchen, only a hot plate. He looked in the cracked mirror and couldn't help smiling. It felt good to be alive, in love, and living in squalor.

Ethan left Nevena's apartment building and walked five minutes down to the outdoor Zhenski Pazar, named the "Ladies Market" because of all the women who brought their goods in from the surrounding small towns to sell from the stands and sidewalks.

He threaded his way through the clothing stands filled with Turkish goods and pirated American brands. A toothless teenage boy whistled and danced while hawking a pile of LEVVI jeans and black-market compact discs. Ethan had gotten a younger cousin a high-school graduation gift at this market. The Rolex watch had cost him twelve bucks.

This was private enterprise. Families opened cafes in their living rooms with only two tables, and would serve espresso and fried bread to anyone they could entice inside. Pensioners would travel in from the villages on the bus to sell a small bag of tomatoes and a single bunch of parsley in the underpasses. For the first time, they could do whatever they wanted, and they were creative. They sold old Soviet caps and uniforms, homemade lace, antique Turkish heirlooms, cotton candy, and fortunes foretold by hamsters. So maybe some of the stuff was junk, Ethan thought, looking around. But what beautiful junk. What historical and hopeful junk.

On Boulevard Stambolijsky he caught his tram. It was so crowded that he was forced to hang from the door, but he liked his unobstructed view of the street. Girls in tight, crotch-length skirts flaunted themselves in front of the shops, and a couple of longhaired boys walked with skateboards tucked under their arms. They were on their way to catch the tram to the Monument to the Soviet Army. There the punk skateboarders convened to try out tricks, as well as stealthily deface the structure depicting Red Army soldiers protecting a peasant woman and child. The severe stone faces of the Russian guardians of Bulgarian conduct now stared placidly out over teenagers in jeans and sneakers hawking loogies on the sacred soil. Ethan took an immense amount of enjoyment in the irony.

Thirty minutes later, Ethan jumped off the tram in Darvenitsa, where he and June had an apartment. He crossed the tracks and walked toward the suburb of high-rise Block tenements, gray, identical, and somehow suicidal. Now, however, he appreciated the flowers on the dingy balconies and felt affection for the children making the best of the sunny morning by playing with scrap metal and rotting wooden two-by-fours. Against their parents' orders, a few clutched ratty kitchen towels and were engaged in a lively tug-of-war with the stray dogs who had taken over the Block garages. Ethan could find inspiration all over the city. It was brand-new and ancient, under construction and coming apart at the seams. It was Mafia bodyguards driving Ferraris down cobblestone alleys past peasants with donkey carts full of melons. Sofia was a miracle, and mostly because it was the home of Nevena Petkova.

So, it was really over with June. For the past year, Ethan had experienced doubt as to whether he could actually end their marriage. In the beginning he had wanted so much to forgive her, wanted so much to accept part of the blame, even though he was not accustomed to doing either. There had been a time when he was ready to say, "Perhaps I shouldn't have been so selfish," but his anger stopped him. The anger led him to Nevena, and there he stayed. In her bed, in her arms, in her world. Ethan had felt an overwhelming duty to Nevena. He loved her, and she needed him—in a way that June never had.

Ethan had never felt that June couldn't live without him. That she loved him, yes. But she was a survivor, and unlike Nevena, she would be fine on her own. Just look at what she had done—finding someone new not long after he had begun the affair with Nevena. And a Mafia Socialist, no less. A terrorism tycoon. He couldn't stand to think about it.

The only thought that bothered him even more was that of June going back to Los Angeles—packing up her books and spices, prints and photos, paints and favorite CDs—and taking everything that was HER away from HIM. It was painful. Of course June would be okay. She would be, after a while, fabulous. Ethan missed her and hated her at the same time. Above all, he wished that he could stop thinking about her. Yes, she should go back to America. Go away so he could forget her once and for all.

There was no doubt that he loved Nevena, but had he really stopped loving June? Nevena might be needy, but she wasn't stupid. Perhaps she was right to worry.

3

Subject: RE: WooHoo, Spring!
Date: Tue, 15 April 1997 14:36:19 -0800
From: June Carver <jcarver@sof.cit>
To: <DD@netcal.com>

Dee! How do you think it feels to be almost thirty in the
Third World? It feels AMAZING, JOYFUL, INSPIRING, and LIFE-
AFFIRMING! Sleeping alone on a foldout couch thrills me.
Strolling through the rat-infested park among the handhold-
ing couples makes me tingle with happiness. And no, I didn't
see the Oscars. I don't have a television. Don't take this
the wrong way, Dee Dee, but if you keep it up with the cute
roller-blading b.s., I am going to block sender.

You know I love you, but please, show some tact. You're from
the South, remember?

Love,

June

*N*EVENA GOT OFF her bus at Orlov Most, the bridge named for the predatory concrete eagle statues that stood like sentries on either end. It was one of the wealthiest parts of Sofia. In most of the Blocks, several generations shared one- and two-bedroom apartments with beds in the kitchen and mattresses on the living room floor and balcony. In this neighborhood, satellite dishes perched on rooftops and balconies, bringing CNN and the Western world into the living rooms of the well connected and well-to-do. Every gate and front door was plastered with bright stickers, declaring the premises insured by one of the city's top four Mafia protection agencies. Racketeering was common and understood and accepted. When Bulgarians talked about the corruption and power of the Mafia, they often sought comfort by referring to the history of the Mafia in the States. Just look at any one of the Scorsese films that could now be rented in the new Sofia video shops. The Mafia was a phase; a necessary evil that was inevitably present during the birth of a Capitalist economy, and like the Turks and the Communists, the thick necks with their fancy foreign cars and cell phones would eventually pass. For now, it was the Wild Wild East, with the bad guys in control.

Nevena let herself into the heavily secured apartment building and noticed that the alarm had already been turned off. Roxanne was up early. As she passed Roxanne's office, she heard fingers flying across a computer keyboard. They suddenly stopped. "What time is it?" called Roxanne.

"It is a quarter after, Roxanne. Sorry to be late. The bus, you know."

Roxanne didn't answer. After a second Nevena heard fingers resume tapping on the keyboard, and she hurried to put on her work clothes. She started her day by changing the cat litter and loading all of Roxanne's clothes into the laundry machine. There was always laundry to be done because Roxanne wore things once and then considered them dirty. Nevena had learned a lot about American excess from working for expatriates for so long, and she kept her mouth shut. Americans didn't like to be made to feel guilty for their behavior. They didn't like to have their wastefulness pointed out. Instead of confronting them, Nevena quietly took the stale crusts of bread out of the garbage and gave them to the stray dogs, and took it upon herself to take back the Americans' glass bottles for the deposit. Nevena also washed, dried, and reused the plastic bags used to carry produce home from the grocery stores. The plastic bags cost only a penny, but it added up, and Nevena could remember nights when a quarter would have saved her and her brother and sister from going to bed on an empty stomach.

NEVENA LOOKED UP from where she squatted next to the litter box. Roxanne was leaning in the doorway of the kitchen, smoking. Her jet-black hair was unruly, and she wore a silk robe and slippers. She looked like she hadn't been out of bed long, and like she hadn't slept well. There were circles under her red-rimmed eyes. Nevena walked to the sink. She wrung out the sponge, turned on the water, and started the dishes.

"So what kept you this morning, the bus? You sure you weren't dilly-dallying in bed with June's husband?" Roxanne flicked her cigarette ash on the floor. They both knew Nevena would clean it up later.

"I waited twenty minutes for the bus. There must have been a, you know, a catastropha, somewhere along the line."

"A catastrophe."

"Yes." Nevena gave all her attention to the soapy water in the sink.

Roxanne stood there for a second and then walked to the breakfast table and sat down. Nevena's back was to Roxanne and she closed her eyes and clenched her teeth. All she'd wanted to do was get her work done and leave. "Nevena," Roxanne started.

"Yes?"

"What's new?"

"Hmm?"

"With you. And Ethan. What's new?"

"Nothing."

"Come on. Let's talk. It's about time."

"It's not so comfortable time now." The quality of Nevena's English suffered when she was nervous.

"Well, sorry, but there's really no time like the present, and I'm in the mood to just jump right in. I don't want to be a bitch, but I've lived twice as long as you have and I've been married five times. I know a thing or two about men and love."

Nevena wanted to say, "That sounds to me like you know nothing about men or love," but she kept silent and scrubbed at curry burnt on the bottom of a frying pan.

"Ethan is married, Nevena. I'm not talking to you from a moral stand-point here. I've played the mistress a time or two and believe me, there's probably not a sin you could commit that would shock me." She got up and poured herself a glass of orange juice from the pitcher in the fridge. Nevena knew that it was heavily spiked with vodka. "June and Ethan might last and they might not, but honey, a married man is not the quick and easy route to an American green card. If you want a ticket to the States, you need to find yourself someone who is available. I'm talking to you as a friend here."

Nevena's hands froze under the running water.

Roxanne sat back down at the breakfast table with her screwdriver. "I could introduce you to Jerry, remember him? He was the man who was here the other night with the Jensen couple. Balding but not bad yet. He's a diplomat from Ohio and he's single. Granted, he's not much to look at but that makes him an easier catch. Now—"

Nevena turned around to face Roxanne, her hands dripping, held away from her body. Her dark eyes were wide. "You think I just want to go to America?"

Roxanne gave a sassy shake of her head. "You're saying you don't want to go?"

Nevena looked up at the ceiling. "But you think that I am . . ." She was searching for the right English word. Not making love, not fucking, not prostituting. "You think that I . . . that me . . . and Ethan . . ."

"Look, Nevena," Roxanne said, standing up. "I'm not making any judgments. It's completely understandable. Middle-aged, overweight American diplomats in underdeveloped countries all over the world come home with beautiful young brides. Lots of frumpy old government spinsters bring home hunks. Life is short, take what you can, that's what I say. But you, honey, you're gold mining in a sand trap. Regardless of how June decides to handle things, Ethan's not going to be free for a while. I don't think he's worth the risk or the wait."

Roxanne arched an eyebrow and gave Nevena a knowing smile. "Hey girl, if you're going to sell it, you want to make sure you're dealing with a real investor. Men go back to their wives all the time, sugar. Wives who aren't half as beautiful and smart as June." Roxanne walked out of the kitchen toward her office. After a second, she peeked her head back in the door. "Come to think of it, Nevie, there might even be another option. I still have that friend from the American embassy I told you about a long time ago. Let me talk to him and see if there's anything he can do. I hope you understand that I'm just trying to help."

"Of course."

"Okay then. Back to work. For both of us."

Nevena waited until she heard the door to Roxanne's office close. Then she wiped her hands on the dish towel and placed them over her mouth. She sat down at the breakfast table and covered her eyes.

Roxanne's suggestion that Ethan might go back to June hurt. That was Nevena's secret fear: that Ethan would desert the quiet and often sullen un-educated mistress for the creative and well-schooled American wife with the friendly smile and shiny hair. What was worse was the insinuation that she was exchanging her body for a visa. This would have hurt Nevena's pride un-der any circumstances, but the fact that she had been raised Muslim made it unbearably offensive. Until she was eleven, Nevena had lived in a small vil-lage in the Rhodope mountains just northwest of the Turkish border. Her earliest memories were of the elderly, stooped women of her town hiking up the stony hillside paths with gnarled wooden walking canes, completely cloaked in hijab that exposed only their faces and fingers. Muslim women were sacred, not even to be looked at in lust.

Even if Roxanne had known that Nevena was raised Muslim she proba-bly wouldn't have understood the impact of her words. But Roxanne didn't know. Nevena was not a Turkish name, not a Muslim name. Neither were Boryana or Georgi, the names of her younger brother and sister. She did not practice Islam and she did not read the Koran or cover her hair with a scarf.

No one could have known unless she had told them, and why would she tell anyone? She had no desire to dramatize the night when she was eleven and the Party soldiers had come to her village. If anything, she wanted to for-get the image of her father answering the door at three in the morning, and squinting at the document thrust in his face by soldiers from Todor Zhivkov's Army. Mehmed didn't have his reading glasses and they wouldn't let him go get them. "Just sign," they had said.

Nevena, who was then called Nashe by her family and friends in the vil-lage, had watched from the upstairs loft where she slept with her sister, who was only eight. The soldiers shouted things at her father, using phrases like "national unification" and "for the good of the Party." The term used more recently in the media was "ethnic cleansing." They told her father they were going to give him back what the Turks, the Ottoman conquerors, had stolen from his family hundreds of years before: the right to a Bulgarian name and true Bulgarian nationality. They dragged Nevena's mother out of her bed and made her stand before them, humiliated with her hair loose. They told her that they were liberating her from the oppression of Islam. She could show her face and hair to the world. Her daughters would each have an education and career opportunities.

Mehmed had shaken his head. Taking his frightened wife into the curve of his arm, he told them that his women were well treated and educated. He refused to sign the document; refused, at middle age, to change his name in a split second by flashlight at the request of a brigade of filthy-mouthed teenage Communist soldiers.

It was at that moment that one of the soldiers, the biggest one with the most angular jaw and the grayest eyes, chanced to look up into the loft. His cold gaze fell on Nevena and changed. She was peeking over the wooden ledge, her long brown hair loose and tousled from sleep. The beam from his flashlight played over her big eyes and red lips. It dropped lower, to where her white nightshirt hung open at the throat because she was on her hands and knees. The soldier used his rifle to shove her father out of the door, and pushed his way inside, followed by four others. Mehmed shouted, enraged that the soldiers dared to enter his house, and then he turned and saw what they saw: the sleeping quarters of his children, and the face of his oldest daughter retreating back into the shadows. Mehmed turned bright red and with outstretched arms threw himself against the soldier with the square face. His words were choked in his throat, "Nehdeh! Nehdeh! Do not!"

Nevena remembered nothing after that moment, until the following afternoon when she awoke in a neighbor's bed, cotton pads between her legs to soak up the blood. The neighbor woman tended her with trembling fingers and a frightened face. Instead of Nashe, she called her Nevena. Over and over again she repeated this name. How do you feel, Nevena? Does it hurt, Nevena? She woke from a nightmare to find that she was a completely different person, with no parents and a home burnt to the ground. The country awoke with thousands less in their Muslim minority. Nevena was her new name. Wasn't it a beautiful Bulgarian name?

At some point much later it was explained to Nevena that her parents had been traitors to the State. After abandoning their children, they had attempted to escape into Turkey in the middle of the night. When detained by the border patrol, Mehmed had gone crazy and attacked a soldier. A fight ensued, and Nevena's mother became involved. It was all very vague and yet all very standard. Needless to say, the hysterical Pomak couple had been killed in the struggle with the border patrol. At eleven, even at that young age when it is normal to believe everything adults say, Nevena knew this story was a lie. Not that her parents wouldn't fight, and not that they wouldn't flee—but they would never leave their children behind.

Nevena had never once said out loud that she had been told lies. In fact, she never talked about that night or the ensuing months at all. Why would she have told anyone this story when it was so impossible to believe? It wasn't until after the "Great Change" that the "Bulgarization of the Turks," as the event came to be called, was publicly acknowledged. It was only recently that some people had begun to raise questions about Todor Zhivkov's flailing attempt to maintain power and preempt the escalation of ethnic conflict that was brewing dangerously in the former Yugoslavia—a conflict that would eventually lead to religious wars and bring American troops to Balkan soil. Zhivkov's plan had been to force a national rebirth through the ethnic cleansing campaign he so gloriously named "vazroditelen protses," or "the regeneration process."

Ethan had once asked Nevena why she hadn't ever taken her old name back, after the Change. "What change?" she had wanted to demand, but she knew it was useless to argue. For all his studies, all his interviews, all his figures and photos and history books, there was much Ethan didn't understand. The Turks had ruled and oppressed the Balkans for five hundred years. They tore down Christian cathedrals and replaced them with mosques. They took over the land and made serfs of the people. Every few years, emissaries from Istanbul had ridden through Bulgaria and the former Yugoslavia and taken away the best children to serve as soldiers and harem girls for the Sultan. The Balkans were completely conquered until the Russians liberated them, and then look into what hands they were delivered!

How could you understand unless you were born here, thought Nevena, the depth of hatred and the desire for revenge? Ethan was American, and so had a great capacity for indignation, forgiveness, and a firm belief in the powers of individual action. The Balkan people were not like that. They had failed, they had faltered, and they had been mistreated, lied to, robbed from, and forgotten. Outrage was for people who thought they could make a difference. Victimization was a word tossed about by those who weren't mortally terrified of becoming a victim yet again. Why didn't she change her name back? What good would it do? And despite what they said, people would think of her differently. Upon hearing her name they would instantly classify her as either the descendant of one of the infidels who stole the Bulgarian Renaissance, or a Pomak, an ethnic Bulgarian whose ancestors had, during the occupation, forsaken their true religion.

Americans, with their smug pride, smiling president, healthy economy, bill of rights, and history of success, might wonder why she didn't honor her parents' memory by resurrecting their name. An American wouldn't understand that the same Party soldiers who killed her parents were now older, and had even more power. They went by another name, wore a different uniform, and had sworn to a change of ideology, but inside they were the same. Ethan would never quite understand that Nashe was a girl from a small village who lived in the same building with the family goats and was raped by five men before being turned over to the short-lived care of her neighbor. Those soldiers had robbed a little girl of her parents, her name, her religion, and her virginity, but on that same night another girl had been born. Her name was Nevena, and she was new. She could study English and dream of leaving the country where her parents had been murdered. She could move to the capital and work for the rich and provide for her younger siblings. All this she could do. What she could not do was get rid of the feeling that those soldiers had ruined her, that they had turned her into something she never ever could have been if her Muslim parents had lived. She was a married man's mistress. She was what Roxanne had made her feel like with those careless words.

Nevena held her stomach and rocked back and forth, picturing her little sister, who had disappeared nearly a year before. The last time she'd seen Boryana, the girl was crying, escaping from a crowd of teenagers outside the National Library. She and Nevena had been sitting on the steps, looking at a book on Ottoman architecture, testing out a few of the words they remembered from their childhood. Nevena had never been able to forget the anger in the boys' voices. She could still see their distorted screaming faces, and their collective sneer of disgust. Boryana hadn't been able to take it. She ran, and as Nevena yelled for her to wait, to come back, the group of teenagers closed in on her and circled, fingers pointing, spitting, that she was nothing but a dirty . . . Turkish . . . whore.

4

Subject: It's okay
Date: Fri, 22 Apr 97 18:14:41 PST
From: James McKinnon <McKinnonJ@smnet.com>
To: June <jcarver@sof.cit>

June, hey darlin'. Of course I'm not missing any big auditions for this vacation. Everything's under control. We start Reiko's interpretation of *Cat on a Hot Tin Roof* when I get back. Maybe you'll be back in Los Angeles to see me on stage in my sweaty white T-shirt yelling my head off like a complete fool. (This could be more humiliating than that postmodern Macbeth you came to see me perform back in Austin—on second hand maybe you should stay far far away.)

Anyway, listen. I totally understand. I don't have any expectations. This is a difficult time for you and I am coming there to be with you as a friend, as the friend I always have been—despite some hurdles. You don't need to worry about what I am thinking. I am an adult (well, most of the time) and I can handle whatever situation you decide to throw at me. Okay?

I saw your sister at the Farmers Market two days ago. She's got a new boyfriend—a nice guy. I think you'd like him. We were talking about how much we wish you would come home. For good.

Miss you, honey.

James

THE CELL PHONE vibrated against his chest, and Chavdar Kozhuharov flinched. It could be her. His heart thumped and he fumbled stupidly for the phone in his suit pocket. Standing at the corner of Bulevard Vitosha and Patriarch Evtimii, the noise from taxis and stereos and shouting people was deafening. "Alo?" he yelled into the phone, placing a hand over his opposite ear. "Alo? Chuvate li? Kazhete!"

It was a bad connection and he could hear nothing but static. After a second he flipped the phone shut and stuck it back in his pocket. He had really grown to hate the damn thing. A couple of years before, it had been his favorite toy. Back then, mostly women called him. Now, it seemed like the calls were usually business: who was unhappy, who had been arrested, who had dropped out of sight. The women still called, but he no longer cared. There was only one personal call he wanted to take and it was the one call that no longer came.

Chavdar scowled, and charged out into the street against the light. A taxi blared its horn. Chavdar turned a cool gaze on the driver, and the taxi halted. Up close, Chavdar looked like he should be allowed to cross the street wherever and whenever he wanted. He was tall, dark, and angry. He looked like he owned not only the street, but also the whole city and everyone in it.

As he walked toward his office off Plaza Baba Nedelya he elicited looks from interested women and envious men. He wore a tailored Italian suit, and in his aloof but brooding and bored expression was the unmistakable confidence that comes with power. He had dark brown eyes touched with a hint of green, thick hair combed back behind his ears, and his shoulders were broad over a slim torso and long but muscular legs. There was something obscene about his beauty; the Roman nose and full lips were too perfect, and the line of his jaw was too sharp. He looked not only like a lady-killer, but like a man capable of murder. Recently Chavdar had begun to go a little wild.

The sidewalks were impossibly crowded, and yet he made physical contact with no one. People made way. These days, he always frowned on his way to work. IZTOK, Chavdar's security agency, had offices all over Sofia. The main office was not far from the Nevski Cathedral, with ten full-time bodyguards at the revolving glass door entrance at all times. There was a marble staircase in the lobby that led up to three floors of suites. The best offices, belonging to the most prominent "family" members, overlooked the monument to the celebrated Bulgarian liberation hero, Vasil Levski, who had devoted his life to the revolt against Ottoman rule. Now, the Sofia Mafia leaders enjoyed a prime view of the cherished monument. They often glanced at it, and more than likely felt a touch of patriotic pride as they went about their daily business of extorting money from the country's struggling working class.

Chavdar could feel eyes on him, but he was used to being stared at with hostility. The memory of the harsh winter revolution, with bread lines, bonfires, and protests in the snow outside the parliament, was still fresh. Hyperinflation and the shortage of gas, water, and electricity had bred fear and anger that could not be erased by a little nice spring weather. Chavdar, with his shiny shoes and tan skin, looked as if he'd spent the winter months comfortably housed in a Greek villa south of the border. In fact, he'd vacationed in Mykonos for just three weeks in January, and he only did that for June; lovely, hateful, ungrateful June.

Chavdar pulled his sunglasses down over his eyes to help distance himself from the sea of hatred in the streets. Behind the glasses he felt protected. He could be anybody. He didn't have to be a Sofia mutra. Instead, he could be a wealthy German in town looking to invest in one of the state corporations about to be privatized. Or maybe he was a film producer from France scouting out inexpensive shooting locations. That was what he'd always wanted to be, anyway—a film producer. The moneyman behind Scorsese or Tarantino or Besson. The moneyman behind the artists, the moneyman behind the tinted sunglasses. With his Western-style shades he was anonymous. No one could blame a stranger.

Chavdar hated to be blamed, and yet he understood the people's anger. He was an educated man, intelligent and aware. He knew, just as well as they did, that he had profited from their loss. When the Change came about, all the old rules had suddenly and shockingly ceased to exist, but no new system of law and order had been effectively implemented. The Balkans became a refuge for outlaws, con artists, and white-collar criminals. Banks were opened by groups of friends from the former Communist Party, using their connections. Time passed, and when people tried to close their accounts, they were asked to come back in a week—in a month—and finally just *"later. Come back later."*

Someone on the inside talked to the newspapers, and the headlines announced that several of the top banks had gone bankrupt. Everyone rushed to reclaim at least part of their life savings. Chaos ensued and the papers announced that ten Bulgarian banks had declared bankruptcy. Then fifteen, then thirty, and then nearly all. The money had, for all intents and purposes, vanished.

Of course, a few people knew where the money had gone. After its initial rest period in Swiss bank accounts, some of it had filtered back into the country and built discos, strip clubs, and casinos. Some of it had gone for jewelry and fur coats, and much of it had found its way into the pockets of law officials. In the Wild East there were no consequences for such criminality, not for the untouchables. It was just as it had been for the previous forty-five years, and the "Credit Millionaires" as the papers called them, went unnamed and unpunished. Foreign attorneys arrived en masse to help write laws to reign in the corruption, but the process was slow. Meanwhile, the same families controlled the money and the country, the same families sent their children to foreign universities, and instead of moving out of their mansions, the former Communist leaders were adding on new wings, digging swimming pools, and planning extravagant real estate purchases on the West Coast of the United States.

As for those who had lost everything, they were no longer naive enough to put their money in banks. They drilled holes in the walls of their homes, canned their leva in the same way that they canned their preserves, and hid it away. The banks failed and never reopened, for each and every Bulgarian family had become its own financial institution, with a jar bank secretly located and closely guarded in the relative security of their own homes.

Chavdar was not immune to guilt. He felt deeply, painfully sorry for the pensioners who had died over the course of the winter because they had disconnected their central heating for lack of leva to pay the bill, but he also was a realist. Bulgaria was not yet a Democracy. He wasn't sure what it was. It was like something unformed in the womb, its characteristics too blurred or perhaps even deformed for anyone to make a definitive statement about the nature of the creature that was growing and growing. It could be a monster, but Capitalism was monstrous, was it not? Every man for himself? Every woman and every child and every pensioner and every handicapped war veteran and mental patient? Was he to blame for the fact that life was now, just like among the animals, survival of the fittest? Of course not. People needed to learn. People needed to do as Chavdar had done and read the translation of Joseph Kirschner's *New York Times* best-seller, *The Art of Being Selfish*. These kinds of books had just recently found their way into the post-Communist country, and Chavdar was one of the first fans.

On the rare occasions that Chavdar was somehow drawn into a philosophical discussion of the economic crisis in Bulgaria, and the way the people had been exploited, he would not skirt the issue. Instead he would, in a low, steady, and confident voice, explain that his security company provided a very valuable service to the citizens. "It is a researched fact," Chavdar would explain, his eyes focused intently on the unlucky inquisitor, "that in developing countries, whether in Eastern Europe, Africa, or Asia, such security companies must, for a certain amount of time, assume the role of law enforcement. The Bulgarian police are ineffective. Look at them. They drive Russian Ladas! What criminal will they be able to chase down in a Lada?"

Chavdar would then shake his head contemptuously. "When someone's home is robbed, their privacy violated, can the police help? If their car is stolen, will the police come to the rescue? Of course not! The police are underpaid, lazy, and incompetent. But . . ." And at this point Chavdar would lean closer to his partner in conversation and raise his pointer finger. "But if you purchase security from my company, and put our sticker on your car or home or store, it is as if you have hired a policeman to guard it at all times. It is as if a great spotlight is trained on your property twenty-four hours a day. Criminals know what will happen to them if they are caught stealing from one of our clients." This would be followed by a cold, self-assured laugh. "And they are always caught, my friend. Our clients never forfeit their property. Never. That is our guarantee, and until the police become some kind of presence in this country, my security company is the only institution that enables people to sleep at night, with the assurance that their lives and belongings are protected."

After several years of such justification, Chavdar had convinced himself that while what he was doing was questionable at an ideological level, he had no choice, no better choice. His parents had joined the Party so that their son would have a decent education and they would have better occupations and a more comfortable home. His father had risen in the ranks and parlayed his intelligence and naturally conciliating nature into a fruitful career and rewarding life of comparable luxury. Chavdar was sure he would have a wife someday, and children. His fate was not so different from that of his parents. He could either rule or be ruled. He had chosen to rule, and he did so with a silent, terrifying strength.

CHAVDAR SOLEMNLY GREETED a few of his employees with a distracted wave as he headed down the hallway toward his office. Inside, reading a copy of the morning paper *24 Chasa,* was his assistant and head bodyguard, Stoyan Dimitrov. In Stoyan's fleshy hand was a small pile of sunflower seeds, and the ashtray was full of shells glistening with saliva. He looked up when Chavdar entered, spit on the floor, and slammed a fist down on the table. "Where have you been?" Chavdar had a close protection team of five men and was supposed to be flanked by two at all times. "Sasho and Rossen are waiting for you outside your house. What the hell do you think you're doing?"

Stoyan possessed none of the suave, intelligent good looks that made Chavdar so dangerously imperious. Dark, short, and thick in appearance, he looked much like Chavdar's other bodyguards, and all of them looked like what they were: Eastern European Mafia thugs.

Chavdar set down his briefcase and pulled out a paperback. The title was *Kak da Preodoleem Bezpokoistvoto y da ce Radvame na Zhivota,* and it was a translation of one of American self-help guru Dale Carnegie's guides to greater personal fulfillment. "I wanted some privacy. I walked to work, and you see, I am still alive. You should read some of these new books, Stoyan. They say walking improves concentration and relaxation. I think they are on to something."

Stoyan stood up, and his mesomorphic body gave the unsettling impression of being nearly as wide as it was tall. Like many of the bodyguards, he was a former wrestler, lacking common sense, but with an abundance of brutish cruelty. The people called these members of the Mafia the "big necks," and rumor had it that many of them had served, in a similar protective capacity, for the KGB. The people hated these cold-blooded guards even more than they hated the businessmen they protected, because these shifty-eyed cretins were not only rich, arrogant, and cold-blooded. They were, almost invariably, absolutely stupid.

Stoyan was smarter than most, and it made him more ambitious. His nature was incendiary: he was happiest when there was trouble, and if work was too calm, he would stir things up. Despite his cumbersome and intimidating physical dimensions, he had endless energy, an internal fire that he constantly stoked with heavily sugared shots of espresso. "Were you out walking this weekend, too? You should have been at Manev's funeral."

Chavdar shook his head gravely. "I know."

"His wife was insulted. It looks bad. It looks like you are hiding."

"Maybe I am. I need time to think."

"Now is the time to act. Not think."

Suddenly Chavdar looked up. "And what about you? Eh? Why aren't you acting? Get out of here and go find our missing money. Get out of here and go find that girl."

"I thought we had bigger problems."

"Those are my problems, and I'm managing with them. Apostolov is under control."

"How do you know?"

"I spoke to someone last night at the club."

"That's not good enough. When the Interior Ministry opens the rest of those files, we're going to have problems, Chavdar. We need some guarantees. We need to meet with Varezhdov, Zlatarov, and Ognev immediately and decide—"

Chavdar held up a hand to silence Stoyan. He rubbed the bridge of his nose, and then his forehead. "Just be quiet."

Stoyan stood awkwardly beside the desk, frustrated by all he wanted to say.

Chavdar flipped through the messages. "Did anyone call while you were here?"

"Yes. Many people. Many people who want to know what we are going to do this week when Bogomil—"

"I mean June. She didn't call?"

"No."

Chavdar sighed and sat down. He lowered his head and used his long fingers to push back his bangs. "I don't understand it."

"What?" Stoyan asked, exasperated. "What don't you understand?"

"How her feelings could change so quickly. I've been so good to her. One little fight, one instance of losing my temper, and she really doesn't want to ever see me again."

Stoyan took a deep breath. He knew he would have to talk about June before they could move on to any other topic. "When did you talk to her last?" he asked. His tone was as patronizing as allowable, considering that he was dealing with his employer.

"Oh . . ." Chavdar rubbed his chin. "Not since the night at the Tango when the money was stolen."

Stoyan exploded. "The night you said she ran away like a child? That night?"

"She was angry. And frightened. She's American. She shows her emotions, doesn't hide them and tell you what you want to hear. She behaves genuinely and impulsively. That is part of her appeal."

"Oh, I see, Chavdar. She is appealing because she insults the man who has done everything for her." Stoyan stood up and paced in front of Chavdar's desk. "You don't see what I see, Chavdar. I have known you for years. I have watched you take home many women, many lovely, sexy, Bulgarian girls. Respectful girls! Girls who worshiped you, who would have done anything to make you happy. And you are letting this American kuchka—"

Chavdar looked up sharply.

Stoyan raised a pacifying hand. "All right. Sorry. But you have let this woman get under your skin and cloud your judgment. She is attractive, granted. And when she wants to be charming she is quite alluring. But most of the time she is opinionated, independent, feminist, fierce—not normal! My God, Chavdar! Let this unhealthy obsession go! Leave it! Someday you will look back on this winter, this very long, cold winter, and realize that this American was nothing more than a nice warm woman, no different than all the rest."

Chavdar didn't answer. Of course Stoyan would call June opinionated and independent. Of course he wouldn't see the wild appeal of an untamed woman. Much of what Stoyan said was true. Chavdar had had his share of women: pliable, gentle, agreeable, soft, sweet women. They did worship the ground he walked on, and they would have done anything to make him happy. Many of them were educated, self-possessed, and confident while still accepting their role, and from excellent families. It was hard for Chavdar himself to understand why he couldn't settle down with one of these perfect women, so how could he explain it to Stoyan? June had forgiven him for being what he was, and he had been helpless against her mercy.

When he was with June, there were moments when he didn't feel like a serious Balkan businessman. She would puff on his cigars and tickle him in his ribs until he laughed uncontrollably. "Mercy, mercy—say mercy!" It was his favorite game.

He remembered nights when she pulled the waitress and the coat-check girl up to dance with her on the polished wooden bar at his club, shaking her hair like a video vixen. She had tried to pull Chavdar up too, and he had refused. He wished he could let down his guard, be someone else, be wild and good and free all at once. Being beside June was the closest he could get. Of course, there had been quiet times, peaceful moments when she would sit on his lap like a girl and tell him stories about movie stars and directors—who was a genius and who was a prima donna—and in between stories set in Southern California, she would kiss his nose, his eyelids, his cheeks, and finally his lips.

When her marriage was legally dissolved, he dreamed that she would loyally and faithfully give herself, heart, soul, and body, to him for the remainder of her life. She had played a pretty game; she had definitely led him on a merry chase. That was what women did and it was part of the fun. He'd had enough liaisons to appreciate the feminine art of being coy. But now that she had won him, truly won him, he wished she would stop. She must return his phone calls, she must, very soon, be back in his bed because he simply couldn't stomach her absence. Wild June, he thought, I have fallen in love with you and you will be tamed. I must be good enough, I must be good enough for you. You will love me too.

She would come around. Once business was under control he was sure that just as with everything else, his will with June would prevail.

CHAVDAR'S EYES LOOKED a little shiny, as if he had a fever. He massaged his temples for a moment and then put his hand on Stoyan's shoulder. "What I would like for you to do now is to go find June. Wherever she is, whatever she is doing, that is of no importance. When you have found her, please bring her to me. I am sure you can be very convincing."

Stoyan clenched his fists. The International Monetary Fund had just ordered the immediate organization of an antiterrorism commando, and the new democratic government had convinced the Interior Ministry to open the secret police files on prominent bankers, politicians, and insurance *businessmen* such as Chavdar. And what he wanted was for Stoyan to go spy on his bitchy American mistress. The man had a death wish. "As you request," Stoyan said through his teeth. "The persuasion will be a pleasure."

5

Subject: I'm outta here!!
Date: Sat, 26 Apr 1997 15:03:29 -0400 (EDT)
From: June Carver <jcarver@sof.cit>
To: Benny <bgatwick@asb.com>

Benny baby, I am finally taking everyone's advice and getting the heck outta dodge. It is a good thing that I am going away for a while because I was beginning to espouse the
hygienic positives of squat toilets, find the mangy stray
puppies in the streets suitable for cuddling, and enjoy the
faulty phone-lines because they provide an excellent excuse
not to talk to people for weeks. I have eaten brains fried
in butter, constructed tampons out of old socks, used leva
for toilet paper, and recently haggled in Bulgarian over
the price of an uncured sheepskin vest. I am becoming a
barbarian.

How's life there? Big money, big dreams? What film are you
working on these days?

Love, June

*T*HE BARE WHITE ceiling confronted June with its lonely lack of adornments. It looked sad and stark, and it occurred to her that ceilings had never before struck her as having any emotional content one way or another, probably because she usually looked up at them while lying next to or underneath Ethan. Now he was gone. She'd come so far to give up so much. Damn! She'd lost not only Ethan, but also an entire life. She'd really been getting somewhere before they left. She'd been promoted to Unit Manager, and the quality of the films the start-up company was getting improved with every production. Back to square one. Starting from scratch. Alone in bed in the Balkans. This is not where June thought she'd be at the age of thirty.

When she was five, in her blurred vision of her future, she saw a mother in an apron, cooking Betty Crocker cakes and giving bottles to babies who looked like inanimate dolls with synthetic white hair. At fourteen, after being coached by her mother for her third year as a beauty contestant, she would have robotically replied that she wanted either a career in social service or to be a veterinarian because she (big smile, June, show us those teeth!) just loved both animals and people.

Later, June began faking stage fright, and consequently her contest career came to an end. Claire stopped talking to her daughter, and in the silence, June developed in some new directions. In her last year of high school, when she powdered her face to a deathly pallor and wore combat boots to school every day, she only cared about getting away from her mother's constant criticism and diet regimes. (If only the silent treatment had lasted forever.) If anyone had asked this seventeen-year-old June where she would be when she was thirty, the angry girl clad in black would have replied, "As far away from here as physically possible!" Then she would have stormed up to her room, stuffed a Ho Ho in her mouth, cranked up the most suicidal song from The Cure, and painted her windows red as if they were dripping blood.

She had been an unlikely salutatorian—not allowed to speak at graduation for fear that she would accept almost any dare if the price was right. (Rumor had it the promise of a hundred bucks had resulted in a tattoo, but the location of the tattoo had prevented proof and payment.) The principal was afraid of stripteases, buckets of blood, or anti-administration riots. The beauty queen had become trouble.

ETHAN HAD BEEN the rebellious guy she'd been waiting for, more intellectual than hip, but she'd liked that. After living in L.A. for so long, she'd been ready for a change, and he was certainly different. She'd never met a diplomat's son before, and to her he was as exotic as a prince or a duke or a sheik. Besides that, he was smart. Of this she was sure, because of how outspoken he was in the Italian film class they'd had together. He was also militant about campus politics, well known in the avant-garde and artistic edgy circles, and he had a convertible Mustang and penchant for sunset picnics on the beach. June had loved him, for all of those reasons and more, like the fact that he'd taken her away from everything to a secluded hippie hotel in Desert Hot Springs to recover from her mother's suicide.

On a run-down beach chair facing out over skeletal Joshua trees and red hills, he'd held and rocked her. He kissed away her tears and whispered promises that the despair would eventually pass, and that her mother's death would not leave her void of love, in a chasm of loneliness as deep as this heartbreakingly beautiful desert was wide. He would not allow it. He would be by her always. She cocooned in his lap. She thanked God for his protective arms, holding her to the barren, empty earth when she felt two-dimensional enough to be blown away and lost.

When, that weekend, he asked her to be his wife on a rock plateau that looked out over a sunset like endless heaven, she hadn't hesitated. And what luck—Las Vegas had been just a short desert drive away. Within two weeks she had lost a mother and gained a husband.

THE PHONE RANG again and June covered her face with the pillow. Who would let the phone ring for such an embarrassingly endless amount of time? Only Chavdar.

"Chavdar's a knockout, June," Roxanne had said. "A real world-class man. You need to find out what it's like to be with a *real* man." What it was like with Chavdar was this: the telephone ringing at all hours to find out where she was, strange Bulgarian men in slacks and polo shirts watching her apartment from conspicuous sports cars parked across the street, cold champagne, lingering stares, thirty-minute cell-phone conversations with his office in the middle of dinner, and a hairy arm holding her hostage against an equally hairy stomach all night long.

Naked, Chavdar would stand in the kitchen making sandwiches with his cell phone tucked between his cheek and shoulder. From the couch she watched the movement of the muscles in his back, and at the taught buttocks, like the Statue of David, shifting as he reached across the counter for the mayonnaise. Oblivious to her presence in the darkened living room, he chatted about bombs and bribes. Later he would eat his sandwich, giving her a closed-mouth grin as he chewed with his cheeks full. Then he would take a swig of apple soda, spit some on her stomach, and lick it off with his well-trained tongue. It had felt way too right even when she knew it was wrong.

Where would she be at thirty? Now she had the answer. Alone in bed in an apartment with a phone number she had never memorized, in a city of people with whom she could barely speak. In a post-revolution landscape of gray buildings, wild dogs, and trash, where no one returned her smiles. How would she look? Thin, but not from step aerobics at the Hollywood Athletic Club. Instead, her slimness could be attributed to stress and forgetting how to enjoy food without Ethan; and the translucence of her skin was not the product of Clinique, but rather of anemia. Her husband had run off with a maid, her local lover who lunched with assassins was stalking her, and she was about to disappear with a man who quoted Shakespeare, sang Broadway musicals in the shower, and played Frisbee better than anyone—and who had contributed quite enthusiastically to the destruction of her marriage. It was not a pretty picture.

ETHAN DIDN'T ENTER the apartment until after noon. June appeared in the hallway. She was in sweats and a T-shirt, and her hair was in a lopsided ponytail. His nearly empty bottle of rakia was clutched in her left hand, and she suddenly raised it over her head. "Hi there! Zdrasti."

It looked like a military salute, and Ethan wasn't sure how to react. She still made him want to smile. "Hey," he said, setting down his briefcase and starting to pull off his jacket.

June shook the bottle, still holding it up high. "I drank all your rakia."

Her clothes were all over the place. He put his hands on his hips. "Is that . . . grass in your hair?"

June ran a hand over the disheveled ponytail. "Grass? No, no. Well, maybe. I had a little accident." She looked down at her scraped palm. "I fell down last night walking back from the denonoshtno on Popa square."

"You fell, huh? Are you okay?"

"Don't I look okay?"

"No."

"You know what? I am okay. Maybe not right this exact second, but I will be. So don't worry. Seriously. I'm going to Greece and I'm going to buy a rose from one of those women with the mustaches and I'm going to walk through the streets with it clenched right between my pearly-white capped teeth. I'm going to be fine. Better than fine."

"June, stop."

June rubbed her eye with her free fist. "Impossible. I'm on automatic pilot."

"Come here."

The rakia bottle slipped in her hand. She made an awkward attempt to catch it, but it smashed on the floor. June looked at the shattered glass and then up at Ethan. When she laughed there were tears in her eyes. "Whoops!"

Ethan couldn't help himself. "June, come here. I'm sorry. I really—" Ethan was interrupted by the buzzer. "Who's that?"

"I don't know."

"Are you expecting someone?"

"No," she said, turning toward the window, and then back to Ethan. Then she repeated the maneuver, like a distressed caged animal.

"Maybe it's your boyfriend, huh?"

"He's not my boyfriend," June said, making futile attempts to tug the blinds together. "Pull the curtains."

"I'm not going to help you play games with your mutra, June."

Someone knocked on the door. "Alo?"

"Oh God, it's one of Chavdar's thugs. Hide."

"Who?"

"Shhh!"

June grabbed Ethan's hand. They walked on tiptoe into the hallway and climbed into the built-in closet. They tripped over June's shoes, and Ethan's face was wedged against her winter coat. The closet was barely big enough for both of them, and the wooden plank on which they stood creaked and sagged. They sank down and tucked their knees up in front of them. Ethan could hardly believe what he was doing. "This is the most ridiculous thing—"

"Quiet," said June, and in the little bit of light coming through the cracks in the door he saw that she had been scared sober and that her green eyes were wide. Suddenly he became very uncomfortable and silent.

They both heard a key turning in the lock. Ethan elbowed June in the cramped space. "You gave him your key?"

"They don't need keys."

Stoyan walked into the apartment and took in what he considered the pleasant smell of a barroom bash. He stood in the doorway for a second, jangling his keys. "June?"

After a second he walked into the kitchen. It was dirty and there were dishes in the sink. Stoyan shook his head with disgust and twirled on his heel. "June? Tuk li si?"

There was a bowl on the kitchen table full of tomatoes. Stoyan took one of the bright tomatoes and bit into it. After his first bite he found the salt-shaker and salted the inside. While he munched it like an apple, holding it with his left hand, he pulled his cell phone out with his right. He laid it down faceup on the counter and punched in the office's number. With a mouth full of tomato, he said, "Elga, dai mi Chavdar."

June and Ethan could barely hear Stoyan's mumbling voice as he spoke with Chavdar. "She's not here. Where should I look next? What is Roxanne's address again? Hold on, let me find a pen."

Stoyan started rifling through the kitchen drawers. He found a pen, and beside it was a plane ticket with June's name on it. Stoyan picked it up for examination. "Are you taking June out of town? Uh-huh. Because she's leaving tomorrow for Greece. Balkan Air at noon. Let me see . . . Yes, there's something that says Sunset Villas. Da. Da, da. Okay, I'll be back there in twenty minutes."

Stoyan finished his tomato and dropped the green stem on the floor where it landed with a wet smack. "I bet that will be there a month from now," he said under his breath. "Sorry excuse for a homemaker." He whistled as he walked out of the apartment, and Ethan and June could hear him re-locking the dead bolt from the outside.

They waited a few minutes before coming out of their hiding place.

"That was great. What a treat. It's so fun to share in your soap opera from time to time."

June looked like she was going to throw up. "Please don't."

"This might be your new life, but it doesn't happen to me every day. I'm fascinated. That was actually really cool. What are you, playing hard to get now? You brought Hollywood with you, didn't you? The many loves of June Carver. A day in the life of June Carver. You could write a book. How to be a dick tease in ten easy steps."

June walked into the other room and sat down on the foldout bed.

Ethan followed her. "Married to the mob. I was a Bulgarian mutra's bitch, the sensational new screenplay by up-and-coming genius June Carver. Bravo!" He clapped and whistled. "Bravo!"

June took her ponytail out and began combing her fingers through her hair, extracting the leaves.

Ethan dropped to a sitting position next to her. After a second he said, "Okay. Sorry."

"But you're not. It's okay though, because finally I don't care. I mean, I do care, but I can't care. It's over with you and it's over with Chavdar and I'm going away. I am going far away and I am never coming back and I will never think of you anymore because I will be so busy being happy." June stood up and walked toward the bathroom. As part of her grand exit, she bumped her knee on the bedside table.

Ethan shook his head, thinking it was a sad finale to what had, at one long lost time, been a really wonderful production. "June?" he called, feeling that he couldn't leave their love like that. If it was dead then at least they should show some respect for it, bury it, say something pretty. She turned around, and all he could think to say was, "Junie, how the hell did you and I get like this?"

PART TWO

"*The Making of June*"

[JULY 1996—ONE YEAR EARLIER]

6

Subject: Update
Date: Tue, 16 Jul 1996 04:52:44 -0700
From: June Carver <jcarver@sof.cit>
To: Everyone <mail-list>

Hi everyone,

Quick update—Still adjusting to arrival, but doing better
than before. I feel more like I am in the Middle East than
in any recognizable part of Europe. There really are wild
dogs everywhere, and they cry all night long. There is at
least a miserable, bohemian glamour to the life here. There
are a ton of outdoor cafes with people smoking and drinking
rakia, Gypsies leading dancing bears around on leashes, attractive people, glue-sniffing teenage gangs—contradictions
everywhere. My email is hard-wired into a big, gaping hole
in the apartment wall and ants and little spiders keep
crawling out. I am trying to keep an open mind.

I hope you are all happy and enjoying the summer in sunny
L.A. The sky here is gray. But, heads up, young people!
Right? Care packages are welcome—Mrs. Fields chocolate chip
cookies, movie magazines, Mace (for possible protection
against aforementioned wild attack dogs and zombie-eyed
bands of glue sniffers), self-tanning lotion, and Old El
Paso salsa (yes I know no one else likes it but me) topping
my own personal list. Just kidding. The only thing I want
you to send is gossip from home. I miss you all terribly!

Sending love,

June

*I*T WAS THE middle of an unusually muggy July when they arrived, and a summer storm poured down from the murky sky. June wiped away the condensation from the taxi window. In the distance she could make out a skyline consisting of towering tenements the same color as the slate clouds behind them. One after another, there was nothing to break up the monotony. They were all alike: tall slabs of concrete with symmetrical black windows and doors. The Locke-Fields organization had told them their kvartal was called Darvenitsa, and it was surrounded by several other residential housing projects from the era of Socialist construction, with names like Mladost, meaning youth, and Nedezhda, meaning hope.

Block 231, Block 232, Block 233, Block 234. The addresses scrawled on the sides of the buildings with spray paint blended into the graffiti, some of it Cyrillic, and some of it in poor English: "Class War Now!" and "Hitler Lives!" In the rain, the painted numbers bled down the brick tenement walls, making it almost impossible to tell the hideous dwellings apart. June pointed. "Look, Ethan. 'Kill Capitalist Pigs.' Lovely." June giggled and Ethan looked at her hard. She swallowed and let the window fog back up again.

The flight had taken forever and June was so tired she was a bit slaphappy. Her eyes and throat were dry, and her Ann Taylor "breathing light linen" travel suit was stained with tomato juice from her third in-flight Bloody Mary. June's going-away salon splurge at the Beverly Garden Spa was ruined; she had bitten away her French manicure, her massaged muscles were more sore than ever, and her new hair-do hung wet and stringy against her face, sticking to skin that no longer looked peachy from her red-earth mud mask. She needed a hot shower and a good bed. (And another Bloody Mary, though she wasn't likely to get it.)

At last the taxi driver arrived in front of one of the Blocks and switched off the engine. He peered out into the downpour and then turned to face the couple. "Block dvestachetirisetidevet," he mumbled, punching a button on the meter that instantly doubled the fare, "Yours."

The heavy metal front door gave way after a few minutes of working it with the key. They moved their suitcases into the unlighted foyer and stood there dripping while they took in the plywood mailboxes and the dull concrete staircase that led up to a four-person lift. No one was around and the only sound was the rain pelting against the building. "I think the luggage will be all right here for a few minutes," said Ethan. "Let's get the computers and go up and check the place out."

They closed the collapsible wooden slats behind them and took the shaking lift to the thirteenth floor, where they stepped out into another unlighted hallway. June felt her way down the dark hall and activated the light switch while Ethan located number 89.

The metal door swung open, revealing a small living room with a couch and a picture window looking out over a balcony. The rain and fog made it impossible to make out the view.

"It's a one-room studio," said Ethan. "With a foldout couch."

It took only a few more minutes to establish that the apartment had no blankets or towels, the hot-water heater didn't work, the microwave-sized laundry machine drained into the sink, and the bathtub looked more like a metal watering trough for cattle. The phone was a party line and of all the electricity sockets, only two worked. Plugged into them were small, yellowish antique lamps that, when turned on, gave off a sickly hospital glow.

Ethan looked wearily at June. He shrugged his shoulders and his long arms hung at his sides. She hated to see him look so defeated.

"Hey," she said, retying the belt on her raincoat. "Why don't we go get a room in a hotel? Let's get a bottle of wine and room service! Massage each other back to life. After twenty hours on a plane we deserve to treat ourselves. Let's deal with this mess after a good night's sleep."

"We shouldn't. We have to start adjusting. Staying in a hotel is not a healthy way to start dealing with culture shock. It's you I'm thinking about, June. It's you who really needs to jump in headfirst."

June nodded and walked to the window. This was not the spontaneous Ethan who had proposed to her in Desert Hot Springs and wedded her five days later in Vegas. This was not the man who had gotten a hotel room at Chateau Marmont when their apartment was only forty minutes away because he wanted to make love *now*.

June always felt guilty now—but he was guilty too; of reading *The Economist* when she needed to talk about her next job interview, of wearing slippers and crossing his legs while he smoked a pipe with his single-malt scotch, and of staring at the ceiling for hours thinking thoughts that "were complicated and wouldn't interest you." He was guilty. He had let the passion fade. He was no fun.

June was silent and indignant, thinking of her thick down comforter and soft cotton sheets, her special coffee beans in the freezer, her alarm clock that woke her to Elvis, the amaretto and whiskey in the cabinet that she would add to hot chocolate and drink while reading the trades before drifting off to sleep. Her desk in the sunny corner of the office, looking out toward the water, her two new girlfriends in the yoga class in Venice. She'd left all that behind for this—and now she was being asked to jump in headfirst. Fine. She dug an emergency cigarette out of her backpack even though she had quit. She lit up and looked out at the rain. Well, here we are, she thought. At home in the Block.

ETHAN'S IDEA of jumping headfirst into their new lives in Bulgaria was to do what his parents had always done when they were American diplomats relocating biannually around the world. Within three weeks of their arrival, Ethan had already planned a cocktail party at the Locke-Fields sponsor's home, and invited almost the entire international community. He'd asked June to do all the cooking, as she had once said to him, "Maybe catering is something I could do on the side without a work permit in Bulgaria. That sounds kind of fun."

THIS IS GETTING out of control, June thought as she rushed between stirring and chopping and washing and draining. The Locke-Fields sponsor's kitchen was in shambles. On the stove, green peppers and red peppers were overcooking in boiling water because the burner dials had no heat indicators. The oven dial was also worn clean, so there was no way of knowing the temperature inside—but the three baking quiches smelled ready. All of the mixing bowls were marked with European measurements, and June had not paid much attention to conversions in high school, having foolishly never considered that she might one day be called upon to throw a dinner party for sixty in the Balkans. The sink was stopped up with bits of bread, cheese, and vegetable cuttings, and June could not get it to drain. I need to relax, she thought. I can do this; I've done it before, brilliantly. Nothing to it. I just need to relax and get myself together. Nothing to worry about. Nothing except bags of spices labeled in Bulgarian, yogurt that looks like milk, rice that refuses to cook, chicken that smells suspiciously like pork, and a bunch of things I've made with flour that might not be flour after all.

"Oh God," she said, flailing in the strangeness of the kitchen. "This is going to be a major disaster." She took a swig of cooking sherry, her Grandmother Penny's favorite.

When Ethan came into the kitchen to check on her progress, two black
pies sat on the stovetop and one was on the floor. "What is that?" he asked,
joining her where she kneeled over charred chunks of egg and crust.

"I just checked them, Ethan," she said. "I mean, I literally checked them a
minute ago, and they were just right. And then I smelled something and I tried
to get them out in a hurry, and now look! Look at my goddamn quiche."

ETHAN RAN frantically through the party, searching for suggestions. An
American woman named Roxanne claimed that her house girl could be over
in fifteen minutes and have a spectacular feast prepared in an hour.

As June persevered with the meal (and also with the cooking sherry),
Ethan paced in the living room. "Roxanne," he finally said, "it's been almost
a half hour. Should I send someone for takeout?"

"Not to worry," she said, smiling at him with a heavily lipsticked mouth.
"The help has just arrived." She swept out a graceful hand to present the girl,
who wore a gray button-down dress with a business collar, thick-soled black
shoes, and a long, brown sheepskin coat too warm for the weather. Her hair,
which matched the coat, was pulled back in a ponytail, but a few wisps had
escaped in the summer wind. Her cheeks were flushed. Roxanne helped her
out of her jacket and said, "Nevena, this is Ethan Carver."

Straight-faced, the girl offered a courteous but reserved nod. "Pleased to
meet you."

"I can't tell you how great it is to meet you," Ethan said, a little frazzled.
"Let me help you with your packages." He picked up two heavy plastic bags
filled with jars and produce. As he carried them to the kitchen, he looked
over his shoulder at the thin arms of the slender girl. "How did you carry
these all the way here?"

Nevena shrugged, "I manage."

Ethan pushed his way into the kitchen and Nevena followed. The situation had worsened. As Ethan and Nevena entered, they caught June swigging
from the sherry bottle. "Whoops," she said, blushing. "Caught in the act."

"June, for Christ's sake!"

"What? Since when are you such a teetotaler?"

"Forget it. This girl is going to help."

Nevena looked calmly around the kitchen. She immediately went to the sink, crouched beneath it, and loosened the fixture around the pipe. She used her fingers to dig out the soggy food and part of a wine bottle cork that was lodged inside. The filthy water in the sink began to move, and Nevena held a plastic bucket underneath the pipe while she readjusted the washer with a wrench. As she rinsed her hands off, she glanced over her shoulder. "If you wish, you may go on to the party now. Tell Roxanne there will be food in three-quarters of an hour."

"I'll stay and help. Just tell me what to do," said June. "I'm not familiar with a lot of this food and how some of the appliances work, but I promise you I can follow instructions."

"I manage best alone, thank you."

"Oh please. At the very least you could use an extra set of hands for chopping."

June watched Nevena grab a knife and start slicing tomatoes with gourmet skill and speed. "Thank you, but no thank you."

"Well. Okay then. Ethan?"

"Hmm?" He didn't take his eyes off Nevena.

"Are you coming out to the party?"

"Um hmm."

June waited a second and then walked out of the kitchen.

Ethan stood still and observed the girl working. Her hair was not freshly washed but neither was it dirty, just limp.

Nevena tasted the stuffed peppers June had been cooking and set them aside. "She was mistaken with this type of cheese." Nevena looked at Ethan, noticing his face for the first time. "I will make new ones now. But we don't have to tell her. At the least she might think she did one thing which tastes very good. Dobre li e? It is okay?"

"Da, dobre," he answered. Ethan was wondering how old she was. Her body bordered on adolescent, it was so thin and bony and almost awkward, but her face looked drawn and tired. She was not like an American girl. Not only did she lack any coy or flirtatious mannerisms, but she hadn't smiled once since she walked in the door, not even a little. He suddenly felt very uncomfortable alone in the kitchen with her, watching her cook, watching the silent, graceful movements of her childlike arms. "Thank you, Nevena," he said, pulling at the collar of his sweater even though he wore no tie.

She looked up from the tomatoes she was slicing. Her brown eyes met his straight on in a way that seemed dramatic. "It is nothing."

"Oh, it's definitely something. Definitely." Ethan felt flustered. He had an urgent wish to see her smile. He'd had a few swigs of sherry himself and knew it was best to walk away. Instead he said, "Where did you learn to cook?"

"My mother of course," Nevena answered quickly, as if she were being interrogated. "All Bulgarian women cook."

Ethan could tell he was bothering her but was powerless to stop. "Oh, really? I can't wait to taste what you make."

Nevena looked up at him fleetingly, with a strange expression on her face.

Ethan looked away and clapped his hands together. "Okay, I'm going to leave you alone to do your work. I'm headed to the bar to get myself a drink. Can I bring something back for you?"

This time Nevena didn't raise her head. "I am working, not attending a party."

"Right," Ethan said, finally finding the motivation to move away to the door. "Right. Okay, I'll talk to you later, Nevena. Thanks again."

She didn't say a word, and her hands didn't slow their methodical slicing. When the kitchen door had swung shut on his departure, she finally looked up. He left behind a particular scent. Nevena recognized it as a Western shampoo that other American men she had worked for had in their bathrooms. It was for dandruff, and for some reason, today it smelled pleasant. She cocked her head to the side for a split second and blinked. Then she continued to cook.

JUNE DIDN'T JOIN the party, as Nevena had suggested. Instead she went to the upstairs bedroom, took a cigarette from a pack on the bedside table, and shut herself in the bathroom. The door didn't lock and June held it shut with her foot while she sat on the closed lid of the toilet, smoking. Suddenly she felt like she needed a good cry.

So Ethan was disappointed in her and impressed with the girl with Euro-friendly kitchen experience and Ginsu chopping skills. Whatever. Put us in Los Angeles with a Cuisinart, a wok, a pack of seaweed, and a bunch of raw fish and then we'll see who has the last laugh. Screw cooking, anyway. There was plenty of other stuff she could do really well. Plenty!

June imagined the look on Ethan's face if she went down to the party, stood up on a chair, and called the room to attention with a cheerleader clap. Her announcement would go something like this: "My name is June Carver but it used to be June Summer. That's right, my mother named me June Summer but I managed to overcome it and still lead a normal life. How's that for an accomplishment, huh? And that's not all! In the last month alone I fed some mean-ass teamsters, talked down a suicidal actress from a billboard on Sunset Avenue, found a three-story turn-of-the-century farmhouse location *downtown,* and got three B-list actors into first-class from Los Angeles to New York five minutes before takeoff *without* a scene. How do you like them apples? And outside of work, I want each and every one of you to know that there are plenty of things I can do even better than cook. For one, I can tap dance . . ."

At this point she imagined launching into something very Shirley Temple that could be performed on the width of a chair seat. While she danced she could chant out of sync with the rhythm of her clicking feet. "I was Miss Pre-Teen Encino and Miss Teenage Sherman Oaks. Beauty, talent, and extra points for any visible signs of intelligence. I have a master's degree, and what's more . . ." This would be the part Ethan would love. "And what's more, my breasts are real!" She could whip off her dress and unsnap her bra and jiggle them around just like a go-go girl.

Ethan would faint from shame. The mental image of the waifish Bulgarian cook throwing a pail of water in his face to revive him finally made June crack a smile.

SOMEONE KNOCKED ON the door and June turned the faucet on to douse the cigarette. She started waving her hand around in the tiny cubicle, as if the cloud of smoke might magically disappear, even though it had nowhere to go. "Just a minute."

"It's been ten already, hon."

June opened the door to the dressing area with the sink. Smoke billowed out around her, and she couldn't help but cough. A middle-aged woman with jet-black hair and ruby-red lips was seated on the marble counter rolling a joint. She watched as June bent over and hacked and hacked. When June finally recovered, the woman was sealing the joint with her tongue and fishing a lighter out of her purse. "Going to live?"

"Unfortunately. You're the one that called nine-one-one, right?"

"Yeah, she's my cook."

"Well. Thanks."

Roxanne extended the joint to June. "You do, I assume." She smiled sarcastically. "Being from Los Angeles."

"You know where I'm from?"

"The expat community in Sofia is pretty small. If we don't know each other, we know of each other." Roxanne crossed her legs. They were very bony and covered in thick black stockings.

"I was actually born in North Carolina."

"Hey," Roxanne said, leaning back against the mirror. "No one has to know."

June laughed, then coughed some more.

"You think I'm kidding, but I'm not! Oscar Wilde said, 'Never trust a woman who will tell you her real age. If she'll tell you that, she'll tell you anything.' I love it. Writers can get away with anything. One of the reasons I chose to be one."

"You make a living at it? Writing?"

Roxanne snorted. "Hell, no. If I had to make a living at anything I'd be finished. I have been married five times, honey. I'm independently wealthy."

"You're kidding," June said, looking away from the mirror at Roxanne's high cheekbones and smooth skin. "You're kidding, right?"

"I'm older than you think. I have a good doctor in Vienna." Roxanne turned and studied her profile in the mirror. She ran her hand down her jaw and neck.

June stepped closer to Roxanne. "Really? I can't tell. I mean, it must be really good because usually I can tell. Claire had a lot of work done."

"Claire?"

"My mother. I mean, *a lot*. She had her eyes and nose done, and a face-lift too. And a tummy tuck and lipo on her thighs. I think the last thing was the boob job."

Roxanne tilted her head to one side. The bathroom light had an uncomfortable fluorescent quality. "How is she holding up?"

June looked down, and after a second began fumbling in her purse for her lipstick. "Well . . . she's not."

JUNE AND ETHAN did not speak at all on the taxi ride back to Darvenitsa. June couldn't stop thinking about Claire. Her mother hadn't been a very good cook—one of the reasons why June had learned in the first place. There had been a lot of things Claire couldn't do, like, for example, getting out of bed on a cold day. June did not want to believe that she and her mother were alike, but there was no denying the fact that she had royally screwed up the party. Claire hadn't *tried* to be a mess. It had just happened. What if she couldn't help it either? They say that one day you wake up and you've turned into your mother. What would it be like to really lose it, June wondered, and would you know when you started? What were the signs? The irrational desire to perform a striptease to embarrass your husband, or the growing importance of the clandestine shot of whiskey in the nightcap cocoa? Maybe not, but what about recurring nightmares in which you lower your head to accept your sparkling tiara and suddenly whip a semiautomatic from under your ballroom skirt, ready to assassinate a whole crowd of Fashion TV–type models and beauty contest judges? What about conjuring up such obsessive and realistic jealous fantasies about your absent husband's infidelities that in the end you are actually the one to cheat? Perhaps that would be followed by unhealthy flings with cosmetic surgery, Wonderbras, electrolysis, mud masks, waxes, hair dyes and hennas, Prozac, Retin-A, cortisone, gelatin therapy for healthy nails, VO5 hot oil treatments, cellulite cream, delicious shakes for breakfast and lunch, Jane Fonda's video/cookbook package, and the spa secrets of Europe's rich and famous. Maybe when those didn't work out she would try a new, lethal combination of medications guaranteed to ensure that she would stop aging, just like Claire.

AT HOME, ALONE in the kitchen, Ethan finished a rakia and poured himself another. He was thinking of the Bulgarian girl with the moles and big brown eyes. It was just because of the tension with June. He had been short-tempered and she had been moody and he wanted to think about something else. Simple as that. But that *attraction*. It had nearly knocked the wind out of him. Not that he had never thought of other women before. Sure he had. Old girlfriends, students in his classes, beautiful women in the street. Of course there had been the thing with his research assistant Moira, but he preferred not to think about that. In any case, it had not been the same. He had never been so overwhelmed with this kind of urge for action.

He wanted to call Nevena, wanted to follow her home, wanted to contrive an accidental meeting in front of a dark and inviting coffeehouse. It would go away, he told himself. It was a fleeting drunken obsession, like trying to remember the words to an old high-school song. In the morning he would wake with June beside him, her eyes shut, the sheets pulled up under her chin. She would look like an angel and these thoughts would be gone. He wouldn't even remember her name. Nevena. Oh God . . . *Nevena.* He allowed himself the pleasure of saying it aloud, in a hushed whisper. The word itself was a poem. It tasted like sugar on his tongue. What was he thinking? What was he doing, standing in his kitchen whispering the name of a Bulgarian maid in the dark, while his wife was preparing for bed in the next room?

He finished his second rakia, brushed his teeth, and went into the living room. June had already pulled out the sofa bed and was under the covers. Her face was crushed in the pillow.

"Don't make this into a bigger deal than it is, June. Don't dramatize, will you?"

"Thanks for the kind words."

"It's not a tragedy."

"Well, I didn't serve poisonous blowfish filet and murder them all, that's true."

"Come on."

"Maybe I'm upset about something else. Maybe it's not the food at all."

"June . . ." He looked at her distraught expression and sighed. He took her hand and pressed it to his mouth. "What is it?"

"What's going on with us?"

"We're going through a rough time of readjustment."

"But other than that, everything's fine?"

Ethan stared at her in the muted light. She had gone out and bought scarves to hang over all the ugly lamps, and for once, the apartment didn't seem hideous. The soft shadows were rose-colored. "What do you mean?"

"I saw you looking at that girl tonight, Ethan. I saw you scratching at your neck the whole time you were talking to her."

Ethan didn't deny it and June got out of bed. As she walked out of the room she pulled one of the red silk scarves off a lamp. Ethan winced. Now he could see the horrible orange and brown couch, the shabby throw rug, and the black, rotten cracks in the parquet floor. June let the scarf drop into a small, silken heap by her feet. "Everything is not fine, Ethan. It's smoke and mirrors."

7

Subject: What's up party girl?
Date: Mon, 05 Aug 1996 10:30:19 -0700
From: June Carver <jcarver@sof.cit>
To: Laney Nathaniel <laney@smnet.com>

So, remember how I was going to come over here and take pho-
tographs and paint and write and take Bulgarian lessons and
start swimming seriously and teach English and start an herb
garden? Well, so far instead of any of the above, I have
succeeded in drinking no less than a bottle of wine a night,
spending over two hundred dollars on a swimwear ensemble of
cap, Speedo suit, flip-flops, goggles, club membership etc. in
an attempt to turn myself into Esther Williams without having actually gotten in the pool. (I am currently taking the
smoking much more seriously than the swimming and getting in
about thirty minutes a day.) I bought some herbs at the
store, painted the kitchen cabinets (hardly a creative experience) and I did hire a Bulgarian tutor. I will probably
reward myself for these accomplishments by drinking an extra
half bottle of wine tonight and giving myself permission to
skip the first class tomorrow.☺

Write soon, I love you.

June

p.s. I keep dwelling on what happened. I feel guilty and
yucky. I think I might be projecting and accusing Ethan of
things when really it's just me to blame. I am thinking
of telling him.

*R*AINA LIVED ON the twentieth floor of a towering Block in an apartment half the size of June and Ethan's. The elevator was big enough for two thin people and had no light. June stepped into the dark metal cage for the second time. She hadn't liked the elevator on her first short visit, and instead of feeling more comfortable this time, she was embarrassed by her terror. She felt like she was shrinking as she rose toward Raina.

The tutor was waiting for June at the door. "Can you see?" she called. "The light is on the wall beside the lift, do you remember where?"

"Yes, thank you," June called from the other end of the long, concrete, windowless corridor.

Raina's stout figure was silhouetted in the entrance to her apartment. She wore a skirt and sweater, and her thick calves looked even thicker in knitted socks. On her feet she wore house slippers.

The living room contained a small couch facing a table, and two stiff-back chairs against the opposite wall. Raina had June sit on the couch and pulled one of the chairs over so she could sit facing. "Aren't you going to sit on the couch?" asked June.

"No. Last time you were here we were just chatting. This time I have to be the drill sergeant. I need to keep the lesson moving. If we both sit on the couch we're liable to drift off to sleep." Raina's eyes were small in a fleshy face, and her hair was cropped short. Despite this, she looked as if she had once been beautiful. She was examining June closely. After a second, she stood and said, "I'll be right back."

Raina returned from the bedroom and handed June a tube of lotion. "You have a bit of a skin condition."

"I've been told I have to get used to the water, and then it will go back to normal," said June. She squeezed some of the lotion out and applied it to the dry skin at the corners of her mouth. "Nice lotion," she said, smelling her fingertips. "My sister has her own business in Los Angeles. She makes organic skin products. She has a vanilla face mask that smells a little like this. It's selling very well."

"Hmm. Let me just make us some tea."

June sat stiffly on the couch, waiting to hear the whistle of the teakettle. She was surrounded by brown, as if she were imprisoned in a mammoth cardboard box. The smell was sort of a cardboard box smell too, as if the apartment were an attic storage space for forgotten books, clothes, and old newspapers. Even the pale cream ceiling was brown in spots from a slowly spreading leak. The room was too sad for the woman who lived in it. So far, it was like most Bulgarian living rooms June had visited, minus the Serbian pornography. She decided to keep this observation to herself.

When Raina shuffled back in with the tea, she asked June to open up the textbook. "Did you look through it this past week?"

June flipped through the pages. "Yes. I did the introduction to the Cyrillic alphabet. Then it talked about introducing myself and ordering food."

"Were you able to apply any of the lessons?"

"Well, I wanted to buy a pair of mittens. I tried at this stand on Graf Ignatiev. You know, 'kolko struvat' and everything, but the man kept telling me a different price than what was on the gloves and I couldn't understand him. Then he wanted me to let him get in my wallet so he could show me which bill to give him, and at that point I walked away."

"We'll have a different lesson today. You write down everything I say and memorize it for next week."

June took out her pen and paper. "Okay."

Raina spoke slowly. "Az sum chuzhdenka no rasbiram mnogo dobre che me luzhete. Nyama da doida tuk nikoga poveche. Blugodariya, dovizhdane."

It took June several minutes to write down the words. "That's a mouthful. What does it mean?"

Raina wore a sly smile. Then she laughed and her jowls shook. "Ah. It is very formal, very polite. It means, 'I may be a foreigner, but I understand very well that you are lying to me. I will never return here again. Thank you, good-bye.'"

June beamed. "Perfect."

The lesson was supposed to be three hours long, but Raina stopped early. "I think we should watch the news. It will be good for you, and I am interested in hearing about the elections."

Raina turned on the small black-and-white television set and they got a grainy picture. She checked her watch. "We have five minutes. I have many bad habits. I drink and I smoke. I'm going to have a rakia and a cigarette. Would you like something?"

"I'll have the same as you. Rakia. That sounds good."

Raina went into the kitchen and returned with orange soda, a bottle of rakia, and four glasses on a tray. "Homemade," she said, thrusting her chin in the direction of the bottle. "Good and strong." Then she went to the pantry and got out a jar of sardines and some crackers. "It's a tradition to drink rakia with snacks. Not like the Russians, you know, who just drink to get drunk. I like a little snack with the news."

It was the first time June had tasted homemade rakia, and she fought to keep her face expressionless. "Well! Wow. It's good."

"Uh-huh. The next sip will be better. Have some orange soda."

Raina waited until the news started to light her cigarette. June couldn't make out a single word. All she saw was a screen full of middle-aged men shouting at one another. It went on forever. "Hmm," said Raina. "You can't understand. They are just arguing, but saying nothing, buh buh buh buh buh. Anyway, the election is not that important. It is for President. Here it is the Prime Minister that matters."

"Who are you going to vote for?"

"I don't know yet," Raina said, sticking her lower lip out obstinately. "They are all corrupt."

"You don't like any of them?"

"Of course not. Nothing will change without a real revolution. Red, Blue, Socialist, Communist, Monarchist, the Party for Democratic Reform. What I care most about is the price of bread and the election won't affect that." She speared a sardine with a fork and shifted her eyes away from the television toward June. "What are you doing here? If I may ask."

"My husband is a Locke-Fields scholar. He's writing this book and doing his dissertation here—economic transition stuff. I mean, it's more complicated than that but to be honest, I don't understand everything about his research. He's really book-smart, you know? And I'm more street-smart. Like, what I do is work in production. Film production in Los Angeles. You've got to be *really* street-smart for that. For the next year, I don't know. Write, tutor English—I'm not sure yet."

"Why Bulgaria? You will be asked this a lot. Most Bulgarians think the foreigners are here for one of two reasons: to lie and steal from us, or to be lied to and stolen from."

June wiped her brow. Suddenly she was very hot. Raina refilled her shot glass. "Ethan is here because this is a historically important period in Eastern Europe. Bulgaria has only been a Democracy for—"

"False." Raina now poured herself another shot of rakia.

"Excuse me?"

"False. The police still listen to us, there are still secret files. How many private businesses are there in this country? And who owns them? Who are our democratic leaders anyway? Tell me about Videnov, for example. Does your husband know the answers to these questions? Ask anyone on the street how long Bulgaria has been a Democracy and they will laugh in your face. Your husband had best discover this."

"Well, we've been here such a short time." She picked up a sardine by the tail. It was silver, complete with the head, the eyes, and a fin on the tail. She did as Raina had done and popped the entire thing into her mouth. It was slimier and crunchier than it had appeared. "Oh boy," she said, after succeeding in swallowing. "Delicious. Mnogo vkusno."

"Uh-huh." Raina turned back to the news. "This is interesting. You are from Hollywood, you should like it." She listened for a minute. "The former Prime Minister, Andrei Lukanov, is receiving death threats. He has said that before the elections he will make public the names of the government officials who profited from the banking scandal. He will expose some of the highest ranking credit millionaires."

"Credit millionaires?"

"After the Change they formed banks, took the people's money, and never returned it. The banks made loans to the state, to the Mafia, to relatives and friends. And you know what happened?" Raina snapped her fingers in the air. "Poof! No documentation of those loans. The paperwork is gone, vanished."

Raina rubbed her lips together and squinted at the television. "The people were stupid to trust. We listened to them when they said your money is safe, buh buh buh buh, the state will protect you, buh buh buh. I was stupid. I had money there when the banks failed." She motioned toward the window, toward the streets. "Swindlers. Many of them were government officials, many of them Mafia. Kakvo da praviya? What to do?" She extended her open hands toward June and widened her eyes in an exaggerated and sarcastic display of helplessness. "What to do? It's a very dangerous threat that Lukanov makes. He has many enemies now. The mutras will kill him."

"What are the mutras?"

"Mafia. An important word for you to know but never use. Many of them used to be wrestlers, bodyguards, and assassins. The KGB gave them all kinds of dirty work. It is not very pleasant for a country with such beautiful beaches, mountains, and villages to be best known for its clever and cruel killers. Criminals. Cretins. Ehhhh! Shibanite mutri!" Raina slammed down her glass on the television tray and rakia slopped everywhere. She crossed her arms over her bosom again and stared straight ahead.

After a full minute, June cleared her throat. "I've been in the mountains with my husband. It was spectacular."

"Hmmph. You like it here then? You're happy?"

June considered. Like it here? Happy? If June divided her life into parts, befores and afters, it went something like this: before Bulgaria, after arriving, before Ethan began traveling, after he stopped unpacking at home between trips, before what Claire did, after what Claire did. This was still afterward. Actually—since Claire died, everything had always been afterward.

Mrs. Summer had been about to turn fifty. June had just moved in with Ethan and had driven home for the birthday party. She'd hand-painted a ceramic vase for Claire at the Color Me Mine on Montana Street, gotten her a gift certificate for the new Bliss Spa in Beverly Hills, and bought a nonfat frozen yogurt cake from Baskin-Robbins. (June knew Claire counted calories and grams of fat, even on her birthday.) She had all of this in her arms when she opened the door. It was a Saturday afternoon and the house was quiet.

June saw her mother's bare feet on the floor before she saw anything else, and she was angry—not sad, not scared, just angry. It was far from the first time it had happened. She did not run to her mother's side, as she had in the past. Instead she went into the kitchen, set the cake down on the table, and dialed nine-one-one. After summoning the ambulance, she put the cake in the freezer before going back into the living room. Then June dropped to her knees by Claire, whose head was turned to the side, who this time had no drink spilled across her dress. Her lipstick was perfect. June slapped her. "Wake up," she said. "Wake up, Claire." She was always to call her Claire, never Mom.

June slapped her again and the skin felt different. "Wake up, Claire." Her mother did not move. It seemed like June was sitting in a dark movie theater watching a dramatic scene on the screen. It couldn't be possible, not now, not after so many years of this same routine, not after Claire had bought champagne and a new dress for her own party, not after she'd gotten her nails done that morning. Neil was playing golf, Lilly was heading in from Palm Springs, and June knew that this time her mother was gone.

"Mom?" she said. "Oh God, Mom." June fell across her mother's body, cried, and kept touching her cheek. She kissed her own fingers and placed them against her mother's face, stroked her rouged cheeks, and apologized, over and over. "I'm sorry. I'm sorry for slapping you."

When the paramedics arrived, they asked June what happened. June couldn't take her shaking hand away from her mother's face. She had Claire's lipstick all over her palm. She kept running her fingers over Claire's cheeks trying to erase that last offensive gesture.

The female paramedic tried to pull June away, but she wouldn't leave Claire's side. The shaking was getting worse. The paramedic knelt down and asked again, "What happened?"

"I slapped her." June fell backward to a sitting position next to the body. She could not make her legs work. She pointed to Claire's cold cheek. "I slapped her." June looked up at the paramedics. "I slapped Claire. I slapped my mom so goddamn hard."

One of the paramedics turned to the other and whispered, "Okay, I guess she slapped her." The other paramedic laughed under his breath as he picked up Claire's ankles, sending the flowered skirt sliding to her waist. June grabbed the antique end table and knocked over a bowl of potpourri while trying to pull herself to her feet. Claire died wearing control-top panty hose and everyone could see it. June stumbled to the sink in the kitchen and threw up.

Less than a month later, on what should have been the happiest day of her life, June stood looking at the elderly Las Vegas preacher who was marrying her, thinking, "What if he knew I slapped my dead mom?"

"THAT'S A HARD question," she said, finally answering Raina. "I keep up appearances. I don't wallow. But if you want to know the truth, I'm not *really* one of those happy shiny people. Don't get me wrong. I'm not all morbid and depressed and thinking it's glamorous. It's just a circumstantial thing, really. It's nothing against your country."

Raina seemed to like this answer. "We will be all right," she said, topping off the rakia glasses. "We'll get along fine."

8

Subject: Fired
Date: Sat, 28 Sept 1996 12:21:46 +0000
From: Greg Schwartz <gschwartz66@horizon.com>
To: June Carver <jcarver@sof.cit>

Hey June,

Just writing to tell you I got canned. Whatever. Rob tells
Jess to tell me to get the galley of Stephen King's new book
and I call and you-know-who says no. So I tell Jess but she
doesn't tell Rob. So Rob calls and asks where's the galley
and I say it's not ready, they won't let it go. And he says,
did you know it was for Jeff Berg? And I say no. And Jess
says to Rob that she told me. Which she didn't. Which I make
clear to Rob. She then strings me up by my balls for insinu-
ating that she is a liar. Which she is. Which I make clear,
again. Which causes her to cry.

Meanwhile Rob calls up the agent and gets the galley no
sweat but by that time Berg is already on a flight to Cal-
cutta. Or Cancun. I can't remember. And Jess is sitting in
her stupid office squeezing that goddamned little rubber fat
toy that she squeezes when she's stressed and Rob is pretending to be on the speaker phone yelling, "Someone's getting a new asshole ripped over this one Jeff, just you be
assured," when really he is practicing his psychological
terror techniques and Melanie from HR calls me and says,
"Don't touch the computer, don't touch the rolodex, don't
touch the files, don't use the phone."

The point being to respond to your last email: So you feel
you have lost your husband and your career and your family
and all of your friends? Congratulations. You have just done

what every person I know dreams of doing. And you didn't even have to fake your own death. I'm sorry you are miserable, but I can't empathize with your penchant to be back here. I am going to work for my sister's catering business. Oh, the glamour. I was going to be someone.

Can I come live with you?

Love,

Greg

*E*THAN WAS OUT of town with his new friend Stan, a lawyer working at the Center for the Study of Democracy. Stan, with his balding head and tobacco-chewing habit, was an expatriate from Des Moines and had latched onto Ethan immediately. In his mid-thirties, Stan was overweight, nearsighted, and always wore a backward baseball cap. In a lifelong effort to make up for his physical inadequacies, Stan had become a man of loud laughter, competitive handshakes, and derogatory jokes. He had been in the Balkans for two years to perform the ambiguous function of "helping rewrite the books," and had been asked to go with a group from USAID out to the provinces for the presidential elections. Monitors would be placed all over the country to observe balloting and make sure that the Mafia did not try to buy people or strong-arm the locals into voting Red. Included in Stan's weekend getaway would be plenty of rakia, Cuban cigars, hiking in the mountains, and krutchma outings involving him showing off his expensive American belongings for lovely, naive village girls. Ethan had suggested June use the weekend for her language studies.

After spending all of Friday night in bed with a cup of hot chocolate with whiskey and an Anne Tyler novel she had already read once on the plane, June decided to call Roxanne. "It's June, hello! Oh nothing . . . nothing interesting. Ethan went out of town with Stan to Pazardzhik and thought it would be best if I stayed in Sofia and worked on my Bulgarian."

"Oh. How interesting."

"Yeah. I was thinking tonight might be a good time to practice conversation."

"Oh? Really! How *interesting*!"

"When can you pick me up?"

THE TAXI LET the two women off in front of a drab gray building not far from the Party House. It was as if the former inhabitants, upon being burnt out of their headquarters by a torch-wielding mob, had simply taken their big red star down from the roof and quietly moved around the corner to a cozier locale. Unofficially, of course. The club had an air of old money, with couches, gleaming tables, wooden paneling, marble columns, candles, and dim lights behind a staggering selection of alcohol arranged against mirrored shelves. Cigarette smoke was everywhere, and piped in was American jazz with a Dixieland bounce. A bartender in a tuxedo stood against the back wall beside an ice sculpture of a saxophone.

With a glass of red wine clutched in her hand, June descended the stairs behind Roxanne. They wound down and down, and as they neared the bottom, June heard rock and roll. The dance floor was packed with men who had discarded their ties and jackets. They spun women with loose hair around until their dresses flared and revealed exotic underwear.

A blond woman with a British accent yelled at Roxanne from a leather booth against the wall. "Roxy! Yoo-hoo, Roxy!"

Roxanne waved to her with waggling fingers. "Right back," she said to June.

June was not sure she liked this place. It seemed like a place for people who said things like Roxy, yoo-hoo, Roxy. She drained her glass and went to the bar for another.

Roxanne joined her a moment later with a bottle of tequila, two shot glasses, a saltshaker, and a dish of lemon wedges. "Look what I scored!"

"If I drink tequila, I'm warning you."

"Warning me what?"

"I'll be too much fun. You'll die. Death by June. Death by an unstoppable case of obnoxious June."

"Kakvo e tova?" a man with an enormous head asked from the table behind them. He had a scarf draped aristocratically around his thick neck. He pointed at the tequila shots and grinned.

BEFORE LONG, JUNE'S inner elbow was salted. "I like this taki shak," the man, whose name was Petko, said to June. "Let's do another taki shak."

When he licked her arm with his rough tongue, he did seem somewhat like a pet. A poorly behaved pit bull. "I am from sugar factory."

"Excuse me? Sugar factory?"

"Yes. You know Plovdiv?"

"No."

"Plovdiv is best Bulgarian city. That is Stoyan there," Petko said, pointing to a man at the bar screaming into his cell phone. "He is from sugar factory neighborhood too. We are both part of close protection team for a very important man. You know, special force security."

"Bodyguards."

"More than bodyguard! More! Us from sugar factory, we are like security detail. Special police."

"I see."

"When we was boys we stole bons bons from Plovdiv sugar factory. Our neighborhood is famous."

"For bonbon stealing? Great."

"No, not great. Sugar factory is famous for pimps and narco dealers. Only few of us are so powerful. Me and Stoyan, a few others. Not many. You ask around. People know who are Plovdiv sugar factory big men in Sofia. You ask around."

"Okay, I will."

"Yes, you will. Okay. And then maybe one day you will not mind to have my driver come to fetch you to party on villa in mountain where I have my trophies and my Jacuzzi."

"Sure." She looked around for some means of escape, but she was pinned against the wall by Petko's massive body. The crowd was crazy and drunk and she decided no one gave a damn what she did. She had to get away from Petko, whose fat pinkie finger was now lightly tickling her knee. She stood up on the leather seat, hiked up her skirt, and proceeded to climb over the back of the booth. She gave a partial moon of white upper thigh and polka-dot panties to the bar in the center of the room.

Stoyan, still on the phone shouting at the disrespectful owner of Neron's discotheque at the top of his lungs, was privy to June's little display. He covered the mouthpiece for a second and nudged the man sitting next to him. Chavdar was sedately sipping a Ballantine's and engaging in an unfocused and uninspired conversation about opera with Ani, the attractive daughter of one of his business partners. "Chavdar, vizh," said Stoyan.

Chavdar looked. June's behind wriggled for a second before she successfully jumped, high heels and all, to the floor. She flipped her hair up, swayed, and then reached for the back of the booth to steady herself. From across the bar, Chavdar heard her exhale and say, "Whooaa."

A spontaneous laugh escaped Chavdar's mouth, and he covered it to hide his smile. The business partner's daughter continued to talk, unaware that she had lost her listener. "And my father has excellent tickets for Verdi's *Aïda*. Of course, it won't be as spectacular as the outdoor production at the Dimitrov Mausoleum, but perhaps the acoustics in the National Opera will do more justice to the music. Although wasn't it originally performed outdoors? Anyway, when the Arabesque Ballet troop moved to the National Opera from the Palace, they had a lovely . . ."

Ani talked and talked and Chavdar shook his head absentmindedly. His eyes followed June as she walked, or rather weaved, toward the ladies' room. There was something disarming about her bright eyes, her easy and eager smile. June fanned herself with a cocktail napkin as she traversed the room. "She's beautiful," he said to Stoyan.

Stoyan finally hung up the phone. "Nice panties," he said, and took a swig of rakia.

"I want to meet her."

WHEN JUNE EXITED the bathroom Roxanne called her over to a booth. Two bottles of champagne were on the table, and Roxanne looked tiny, seated with three enormous Bulgarian men. Two of the men were thick, their collars brushing against their heavy jaws. The third was tall and slender in comparison. Seated, his torso towered above the others, and he was lean and well built. June gave the tall man with the greenish-brown eyes and statuesque bone structure a once-over as she slid into the booth. "Hi."

Roxanne was at her most gracious. "June, let me introduce you to my new friend Damyan and his associates, Gospodin Samardjiev and Gospodin Kozhuharov."

Chavdar extended his hand courteously. "Chavdar. Call me Chavdar, please."

June gave him her hand, which he held delicately between his thumb and fingers as he bowed his head. "Nice to meet you," she said. He had manicured nails and tan skin. The dark brown hair on the back of his hand crawled up his arm, partially hiding a gold watch at the edge of a crisp cuff.

Chavdar tickled her palm before releasing her hand. "Likewise," he said, giving her a suggestive wink. After the grope Petko had given her under the table earlier, June was starting to suspect that palm scratches and pinkie tickles were par for the course in the Bulgarian pickup scene.

June quickly found Chavdar extraordinarily amusing. A real crack-up, actually, with his suave suit, jewelry, palm tickles, and bedroom winks. His face, while devastatingly handsome, was too debonair. Every dark hair was swept back and in place. His lips were too full and soft and looked as if they had never once been chapped. His fingernails sparkled, and she realized that he wore a clear coat of polish. June wanted to laugh out loud. She had met her first dandy.

June cleared her throat and resolved to devote herself to conversation that seemed worthy of champagne providers. Squash, cigars, whiskey, cars, politics, the Concorde, and sex with stewardesses. "So," she said, "what do you all do?"

"We're with IZTOK, the insurance security firm," answered Damyan.

"Security. A good thing to have in Sofia, I assume."

"Yes." Chavdar smiled and winked at June again. She could feel his knee against her leg under the table.

"This is great champagne. Thank you so much," June said, toasting the table.

"Wonderful," agreed Roxanne.

"Nishto, nishto," said Damyan and Chavdar simultaneously.

"Um hmm . . ." June cleared her throat and felt the need to fill the silence, especially since Chavdar's leg was pressing harder against hers. It seemed he was trying to pry her thighs apart. June paused mid-sentence in disbelief. This businessman in his thirties was coming on like a high-school boy who had just discovered the joy of sex. "So, okay. Security in Sofia. Hey, what about that assassination recently?" June was pleased that she could actually remember the murdered man's name. "Lukanov, wasn't it? What's up with that?"

There was an uncomfortable silence at the table and Roxanne reached for her lipstick. Stoyan looked from Damyan to Chavdar and then back to Damyan. Chavdar scratched his neck and his face wrinkled in consternation. Then he laughed. "What's up with that?" he asked, looking at Stoyan and enjoying the feel of the American slang coming from his lips. "Kato, kakvo stava sus tova, nali? Good question. Damyan . . ." Now Chavdar put a particular emphasis on the phrase. "What's *up* with that?"

Now it was Damyan's turn to laugh. Roxanne finished putting on her lipstick and allowed herself a belated gratuitous giggle. Only Stoyan remained quiet. His beady eyes slid to the side and focused on June.

"Anyway," Roxanne said, finishing her champagne. "I say we blow this joint. It's starting to get stuffy and I feel like dancing."

Damyan nodded and slung an arm around Roxanne's shoulders. "That is good with me."

"I like the disco under the Palace," said Roxanne. "Neron's."

The three men exchanged looks, and Chavdar stood up. "Not tonight."

"Why?" asked Roxanne.

Chavdar helped June out of the seat. His thumb massaged the palm of her hand again. "They are having something special there tonight. A private event."

Stoyan grunted. "Exactly. Tochno taka."

Chavdar gave his most charming smile to Roxanne. "Why not some jazz instead? Or is that . . ." He glanced at June. "Too tame for you?"

Roxanne shrugged and grabbed her purse. "I like jazz. How about you, June?"

"Yeah. Super."

Stoyan glared at June. "*Super* then. I'm going home."

Chavdar leaned in and whispered something in Stoyan's ear. June thought she heard him say, "Call me when you are finished at Neron." June shook her head. Her Bulgarian was still so bad. She couldn't understand a thing.

THERE WERE NO tables available at the jazz club, and June started to make her way toward the bar where she could fight for leaning space. Chavdar gently took her arm. "Would you like to sit down, June?" She turned around to tell him that there were no tables, but he was motioning to an empty chair. The group who had been seated at the table were standing up and counting money. The women looked irritated, but the men moved away quietly, nodding briefly at Chavdar. He then pulled the chair out for June. "Have a seat. What can I get you to drink?"

"Red wine?"

"One moment," he said, and touched her shoulder. It was an unusually long touch, and his fingers trailed across the back of her neck as he walked away.

Roxanne leaned over to whisper, "He's one of the most interesting men in Sofia!"

"Who?"

"Chavdar, you silly!" Roxanne said. "I have wanted to meet him for ages."

June turned to look at him at the bar, counting his wad of cash as if he were a blackjack dealer. "I think he's corny," she whispered. "Rico Suave. Don Juan—"

"Shhh," Roxanne said, as Chavdar arrived back at the table with drinks for all.

"So, June," Chavdar said, zeroing in on her with an inquisitive expression. "How long are you in town?"

"I live here, actually. My husband is doing research for a book."

"And what do you do?"

"On my last film in Los Angeles I was the Unit Manager. I would like to work here, but things haven't fallen into place yet."

"Film?" he said, genuinely delighted. He shook his head as if that explained everything. "It might be a good time for film in Bulgaria. Inexpensive locations, well-educated crews, a lot of unused studio space and equipment."

"So you know about film."

"Well, it was my dream once. I wanted to be a filmmaker before, many years before. A colleague of mine is now in the Czech Republic making films. Prague is becoming very famous with Hollywood filmmakers. I hope perhaps Bulgaria can become like that someday. But Bulgaria is different. Maybe not soon, here. Maybe not ever, here."

"Did you study film?"

"Oh no. It's just, how do you call it? Something I enjoy."

"A hobby."

"Yes. A hobby." He was speaking plainly, and had forgotten about brushing her leg under the table with his foot. He actually had a big, beautiful, boyish smile. "What do you think of Martin Scorsese?"

"Genius."

"I admire him very much. *Raging Bull, The Godfather, Scarface.* You know them?"

"Of course, but *Taxi Driver* is my favorite. Jodie Foster in that big-brimmed hat and white platform shoes. Hot pants and juice-can curls. Travis— I *loved* Travis."

"I wanted to *be* Travis." He squinted an eye, giving her a Robert De Niro smirk. "All the animals come out at night."

"But someday a real rain will come and—"

"Wash all this scum off the streets." He leaned back to look at her. "Mnogo si hubava," he said. "Do you know what that means?"

"Yes. Thank you."

"It means you are very beautiful."

"I know. I'm taking Bulgarian lessons."

"Really? Most foreigners come here and don't take the time to learn even one word of our unimportant little language. They expect us to speak to them in their language, their superior tongue."

"Well, that's sort of awful."

"Yes."

June felt uncomfortable under his gaze. Chavdar bit his lower lip and didn't try to hide the path of his eyes from her face, to her breasts, to the curve her hips made with her legs crossed. Then he smiled in a way that left no doubt as to what he was thinking. He leaned forward, put his hand on her knee, and whispered. "Iskam da te izpapkam."

"What?" June asked, her voice catching. "I—I haven't learned that one yet."

"It means, I want to devour you."

"Well. Well, that's—not in my book."

He smiled, took her hand, and folded it into a fist. He lowered his mouth and gently touched his tongue to the crevice between her middle and pointer finger.

"Oh." June watched him and he watched her, from under his swooping bangs. He never moved his mouth from her hand. His lips surrounded one knuckle and he sucked gently. "Oh *God*."

"You like that?"

Suddenly June stood up. "Roxanne? Sweetie, thanks, but I have to go. Thank you all for everything. For a great night. I am suddenly very tired."

Chavdar stood up right after her, almost knocking over his chair. "What?"

"I'm sorry," June said, tugging on her coat sleeve, which had become tangled around the chair. "It's time for me to go home."

"Let me take you."

"Oh, thank you but I'd prefer to catch a taxi."

"Absolutely not. I won't allow you to go home by yourself in a taxi." Chavdar turned his back for a second to grab his trench coat, and when he turned around, she was gone.

"She's quick, ain't she?" asked Roxanne. "Poof!"

Chavdar sat down, crumpled a cocktail napkin in his hand, and glanced irritably at Damyan. "What? Why are you laughing?"

"Because I have never seen that expression on your face before, and I doubt I ever will again."

JUNE HAILED A cab and sped through Sofia toward the suburbs. She felt a bit foolish for her quick exit, but it was late, she was tired, and Ethan was where she had become accustomed to him being—far away. She wanted to lie down and put her head on the pillow that smelled like her husband so as not to smell Chavdar's cologne. She wanted to fall asleep thinking of the way things had been with Ethan once upon a time. Chavdar was very good at his cheesy ladies' game, but June was not interested in playing. She told herself this again and again, even as the smell of his cologne lingered on her clothes, and the feel of his hand on her shoulder stayed in her mind. It had been such a long time since anyone had paid her so much special attention. In bed alone, her pulse quickened, thinking of the words *I want to devour you.*

"Ughhh!" she said out loud, flipping onto her side. She tried to think of Ethan, returning to her, kissing her—but instead she saw him clawing at his collar while ogling that teenage Bulgarian cook. She reached over, grabbed his pillow, and wrapped herself around the scent of his dandruff shampoo. It didn't help at all.

9

Subject: I miss you, flesh of my flesh
Date: Sat, 09 Nov 1996 04:08:59 -0700
From: Lilly Summer <org.beauty@ink.net>
To: June Carver <jcarver@sof.cit>

Hermana mía, cómo estás? (I am dating a beautiful angel
named Joaquín from Mexico City. He makes Day of the Dead
ceramics and is teaching me Spanish.) I met him at my new
kickboxing class. My chiropractor said this kind of fitness
would be beneficial for my circulation, and the tingling cucumber masks are not doing the trick on the face and feet
for me these days. Don't tell my customers.

So, no one can believe it when I say my sister is living in
Bulgaria. My acupuncturist insists, however, that Bulgaria
is famous for healing mineral baths and homeopathic medicine. I hope you aren't neglecting your physical and mental
well-being if such rare luxuries are really as accessible as
he told me. In any case, I still think you should come home
for the holidays. I need you and love you and want to talk
with you face to face so that I can be sure that you are not
running away from your problems. If you will not be home for
the holidays please give me an address where I can send the
Teach Yourself Yoga instruction manual. June, is everything
okay? Answer me.

Health and happiness,

Lilly

JUNE WAS IN her new favorite place in Sofia: the ugly claw-foot bathtub. She had developed a wonderful yet dependent relationship with the metal trough. She cried in it on the nights Ethan was away, guiltily reliving her indiscretion with James. The tub knew her well from cradling her bare bottom and the pads of her feet. It welcomed her salty tears along with the stubble from her shaver.

"JUNE?" ETHAN KNOCKED on the door to the bathroom. June jumped and almost spilled her whiskey into the bathwater. She had started cutting out the hot chocolate entirely.

"What?"

"Phone."

June had only one friend. "Tell Roxanne I'll call her back, please?"

"It's some Kozhuharov guy."

Ethan heard a thump followed by a veritable tidal wave of water sloshing onto the tiled floor. "Just a second."

June emerged from the bathroom a second later in a towel. She dripped and slipped her way toward the phone. "Hello?"

"June, this is Chavdar Kozhuharov."

"Really? What a nice surprise."

"Well, I hope. Damyan acquired your telephone from Roxanne. I'm not bothering you?"

"Bothering me? No, no. Not at all. How are you?"

"Fine." He sounded very to the point. "I call you now because I remember you said you were looking for work. For something to 'fall into place,' I think you said. Yes?"

"Yes." June was genuinely surprised.

"So. Do you know this newspaper the *Sofia Sentinel*?"

"I've heard of it."

"Well, then you know it is an English-language newspaper. It has an entertainment section but only a very small one."

June released her grip on the phone and wiped her sweaty palm on the towel. "Umm hmm?"

"I know the editor, and I told him how I met a lovely young woman from Los Angeles who worked in film, is a writer, and has an academic background—a master's degree, as well."

June took a breath. It sounded so good the way he said it, academic background and all. "That was very nice of you."

"Well, he told me that they require a journalist for this entertainment section, concerning ballet, opera, and of course film and theater. They lack native English speakers at this paper. This journalist they require would also need to be available for night editing twice per week. Does this interest you?"

"Of course!" June burst out. "It interests me so much you can't imagine! Thank you so much for the recommendation."

"It is nothing. The editor will thank me when he meets you."

"What's his number? So I can arrange an interview?"

"An interview is not obligatory. You are hired."

"But, well, there's a small problem. I don't have a permit to work in Bulgaria."

"No problem. Now it is just to determine salary."

June would have done it for free. She didn't care if they paid her in baklava. "Oh, this is just too generous."

"No, I fear you will not find the pay generous. Not by the American standard."

"Oh, that's all right. I completely understand."

"Roxanne tells me you live in Darvenitsa and you want to move to the city."

"That's true. My husband and I are giving it a lot of thought. I feel very isolated out here sometimes."

"I expect you could find a very comfortable situation in the center for not so much."

"That's what I've been told."

Chavdar's voice was low and confident. "I will keep my eyes open for you, June."

ROXANNE WAS OUT of town for the weekend. Nevena had the keys to the apartment, and had been instructed to feed the cats, do the laundry, and have a casserole waiting.

Instead, Nevena fed the cats, started the laundry, turned the stereo on, took a bubble bath, read several imported issues of *People* magazine, drank two Coca-Colas and one orange Fanta, smoked two of Roxanne's Cartier cigarettes, watched a half hour of Euro MTV on cable, smelled all of Roxanne's perfumes, and had just started trying on Roxanne's clothes, including her underwear.

Nevena stood in front of Roxanne's full-length mirror wearing a black miniskirt, knee-high boots, and an oversized vermilion bra that gaped loosely over her small breasts. Her face had no trace of makeup, and her limp hair was straggly on her shoulders. She stared at her reflection and felt like a stranger. She couldn't smile like the celebrities in the fashion magazines, she couldn't pose or blow kisses. All she could do was dolefully flip through Roxanne's endless sea of clothes, make a halfhearted selection, and pull the oversized garment on over her gaunt body. Flashy tube tops, sequined camisoles, silk stockings with mauve garters. Then she would stand, as she was doing now, and stare forlornly at the mirror, seeing only her bony knees and the rings under her eyes.

Nevena could stand and stare into the endless double mirror reflections forever. There were a million of her, life-size and smaller and smaller, stretching all the way back into the mirror, until her image resembled a tiny doll in the distance. The time would slip away like sleep because she was daydreaming. She was an American woman with a closet full of short plaid skirts and a gentleman friend who brought her flowers. She was studying at a university, had her own car and parents who were alive, as well as a number of good job offers waiting for her upon graduation. Or, she was Roxanne, a writer, a woman of sophistication and elegance, a woman who threw dinner parties every week and let her maid clean up the mess.

Her favorite dream was the simplest. She was just herself, ordinary Nevena, and she won the visa lottery. Overcome with joy, she would get to go to America, where she would find a good job as a housekeeper or nanny for a rich family, and send for her brother and sister. They would all live together in the mountains, maybe Colorado or California or New Mexico, and with all the money they would make they could go to night school. She was Nevena and no one else, and she could afford clothes like the ones she wore now, not just for herself but for her siblings too, and she could buy her own magazines and rose water and speak English fluently. She would look in the mirror and be able to smile.

Nevena was standing stock still, completely withdrawn inside herself, her eyes fixed on the patent leather boots on her feet, when the doorbell rang. Immediately she tore off the lacy red bra, dropped onto her behind, and stuck her feet up into the air to try to pull the tight leather boots away from where they were stuck.

ETHAN WAS WHISTLING a little tune and checking his watch as he waited for Roxanne to answer the door. June had made holiday gift baskets for her friends and Ethan's research colleagues, and Ethan had agreed to drop one off for Roxanne, even though he was in a rush. He had a lunch date to interview the commercial attaché from Switzerland and later in the afternoon he had an appointment to discuss the progress of banking reform in Bulgaria with a representative from Balkan National. It was sometimes tedious work, but Ethan enjoyed the research. He truly believed that he could write a worthwhile book and dissertation. Ethan was optimistic that his work would play an important part in developing a model of reform that could pull countries like Bulgaria out of economic crisis. He felt like he was doing something meaningful, and he was happier than he'd been in a long time.

His thoughts were on his work, and when the door finally opened it took him a second to recognize the girl standing before him. Nevena wore her housecoat and sneakers with no socks, and she kept switching her weight from one foot to the other. Her hair was pulled back in a sloppy ponytail. "Yes?" she said, avoiding his eyes.

"Hi!" said Ethan. "Nevena! What are you doing here?"

Nevena opened the door an inch more and narrowed her eyes. Before her stood a man who was so bundled up in winter clothes that she could barely see his face. Even stranger, he wore an old Soviet commander's coat and was carrying a ridiculously feminine basket smothered in bows and other frivolous decorations. Her fingers closed around the chain, making sure the door was secured against this obvious psychopath. "I work here. Who are you?"

Ethan paused, taken aback. Then he whipped off his hat and tugged on the scarf surrounding his throat. "I'm Ethan. A friend of Roxanne's? I met you at that dinner party."

"Which dinner party?"

"Uh, the one where you and I, we talked for a while and, uh . . ."

"Never mind. It is not important."

"You came in at the last minute to help, and I was in the kitchen with you."

Nevena looked him over and nodded curtly. "Yes. Anyway, never mind. Roxanne is not at home." She was eager to close the door, lock up, and leave. Her fun for the day had been interrupted, and she had other homes to clean in the afternoon.

"Can I bring this in and set it down?" Ethan asked, nodding at the basket in his arms.

"I will take it," she said, finally undoing the chain lock.

"It's pretty heavy. Why don't you let me?"

"I prefer to take it alone," Nevena said, extending her arms for the basket. As soon as she did so, however, several of Roxanne's bracelets slid down her arm toward her hand, clanking as they fell. Nevena immediately snatched her hands back and clasped them behind her back. "But do as you please. Continue to carry it inside if you wish."

Ethan carried the fruit basket into the apartment. The television was on, playing the European countdown, and from the other room the stereo was blasting a Middle Eastern beat with Turkish words.

Nevena looked at the floor and kept her jeweled arms hidden. "Just put it on the table."

The empty soda cans, cigarette butts, and movie magazines were still where Nevena had left them. It didn't take a genius to figure it out. Ethan looked over at Nevena with a smile and noticed that her pink housecoat was on inside out, the buttons pulling away from the holes. "Where's Roxanne?"

"She is not here, I said." The room was not well lit and Ethan couldn't see Nevena's face turning pink, or the subtle quivering of her lower lip.

Ethan was thoroughly charmed by the sodas and magazines, and felt that some teasing was in order. Finally he had come up with a decent subject of conversation. He set the fruit basket down and gave Nevena his most winning grin. "She's out of town, isn't she?"

Nevena's face turned bright red with the effort to hold back her tears. She stamped her sneaker down on the tile and wiped her nose. "I do good work here!" she said, angrily switching off the television. "I work like a horse, do everything right!" She jerked the bracelets off her wrist and closed her fist around them. "Say whatever you want, I don't care."

"What do you think I want to say?"

Nevena held out the bracelets in her shaking hand. "You will tell about this."

"No I won't. I don't care if you raided the refrigerator and watched television while she was out of town. If it was me I probably would have thrown a party. And if I was your age I definitely would have thrown a party."

Nevena looked at Ethan warily. "I did not make any such party."

"I know. Are you . . ." Ethan motioned with one finger to her dress. "Are you going to leave the house like that?"

"Like what?"

"Your dress is on inside out."

Nevena looked down and fiddled with the buttons unsuccessfully for a second. "That is like that on purpose," she said unconvincingly. "That is so it does not dirty when I clean." She looked up, but her fingers stayed glued to her buttons. "Did you know this, what you wear, is one old coat that was Soviet commander's?"

Ethan laughed. "You mean this belonged to a Soviet commander?"

"Yes, that is what I said."

"Is that bad?"

Nevena shrugged. "Some people might not consider it to be, uh . . . dobur vkous?"

"Good taste?"

"Yes, maybe some say it is not so good of taste."

"Are you one of them?"

"Yes."

Ethan had forgotten about his afternoon appointments. "Can I buy you a cup of coffee?" He glanced at the table. "Or a soda? It looks like you really like soda."

"I had enough soda already."

"Cappuccino?"

Now that his Soviet coat was open she could see the rumpled suit and tie beneath. All over his head reddish blond hair was sticking up, full of static from the stocking cap he had just removed. His cheeks were ruddy from the wind outside, he was smiling, and he had brought Roxanne fruit and bows in a basket. Nevena didn't know any Bulgarian men who would walk through the street carrying such a gift. "I like cappuccino," she said softly. "But it is necessary I change the clothes first."

"Great." He motioned to the couch. "I'll just read Roxanne's magazines, pop open a cold one, and watch some MTV."

Nevena hesitated in the doorway. "Are you joking with me?"

Ethan nodded. "Yes."

Nevena looked at him for a long, quiet moment and then smiled. Her brown eyes tilted and her lips parted. Just barely, no teeth. "Okay," she said. Her dimples showed.

"THIS IS THE PLACE," Nevena said, pointing to a depressing little coffee shop. Inside were five white plastic tables and red and yellow plastic chairs. The addition of the bright colors didn't do much for the shop, could not cancel out the dingy walls or the scowl of the woman behind the counter.

"Great," Ethan said, holding the door open so she could enter.

Nevena took off her heavy coat, and Ethan was met with the very subtle scent of her body. By now he was used to this odor, on the trams, in the small offices cramped back-to-back with desks and too many people. He no longer minded the absence of hair sprays, body lotions, perfumes, and deodorants, but he was not prepared for the arousing effect of Nevena's natural smell. It wasn't sweat or dirt exactly, just something musky and feminine—something profoundly sexual. Ethan looked away as he removed his own coat. "Cappuccino then?"

"Yes." Nevena started to walk toward the counter.

Ethan touched her elbow. "Sit down. I'll get it."

Nevena looked at him oddly. "You will?"

"Sure."

"I mean to say, you will serve me?"

"Yeah."

"Oh. Okay."

"Anything to eat?"

"No thank you."

"You sure? I'm going to get something."

Nevena was starving. "I want nothing else, thank you."

Ethan made two trips back to the table, first with the cappuccinos and the second time with one baklava, one banichka, and one chocolate-filled croissant. "I got a few things just in case you wanted a bite. I didn't know what you would like."

Nevena bit at some skin on her chapped lips while she looked at the food-laden table. Cappuccinos were twice as much as a shot of espresso and she rarely treated herself. She never had three desserts, and definitely never had a man bring them to her and smile and wait for her to take the first bite.

She looked around self-consciously. Yes, people were already staring. "Thank you," she said. "That was very kind."

"Dig in," Ethan said.

"Dig in," she repeated softly, picking up her fork. "That is a new phrase for me. Dig in. Okay." Nevena took a delicate bite of the baklava and then set her fork down. "This is much too generous. Really."

"Too late," Ethan said, taking a big bite of chocolate croissant. "We have to eat it now. It's my way of apologizing."

"No apology is obligatory."

Ethan dismissed this with a wave of his hand. "You must really like working for Roxanne, to get that upset."

Nevena took another delicate bite of the baklava, trying not to give away the fact that she hadn't eaten all day and wanted to wolf it down with her fingers. "I don't like working for her. That was not why I was upset."

"Why then?"

"I work for fifteen different families, and I need every hour of work. She pays me well. If I lose her house I have to take two more to make up for it, and I have very little free time as it is."

"Fifteen houses?" asked Ethan.

"Fifteen. Yes."

"How many hours a week do you work?"

Nevena looked confused. "All."

Ethan set down his cappuccino. "You work from when you get up in the morning until you go to bed at night, Monday through Friday?"

"Oh, no. I misunderstood."

"Oh. Okay."

"Saturday and Sunday too."

Ethan leaned back in his chair and shook his head. "How do you do that?"

"I take coffee breaks. Several a day."

"That's a lot of work."

Nevena shrugged. "Some people do more. Some people do less." Nevena sat quietly, but Ethan's fixed look was unnerving. She sighed. "I have one younger sister and one brother who I must help, you see."

"They live with you?"

"No." Nevena paused and glanced around the coffee shop. People continued to look at them, studying the Bulgarian girl having what looked like a personal and possibly inappropriate conversation with a man who was obviously a foreigner. The coffee talk was getting too deep too quickly. They should have been talking about the weather, about the rising inflation, about the price of bread in the store next door. Nevena should have brought Ethan's coffee to him, and there should not have been three desserts for two people.

Nevena cleared her throat and looked at the table. "My sister used to live with me, but I have not seen her so suddenly."

"You mean recently?"

"Yes, that's what I mean." Nevena seemed intent on examining her sugar packet. "Actually I have not have word of her since . . . Well, it makes many months now. And my brother, he works in a factory, one hour outside Sofia. It is too far to drive each day."

"These are your younger siblings?"

"Yes."

"How old are they?"

Nevena stirred her cappuccino nervously.

"Do you want to talk about something else?"

"No, it is no problem. Boryana is twenty and Georgi is nineteen."

"Why haven't you heard from your sister?"

Nevena looked up suddenly. "I don't know this! How can I know this?"

"Don't your parents know?"

"Oh, my parents? They . . . they . . ." Nevena realized that as nice as Ethan was, she couldn't take this scrutiny any longer. She drained her cappuccino. "I'm sorry to be so impolite but I must go. Or I risk to be late for my next appointment. It is across town and . . ." Nevena trailed off. Ethan was looking at her with such disappointment.

"Did I say something to offend you? I was just trying to make conversation. Sometimes I'm too, I don't know. Sometimes I just don't say what I mean."

"It's okay."

"No, it's not. It's just that I'm interested in you. I mean, interested in a nice way. Not in the American slang way. In a respectable way—"

"Please! You have just only met me!" Everyone was now staring blatantly from behind newspapers. A big man with rolls of fat on the back of his neck had turned all the way around in his seat to watch over his shoulder. He narrowed his eyes at the disrespectful foreigner being pushy and loud with a nice Bulgarian girl who was trying to remain demure and quiet. Ethan's friendly forwardness, so effective in California, was viewed here as merely fake and suspicious, even childish and rude.

Nevena saw the man put down his paper and cock his head just enough to signal he was ready to assist. There was going to be trouble. She quickly stood, pulled on her coat, and tried to ignore Ethan's wounded expression. She turned and walked to the front door. Before stepping back out into the cold she looked back. "Thank you, Ethan."

Ethan waved. He had wanted to make her laugh and instead he had made her run away. He sank bank into his chair and sighed. It was probably for the best.

10

Subject: Re: the wild wild east
Date: Fri, 15 Nov 1996 03:05:04 -0700
From: Benny <bgatwick@asb.com>
To: June <jcarver@sof.cit>

Hey there, you. Okay, you want gossip? You got it.

We were informed last Thursday that our movie is $5 mil over
budget. The producers were turning in estimates for $50 mil,
and now we are shutting down production immediately for re-
evaluation. All the local hire people were laid off. Remember Sarah, the cute lesbian from Sandcastle Productions? She
just got a deal for a script assignment with Global. It's a
modern-day continuation of the Snow White story, only it's a
hippie girl/princess from Haight Street with seven fucked up
transient kids (the weirdo dwarves) living with her, and the
evil witch is some rich Pacific Palisades socialite. Of
course, prince charming is a do-gooder environmentalist who
is still hip enough to drive a motorcycle or some such junk.
That's what's worth one hundred thou these days.

If you write anything meaningful over there, June, keep it
far away from this city. They will turn a story about glue-
addicted gypsy children in the Balkans into an animated
musical about a tribe of pixie-sized fairy-dust-loving
flamenco dancers who live happily ever after with their
dancing bears.

And lastly, about the situation with Ethan—you've had a suc-
cessful relationship for almost a decade. I'm still unat-
tached, untamed, and inexperienced at surviving something
longer than six months. If being almost thirty with relationship problems is as tragic as you make it out to be, we
might as well form some kind of "Lost Souls" club together
or something. Or maybe a bowling team.

Take care sugar,

Benny

THE TAVERN WAS smoky and full, even in the afternoon. Most of the pa-
trons were middle-aged men with weathered faces and rumpled clothing. The
room was small and dark, with many tables pushed close together. Nuts,
crumbly brown bread, hard ovals of black sausage, and yellow wedges of
cheese sat on the tables between many short glasses of rakia and soda water.
Chalga, a Bulgarian combination of Serbian, Greek, and Turkish folk music,
played at a low volume from a portable radio on the bar. Raina sank heavily
into a chair in the corner. "Here we are," she said to June, getting out her cigarettes. "It is interesting for you, yes?"

"Extremely. Thank you so much for bringing me—for getting me out of
the house."

"Hmmph. It is like going back in time."

"To when?"

"Back to the time when we would come to places like this on break and
stay until the early evening. Back to the time when the government pretended
to pay us and we pretended to work." Raina turned toward the bar, held up
two fingers, and then turned back to June.

"I don't understand how anyone had any money for anything."

Raina looked at June incredulously. "No one had much. Just enough. Except for the privileged party. If the winter is as bad as they say, you will see
something from the past on the streets." She touched her badly cut graying
brown hair. "There won't be any imported hair dyes, for example. All the
women with the same color hair, probably orange, just like in the Communist days." Raina laughed. She tapped on the cigarette pack and discovered it

was empty. She didn't stop talking as she reached for the ashtray and retrieved the stubs of the cigarettes left behind in the unemptied ashtray. June tried not to stare as Raina tore open the stubs and heaped the remaining tobacco in a little pile on the counter.

Then Raina took out her pipe, filled it, and continued smoking. "Westerners who visited back then thought we had such bad taste, such ugly clothes, such tacky hair. They didn't know that we all looked the same because there was no way to look different. We bought what was in the stores, we had no choice. One kind of awful toilet paper that is murder on the behind, outdated baby formula that we were scared to give our infants, one hair color for all women to cover their gray, one pair of ugly white boots that everyone owned."

"If it would have been easier for you and your family, why didn't you join the Party?"

Raina readjusted her bulky body on the small wooden chair. "Good question. I am surprised more people don't ask."

"Americans anyway, they probably assume they know the answer."

"You have heard of the American College? It was reopened after the Change. It had been closed for forty-five years. Of course."

"Of course."

"My parents went to the American College. That's where they met, back before the war. The Second World War, you know. My father studied economics and my mother studied history. Their professors were Americans, good people. My parents both spoke impeccable English. My father also spoke German and my mother French. They were highly educated. Not very rich, you understand, but comfortable. My mother taught school and my father worked as an economist for an investment firm. That was until the war."

"And then what happened?"

"Liberation Day," Raina said simply. "The birth of the People's Republic, you know. The implementation of the celebrated Five Year Plan. And so then the life that my parents knew was gone. The Communists were suspicious of all graduates of the American University." Raina leaned forward, cupped her hand to the side of her mouth so that no one could read her lips, and whispered sarcastically, "Spies, you know, spies! All over, those American-educated spies!"

She leaned back and crossed her arms across her formidable bosom. "My parents were transported, like cattle you understand, to the countryside outside Borovetz, where jobs were arranged for them. My mother worked in a factory and my father was assigned a position as a porter. He carried packages. For the rest of his life, you understand, my father carried packages and trunks, suitcases and boxes."

Raina paused, tilted her head to one side, and let her eyes wander across the many weary-looking men sitting hunched over their drinks at the surrounding tables. Some of them played cards with friends and several sat alone, staring at the slowly burning cigarettes clenched between stained fingers. "And then my father died. He died a very tired man, and disappointed, and afraid for the future. Whenever someone close to you dies, you take a second look at life. It is inevitable that you will change. I did much thinking and I refused to join. My husband wanted very much to be a member of the Party, you see. Raina, he said, please stop your foolishness. He wanted a better job, classy friends, a nicer apartment. Please, Raina, he said. It would be so good, buh buh buh buh, it would mean so much for us, buh buh buh buh. Please, Raina, think about it Raina, don't be so stubborn. It went on for years, buh buh buh."

"You still refused?"

"Umm hmm. Finally we divorced."

"Do you ever consider remarrying?"

Raina fingered a piece of dry, lusterless hair from her bangs and pulled it down in front of her eyes to examine. "Look at this. So ugly. Our hair was gray before it should have been. There was no time to be a woman, to try to be beautiful or feminine. I never saw a negligee or camisole except in a French magazine until recently when they appeared in our stores. Imagine what I would look like wearing one of those things now! And yet I do wish. Sometimes . . ." She trailed off. "Anyway, we were animals, beasts of labor. And the men looked at us and said, buh buh buh, this is not a woman; this is not a zhena, buh buh buh. What is this that I have married?" She pulled heavily on the pipe. "I married when I was young and beautiful. By the time I was divorced, it was too late."

June reached over, took Raina's warm hand in her cool one, and squeezed. "You're still beautiful, and it's never too late."

Raina snorted. "What an American thing to say."

"Well, occasionally us Yankee yahoos know what we're talking about."

After a second, both women laughed. They toasted, and drank.

Raina and June were tipsy when they left the tavern. The sun was setting and the streets were colder than they had been before. Raina slipped her arm through June's. "Thank you, my dear. That was lovely."

"It was nothing," June said, meaning it. All the drinks and food had cost her less than three dollars, and here Raina was, behaving as if June had treated her to something special.

"Oh lei lei! My ears," Raina said, putting her hands over them. "The first snowfall can't be far away." They were passing a small boutique, and in the window was a mannequin wearing a fuzzy pink hat. It looked incredibly soft, like angora. Raina paused. "Do you think I am too old and sensible for this hat?"

"Definitely not," said June. "Why don't you try it on?"

"I don't think so," Raina said, sniffing. "I am not so elegant, I don't think."

"Come on, just for fun."

"Just for fun you say," Raina said, still looking at the hat. "It's not fun to be foolish."

June took Raina's arm and pulled her into the store. "It's *always* fun to try on hats."

The store was small and warmed by an electric floor heater. A middle-aged woman with the carrot orange color of hair Raina had spoken about jumped up from her chair when they entered. "Moga li da vi pomogna?" she asked, her voice too urgent, her hands clasped together in front of her almost as if in prayer.

"Only looking," answered Raina. "We saw the nice hat in the window."

"I have many of them," said the shopkeeper. "I have them in every color. I will bring them out. You can choose. Just one minute." She hurried through a curtain into a closet, and Raina and June could hear her digging through boxes and tissue paper.

Raina scratched her head. Under her breath in English she whispered to June, "This was a mistake. We should not pretend we might buy for fun."

The shopkeeper came out of the back room with a bundle of hats clutched against her chest. She had not lied; they came in every color. "Please," she said, extending the armful of hats. "Take one and try it on. Feel how soft they are. Only two thousand lev. They are a very good deal."

Raina sighed and picked up the pink one. June pulled an orange one on over her light hair. Standing side by side, she and Raina looked into a mirror that the shopkeeper held up for them. "Very nice," the saleslady said, nervously touching a lock of June's hair.

June wanted to laugh. Raina looked ridiculous, her fleshy face topped by such a pink puffball, and June thought that her own hat made her look like a pumpkin. Raina turned from side to side. Her thick, ruddy cheeks looked even plumper and fuller, and the color brought out the red rims around the bloodshot whites of her eyes. "I don't think so," she said, taking the hat off and handing it back.

"It wasn't the best color for you," said the saleslady. Her hands were shaking as she searched through the pile of hats for one of forest green. "This is the one for you. It will complement your coloring." She held the hat out toward Raina, and her eyes were pleading. "This hat will keep you warm in the long cold winter." The saleslady turned to June. "It's going to be a very bad winter. You can't have enough warm clothes."

June handed the orange hat back. "Thank you, but no. It's not quite right for me."

The saleslady noticed her accent immediately. "Ah! A foreigner! This hat, you won't find it anywhere else in Sofia. And for you it is not just a good deal, it is a steal! It is so cheap you cannot say no. Not when it looks so nice on you and is so comfortable. Please, if you don't like the orange one, try another."

Raina took June's arm. "I think we are finished."

"Please!" the saleswoman said, holding out two hats, one black and one green. "Please try them. Just put them on and see! Maybe you will like them! Maybe you will!"

June was unable to walk away from those beseeching open arms, that falling face that had been so hopeful seconds before. The woman's eyes were actually wet. Raina dragged June out the door and led her down the street.

Sitting down on a concrete window ledge, Raina put her hand over her heart and took a few deep breaths. After a second she pulled out her cigarette pack. It was as empty as it had been the last time she checked. She crumpled it in her fist, swearing.

"She was crying because we didn't buy the hat?" June felt inexplicably guilty. "I should go back and buy it!"

"No," said Raina. "It's not just that. She was crying because of the winter. People with little shops like hers, they wonder how they will live. Forty-five years, these people were provided for. Not with much, you understand, but there weren't beggars in the streets or homeless people. Now everyone must figure out a new way to make a living. Selling hats or popcorn or flowers or coffee, there's not much difference. They are scared." Raina stood up straight and began to walk. "The truth is, I am scared too."

THE TRAM TRACKS BESIDE them made a humming noise, and in the distance they could see the lights approaching. "This is my tram," said Raina. "I'll take this home now. Do you want to come with me? For coffee, some television?"

June swung an arm around Raina's shoulders. "I have taken up too much of your time already."

Raina laughed and then doubled over, hacking. June patted her on the back, and when she stood up, Raina smiled. "Well, you are paying me, after all."

"I'm sure you have to do some preparations for your other students."

"Um hm," Raina said, looking away. "But you know, the embassy has found a young woman who will run around from place to place all day and tutor the employees and their spouses in the comfort of their own homes and offices. I can't compete. I do not even want to enter this competition." The tram barreled up and screeched to a stop, its rusty orange doors opening with a squeak and a bang.

"Raina," June began, helping her step onto the tram. "That doesn't seem fair."

"Quiet," Raina said, letting go of June's hand and putting one finger to her lips. "Stop this American foolishness about fair, fair, fair. You are in Bulgaria now. If you like, why not plan on staying for dinner after next week's lesson? I don't have anything more important. June, you are my only student."

11

Subject: Message for June from Dad
Date: Tue, 19 Nov 1996 21:47:35, -0500
From: Dad <Summer2@ncal.tech>
To: June <jcarver@sof.cit>

Hello June,

This is Tues. night and I just got back from San Antonio. I
went for four days to the CCC (Classic Car Convention) with
Adelaide, that woman I mentioned to you. We were entertained
royally and got to see Kenny Rogers. I worked on the brakes
of the Nomad before the convention. The front calipers were
sticking. I discovered this when I went to change the front
wheels for the show. It's much faster now that the brakes
aren't dragging.

Shelby died while we were gone, but she had a good long
life. Her hips were bad (that apparently is common among
German Shepherds) and she got hit by a car. Seth from next
door was feeding her, and he found her. I gave him one
hundred dollars. I had her buried at the pet cemetery in
Encino. We can visit the site when you get back. It's a
nice park.

Tomorrow it is back to work. Why don't you ever mention
Ethan's work there?

By the way, just so you know, back in my day, most women
were "housewives." You act like it's a dirty word. "Frig-

gin," "piss," and "screw," which keep recurring in your emails, are the real dirty words. I don't want to hear how "frigged up" the country is or about how Ethan is constantly "pissy."

But most importantly, stop complaining about how your career is now "screwed." If you want something important to do, have a baby. You should see the way Lilly is aging, the way she works at that beauty business of hers. If it's not one thing it's another.

Best,

Dad

*T*HE BUS STATION in the center of Sofia was like another country, or many countries side by side inside the perimeter of a parking lot. The aromas of exotic foods mingled in the air with diesel fuel and the stench from the outhouse. People ate Bulgarian kebapche meatballs, fried bread, Turkish doner kebabs, and Belgian French fries with mayonnaise while they waited for the buses that would take them away to Sarajevo, Skopje, Athens, Tirana, Ankara, and Belgrade. It was early in the morning, and the sun had just begun its ascent into the polluted sky. People pushed and shoved, lining up for shots of espresso. Cigarettes dangled from mouths everywhere.

June and Ethan located Mataruk, the bus line that linked Sofia and Istanbul. The trip had been June's idea.

"A romantic weekend, just the two of us! Think about it. Turkish coffee, shopping, museums, and mosques. We'll sit on big pillows in front of a water hookah and watch belly dancers. It will be like those stories you told me about going to Istanbul with your dad when you were thirteen. What do you think, Ethan? I've finished my movie reviews for the paper. Can you take a few days off?" There had been a long pause while Ethan polished his reading glasses. "Come on, you old fart," June said, tickling him. "What better place to spend Thanksgiving than in *Turkey*?"

He smiled. "You're right. It's a great idea."

IT TOOK HOURS, and many bribes of cigarettes and whiskey, to cross the border from Bulgaria to Turkey. Ten hours after leaving Sofia, a ramshackle, smoky, two-tiered bus filled with veiled women and screaming children deposited June and Ethan in Istanbul. After scouring the city in vain for a hotel with a vacancy, June and Ethan finally collapsed onto two narrow beds lining the walls of their closet-size hotel room. Outside the window was a construction sight, and the smell from the bathroom next door was awful. The sheets on the bed were a dingy gray and the blankets looked as if they were just downright dirty. June sat up, hugged her knees, and looked around at the walls. They were a light lime green, and in places they looked like they had been smeared with something brown. The only attempt at decoration was a cheap print behind plastic, of the ocean and palm trees.

Ethan had gone to buy a newspaper, and June sat on the soiled blankets and combed out her hair. She stared at the print. There was something familiar about it. She stood up, walked over, and leaned down to look at the photo credit. The brilliant blue beach scene hanging on the wall of the Turkish slum hostel had been shot in Malibu. Suddenly June was terribly homesick for her little corner office, for their old apartment, for bright outdoor restaurants with handsome waiters, umbrellas, and flowers, and a sky as clean, uncluttered, and nonthreatening as a Santa Monica sidewalk.

The shop windows on Main Street did not show winter hats, practical shoes, or a secondhand assortment of mended stockings, like the stores in Bulgaria. Instead, the window mannequins were as slim and smooth as the people peering in from the street, the plastic faces equally void of expression. The tan, fit, and perpetually youthful sat at outdoor coffeehouses, their mobile phones resting next to their bagel and lox. When June passed by, neighbors, coworkers, and old film-school friends would often wave and call her over to discuss the weekend box-office draws and new productions. They smiled at each other with straight white teeth, inquired after each other, and with shining eyes asserted to each other that they were doing great, really really great. Super. Fantastic. Busy and happy. Smoke and mirrors?

June felt a rush of longing so strong that it made her stomach knot. Sushi and Mexican food, picnics on the sand at sunset, the smell of the Santa Anas, thrift stores on Melrose, college kids on bicycles heading for State beach, transvestites on Santa Monica Boulevard, parties in the desert, thunderous applause and standing ovations at the end of movie premieres. Too much beauty to take in, too much stimulus to sleep. The feeling of nostalgia was really a nauseating one, and June realized that the knot in her stomach felt like fear. For the first time since leaving Los Angeles, she realized what it was she had left behind. The vacant eyes of the flawless mannequins floated in front of her, indistinguishable from the silicone bodies and coached smiles of actors and actresses. From this great distance, June suddenly saw emptiness in what she had come to love so much. She saw Dee in her cute Rollerblading combo, Janice lunching with her psychic, and James in his isolation tank meditating on Macbeth. She saw her sister burning incense in the lotus position and praying for profits, and saw herself at the Beverly Garden Spa stepping nude into a vat of red clay. Buh, buh, buh, buh. Despite the homesickness, June did not like what she saw.

SHE AND ETHAN SPENT their first morning walking along the harbor. Other couples strolled the waterfront as well. Women with purdah scarves covering their hair and long dresses disguising their bodies were out walking arm in arm with husbands who dressed in jeans and sport shirts. After breakfast, June and Ethan crossed the enormous bridge over the Golden Horn. Underneath, sailboats and tourist cruises passed back and forth in the murky water. They took photos of the hundreds of fishermen hanging over the railings hauling up the wriggling fish that had managed to survive in the pollution.

Eventually, they meandered through the winding alleyways to the world-famous Grand Bazaar. Archway after archway spread out before them in every direction, leading to endless vaulted rooms and domed ceilings. It was like an optical illusion; a room with hundreds of mirrors all reflecting curved passages and white pillars, making them multiply to infinity.

Gold and silver kettles were haphazardly displayed in shining heaps on the earthen floor. Persian carpets hung from the ceiling and were stacked on the ground in such great quantities that the piles were taller than the shopkeepers. Men dressed in all white ran about with barrels of tea strapped to their backs delivering it to those workers who couldn't leave their products unattended. The stalls went on forever and contained packs of exotic spices, precious jewelry, children's clothes, leather jackets, running shoes, belly dancing costumes, lamps, china, birds, rugs, and tacky souvenirs.

June pulled Ethan aside. "I know this place is a tourist trap but maybe it would be fun to buy a carpet for the apartment? It really needs one, you know." She saw a carpet strung from the ceiling with blue and turquoise tassels on the edges. In the center of the carpet were hexagonal shapes containing hyacinths and dagger-leafs of green, turquoise, and rose, radiating out against a blue background. Twining vines of dark black twisted out toward the edges. "That one's gorgeous," she said, pointing. "Maybe we should just take a look."

Ethan walked over and haggled with the shopkeeper for a few minutes while June hung back, watching. Finally the shopkeeper got out a stick with a claw on the end and used it to fish the heavy carpet down from the ceiling. As the shopkeeper rolled up the carpet, he pointed to the black vines at the edges. "This type of border dates back to the Damascus period. In the center you have a design that is more Rhodian. You have selected an eclectic carpet, a very nice one. You must cherish it forever."

"CLOSE YOUR EYES," Ethan said.

June did as she was told. She was sitting cross-legged on the floor of their pension, the Turkish rug spread out beneath her. In her hand was a glass of red wine and the air in the room smelled of the harem musk incense they had bought to mask the odor from the hotel bathroom. "I'm feeling sort of buzzed, Ethan. I might get a little crazy if we don't eat something soon."

Ethan sat facing her, also cross-legged. Candles were burning on the nightstand and in several places on the floor. "After we play a little game," he answered. "Okay, do you remember the story you told me about your dad's mom, your Grandmother Penelope?"

June took a sip of wine but kept her eyes closed. "I probably told you a lot of stories about her. She was a kooky lady."

"The story where she would take you and Lilly up into the attic of their house and have you sit on the magic carpet."

"That one. Yeah." June remembered it with a smile.

"Ah-ah! Keep your eyes closed! It's the same rules. I'm going to take you on a magic carpet ride and describe to you everything that I see below us, but if you open your eyes the spell will be broken and we'll just be back in this crappy hole-in-the-wall hotel. Okay?"

June nodded, still smiling with her lips pressed together.

"Now, tell me where you want to go. Anywhere you want, my special girl. Money's no object, the sky is the limit. And don't say I never pamper you."

If she answered truthfully, she would say back to Los Angeles, back to a time before Ethan had starting locking himself in the study, before James had come over with a bottle of Four Roses saying it was the cure for both a sore throat *and* heartbreak.

"June? Your travel agent awaits your answer. Ah-ah! Don't break the spell!"

"Can I take it back in time?" she asked. "Can you take me to Westwood circa 'eighty-five? To an apartment party on Gayley thrown by that girl who always wore the overalls and Birkenstocks. Illona, I think her name was? The granola girl with the dyed red hair and the Jimi Hendrix sheet hanging out over her balcony. Do you know what night I mean?"

"I do, and I think it'll work. It is, after all, a magic carpet. Get ready for takeoff . . ." Ethan leaned toward June and blew in her face. "Feel that wind? We're rising now, floating above Istanbul." He blew on her face again.

"Strange," June said. "The wind smells like chicken kebab."

"Quiet," Ethan said. "You'll break the spell. We're moving west, we're going fast. Below us is the Aegean Sea, so hold on tight. I don't want you to fall off and get lost in all that water. Okay, we are approaching land. Over Greece now and moving on. I'm hitting warp speed so brace yourself. We're over Italy, the Mediterranean, Spain—"

"Oh, shouldn't we stop in Spain?"

"Impossible. I have already set our destination and the magic carpet is not at all flexible. Okay, all this time we've been talking we've been hurtling over the Atlantic Ocean and now we're reaching the States. As we cross each time zone we'll move a few years into the past and by the time we hit L.A. it will be 1985. I see wheat fields and the world's biggest ball of twine. I see the Rocky Mountains and some macho mountain men drinking Coors . . ."

June was now laughing and Ethan covered her eyes with his hand. "Watch it there, you're on the verge of peeping and sending us down for a crash landing right on a cactus in Joshua Tree. Okay, we're leaving the desert, and looming up on the horizon is the west coast of the good old U.S. of A. We're going down, down, we're slowing down. Okay, we're drifting in over Silverlake. The skyscrapers of the City of Angels are just behind us, with all the office windows lit in the dark—American workaholics. Hollywood is coming up on our right. There's the Observatory and the Hollywood Bowl. They're having a concert tonight, looks like a bunch of people are out picnicking. We're passing the Hollywood sign and a couple of kids are making out underneath it on a blanket. Looking down on Beverly Boulevard right now I see our favorite Mexican place."

"Oh! I miss El Coyote."

"Wait! I think I see Lilly. Yeah, that's her. Your sister is sitting on the patio having a virgin frozen margarita."

"That figures. What else?"

"We're continuing on, coming to Beverly Hills. Not much of interest here, just a bunch of idiots paying ten bucks a beer. Let's get out of here and proceed to Westwood. Uh-huh, we're moving up Wilshire, floating low over traffic. Now we're over Westwood. Since it's 'eighty-five all the streets are closed off and the Hare Krishnas with their orange gowns and shaved heads are shaking tambourines and dancing in the main square. Students are everywhere. There's a street band in front of the Chart House, and about thirty people carrying pint glasses are lined up to get into Strattons. We're flying up the street and into the window of Illona's apartment. The music's loud and all the retro kids are here wearing Guatemalan pants and Indian-print dresses."

Ethan's voice changed to more of a whisper. "There's a beautiful girl in the corner. She has long brown hair in braids and green eyes and a great smile. God, June, you were beautiful. Look at you, only nineteen years old, with holes in your jeans. I'm at the party too, watching you from the kitchen, feeling weak in the knees. Your white peasant blouse is off your shoulders—which are tan and peeling through to little pink patches. Those shoulders. I'm dying to kiss them. I ask someone who you are and they tell me you're a film student. Now I'm walking over and pretending to be really into movies. I'm saying something very sensitive, like that the world needs more films with sad endings. You're looking at me like I'm crazy, you're recognizing me for the geek that I am—"

"No I'm not," protested June. "I am thinking how blue your eyes are and how much I love the Japanese fish hanging around your neck on that piece of leather. I'm thinking corny nineteen-year-old thoughts like that no movie would be sad if you were sitting next to me and holding my hand."

"Really? I wish I had known that then. Now our hero, the incredibly awkward and nervous twenty-one-year-old Ethan Carver, is being very gentlemanly and suave and sophisticated by inviting you onto the patio to share a double beer bong with me. I am promising you something along the lines of 'I'll make sure you don't get too much foam, babe.' Now you're being all cool and holding up your joint and telling me you're not drinking."

"Oh come off it, Ethan," June said, laughing. "I wasn't trying to be cool."

"Yes you were. But okay, whatever, you're still blowing me off. But not before telling me that you're taking Italian Cinema next quarter."

June couldn't play along anymore. She opened her eyes and Ethan didn't complain. "I told you that night that I was taking Italian Cinema the next quarter?"

"Yeah. Why do you think I took it? Why do you think I was such an obnoxious jerk in that class, always talking and arguing?"

"You met me for five minutes and decided you wanted to spend forty hours hearing lectures on *The Bicycle Thief* and *La Dolce Vita* just to get to know me?"

Ethan took June's hand and kissed it. "Yeah, sweetie. I thought I'd told you that before. It was love at first sight. It took me less than five minutes to see how wonderful you were, inside and out. A split second to know I wanted to spend my life with you."

"Oh God," June said, standing up.

Ethan misinterpreted her action. "Surprised, huh? Isn't that weird that after all these years we can still sit down and talk and discover new things about each other?"

June covered her mouth with her hand and stared at Ethan, still sitting on the floor. In the candlelight he looked like an angel. He was smiling innocently and he had fallen in love with her in five minutes and she had betrayed him. "Ethan, you don't know. But you should, you really should. I should tell you."

June began pacing back and forth and her eyes were distraught. She took a giant swig of her wine. When she turned and the candlelight hit her eyes, he could see that she was crying, her lower lip trembling uncontrollably. "Junie," he said, holding out his hands helplessly. "What is it?"

"Oh, Ethan," she said. "I love you. I love you so goddamned much. It was the same with me, how I felt about you at first sight, how I felt after our first date to the planetarium. I do love you."

"I know. I love you too."

"I'm so sorry. I did something. Things changed and you wouldn't talk to me and you left so suddenly for South Africa and you even told me you were going to see that Dutch—South African—whatever ex-girlfriend of yours, and you barely wrote!"

"I told you how busy I was."

"I know, but that year suddenly you were always busy! And arrogant and cold and distant."

"You're scaring me. Get to the point, June."

"I did something wrong. I made a mistake."

"With who?"

"James McKinnon."

"Jimmy?"

"Yes."

"When?"

"Your last month in South Africa."

"What did you do?"

"Oh God, Ethan. Just once. I am so sorry. I don't know what to say. I'm so sorry I never told you. And I'm so sorry for telling you. I am just so sorry."

Ethan blinked and didn't appear to register the information. "You *slept* with Jimmy?"

June was sobbing. She couldn't speak so she only nodded her head and hugged herself.

Ethan looked as if he'd had the wind knocked out of him. He couldn't look at June. The only place he could steer his eyes was to the floor. His shoulders hunched and quivered and he put both hands over his face. When he finally spoke his voice was muffled, his lips pressed against his palms. "I was just talking about how great it was that we could still discover new things about each other. Isn't that ironic? Isn't that completely ironic?"

12

Subject: Life in the wacky states
Date: Sun, 30 Nov 1996 00:27:10 -0500
From: The Carvers <M&Dcarver@tech.com>
To: Ethan <ecarver@sof.cit>

Dear Ethan,

I thought I would send a letter while the endless football
games drone on. Dallas won again today. All the bums are
having a winning week, including Clinton. Another four years
of indecisiveness, boring speeches, embarrassments, bimbo
eruptions, and flip-flops.

I saw Mrs. Camarillo at Ralph's yesterday. She said the
Berringers are building a huge gazebo in their front yard.
She said it looks like the Taj Mahal and the cement mixers
have been running every day since October. I know you were
good friends with Daphne, but Sandy Berringer really tires
me. Always trying to outdo everybody else. Well, that's
about it, except—well, I am butting in but I don't care . . .

We received a VERY strange email from June not long ago. She
sounded a bit down, and also a bit scattered. Don't tell her
I asked this, but is she drinking? You, better than anyone,
should know about the family history. Just be sure you're
taking care of her over there. I spent years following your
father around the globe and I know how lonely it can be.
Remember, she is thousands of miles away from her home in
order to be with you during your project. I don't want to
receive any more emails like the last one. Dad says watch
it. Anyway . . .

How is the dissertation going? We haven't heard a peep in a
while!

Much love, M & D

*E*THAN HUNG THE secondhand Soviet commander's coat in the back of the closet and bought himself a new black trench coat. He was wearing it as he walked down Ivan Assen Street toward Roxanne's house. Ever since moving to Sofia, Ethan had elicited stares on the streets. It wasn't just his strawberry blond hair, blue eyes, or Western clothes, though all of that did make him stand out. More than anything it had been his expression and the way he carried himself. When he passed through the streets in the sunshine he acknowledged passersby and kept a slight smile on his face. He stood up straight and walked with the stride of a man who was getting things done. He was so dapper, in fact, that had he lived in another era he might have been swinging a cane, tipping his hat at the ladies, and whistling a merry tune. To Bulgarians, Ethan had always looked like a busy man, but one who might actually stop to smell the flowers. Ethan had stood out among the masses because he looked confident and happy.

Not so anymore. In his black trench coat, trudging through the sloppy, muddy remains of the first snow with his hands thrust deep in his pockets, Ethan looked a wreck. There were rings under his eyes, his beard was coming in thick, and he was hunched over in the cold. His long, narrow body was hidden by the shapeless coat, and his reddish gold hair was unwashed, poking out from a gray stocking cap. No one on the streets noticed him at all.

That morning the lev had taken a nosedive. Prices had tripled and the word "hyperinflation" was on the tip of every tongue. The country was going under, falling ill in an economic crisis that would be catastrophic. Everyone was miserable, pushing and shoving in lines to change their lev to dollars. A loaf of bread that had cost forty leva a month before now cost over a hundred.

With the economy taking such a drastic turn for the worse, Ethan should have been interviewing the people in the streets and consulting with his contacts at the banks or the Center for the Study of Democracy. He should have been at the library, finding precedents for the current situation and researching both short- and long-term solutions. He wasn't doing any of this, and he didn't feel guilty. Quite the opposite, in fact. Instead he felt vengeful. Instead he was on a mission. He was in Roxanne's neighborhood, on the prowl for Nevena.

Roxanne's front door opened. Ethan ducked behind a partially torn-down brick wall and watched the porch. Nevena walked out and paused on the landing. As she lifted her brown hair out of the collar of her sheepskin coat, Ethan felt his heart speed up. Adrenaline began to pump through him as Nevena walked slowly down the stairs, pulling on black mittens. She wore the same gray dress, brown coat, and shoes that she had worn to the dinner party. In the cold she wore heavy black leggings, and on her head, an off-white wool stocking cap. Over her shoulder was slung an army satchel of military green. She turned to the left out of the gate and Ethan breathed a sigh of relief. It would be easy now. He had only to wait for her on the side street, and she would run into him. It would be very inconspicuous.

Ethan loosened the scarf that was wrapped around his neck so that Nevena could see his face, and then turned to stare into the window of a barber-shop, as if fascinated by the boy getting a trim in the swivel chair. He fidgeted as he watched her in the reflective glass. She was rounding the corner, she was approaching, she was only a few feet away . . . Ethan stepped back from the barbershop window as naturally as he could. He faced her and their eyes met.

Nevena stopped in her tracks and looked Ethan up and down. He looked very different than he had before. Much more handsome, she thought. More human. Not so gaudy and phony and slaphappy. Nevena suddenly realized that she had just eyed him up and down as if he were a slab of pork for sale in the market, and she turned bright red.

"Hi there."

Nevena turned her flushed face away. "Hello. Good day." She managed to give him a polite nod and then stepped around him to move on.

"Good day?" Ethan repeated, watching her walk past him. "Wait. Hold on a second. Where are you going?"

Nevena turned around. His voice had been inappropriately demanding. "Pardon me?"

Ethan was angry not only with Nevena for being aloof, but also with himself for actually caring. He was just angry, period. "I know you. We had coffee together. Can't you stop for one second to be civil?"

Nevena didn't say a word but she didn't walk away either.

Ethan threw his hands up in the air. "I mean, if I made some culturally insensitive remark the other day, or I did some rude boorish American thing to offend you, I'm sorry. I am sorry, okay? But you don't have to act like I'm a leper. You can stop on the street and exchange two words with me. About the weather even, if you want."

Nevena tightened her wool cap over her ears. Her nose was bright red. "The weather is getting worse," she said, after a second.

Ethan stared at her and wondered what the hell he was doing. Maybe she didn't have a brain in her head or the slightest speck of personality in her body. "Whatever," he said, giving up. "Okay, Nevena. Bye." Disgusted, defeated, and feeling foolish for wasting his time, Ethan turned on his heel and started walking away.

Nevena called after him. "Ethan?"

He looked back. His breath was frozen, rising in front of his face. "What?"

Nevena took a step toward him. He could see that her lips were chapped, their pink color bleeding out into her face as if she had smeared her lipstick. "Well," she said, hefting the army satchel higher on her shoulder. "I just wonder if anything has happened with you. You are very different from last time when we met."

"Nothing happened." He didn't walk toward her. The reserved thing was working.

Nevena looked at the ground. "It is just to live here then," she said. "It must be that just to live here is to change you."

"Probably," he said, shrugging.

Nevena took another tentative step toward him. "You know, I am sorry if I was rude. I don't think anyone is, uh . . . how you say . . . v chas dneska?"

"In a good mood today."

"Yes. Everyone is a stranger today. You understand?"

"Don't worry about it," he said, hitting his gloved hands together. "I'll see you later."

"Ethan, wait." Nevena felt bad now. Ethan was suddenly less threatening. Now when he spoke to her he looked at her, not down upon her as if he were speaking from some high pulpit of money and power and luxury. The brash jokester who had made her feel underprivileged by inundating her with desserts and loud conversation had been replaced with someone more subdued, maybe even the kind of person with whom she could sit comfortably in silence. There was a sadness in him that she identified with and found compelling. He was as brand-new to her as his coat. "There is somewhere you must be right now?" she asked.

"Not right away. Why?"

"I am walking through the park now. If you are free we can walk together."

"That sounds all right."

"I like to have your company," she said, and the simple honesty convinced Ethan that he was not wrong to have come looking for her. He was careful not to touch her or look at her too long. He was beginning to discover the risk and reward involved in courting Nevena.

THEY EMERGED FROM the highway underpass at the western end of the park. The pond by the athletic stadium had a bit of ice frozen at its edges, and the wreckage of peeling paddleboats were stacked for the winter. Despite the cold, a woman sat outside with her portable soft ice cream dispenser. She was selling chocolate and vanilla cones, and the price on her cardboard sign had been crossed out and raised twice to keep up with the day's inflation.

"I heard a joke today," said Nevena. "It says, pay for your beer when you buy it. By the time you drink it, it will cost twice as much."

"Mmm. That's . . . funny."

"It's not. Today the bus ticket from here to Kardzhali went from four hundred leva to nine hundred and fifty."

"Where is Kardzhali?"

"South of Plovdiv. Further east. Close to the borders of both Greece and Turkey. It is in a very wild part, a very remote part of Bulgaria. It is still unknown."

"And why were you going to go there?"

"I was born in a village, near to there. It is called Vodenicharsko. I go every year."

"To visit your parents?"

"No," she answered. "To commemorate their death."

Ethan stopped walking and looked at her.

"They died in 'eighty-five. Every year I put up the . . ." She stopped and searched for the word. "Again, I don't know if you have such a word in English. Perhaps when you walk in Sofia you have seen papers on trees or on walls, and these papers, they have on them a cross and a photograph of someone who is dead?"

"Yeah, I've seen them nailed up," answered Ethan. "And when I was in Bansko I saw a lot. Sometimes they were hung on a door next to a black ribbon."

"Um hm," said Nevena. "That's it. It is tradition. Not so much anymore in Sofia, though some people still do it. But in the villages it is very important that each year, on the day of your loved one dying, you remember them and say to others to remember them. The papers have a photograph, and tell how many years you have been missing this person. That is the most important thing. The dead must know how much they are missing to us."

"That's the kind of thing I can't learn about from the library."

"True. People who think they can learn this country from books, they make a big mistake. Bulgaria has many secrets, many layers. The people do not give out information so easy. To understand Bulgaria, you must live here a long time, be intimate with people, live like a Bulgarian, and speak our language. Even then I don't know how close you can be to real truth. All you see is what is left of us. Maybe if you live ten years in one-room apartment with all the family and worry about what we worry. Maybe then you would know what we know. That we live in the darkest corner of Europe, and that we have been forgotten."

"Let me take you to Kardzhali. Let me buy your ticket and go with you. I need to see the country, for my project. It is you who would be doing me a favor. Please."

Nevena felt the weight of her package pulling down her shoulder. Boryana did not go to Vodenicharsko, and neither did Georgi. They barely remembered their parents. It was Nevena's duty, and she was a dedicated daughter. She looked at Ethan, sniffling in the cold, his blue eyes barely visible because he was squinting against the breeze. "All right."

Ethan allowed himself to enjoy the gift of her smile for a second. The front four upper teeth overlapped a little, and her lips were too thin. He found these faults beautiful. "We'll leave Friday then?"

"Okay. The bus leaves at half past nine. I can meet you at the station at nine."

"That sounds good." Ethan shoved his hands down into his pockets. He was doing his best to resist the urge to take her arm, touch her shoulder, hug her good-bye.

"All right then." Nevena checked her watch. "I need to go to my next appointment. I must catch the bus there," she said, pointing to the exit to the main road.

"Okay. Have a good day."

A big, dirty number two-eighty bus came limping up the street, one side riding lower than the other. Nevena started running toward the stop, which was clouded in exhaust fumes. When she was halfway there, she twirled around and waved. "Thank you, Ethan," she called, cupping her mittened hand to her mouth. "You have made me very happy."

To his dismay, Ethan blushed bright red.

13

Subject: Uncle Bob writing
Date: Sun, 8, Dec. 1996 23:13:45 -0500
From: Uncle Bob <bsum@link.com>
To: Little Princess <jcarver@sof.cit>

Hey little Princess, it's Uncle Bob.

Your dad told me about your email saying some guy Stan, some
friend of Ethan's, got beaten up in a barroom brawl, and I
wanted to drop you a note. Sounds like things are getting
worse and worse with people getting beaten for no reason.
You need to make sure that you are not putting your life in
danger to stay in the Balkans, since you didn't sign up to
risk your life. There is a lot of stuff going on that could
get pretty nasty over there. If you get really concerned it
is time to get out. I know about this stuff. The US wants to
help these countries but I am not sure if they always know
what they are doing. Clinton is sending troops and people
all over the world but of course he would not fight for the
freedom of the Vietnamese. I think that Clinton will probably be impeached sometime in the next four years. There are
a lot of unanswered questions and they continue to have all
these investigations going on.

Well anyway, use your head.

Love,

Uncle Bob

R*ANDOM CHUNKS OF* sunlight broke through the clouds and fell on rotten wooden donkey carts as they rattled over streets of stone and mud, past macabre cemeteries and concrete tenements. On the street opposite June, closed factories fell into disrepair. Broken glass hung in shards from the windows, and the metal doors were brown and orange with rust. Barbed wire fences did not keep Gypsies from scouring through the piles of garbage, and wild dogs nosed through dirty rags, iron scraps, and crumbling cement bricks to find edible refuse. Sofia had seemed ugly to June at one point in time. Now that Ethan wouldn't speak to her and had spent most of the past week at Stan's, the city seemed intolerable. Walking to work was a funeral march. June stared at the ground.

IVAN ZLATAROV, the owner of the Sofia Sentinel, was intense and arrogant. He spoke English impeccably, with a British accent. Ivan was not happy that economic and political circumstances in his country had relegated him to owning a middling English-language publication with a small circulation of foreigners.

The eraser of his pencil was pressed into his bottom lip, and the dark eyes behind thick reading glasses flitted across the page at a rapid speed. June leaned back in the chair and listened as Ivan read her words out loud. " 'William Hurt possesses a gruff charm. Though not as swarthy and arrogant as the Rochester of the novel, he manages to both repel and attract, to be cruel and callous yet vulnerable and sympathetic.' " Ivan paused, and made notes in the margin. June watched uneasily until he said, "Not bad."

After a few more minutes of mouthing the words to the rest of the article, Ivan adjusted his glasses and sat up straight. "Not bad, Mrs. Carver. It's not an incredibly *academic* exploration of the film adaptation of a classic of literature, but it's . . . how do you say . . . snappy?" There was a knock on the office door. "Come in," Ivan barked.

"Zdrasti, Ivane." There was a pause. "Zdravei, June."

June looked over her shoulder and there, leaning against the doorjamb, was Chavdar. He wore a dark suit with a shirt that looked impossibly white against his gorgeous olive skin.

Ivan waved his pencil. "Hello, Kozhuharov. I was just being pedantic and dogmatic with my new employee."

Chavdar winked at June before leaning over Ivan's desk. "Ivan, you know the level of my English. Are you just trying to make me look bad in front of this beautiful woman so you can have her for yourself?"

"If I am being pedantic and dogmatic, Chavdar, it means that I am acting like a rude old schoolteacher. Forcing my opinions on everyone."

"Oh yes. I know these words. They describe how you were when you were drunk like a crazy man out in the backyard with my father. Always ready to start an argument."

"Nonsense," Ivan said, leaning back. "No one ever enjoyed my drunken dogma as much as your father."

"So what do you think of the journalist I brought to you?" Chavdar asked, smiling at June. "That's why I am passing by. To see what is the official opinion."

"I guess I should be on my way," June said, standing up.

"She's wonderful, Chavdar," Ivan said, holding up a hand to keep her from leaving. "Prompt and pretty. A very pretty girl to have around. Very pretty for an American."

"Well, that's . . . always pleasant to hear." June picked up her briefcase. "Nice to see you again, Chavdar. And thanks again—both of you. I'm really enjoying the work."

"An important appointment?" asked Chavdar. "Or have we scared you away?"

"Oh, not at all," said June. "I just need to . . ." It was as if she could feel Chavdar's body heat from across the room. "I just need to go eat." She nodded. "Get some food. I'm starving, and I don't think very well when my blood sugar level is low. And it's low right now. I can tell because I get dizzy when I stand. In fact I'm dizzy right now." She glanced longingly at the closed door. "Very . . . uh . . . dizzy."

"Why not eat with some company?" asked Chavdar. "A business lunch? I know of a very nice place."

"Oh, that's nice of you! But I really can't today. Back-to-back appointments."

"Please, June," said Chavdar. "I insist."

"It sounds great, but no thank you."

"But I *insist*."

June paused, surprised by the annoyance, even anger, in his voice. "I guess I could rearrange my schedule."

AS THEY RODE the elevator down, Chavdar took his cell phone out from his pocket. "Sasho, it's Chavdar. I am across from the Dutch Embassy right now and I'm going to walk to lunch with a friend. No, no, I would rather go alone, so have Doichin and Anton proceed to the Club Marmonte. Anton should have Zhanetta prepare a table for two and be outside with the car at sixteen hundred. All right. No, I won't forget. Thank you, Sasho. Ciao."

"I hope you're not going to any trouble," she said. "It's not necessary. Really."

Chavdar gave June a cool smile. "If it makes you feel better, June, it is no trouble. It is like any other day."

"Oh." June nodded. "Okay." Then she resorted to staring at the floor numbers at the top of the lift. It was the first time in her life she actually wished for some elevator music.

THEY WALKED THROUGH a garden that had lost its bloom. Stone benches and wooden latticed fences looked stark and out of place in a courtyard filled with bare gray trees and gnarled vines with knobby stubs that bore no fruit. The walkway led up to a staircase and front porch with a gothic lamp hanging from the vaulted concrete ceiling. There was a large brass knocker in the center of the white door. Chavdar was reaching for it when the door was opened by an attractive woman in a tight black dress, black stockings, and black heels. Her hair was a gorgeous and startling shade of red, and her eyes were as dark as the clothes she wore. "Gospodin Kozhuharov," she said, motioning them inside. "Come in out of the cold."

The woman smiled warmly at June and helped her out of her winter coat. "Follow me," she said over her shoulder. "Your table is ready."

Inside, the house was a mix of modern elegance and ancient charm. The walls in the dining room were exposed red brick, lit by soft torch lamps. A fire was blazing, and two Doberman pinschers rested in front of it on a fluffy beige wool rug.

The hostess led Chavdar and June to a spot not far from the fire. A bottle of Chardonnay was already chilling in a silver bucket on the table. "Enjoy your lunch," the hostess said, gracefully pulling June's chair out and extending a menu at the same time.

"Merci, Zhanetta," Chavdar said, as the woman retreated from sight. He put his hands together and leaned forward. "So, do you like it?"

"It's beautiful."

"Good. I am glad it pleases you. I want you to see that here in Bulgaria we have many high-quality things to offer. Everything is not just what you see on the streets, you know? This is a safe place. A protected place."

"Those dogs," she said, looking toward the fire. "Are they to increase the ambience or are they of the attack variety?"

"Both probably," Chavdar answered, pouring the Chardonnay.

"Suddenly I'm wondering—from what, exactly, am I being protected?"

Chavdar took a sip of the white wine. "Harm, June. This city, it is a dangerous one. A dangerous country. But in this place, you can, if only for a few hours, forget to fear."

"Forget to fear," she repeated. "I've heard that somewhere before. And it's not a movie I worked on—though it wouldn't make a bad title."

"I am glad you approve. I think it's catchy. It is the advertising slogan for my company. It is a security firm. Well, it was once a security firm until the government changed the laws and outlawed security. Now we call ourselves an insurance firm."

"People have told me about the insurance firms here."

"Really. I'm not surprised. What have you heard? That we are all KGB? That before the Change we were all wrestlers and afterwards we decided to form one elite sports team to rule the country? Or something even more? What is it you have heard?"

"I heard that the security companies were racketeers and that the insurance companies aren't much better. I heard there is a 'criminal element,' I guess you could say."

"You have been living here how long?"

"Since summer."

"Then you have been to Ploshtad Slaveikov, yes? The square in the center where all the black-market music, books, and software are sold? Bulgaria is the number-one producer of pirated music, literature, and computer programs in the world. Or, June, if you have been stopped by the police here, you know that the only way to negotiate is to bribe. If you move to a new flat and want to hook up a telephone, there is a three-year waiting list . . . unless you know who to pay. Whoever this was that told you that they suspect there might be a 'criminal element' in the Sofia security companies, this person is a fool. Of course there is. There is a 'criminal element' in everything in this country. Everything."

Just then the waiter approached. "Ready?" he asked.

When Chavdar turned to the waiter June was able to study his profile. His Roman nose was straight and perfect, and his cheekbones were high and pronounced. There was something obscene about his animal magnetism. "To start, mineral water with ice, house salads, and quiche aux crevettes. For the lady, filets de poisson en soufflé, and for myself the moussaka. Also, a side dish of sautéed mushrooms, and some . . . sausage, sirine, and toasted bread. For dessert, one crème brûlée, and one crepe with ice cream, chocolate, and fresh fruit."

"Will that be all, Gospodine?"

"Yes," said Chavdar. "No, wait. And a rakia for me with my salad. June? Rakia?"

"No thank you."

"The lady will just have wine. Would you have preferred caviar to quiche?"

"I think you did a fantastic job of ordering. I'm very pleased."

"Good." Chavdar turned to the waiter. "All right. That will be all."

"Nice accent," said June. "Do you speak French?"

"Yes, a little. English of course, and some Russian and German."

"How did you learn to speak English so well?"

"Life here was not so backwards as you must think from your American propaganda."

"That wasn't what I was implying. I simply thought that it must have been challenging for you to master English under Communism."

"English could be heard. If I told you that Led Zeppelin was my favorite band in secondary school, will that make me seem very old to you?"

"You're not that much older than me."

"What did you listen to in secondary school? No, better yet, why don't you tell me something more interesting about your childhood?"

"You could not have brought up a less interesting topic. Really."

"That I don't believe."

"Believe it. I had an average childhood. The whole nuclear family spiel, you know. Normal boring parents." She averted her eyes.

"Roxanne tells me you were a beauty queen."

"It's not what you're thinking. My mom made me do it. I hated it."

"For me it is quite interesting."

"No. I'm sure you think I'm holding back stories of scantily clad teenage beauties having catfights over diamond tiaras, but it's actually *really* boring."

"Okay, okay," Chavdar said, laughing. "I relent. I won't continue with this subject."

"I'm sorry," said June. "It's just that it's not my favorite thing to talk about."

"What is your favorite thing to talk about?"

"Gosh," said June. "You really have a great knack for putting people on the spot. Do you work at it or does it just come naturally?"

Chavdar laughed and toyed with his fork. "It is natural. It helps me with business."

"That's what I want to talk about. Your business."

"To quote you, 'I cannot think of a less interesting topic.'"

"Are you *kidding* me? You go to private clubs, drink champagne, have bodyguards, personal drivers, and cell phones, and you're the recipient of the most ardent displays of brownnosing I've ever seen. Now that's a topic for conversation. For a movie, even."

Chavdar looked pleased. "I suppose some parts might have dramatic potential."

"You bet."

"Not just mystery or action adventure, but also *erotica*."

June choked on her water and tried not to laugh out loud. Luckily, the waiter appeared and unobtrusively slipped a side salad and several mini-quiches in front of each of them. Chavdar ignored the food while June began to eat. "Roxanne also tells me you once wrote for the movies."

"Not quite. Working in production, you end up reading a lot of scripts. Most of them were bad. I thought I could do better. I wanted to do something really great, you know? Something worthwhile, but I figured that even if I couldn't make my stories as beautiful on paper as they were in my head, someone might still buy them and make me rich." She smiled. "Didn't pan out exactly. As much as I like the job you got for me, I can't claim that I would have given up studio screenwriting to do Jean-Claude Van Damme reviews for the *Sofia Sentinel*."

"I like the part about the beautiful stories in your head."

"They were beautiful to me, but I don't know. They weren't *Cinema Paradiso* or *Il Postino*. I have a soft spot for Italian films. Studied them too much, probably."

"*La Dolce Vita?*"

"Brilliant but depressing."

"Man as beast. Decadence and hedonism."

"I get enough of that in the real world. Lately I'm more into love and forgiveness."

"Is that right?"

"Well, yeah. I mean, not in a bunnies-and-flowers, hearts-and-moons kind of way."

"No wonder you love *Cinema Paradiso,* June. All those stolen, forbidden moments. All those beautiful scenes of incredible passion censored by the Fascists. An amazing film."

"I thought your taste in films ran to the more violent side. Scorsese and so on."

"You are just beginning to know me, just as I have much to discover about you. I can tell you now though, that I have a *wide* range of tastes. Very wide, June." Under the table, Chavdar's knee insinuated itself between June's thighs. "Tell me, June. I felt that there was something between us that one night. And I felt that you looked at me in a special way. And so I began to think you have a lot of problems."

"I have a lot of problems? I *really* hope there's a language barrier thing going on here."

"I'm not trying to insult you. I simply thought you might have problems with your husband. I spoke with Roxanne. I thought that maybe I am a man who can help you."

June pushed back from the table. "Help me how?"

Chavdar glanced around the restaurant. He held out a pacifying hand. "Now, June, don't think something bad. I don't mean anything disrespectful."

"Please tell me, what exactly do you mean?"

"I found an apartment for you."

"You . . ." June shook her head in confusion. "What?"

"A colleague of mine has lived out of the country for several years, now that his work requires him in Vienna. Recently he inherited an apartment through restitution, you know what this is?"

"They're returning the property that was taken from the people by the Communists."

"More or less. It is a very nice place on ulitza Shishman. It has a bedroom, a big kitchen, and a balcony looking out over a courtyard. He would like to rent, but he is not here to find a suitable person. I told him I knew a young lady who might want the apartment. The rent is cheap, considering it is the best location in the city, and it is furnished and has a phone. My friend does not need the money, you see, and has been out of the country so long he forgets what prices are like here in these days."

"How much?"

"Probably it is worth two hundred but I think my friend would agree to one hundred."

"When someone is this nice to me, I start getting suspicious."

"Good for you," Chavdar said, laughing, "but this is simply a lucky co-incidence."

June took a deep breath. "Wow."

"Besides, I want you to be happy." Chavdar reached across the table and his strong hand closed over hers. "And, June, I think we both know there is something else I want."

"Chavdar," she said softly, "I can't do that. That's impossible."

"I understand. It is not a deal, or an exchange. Certainly not, that would be insulting. I just did not want to play any games with you. I don't want you to wonder, 'What are his intentions?' when my intentions are very simple. I like you, but for now, we are friends. I have given you my invitation to be-come more, my invitation to be with me, for me to treat you like a princess and make you feel wonderful. I ask nothing from you, but for you to be so honest with me as I am with you."

June blinked, and realized that their hands were now interlocked in a tight hold. "Okay," she said, and it came out a whisper.

"Then we agree," Chavdar said, letting her hand go and leaning back in his chair. "Now, with that over, I think we both feel more comfortable and can enjoy the meal."

"I can't take the apartment, Chavdar."

"I said it wasn't an exchange."

"It doesn't matter."

"Fine. Let me know if you change your mind." Chavdar looked up, and as if by magic, the waiter arrived with two silver platters of steaming food. His timing was amazing. It seemed that he had only to wish for something and it would immediately and miraculously come true.

14

Subject: Sunday
Date: Sun, 15 Dec 1996 12:21:46 +0000
From: Greg Schwartz <crazycatering!@netcal.com>
To: June Carver <jcarver@sof.cit>

Hey June,

Wow. Amazing that you can get a cappuccino at a gas station
in L.A. at four in the morning and you can't buy a stamp at
the post office in Sofia. Don't worry, I'd rather have a nice
update email from you than a holiday card anyway. No gas, no
toilet paper, no soft drinks, no meat, no shampoo, no Ethan?
Sounds serious there. Maybe you should come home.

Or maybe not.

Catering still sucks, but it's better than the agency. Well,
I'll break down my weekend for you. Friday night I met Ray
at the Lava Lounge and then we went to the Garage to see
Lisp and they sucked. Had too many beers and then went to
Barneys for more. Saturday I went to lunch with Gannon. Had
a huge Bloody Mary at one o'clock, which set a precedent for
the rest of the weekend. Went to Manhattan Beach to watch
the Tyson fight and then to the Road House for pitchers of
Bud. In the meantime, the girl that came up from Orange
County to see me, who I was not very impressed with, found
out that I was very impressed with her friend. A huge fight

ensued and I went home with neither. Left Manhattan Beach at
2:30 in the morning to drive to Newport to see another girl
I have been dating. Arrived around 3:30 and went to bed
around 6:00 am. Got up at 11:00 to go to her cousin's birthday party. Drank beer and ate cake. Left the party to meet
her friends at a sports bar for more drinks. Then back to
her apartment so she could play her guitar for me and act
soulful and silly. Unimpressed with her musical ability, I
left to drive home 40 minutes later. I am emailing you and
having one last weekend beer. In the morning I will put on
my apron and be a fucking caterer again.

I know how upset you are about this thing with Ethan—but I
think he will forgive you and it's not, as you say, the end
of the world. But I agree with you about the stupid irony of
telling the truth. Good old truth, the stuff that people try
to tell you will *set you free.*

Anyway, the grass is ALWAYS greener—

Greg

*R*OXANNE'S BARE LEGS were propped up on her desk and her hand
rested against her cup of tea. She was partially silhouetted against the window, and behind her June could see the backyard, where the branches of bare
trees crisscrossed through the view of the other apartment buildings. The sky
was an uninterrupted expanse of gray, a shade lighter than the muddy yard
and black trees. Roxanne blew on her tea and took a sip. "I don't know what
your dilemma is, June," she said. "Chavdar's offering you the deal of a lifetime and told you he expects nothing in return."

"He does want something, though, and I'm trying to fix things with
Ethan."

"Yeah, and while you give up the chance of a lifetime, Ethan's moving on.
He knows what he wants and he's going after it, not sitting around mooning
about lost love and guilt."

"What do you mean he's going after it?"

Roxanne tucked her legs up underneath her silk robe and spun her chair back toward her computer. "Ask him what he's doing this weekend. And who he's doing it with."

❦

ETHAN HAD THE APARTMENT to himself. Instead of using the peace and quiet to get a lot of work done on his project, he was busy going through a complicated hygiene ritual that he had more or less given up years before. He flossed his teeth—all of them thoroughly—and used June's tweezers to pluck out the stray red hairs that grew in odd places on his face. Aftershave, and a dab of gel in the hair. Lots of antiperspirant. He was like a teenager preparing for his first date.

June's hands were shaking as she inserted her key into the door to their Darvenitsa apartment. Ethan had finished his personal grooming routine and was now in the living room with several textbooks spread out on the floor, tapping away at the computer. He pretended not to hear June come in.

"Ethan, turn around."

He continued to type.

"I want to talk to you," she said, taking a step toward him. "I've put up with the silent treatment as long as I can and now we're going to talk."

Ethan turned around. "What?"

"What are you doing this weekend?"

Ethan stared at her for a second and then went back to his computer. "I'm going down south to talk to some villagers in the Rhodope mountains."

"What for?"

"To find out how their lives have changed since 'eighty-nine for my project."

"Alone?"

"What?"

"Are you going alone?"

Ethan rubbed his eyes and stood up to stretch. He faced June, and something about the way he held himself looked like a fighting stance. "I'm going with Nevena Petkova. She's from one of the villages down there and she's going to act as my tour guide."

"Act as your tour guide!"

"Yes."

"Roxanne's cook? The sixteen-year-old Kate Moss waif with the pouty face?"

"She is not sixteen."

"You're really going to do this?"

"Do what? Go away on a research trip with someone who can help me? Yeah. Am I going to have an affair with her and make a fool out of you? Probably not."

"I never had an *affair*!"

"What do you call fucking someone else? Maybe you would be more comfortable with the term 'one-night stand,' but doesn't that make you look like even more of a whore?"

"Ethan!"

"What? You brought this on yourself!"

June sat down on the couch. "Ethan, I know how you must feel right now—"

"Bullshit."

June took a deep breath and continued. "I can see it your way. I did it so you should be able to do it too. But I left everything I had to come here with you because *I love you. You.* It wasn't an affair, it was a *mistake*. If you do this, if you have an affair now with us the way we are, it'll be over. I'm not making stupid threats, and I'm not giving you an ultimatum. What I am do-ing is *apologizing*, and stating what I think are the facts: that we won't survive another round of this swingers game. You think it's one of your prep school competitions for power, but the guilt gets out of control so quickly! We won't make it, Ethan. There are other ways to get past this."

"Okay, start spouting your mom's clichés. Two wrongs don't make a right."

"It's true. By hurting that girl and by hurting me you'll hurt yourself."

"Goddamnit, I'm only going away for the weekend with a friend!"

She went to stand beside him, and her voice was imploring. "Ethan, how do you think I felt all those afternoons you said you needed a 'writing retreat' and you got in the car and just took off?"

"My workload was hell! You think it was easy for me?"

"Look, the truth is things were screwed up before James, and I don't know, I guess I was looking for something that would make me feel good. I was looking for someone who would make me feel wanted, and all you ever did was leave me, ignore me, correct me—"

"Stop blaming me for your affair!"

"I always loved you, I just felt unloved! I hoped things would get better. That we'd hold hands in our rocking chairs. That we'd die in each other's arms. You're my best friend."

June touched his shoulder and he recoiled. "I don't feel any friendship for you right now, June. Right now I hate you." His eyes betrayed him. They were full of wounded pride and love. "I've eaten dinner with your family and *him;* I've played racquetball with your dad, your uncle, and *him.* You said he was just one of your arty, freaky film friends and paraded him in front of my face. You laughed at me—"

"I never laughed at you! And he was just a friend. My whole life he was just a friend, and he is *still* just a friend."

"Don't tell me you're still in touch with him?"

"What? Well . . . yes. Ethan! I've known him since I was in kindergarten!"

"Shut up! Really, June, just shut up. If you honestly think that I can simply forgive you for what you did, then you're crazy. And if you think anything you can say will stop me from going away with Nevena this weekend, you're even more messed up than I thought."

June laughed. "This is more like it. Tell me how messed up I really am, Ethan."

"You're egotistical with no reason to be."

"So the problem is not that I'm egotistical, but that I'm egotistical with no reason? I guess it would be okay to be egotistical if I was a Ph. fucking D. Locke-Fields scholar, productive global citizen?"

"It is egotistical of you to think that you can sleep with someone else and that I'll take you back. It is egotistical of you to think that you can do it and I can't."

"Stop acting like some bully on the playground, Ethan! *If you do it, I do it. An eye for an eye.* You're the scholar, for Christ's sake! How can you act like our marriage is an arm-wrestling contest? You're above this! Let's not sit here and insult each other, please! You've always known who you are. Don't do this to me, or to that girl. Just don't."

"I'm tired of being the good one, June. Good people get taken advantage of."

June's eyes filled with tears. "Ethan, I hate to see you this way."

Ethan smiled. "I know you do. And that gives me a great deal of pleasure."

AFTER THE BUS PASSED Plovdiv, the scenery around Pamporovo started to take on surreal shapes, with rock formations projecting out of the mountains and rising from the valleys. While Nevena slept, Ethan took in the different colors in the rock strata, ranging from gray to light yellow to dusty oranges and reds. With Bulgarian *Chalga* music piped in from above, the otherworldly landscape speeding by, and Nevena's head—the head of a virtual stranger—on his shoulder, Ethan felt he'd left everything known behind and departed for another life.

June had always said that one of the tragedies of existence was that each person got only one life, could only ever know what it was like to be one person. He remembered her saying to him, "I'll never know what it's like to grow up in the Balearic Islands, speaking Spanish and working at a beach cafe. Think about it, Ethan. You and I will never know what it's like to be a boy growing up in Brazil or a prostitute in Amsterdam. Or the daughter of a Russian tsar, or a monk in a Tibetan monastery. It's impossible to get inside any of those people. Isn't that sad? Isn't it tragic that we only get our own two eyes to look at such a big world?"

It was only now that, for the first time, he understood the exhilaration of beating the system and living two lives or more, in one lifetime. With Nevena's eyelashes dark brown against her cheek and the mist from her breath warming his jaw, he wanted to break himself into pieces, give a little out to everyone, and leave a small chunk behind wherever he went.

THE LANDSCAPE CHANGED yet again when they approached Kardzhali. Nevena woke abruptly, wiping her mouth and looking at Ethan as if he were somehow to blame for the fact that she had fallen asleep on his shoulder. He smiled at her. "You were out for a while."

"Excuse me," she said, self-consciously fixing her hat, which had slipped down over one eye at an awkward angle. "That was unintentional."

"I know. You were fast asleep."

"Um hmm," Nevena said, embarrassed. She was still not entirely awake and rubbed her eyes with mitten-covered fists. A piece of wool fluff caught in her eyelashes.

Ethan reached out a finger. "You have something . . ." He gestured to her eye.

"What is it?" she asked sleepily.

"Just a piece of your mitten. A piece of fuzz caught in your lashes."

Nevena leaned toward him and closed her eyes. "Can you get it, please?"

"Sure," he said. "Hold still." Ethan picked the bit of fabric up between his fingers, all the while staring at the face she offered so trustingly. The way she leaned forward looked almost as if she were waiting for a kiss, and Ethan wanted nothing more than to bestow one, right on the round tip of her nose.

A *SINGLE ROCKY* dirt road wound up into Nevena's village, and from it, footpaths led up toward the homes and taverns. Above everything, on the uneven side of the mountain, a man was leading a donkey into the corral around his house. His rickety cart sat outside, piled high with firewood.

Ethan and Nevena started up the mountain, passing small homes with rock roof patios supported by wooden beams. Animal skins were stretched and nailed to the posts and withering vegetables hung out to dry. Heavy, longhaired carpets were strung across walls as both decoration and insulation. The doors into the homes were dark, and the interiors seemed like caves. As they walked higher, more of the homes were enclosed by thick wooden gates.

Nevena stopped at one of the gates with a peculiar expression on her face. She trailed her fingers across a rose carved in the wood. "In most of the old towns of Bulgaria, these gates were constructed during the years of the Ottoman occupation. The Turks would ride through the town demanding taxes, food, shelter, and children. You've heard of the Enichari?"

"The blood tax? The eldest sons that were sent to serve the Sultan?"

"Yes."

"We call them the Janissaries."

"The same, I think. So, clearly the Turks were feared and the people thought that the gates could keep them out. It's different in this town, though."

"What's different here?"

"This was a Pomak town. We are close to the border of Turkey and for five hundred years the people in these mountains practiced Islam. There is much controversy about this, though. Whether the villagers in the Rhodopes were ethnic Bulgarians who were forced to accept Islam or if they were ethnic Turks who settled at the beginning of the Ottoman occupation. Either way, they were Muslims, and the Turkish invaders did not attack in the Muslim villages. There was never any need for high walls and gates until the liberation."

"When the Russians came in and helped the Bulgarian revolutionaries fight the Turks, was there a backlash against these kind of villages?"

Nevena nodded. "During the uprising of 1872, in a town north of here called Batak, the Turks killed five thousand Christians. Something like that is not ignored. Muslim families fled across the border and some built gates to protect themselves."

Nevena swept her hand out toward the natural protection provided by the treacherous mountain range. "For the most part, the villages here in the Rhodopes were left in peace. They are very isolated, hard to reach, and not very profitable to plunder. The Muslim families lived calmly here. After a while, the hatred became less and there was some forgiveness between the Christian and the Muslim villages. Which, as you know, is some kind of miracle in the Balkans. The Muslims found that they did not need their great wooden walls." Nevena paused, and leaned in to kiss the rose carved in the gate. "Not until Todor Zhivkov."

NEVENA'S BABA'S HOUSE was at the farthest and highest end of the village. Built against the slope of the mountain, it was two stories, made of sand-colored stones, and had two wooden balconies on the upper level. The only entrance was an arch-shaped doorway in the center of the building. Ethan followed Nevena under the dark archway and found himself in a narrow tunnel. They immediately began to climb stairs toward light. The exit from the staircase lead out into a dirt courtyard where chickens paced around the charred remains of a bonfire. Bunches of dry corn hung from the brick walls, as well as strings of red peppers, garlic, and hollow gourds. Two mangy dogs came running out to greet Ethan and Nevena, wagging straggly tails.

A stout woman in a loose black skirt and a heavy sweater emerged from the doorway behind the dogs. She was removing a stained apron as she walked, but upon seeing Ethan, one of her hands flew up to check her hair bun. Around her face, loose strands of gray hair danced crazily in the wind.

"Baba Safi," Nevena said, kissing the woman on both cheeks and then pulling her in for a close hug. Baba Safi held Nevena's hand and, speaking in an incomprehensible dialect, gestured toward Ethan. It was not a welcoming gesture.

Nevena put an affectionate arm around the old woman's shoulders and began talking. Baba Safi stared at Ethan, and the eyes that had been kind when fixed on Nevena were now narrow and suspicious. Nevena pointed up toward the top of the mountain and the Baba's slit eyes widened, revealing a hint of white. She looked at Nevena and then back at Ethan. After a second she clasped her hands together, brought them to her heart, and strode over to

Ethan. With a sympathetic and motherly touch, she patted his cheek, kissed the palm of his hand, and led him into her home.

"Act penitent," said Nevena. "I'll explain later."

IN THE EVENING, Ethan and Nevena strolled through the village. Each and every house was a reminder of her childhood, and every smell that met her nostrils from the kitchen hearths carried with it the image of her mother. Nevena hadn't come to Vodenicharsko to honor her parents until the Change, but since then she'd come every year. That first year had been the hardest. Even at fifteen years old, after living on her own and supporting herself and her siblings in Sofia, she had been afraid to come back. She'd walked up into the village not knowing who would be left and who would have passed away. Part of her expected to find a ghost town as empty as her heart, as lonely as her life had been since leaving.

Instead she found that her home, which had been burnt almost entirely to the ground when she left, had been rebuilt and was inhabited by a family. The gate with the rose that her grandfather had carved had miraculously survived the fire and been rescued from the ashes. Now it was standing once again, guarding the lives of strangers, forming a barrier between Nevena and her past. It didn't belong to her anymore. Just like her parents, her birth name, and all their family heirlooms, the gate and the home it protected were no longer hers.

Now, seven years later, it was still hard for Nevena to pass where she'd lived as a child. There was a part of her that wanted to open the gate and walk in, calling for her parents. It seemed like they might be inside tending the chickens and goats, waiting for their children to come looking for them after all these years. She wanted so much to walk in and see the kitchen where her mother stuffed aubergines, or the garden where her father, like his father and his father's father, grew roses in the summer. If she went in she would also see the door that the Red soldiers broke down. Her eyes would fall to the new floor that had been put in to replace the old wooden boards that had been stained with her father's blood. If she went in, her mother and father would certainly not be home, and the dream of their existence would disappear like innocence. The illusion would be broken, like a hymen, or a spirit, or a home.

Nevena turned to Ethan, who was walking beside her quietly. "Let's go back. I would like to be alone for a while before we have dinner."

Ethan nodded. "Of course."

Nevena touched his arm, wordlessly thanking him for respecting the silence.

DINNER WAS EATEN in the long section of the house that resembled a tavern. Baba Safi was seated at the head of the table in front of the fire, and Ethan and Nevena faced each other to her right and left. In front of each was a bowl and a shot glass. Community property in the middle of the table was a salad of green tomatoes, baby onions, and parsley, a ceramic jug of mountain spring water, and a plastic Fanta bottle filled with homemade rakia. First, Safi scooped bean and sausage soup into the bowls, and they ate it with flat bread baked in the outdoor oven, greased with a hunk of goat butter. After that, she brought out the mutton stew, which was thick and stringy. Ethan ate two helpings, and Baba Safi greatly approved of his hearty appetite. She continued to toast him with rakia and kept all the shot glasses full throughout the meal. By the time Nevena brought out dessert, Safi was snoozing at the table.

Nevena helped her Baba into the kitchen, where a cot was set up next to the stove. It was the warmest spot in the house. Nevena returned to the table and sat back down. "There is wine or water if you would prefer that to more rakia."

"Are you having anything else?"

"Some wine maybe," Nevena said, taking a bottle off a side table. It was wrapped in a leather casing, and the cork had already been removed. Nevena smelled it. "It's homemade too. I don't know if you will like it."

"Do you like it?"

"Very much. But I am accustomed to the homemade taste. It is different than the bottled, big-company wines to which the foreigners and Sofia city people are accustomed."

She poured some for each of them and then leaned back in her chair. The fire shone in her eyes and her hair was loose. Ethan had rarely seen her without a heavy coat and concealing hat. "So," he said. "What did you tell Baba Safi about me that transformed me from a frog into a prince?"

Nevena arched an eyebrow playfully. "Wouldn't you like to know?"

"Please."

"At first she was offended that I brought a strange man with me and wished for him to sleep in this house."

"That much I could tell."

"Well, I had to tell a lie." Nevena took a sip of her wine and smiled.

"You're just going to torture me with suspense, aren't you?"

"I told her that your wife was ill and that you were making a pilgrimage to the Eagle's Monastery to pray for her recovery. I am serving as your guide."

Ethan pulled back. For a second he had slipped into a delicious fantasy that they were having an intimate dinner and that somewhere in the hazy future was the possibility of romance. The mention of his wife shattered that illusion and made him feel tired and heavy, full of mutton and brandy. "The Eagle's Monastery? What is that?"

"It's a holy place high on the mountain. There was a cave there, and they say two hermit monks lived in it long ago, maybe a thousand years. They called it the Eagle's Monastery because only the birds could find it. A very little church was built outside the cave, and then later it became a mosque. Then for some time it was an Orthodox church again. Now it is full of superstition and legend. We will have to go. It is a nice hike."

"Hmm," Ethan said, rubbing his beard. "And Safi thinks that I believe in this place?"

"She believes in it herself."

"What religion is she?"

"Safi is short for Safiwa. It's a Muslim name."

"What about Nevena? That's a Bulgarian name, isn't it?"

Nevena looked down into her wine. "Yes. A very common, very nationalistic name."

"But, were your parents Muslims?"

Nevena nodded almost imperceptibly.

Ethan was looking at the ceiling. Even there, goat skins and rabbit furs were stretched and hung. "So why didn't they—"

Nevena held up a hand and interrupted. "Look, Ethan, there are a lot of things you still don't understand. It's late. I think tomorrow many things will become clear to you. Why don't we go to sleep?"

She walked away, leaving her glass of wine. Ethan stayed behind by the fire, finishing first his own drink, and then Nevena's. He imagined slipping into her freezing room and joining her beneath the furs on the bed. He wanted to know her secrets. He pictured kissing her lips, reveling in the heat of her mouth, and raising her white cotton nightgown to touch her other source of heat. It was if he already knew how smooth her skin would be, how soft her hair, and how sweet her breath. . . . Ethan imagined her whispering, "Iskam te. Obicham te. Molya ti se." *I want you. I love you. Please.*

The door to Nevena's room opened and she peered out with sleepy eyes. "Ethan? What are you doing?"

His voice caught when he answered, "I have no idea."

THE NEXT MORNING, after finishing Baba Safi's breakfast of fried bread, goat cheese omelets, homemade sausages, and a stove-pot of coffee thick with grounds, Ethan and Nevena prepared to go out into the cold and hang the memorials. As Ethan pulled on his warm clothes, Safi came out of the back room with a pile of papers. She handed them to Nevena, with a few soft words. She touched Nevena's hair and then turned away, clutching her bosom. She left the room in a hurry.

"What are these?" Ethan asked, looking at the papers.

"Memorials for Baba Safi. She wants us to post these as well. Can you hold them?"

"Of course." He turned one of the papers right side up. "This is her son?"

"Yes," Nevena answered, taking a handful of tacks out of a rusty tin in the courtyard.

"He died the same night as your parents?"

"Yes," Nevena said again, walking down the slick, stone stairs to the street.

Ethan followed her, still reading Safi's son's memorial. "Is that just a co-incidence? Is that just—" His sentence died as soon as he stepped out of the darkness of the tunnel. Yesterday the footpath had been deserted. Now it was teeming with life. Elderly couples as well as young people were slowly walking the cobbled streets. They huddled together in groups, some holding candles, others holding piles of papers, and still others tying black bows around the wooden gates. "I guess it's not a coincidence."

"No," she said. "I told you many things would become clear to you today."

Ethan followed Nevena to the nearest wooden gate. It was already papered with photos. Women and men, young and old. There was even a little boy who could not have been older than ten. Fifteen smiling faces looked out at them, fifteen people who had lost their lives the same night.

Nevena handed Ethan a tack. "Why don't you put up one of Yusef's here?"

"I can't believe it," he said, standing back and taking in the magnitude of death and suffering the gate represented. "Was there an earthquake?"

Nevena shook her head. "No. Have you heard of Todor Zhivkov's plan in the eighties to unify Bulgaria? The same kind of 'unification' they are starting in Yugoslavia?"

"Yes, but the article I read didn't say anything about massacres."

"Well," Nevena said, "look around. You don't need an article to see what took place here. People were killed." She paused, her hand curling against her stomach. "And even more people were hurt."

"How old were you?" Ethan asked, as they moved down the hill toward the next gate.

"I was eleven," Nevena said. "Todor Zhivkov's army came to the town with papers for everyone to sign. They arrived in the middle of the night in order to scare us."

"What were the papers?"

"Agreements to change the family names from Turkish to Bulgarian, to give up Islam. The official version is that those who refused to sign were detained by the police. According to the official version the people who refused to sign instigated riots and there was mutual bloodshed."

"What about now? The truth could be exposed. You could find out what happened."

"What about now? Now there is censorship. Now there are lies and cover-ups. Todor Zhivkov is already under house arrest for embezzling twenty-five million U.S. dollars and spending it on houses and cars for his family and friends. But when comes the trial? And when comes the truth? Never. Nothing will come out. Definitely not Zhivkov, from behind the wall that protects him in comfort from the accusations of ethnic cleansing."

From the second he had laid eyes upon her, Ethan had known instinctively that Nevena possessed secrets. Now, rather than feeling as if he had learned something about her, he felt she had become ten times as unknowable. He walked up behind her. "Let me help you," he said, taking the thumbtack. He pressed it in while she stood back watching, wiping her nose. As they started down the hill, Ethan took her elbow in his hand to keep her from slipping on the icy stones. The touch was tender, without pressure of any kind. She didn't object and he did not feel intrusive. Everything had changed. Ethan now felt so much genuine affection and respect for her that he wanted to be her friend. Only her friend. Something told him that was what she desperately needed.

ETHAN WOKE SUNDAY morning dreading his return home. He would have e-mails from the university and phone messages confirming appointments for the week. Nevena would walk away from him at the bus station and he would wave and smile and promise himself that he would leave her alone. The thought was unbearable.

Nevena seemed to be in good spirits when she joined him in the kitchen. "Let's go for a hike," she said, pulling on a thick sweater over her T-shirt. "It's been a nice weekend. Let's make it last a little longer."

Ethan watched her struggling into the oversized wool sleeves, and when her head finally popped out of the neck hole he nodded slowly. "Yeah, it has been nice."

"Besides that," she said, glancing into the kitchen, "Baba Safi expects us to go to the Eagle's Monastery. Appearances, you know."

"Okay. I'll go get a jacket and put on my boots."

The hiking trail started right outside the village. Baba Safi walked with them up to the trailhead in her fur boots. Before they parted, she pressed a twenty-leva coin into Ethan's hand and murmured something that he couldn't understand.

"Baba Safi said for you to buy a candle and wish for your wife's recovery."

"Oh," Ethan said, watching the ground that was covered with loose stones.

"Did I say something wrong?"

"No."

"Do you not like to talk about your wife?"

Ethan tripped and caught himself.

"I'm sorry. Do you find my questions prying?"

"No," he said. "They're just hard to answer."

"I don't think I am ever going to get married."

"Aren't you a little young to decide that?"

Nevena shrugged. "I just don't see very many people who make each other happy. I have had boyfriends, and I don't like it very much. Do this, do that, change your hair, put on some weight. The Mafia boys are mean because they have power and want to show it. The other boys are mean because they are poor and tired, and like their fathers, they drink too much because they need to forget."

"You don't think anyone can make you happy?"

"If someone like you, who seems to have everything in the world—a beautiful wife, education, money, an American passport . . . if you aren't happy with marriage, then I think that is not the right hope for me. Not to find happiness through another person, anyway."

"How do you know I'm not happy?"

Nevena cocked her head to one side. The wind blew thin hairs and the first flakes of a snowfall across her face, so that Ethan couldn't read her expression. "Because you are not home but rather here with me."

Her cheeks were flushed, and the glare of the snow coming up off the frozen earth glinted in her eyes. He felt a sense of vertigo that wasn't from the altitude.

"Ethan, what's wrong?" she asked, taking one of his hands in hers. "Tell me."

"It's being here with you. It's everything about you. Nevena, I'm sorry. I just . . ."

Nevena did not let go of his hand. She took his other one, pressed them together, and kissed them. "It's okay," she said. And then she did what he had wanted her to do for so long. She opened his jacket, slid her arms inside, and stepped forward until they touched. They stood like that, motionless, below the Eagle's Monastery. Up above, a Balkan bagpipe wailed, and the opening strains of an Orthodox hymn echoed throughout the mountain gorge. Ethan and Nevena listened, and continued to hold each other as the white sky began to float down around them.

15

Subject: Me again
Date: Sun, 22 Dec 1996 01:11:02 -0500
From: June <jcarver@sof.cit>
To: Uncle Bob <bsum@link.com>

Uncle Bob, hi! I know you like international news, so I thought maybe you've been watching CNN lately. Have you heard about the protests here in Sofia? Just in case, I wanted to drop you a note to let you know I am fine, and there's nothing to worry about.

It's true there have been a bunch of marches and rallies organized by the Union of Democratic Forces and this group called "Say No to the Fear," which really means, "Say no to Mafia terror control." Supposedly (supposedly because all the news has conveniently been "turned off" for the state enforced two week holiday) there is pressure for the Prime Minister and parliament to abdicate. In general, the news probably looks worse than it really is—for most of us here life is going on as usual, including the shortages.

My hot water is off so I have to boil three big pots of water, and then do an old-fashioned birdbath to get clean. The water is off all over the city. It's not just me, so you can't get too upset. Weird but I'm getting used to these things. Isn't that wild? And good, I think? I like being low-maintenance. Are you getting together with my dad at all over Christmas?

Love, June

p.s. Do you think a divorced woman is damaged goods? Claire told me that a long time ago. I know, I know, but I can't be rational when it comes to her. Like my dad, huh?

*F*OR THE RESIDENTS of Sofia, it would be a white Christmas. A cold and quiet white Christmas, with stillness in the streets and workplaces. The government had declared an official two-week holiday. Newspapers would be scarce, offices would be closed, and even the police stations and post offices would drastically reduce their hours. Most of the currency exchange offices had shut down as well, due to a shortage of leva. Bread lines stretched for blocks. It seemed more like a period of national mourning than the holiday season.

JUNE RUSHED THROUGH the door of the *Sofia Sentinel,* eager to get out of the cold and shed her thick winter coat. Inside the office, however, the temperature was the same as outside. The secretary had a space heater under her desk, and typed wearing gloves with the fingertips cut out. June cinched her coat around her waist and knocked on Ivan's door.

"Come in!"

June poked her head in the door and saw that Ivan was meeting with Kyril, the young, curly-haired photographer. Kyril was pacing, and glanced at June. "I'm sorry to interrupt," she said. "I just want to drop off my stories."

"What do you have this week?" asked Ivan.

"Two movie reviews and a write-up on Theater 199's version of Eric Bogozhian's *Sex, Drugs and Rock-n-Roll.* The one-man show starring Andrei Batashov."

"Oh, fantastic!" Kyril said, turning to Ivan. "These things are more newsworthy than one of the biggest student rallies since the Change? Because of some movie reviews you don't have room for a photo essay on the revolt? This isn't a newspaper, it's a tourist brochure!"

"That's it. Get out," shouted Ivan. "Don't come back until you've calmed down!"

Kyril grabbed his bag off the chair and stormed past June, out the door.

"I'm sorry," June said to Ivan. "I'll just drop my disk off with Natalia."

"No, no. Come in. Sit down. I'm glad you interrupted. That temperamental prima donna was about to give me a heart attack."

"What student rally is he talking about?" June asked, taking a seat across from Ivan. In front of her was a stack of black-and-white photos that Kyril had obviously forgotten. She picked up one and saw a sea of people gathered in front of the Nevski Cathedral. Many were carrying picket signs. Some read, "Say No to the Fear" and others, "Down with the BSP."

Ivan gestured at the photos. "Nothing. It was nothing. Just a foolish outdoor concert attended by a lot of teenagers with too much time on their hands."

"That means *Down with the Bulgarian Socialist Party,* right?"

"Yes, yes." Ivan dismissed the photos with a wave of his hand.

"This is really a great shot," she said, picking up the next photo. It was a close-up of two young girls, stretching open a banner that read, *"BSP is Mafia."*

"Foolishness. Forget about it."

June shrugged and searched through her bag for the disk containing her week of work. "I'm afraid my movie reviews aren't nearly as exciting as that stuff."

"Forget about it!" Ivan yelled, whacking his hand down on the table. "You hear me? Just leave the disk and get out. I can't stand any more of this!"

June stood up and opened the door to leave just as Kyril burst back into the room.

"I forgot my foolish photos," he said. "I need them so I can try to sell them to a real newspaper. One that prints more than bullshit and Communist Mafia propaganda." Kyril grabbed his photos off the desk. He and June exited the office at the same time, and were forced to ride the lift down together. Kyril fumed silently, staring at the ceiling. He acted as if June didn't exist.

June shivered in the cold lift and looked covertly at Kyril. His jaw was clenched. As the lift halted at the bottom of the building, June said, "I saw your photos. I think they're brilliant."

"Don't talk to me."

June wrenched open the metal gate that Kyril had let slam in her face, and went after him. "Hey!" she yelled, running down the steps to the street. "Hey, wait a minute. Hey!"

Kyril turned around. "Screw you, mutressa!"

"Mutressa? Stop! Stop right there!" Kyril glared at her as she walked toward him. "You just called me mutressa?"

"You don't even know what that is."

"Bullshit. I speak enough Bulgarian. You called me a Mafia bitch?"

"Who got you the job at the paper?"

"What does that have to do with anything?"

"Because of the person who got you the job at the paper, and because of all the other people like him in this city, I can't publish my pictures. Instead they run safe little movie and theater reviews written by American girlfriends of the Mafia. You better watch yourself, or go home to your safe American suburb as fast as your daddy can send for you. You don't know what you're messing with. Be blind if you want to, but do it at home. Yanki Mafia bitch."

THE OVERWEIGHT GERMAN kept stuffing Deutsche marks into the girl's G-string. Each time he waved a fat fistful of money, Boryana sauntered over in thigh-high platform boots with six-inch stiletto steel heels and gyrated her pelvis in front of his slack mouth. The management had asked Boryana to wear thigh-high boots to cover her scrawny calves. She was too thin, and men wanted to see a healthy woman dancing and touching her own ripe flesh.

Aside from her toothpick calves, the rest of Boryana's body measured up. Her thighs were long, her ass was small and firm, and her stomach was hollow and taut. Boryana hardly ever ate. Her breasts were not as big as those of some of the other dancers, but they had perfect dark nipples pointing upward, and when she danced they bounced girlishly. Boryana was popular for all these reasons, but the true secret to her appeal was in her face; her very plain, sweet, sad face. The men who came to the Tango to watch the strippers looked up into Boryana's wide, solemn eyes and saw a girl that they could dream of taking home and keeping forever. Unlike the other dancers with their perfect features and Mafia boyfriends watching from the back of the bar, Boryana appeared accessible and quiet. She looked like a shy niece, the girl next door, or the waitress in the coffee shop around the corner. Aside from her naked body, Boryana was average in a very non-average way. The men couldn't stop staring at her because, unlike centerfolds and movie stars and the club's most popular Hungarian blond stripper with enormous silicone breasts, Boryana looked like she could one day be theirs.

❧

BEER BOTTLES LITTERED the floor, cigarettes overflowed from mayonnaise jar lids serving as ashtrays, and girlie calendars hung over unmade beds. Ethan was doing his best to enjoy his new pseudo-bachelor status by playing pool and getting shitfaced with Stan and the MBA Enterprise boys at the Marine House. Drinks, sports, loud music, and smoke—it all seemed like a very single-man kind of thing to do. A three-story tenement in the center, the Marine House was home to the unmarried soldiers who worked for the American Embassy.

Ethan bent over the pool table and surveyed the layout. His words were slurred. "Prepare to be bested, my good man. That's right, Stan the man, I am about to emerge victorious. Eight ball in the corner pocket," he said, pointing with his pool stick.

"No way, you lousy drunk son of a bitch." In his sight-correction spectacles, Stan had a hard time pulling off the macho act. Years of living in Des Moines had, at least, provided him with plenty of pointers. "Or, as I should say, prepare to eat thine words when your eyes alight upon the folly of your imminent botched shot, my good man. So sayeth Stan."

Danny and Michael, two American MBA graduates in Bulgaria doing volunteer work, sat on stools drinking beer. They were watching Ethan and Stan's game, and behind them was a lounge, which served as the common room for the marines. The television was turned to Euro MTV and two clean-cut, brawny boys were drinking with a couple of prostitutes. The girls were thin and heavily made up, wearing short skirts, nylons, and stiletto heels.

Ethan closed one eye, aimed, and sunk the eight ball, winning the game. "Take that, you talentless motherfuckers." He threw the pool stick down, tripped over a pair of sneakers, and fell to a sitting position on the plaid couch. He belched long and loudly. "What? What are all you assholes looking at?"

Danny glanced at Stan and back at Ethan. "Anyway, what happened with June?"

"Why are you asking him that shit?" Stan said, lighting a cigar. "Can't you tell he's trying to forget about it for a while? Jeez."

"I thought it might be on his mind. That's all."

"Well, kiddo, guess what? It's our job to keep it off his mind, so would you kindly keep your sensitive, inquisitive trap shut?"

"It's okay," said Ethan. "We are on hiatus. I've even been spending time with someone."

"Already?" asked Danny. "Don't give up so easily, man."

"He's not giving up," said Stan. "He's moving on."

"But June is cool."

"Man, we suck," said Michael, watching the cue ball he'd shot roll harmlessly to a stop without contacting any other balls. He handed over the stick and wiggled his eyebrows. "Did you hear that, Dan? The old man's already got someone. Not only is he married, but he's been at the dating game all of one measly week and he's already hooked up. You've been here five months, single the whole time, and you haven't seen dick for action."

"Shut up, Michael," Danny said, finally getting one solid in the pocket.

Michael watched the table and just as Danny was about to shoot again, he said, "Even your American passport won't get you laid."

Danny missed his shot and swung the stick around and into Michael's back. "Not like you're any gigolo with the Bulgarian girls. Like Radost was some prize."

"Hey, watch the chalk," Michael said, pulling his shirt out to look for stains. "And you only wish you could have had Radost. Jealous."

One of the marines turned around. "Whoever's bitching, just go and get laid."

"It wouldn't hurt to look a little," Michael said, turning to Danny.

Stan nodded. "I like to look. Ethan? Titty bar?"

"Any bar, gentlemen. Any bar at all."

TWO TAXIS LET Danny, Michael, Stan, Ethan, and a couple of marines off in Ovcha Kopel at the brightly lit entrance of the Tango. The club looked like a casino, with two oversize glass doors flickering with the red hue of the inner pulsing lights. The sign over the entrance was ambiguous without being subtle. Three phallic swords crossed over the silhouetted full figure of a woman. Two bouncers dressed in winter coats sat drinking coffee and playing cards outside the entrance.

Looking up, they saw the group of Americans arriving. It took only seconds to categorize the incoming clients: foreign and drunk. Their varying skin colors, clean-cut hair, and shiny shoes would have given them away even if their slurred English had not. To the bouncers these men represented two things: money and trouble. The key was to get a lot of the former before they had to encounter much of the latter.

The bouncers took the group's cover charge and opened the tinted double doors. As the Americans walked in, one bouncer said in heavily accented English, "No touch girlz. No tak wid girlz. You hear me? No touch girlz. No tak wid girlz."

THEY FOUND A TABLE with a good view and ordered a round of beers. Despite a slightly uncomfortable tension produced by the marginal crowd and the observant eyes of the Mafia, Ethan felt a drunken sense of male camaraderie. Though he'd had his share of adventures doing social work in various countries in economic crisis, he'd rarely felt so manly, so uncomplicated and common. He searched his mind for the source of the pleasure he was deriving from being at a strip club with marines. Maybe it was because for once, instead of studying the behavior of the working class, he was taking part in the life himself. This drunk revelation caused Ethan to raise his beer high in the air and holler, "Cheers!"

Everyone at the table enthusiastically responded to his toast, and Ethan obliged them by doing what was expected; he slugged half of his beer and wiped his mouth with his sleeve. He was having a great time. He had successfully put the hurt created by June and the frustration created by Nevena out of his head. In front of him were naked women and in his hand was a beer. Ethan had never realized that the recipe for rugged fun was so simple, natural, instinctual, and what's more . . . easily obtainable.

The other guys were whistling and clapping and waving dollar bills. Michael shouted over the music, "You gotta see what these girls will do for a dollar!"

Ethan put both his fingers in his mouth and whistled. A busty blonde descended from the dance floor, the neon lights implanted in the stage illuminating her crotch with each step. Behind her came a long, leggy brunette. The two women approached the new clients with their slinkiest movements. The blonde dropped onto her hands and knees and took Danny's dollar bill in her teeth while the dark-haired one bent over in front of the marine named Terrence and accepted his money between her buttocks in the strip of her thong. After a second they stood up and continued to dance. The guys got out their wallets to keep the girls close at hand.

Michael elbowed Ethan. "Give her some moola, man. Get her to shimmy."

Stan whistled and sang, shaking his rear end in his chair. "I wanna see you wiggle it, just a little bit. Wiggle it, just a little bit!"

Ethan felt Michael crush a bill in his hand. The blonde saw it and lifted her leg up to put one high-heeled shoe on the table. She tilted herself toward them and kept rolling her hips to the music. All the guys at the table stared, entranced at the rhythmic motion of her nearly exposed crotch. She slipped a finger inside the front of her thin strip of panties and wiggled it at Ethan. The guys were all clapping now and Ethan gave her the money slowly, using his fingers to tuck it in so it wouldn't fall out. The blonde smiled at him as he did it, and Ethan became embarrassed by all the attention. He looked up from the flesh show in front of his face and suddenly caught his breath.

There, walking out onto the stage in six-inch stiletto heels was a girl he recognized. She had stringy brown hair of a familiar color, and the thin, serious smile that he loved. He stood up abruptly, startling the blond stripper as well as the bodyguards in the back.

Ethan was staring at the stripper with such craven shock and sadness that Danny stood up beside him. "What's wrong, buddy?"

"I know that girl." He continued to stare at the breasts he had wanted to touch and kiss, at the bare skin he had thought was too precious to violate. Then he looked up at the face and was suddenly confused. The eyes were the same but different. The hair was the same color but longer. "I mean," he said, rubbing his eyes, "I think I know that girl."

"No way," said Michael. "What's her name?"

Ethan was still looking at the dancer in a forlorn way. Her hair was flying in front of her face, she was twisting and turning, and he was drunker than he'd been in ages. It was hard for him to be sure. "Nevena," he said doubtfully.

Stan knocked over his chair as he stood up. He cupped his hands over his mouth and yelled, "Nevena! Hey there, little girl, you have a friend here!" He pointed at Ethan. "Nevena, surprise! You know this guy, little girl?"

The head bouncer and two of his colleagues were at the table within seconds. Terrence stood up to try to reason with them. "Look, wait a minute—"

The guard opened his eyes in mock disbelief. "What? You talking to me, nigger?"

"What the fuck? You townie piece of Balkan shit—"

Two other thugs shoved Terrence. "No tak wid girlz," one said. "Out."

Ethan gestured toward the stage and began to talk in drunk, butchered Bulgarian. "Sezhulavam. Izvinaivete, mnogo, mnogo. I'm sorry, I just thought for a second—"

Another bouncer stepped up. "No tak, wize guy. Out."

Ethan made one final attempt. "Just tell me her name. Is it Nevena?"

"Shut up, azzhul," he answered, bulldozing Ethan out into the alley. Terrence was ready to jump at him when the mutra pulled a gun from the waistband of his Nike sweatpants. He waved it menacingly in the air. "Not to come back. Nikoga, chu li? Nikoga!"

Then Stan, Terrence, Danny, and Michael were pushed out the door as well. Stan fell to his knees. "Aw fuck," he said, pushing his fingers into a rip in his corduroys. "My last good pair of American cords, shot to hell."

Terrence threw his hands up in the air. "For fuck's sake! Can someone tell me what that was all about?"

Stan looked up from the ground. "Ethan said he knew that stripper."

Terrence looked at Ethan. "Did you know one of those girls or what?"

Ethan nodded. "I think so."

Terrence pointed down to the end of the block, back deeper into the dark alleyway. "Look," he said. "Those girls Bill and Joey had tonight work here. The only reason you're not allowed to talk to the dancers is because the bosses don't want you making private arrangements with them. They want to get their cut. But if you go down the alley and turn right, there's another door to the place. There's a guy there you can talk to."

THE WALK TO the end of the alley and around the corner seemed to take forever. Ethan trudged, wondering if he was doing the right thing. If it was Nevena, what would he say? He knew enough about the economic situation in Bulgaria to realize that a lot of people were being forced to do things they'd never before considered for money. Nevena probably wouldn't be the first, or the smartest, or the sweetest girl in Sofia to dance nude. She would just be the first one that Ethan had cared for so much.

Ethan approached the dark back door with his hands in his pockets and his stocking cap pulled over his ears, hoping not to be recognized as one of the troublemakers from inside.

A mustached man in a big black ski parka was guarding the door. "K'vo iskash bay?"

"A girl," Ethan answered in his most curt Bulgarian.

"Marks or dollars?"

"Dollars."

"Forty."

"Ne," Ethan said, clucking his tongue to show his contempt. "Thirty."

The man stared Ethan down for a second and then acquiesced. He started to open the door to go inside. "Stop," said Ethan. "I want a certain girl. The one in the tall boots."

Now it was the other man's turn to make the contemptuous noise with his tongue. "Ne," he said. "Forget about her."

"What's her name?"

"Forget about her," he said again. "Not for thirty anyway."

"How much?" asked Ethan.

"I'd have to ask."

"How much for you to just tell me her name?"

"What?" asked the man, now growing impatient and confused.

"I said how much would it cost for you just—" Ethan stopped in mid-sentence.

Boryana had pushed the door open and was now standing before them, wrapped in a fur. "Were you the one asking for Nevena?"

Ethan couldn't speak. It wasn't Nevena, but it could have been her twin. He nodded his head in answer to her question.

The girl motioned with her head. "Come in here." The man started to protest and Boryana held up a hand. "Raiko knows about this, Yuri. He said it was okay."

The hall Boryana led Ethan down was painted red. She turned into a small dressing room and he followed. Boryana took off her fur and sat down in the chair. Underneath she wore a thin robe with a belt tie, and it slid over her legs when she crossed them. Ethan had no choice but to sink down into the cushions of the chaise lounge. He felt ridiculous.

Boryana opened a pack of cigarettes and offered one. Ethan declined and she shrugged. Her head tilted to the side, she eyed him warily. "I shouldn't be talking to you."

"Apparently."

"Normally I wouldn't."

Ethan stood up. "This is just a case of mistaken identity. It's my fault. I'll go."

Boryana dragged on the cigarette and watched him walk to the door. "What kind of accent is that?"

"American."

"You speak Bulgarian very well. For an American."

"Thank you." He paused but didn't know what else to say. "Well. Ciao."

"Wait."

"What?"

"You know my sister. I want to know how she is."

"That's it," he said softly. He looked her up and down. He knew that she was younger than Nevena, and yet she looked just as old or older. In this light he could see there were circles under her eyes and a jaundiced tint to her skin. "You're Nevena's little sister?"

Boryana was studying Ethan as well. "Um hm," she said. "And you are Nevena's . . . ?"

"Friend," he answered, sitting back down on the couch.

Boryana swigged from a bottle of mineral water on her desk. "I didn't know Nevena had any American friends."

"I'm a new friend."

"Is that right?"

"Yes."

"So . . . answer my question. How is she?"

"She's good. You two look a lot alike."

"The truth is we're not much alike at all."

They sat there without saying anything for a minute. It was not a comfortable silence and Ethan could think of no way to fill it. "Well. I was on my way, wasn't I?"

Boryana looked up and Ethan saw that she was wearing fake eyelashes. "Listen," she said. "I didn't want you to think I was Nevena in case you decided to say something to her. If she knew someone who looked like her was dancing here she would know it's me. I don't want her to know."

"Why?"

"That is personal, isn't it?"

"She has talked to me about you. She told me she hasn't heard from you in months and she sounded worried. I think she would like to see you. She'd like to know that you're okay."

"I am okay, but she won't think so. Even though I'm making good money she won't think this is okay. She is very old-fashioned. You would not understand the situation."

"I know about your parents."

Boryana's eyes widened in surprise. "Well! But do you know how many years Nevena worked to support me and Georgi? Since she was thirteen. She worked so we didn't have to, and so we could go to school. Someone else has to make some money for a change."

"What about your brother?"

"Georgi works in a chemical factory in Pernik. He never made much money, but now, this winter, it's nothing. He's still young. If we can scrape the money together he can go to school. He wants to get a law degree. So, you see why it is important that I make money too. If Nevena knew, she wouldn't let me dance here. She'd try to give me her money and make me go to secretary school or something like that."

"That doesn't sound so bad."

Boryana flicked an ash on the ground and gave Ethan a shrewd look. "A lot you know, being from America."

"Tell me what I should know."

"In America do secretaries make as much money as exotic dancers?"

"No idea."

"Well, here in Bulgaria the secretaries barely get by." She gestured around at the ornate dressing room. "When these places opened up after the Change, the secretaries were lining up to try and get jobs as dancers. Some of the dancers here are still secretaries. And English teachers and accountants and shopkeepers and maids. What good would it do me to get a job as a secretary? I'd still have to strip to eat. Now at least I have some free time to study English in the day. Now at least Nevena can save her extra money for Georgi's school." Boryana laughed, and it sounded harsh. "You know, Georgi has no choice but school. No one will pay my brother so well to take off his clothes."

Ethan had no good comeback. What she said was true.

"Will you promise not to tell Nevena about this? No matter what?"

"I think you should call her. I think you should see her."

"Do you promise or not?"

"Boryana . . ."

"You fucking Americans think everything is your business! This is not your secret to give away! This has nothing to do with you!"

"Okay. Okay, I promise."

Boryana studied him with narrowed eyes. "Good. I have your word then. In exchange you have my word. I will never tell my sister—*your friend*—that you were here. She wouldn't like that either. She has high standards for her family and *friends*. Do we understand each other?"

"I think so."

"Good. Then you can go."

16

Subject: Merry Christmas!!!
Date: Wed. 25, Dec 1996 07:42:35 -0800
From: Mom and Dad <M&Dcarver@tech.com>
To: June and Ethan <ecarver@sof.cit>

Dear Ethan and June, It's Aunt Fran. I was just in the middle of making the Christmas casserole when your mom said we were going to email. How are you? I was very concerned about you when we read in the paper that Sofia only had three more weeks of heat left. When the *Oregon Post* is worried about people in Bulgaria you know that there is a serious concern. I hope with all my heart that you and June are okay and have a happy Christmas. We miss you terribly.

Ethan, this is Mom. We are getting ready to eat one of Aunt Fran's famous meals. We will have ham, filet mignon, shrimp cocktail, green beans, oyster and mushroom dressing, two desserts, cookies, cheese balls and etc, etc. Enough food for twenty people and there will only be eight and three children. We miss you! Here's your Grandma Bea.

Dear Ethan and June, I can't wait to hear about Christmas in Bulgaria. I wonder if you will be going to a midnight Mass in one of the Churches to see the way the local people celebrate. I have just been to the Lloyd Museum to see the hand blown glass by an artist by the name of Chihuly. This particular exhibition is of ten chandeliers anywhere from 8 to 10 feet tall, made with small bubbles of hand blown glass. They are so handsome and so beautiful. The Baringtons commissioned one for the new art museum at Stanford for $85,000. Love to both of you. Come to Solvang when you get home for a visit, and we'll have a picnic like old times.

Love from all, and peace and joy to the world!

DURING A WEEKEND of shared secrets, against a backdrop of death papers and poverty, Ethan had promised himself that he would be Nevena's friend—he might want her secretly, but he would not touch her or hurt her. Instead he would help her. A few days after the drunken night at Tango and the clandestine conversation with Boryana, he called Nevena at Roxanne's. Ethan told her that he had an attorney friend named Stan who worked at the Center for the Study of Democracy. "He's rewriting Bulgarian laws and is swamped with too much work," Ethan explained.

"Yes?"

"Anyway, I'm calling to see if you know of anyone interested in law who would like to go to work at the Center assisting my friend." Ethan tried to sound as nonchalant as possible. "You know," he said, "by current standards, the Center, which is funded internationally, pays its employees well."

Nevena had been strangely silent, and had then answered that in fact her brother would probably be very interested in such a position. Stan gave a quick interview and offered Georgi a position as his research assistant at a wage that was twice what the young man had been making at the factory. Georgi made plans to leave behind the polluted sky and chemically poisoned river in Pernik. He would move in with his girlfriend, Ivanka, in Sofia, and would start work a week later, in the New Year.

It was the best Christmas present Ethan could have given either Georgi or Nevena, and he felt an extreme contentment for having done the good deed while keeping his motives and meeting with Boryana a secret.

To express her thanks, Nevena wanted to treat Ethan to dinner. "It won't be much," she said. "Something home-cooked, at my apartment. I'm sorry I can't take you to a restaurant. I know how much you Americans love to eat out."

Ethan, who was speaking on the phone from the Darvenitsa apartment, turned to look in the hallway mirror. He ran a hand through his hair and straightened his shirt. "On the contrary. Dinner at your place would be perfect."

After hanging up the phone, he frowned at his reflection. "Cut it out, rebound boy," he said. "Get a grip."

Nevena's apartment was in an area that Ethan had once heard called the Turkish quarter. It was not far from the Luvov Bridge, named for the stone statues of lions sitting regally on either end of the canal. At the southern end of the bridge, prostitutes smoked cigarettes and chatted, standing underneath the single working street lamp. The Zhenski Pazar outdoor market was around the corner, as was the police station, and the area was always bustling and lively. Trucks stopped in the middle of the cobblestone streets to unload produce into wheelbarrows, and secondhand stores with clothes for sale by the kilo lined the sidewalks. In between these retail outlets, cafes played exotic Middle Eastern music. Red lanterns from Asian restaurants glowed in the distance down dark alleys.

The tram tracks ran in and out through the middle of the neighborhood, and at each stop were stands selling salad-stuffed pitas and kebapche meatballs on bread. Young people were out carousing with plastic liter bottles filled with a mixture of Fanta and cheap vodka. The Bulgarian Mafia more or less ignored the area, allowing the immigrants and Gypsies to live and fight amongst themselves.

NEVENA'S APARTMENT WAS in a turn-of-the-century building with fading paint and a sagging structure. As they walked up to her room on the eighth floor, Ethan had to keep a hand on the railing. The warped stairs sloped, and the light switch was on a timer. He had no idea at what moment the light would automatically switch off and plunge them into darkness.

Inside, it was much smaller than Ethan's apartment in Darvenitsa. It was a studio, with a bathroom that looked like a tiny closet, and a balcony with an adjacent alcove that could serve as a breakfast nook. The door to the bathroom was ajar, and he could see that there was barely enough room inside for the toilet. High above the toilet was a pipe sticking out of the wall, which served as the showerhead. Nevena shut the door to the bathroom and motioned him toward the other end of the apartment. On a table by the window was a hot plate, and underneath it was a mini refrigerator.

Nevena turned on a radio held together with masking tape. It looked like an antique that should have stopped working years before. The station she chose played music that was exotic and incomprehensible. It seemed appropriate.

"Are you cold?" she asked.

"I'm all right," Ethan answered, though he wished he had worn a thicker sweater.

"If you're cold, there is a blanket folded up next to the couch." Nevena lit several candles. "The overhead light doesn't work. The outlet failed a couple of weeks ago."

Ethan stood and peered up at the light fixture. "Maybe I could take a look at it."

"Don't bother. The socket is, how do you say, decayed? Water has been seeping down into it from upstairs. I think it is dangerous."

Ethan paced back and forth underneath the light, looking up. "Hmm. It does look corroded. Rusted out. What did your landlord say?"

"The landlord is too busy putting off fixing the lift that's been broken for a year and a half. He hasn't been by to see my problem."

"So what are you going to do?"

Nevena moved the candles to a higher position on her bookshelf, and it lit the room with orange flames. "I'm going to open a bottle of wine and make you something to eat."

"I mean about the socket."

"I'm going to spend my nights by candlelight. And learn to enjoy it."

Ethan put his hands on his hips. "Nevena—"

"No," she said, taking a bottle of wine out of her cupboard. "Please, Ethan. Just forget it. You don't have to fix everything. Not everything works all the time, not here. Let's just pretend there's no problem. I don't want to think about problems tonight. Okay?"

She went to the small refrigerator and took out yogurt, vegetables, herbs, cheese, and butter. From the cupboard above her head she withdrew several jars of preserves and a package of pita bread. Ethan sipped his wine and watched as she used the hot plate to prepare warm dips for the bread, and the counter to mix together the ingredients for cold salads.

After a half hour of preparation, Nevena and Ethan carried their meal to the living room. On the coffee table they placed dishes of yogurt, cucumber and dill snezhanka, hummus, a paste made from red peppers and eggplant, garlic and caviar dip, cheese, and sautéed mushrooms. The last addition was a platter of sausage-and-rice-stuffed grape leaves that Nevena had cooked earlier that day at one of the houses where she cleaned. They sat on the floor on pillows and ate their meal with their crossed legs touching each other at the knees.

"What you did for Georgi was so nice," she said. "And what you did for me, taking me to Vodenicharsko when I couldn't afford it, that was also very nice of you."

"Come on. It was nothing."

"No. It was something. You deserve many, many thanks." Nevena reached out and touched Ethan's cheek. She ran her fingers down the length of his jawbone, all the while staring at the contours of his face with something like awe.

Ethan covered her hand with his own. "Nevena, if you're touching me now because you think you owe me, please stop."

Her eyes narrowed with a subtle flicker of hurt. "Stop?"

"But if you're touching me now because you feel the same way about me that I do about you, then go on."

"Ethan, how can we feel the same way about each other? You are married. You care for someone else and I care only for you."

These words, said so simply and with such a lack of calculation, convinced Ethan that Nevena was the most artless creature he had ever met. This girl, with her moles and dimples and tragic past, was like no one he had ever known, and what had once been curiosity was now reverence. "Nevena, I have never cared about anyone the way I care about you."

"I am happy then." Tonight she wanted to give him her love and her body, and she knew he would value them. Nevena did not want to burden him with the weight of her offering. She chose not to tell him that he was the first man she could make love to since that day more than a decade before, the day she had been renamed.

Ethan leaned in close to Nevena. He stopped short of kissing her because he only wanted to smell her breath and skin. The anticipation of this moment had been enormous, and now that he knew he would have her, he wanted to make it last. When his lips finally touched hers, he knew that every moment of frustrated longing had been worth it. Their first kiss was just as he had imagined. The kiss was like Nevena herself: straightforward and serious, but possessing an indefinable magic.

His head was spinning. The apartment was cold and yet he was burning. He touched her lips with his finger and buried his face in her fine hair. Nevena's hands ran up and down his back and they kissed again, finding that they couldn't stop. They fell back into the pillows and Ethan's lips were on her neck, her collarbone, and then the hollows of her elbows. He kissed her small arms with a strange passion, for it was their combination of fragility and strength that had first made him notice her, carrying groceries in from the humid summer street. Nevena sighed as his lips traversed her wrist, looking down and lightly touching his reddish-blond hair with her other hand, wanting him closer still.

On that narrow threadbare couch with Ethan, Nevena was no longer the girl who kept her mouth shut and her eyes averted. Instead she let her hands roam with abandon and her back arch with lust. Springs poked through the foam rubber of the cushions but they didn't feel a thing. Someone downstairs banged against the ceiling with a broom handle but they did not stop. Eventually, the music from the late night station on the broken radio turned to static, but Ethan and Nevena were oblivious. They were somewhere far from a foldout sofa in a dingy flat in the Turkish slums of a Balkan capital.

Later, he kissed her forehead and let his face rest against her neck. They clung to each other, both breathing softly, silent and stunned. Nevena's eyes were wide open, staring at the ceiling in amazement. A tear slipped out of her eye, and for the first time in a decade, it wasn't shed in anger.

JUNE LOOKED OUT THE window of the tram. The electrical connection between the tram and the cables above sparked, momentarily illuminating the haggard faces, gray clothes, and hollow eyes of people waiting in line to fill water jugs from a fountain in a plaza. June recognized the square. They were beside the Turkish baths. She pushed her way to the door of the tram and jumped out, suddenly wanting to stand by the baths in the snow.

A bald blind man sat on a wooden crate, clutching a portable radio. Dressed in rags and with his twisted blue feet exposed to the cold, he sang at the top of his lungs. He was fat, his buttocks hanging off the edges of his makeshift seat. He was always there singing with his filmy eyes rolled back in his head. June had grown used to him, and dropped money onto the filthy blanket bunched underneath the wooden crate.

June walked past the baths and entered a tavern where she had spent one afternoon with Raina. She was glad for the anonymity provided by her hat and scarf. No one looked up. They were too busy staring into their drinks. June went to the bar and sat down on a stool. A woman in an apron walked over, and June ordered a rakia and a soda.

The tavern, even with all the bodies huddled close together, was not warm, and everyone was drinking in their coats and hats. A few men gripped their glasses with thick gloves. June turned toward the bar to motion for some nuts, and there, behind the bottles and hanging bags of stale pretzels, was a streaked round mirror. The waitress was looking in it, trying to wipe away the circles under her eyes, as if they were only smudges of dirt.

June was also reflected in the mirror, bundled up heavily, only a single wisp of her light hair escaping from the black cap. She stared at her image with disbelief. Her eyes were deep-set pools of liquid green, as if filled with unshed tears. Lately she had not even been able to cry. She was dressed in dark neutrals, against a sea of other drab colors, hunched over a shot of rakia, preparing to have another. Smoke rose all around her and the sound of the language she had once found sinister—but now spoke—filled her ears. The faces of men and women with tired eyes and deeply creased skin swam together, forming a backdrop of destitution. Underneath the tables their work boots were identical, all black and snow-proofed. She was sitting on a ripped plastic cushion on a wobbly stool, and she had arrived at this destination on a tram with no headlights and two broken doors that flapped open and closed, open and closed, letting in gusts of snow. Her nose was red, her hands were chapped, and her feet hurt. Her heart was broken and in her pocket was a crumpled wad of leva. She was utterly alone. Ethan was probably with the other woman now, even though June had given up everything to move with him to, as she had heard the Balkans referred to so many times, the darkest corner of Eastern Europe.

June dropped too much money on the bar and walked unsteadily to the door, escaping the sight of her changed face. Outside it was pitch-dark, and it had begun to snow. She walked down the gutted sidewalk, careful to skirt the deep potholes and loose bricks. She put her hand out toward a building to steady herself, and looked up. There was the pink, fuzzy hat that Raina had admired but not been able to buy. Behind the streaked window was the pale saleswoman whom June had accidentally made cry. A small boy in pajamas was holding up his leg, and the woman was stitching closed the stocking-foot where his toes poked out.

Raina will kill me, June thought.

She didn't care. Broken heart or not, she refused to let herself become the woman she had just seen staring disconsolately out at her from the mirror in the tavern. Ethan could refuse to talk to her, he could ignore her apologies and make her suffer—but neither he nor the country he brought her to could make her roll over and die. There was something sunny inside her that would still be there regardless of how long the winter and Ethan's anger lasted, and she would continue to be herself in this world, even if she didn't belong. June pushed open the door to the shop. The saleswoman was so startled she nearly speared her grandson's toe with the sewing needle. "Dobur vecher?"

"Dobur vecher. I would like to buy some gifts for a friend." The woman recognized June and her foreign voice, and tripped over her grandson in her haste to haul out the merchandise.

Thirty minutes later, June said good-bye to the beaming saleswoman. She left the shop with a package of several frivolous pink angora presents for Raina, and a smile on her own thinning face. It was the first time she had smiled since Istanbul, and it was real. She herself wore a pumpkin-colored hat along with bright orange mittens and a matching scarf—an ensemble that her friends in Los Angeles would have found appalling. This thought made her laugh—a retaliation against the looming lonesomeness of the empty apartment. As she walked through the worsening storm between the desolate buildings, the snow and moon reflected off her bright new adornments. "To hell with careful," she whispered.

She let go of the tram-stop rail, ran a few feet, and then slid on her boot soles through the slush. The ice between the tram tracks led her in a circle, and she lost her balance—twirling and slipping out of control. Instead of fighting it, she went with the skid, like in high-school driver's ed. Holding her orange-trimmed arms out to her sides, she raised her face to the sky, reveling in the absurdity. She imagined she must look like a Third World Mary Tyler Moore, doing the "You're going to make it after all" spin in an abandoned tram station between piles of trash and dirt-stained snow. Had it not been so damn cold, she might even have ripped off the pumpkin hat and flung it into the air in a true sitcom finale.

When she finally fell backward into a deep and icy drift, her boots sticking up and out, she laughed and laughed and the full green eyes spilled forth all the sadness and just let it go. An old and isolated onlooker from a balcony above blinked and rubbed his eyes; he thought he had seen fiery star-spots burning a winding trail through the foggy darkness. He'd imagined for an impossible moment that he had heard peals of beautiful laughter out in the dismal, freezing Balkan night.

17

Subject: Hi from home
Date: Sat, 21 Dec 1996 01:11:02 -0500
From: Mom and Dad <M&Dcarver@tech.com>
To: Ethan and June <ecarver@sof.cit>

The avocados are about ready to be picked so I hope we
don't get a Christmas freeze. We went to Mary and Mark
Martellini's in Palo Alto last night. I made the antipasto
today. I give some of it to Loraine and Steve every year and
I am a little late in making it. Every year it turns out
different and for some reason a lot different than when my
Grandmother used to make it. She used anchovies but no one
seems to like them these days except me. What are your plans
for Christmas? I suppose it will be a warm, cozy, romantic
celebration for two. Enjoy it now before you have a whole
crew of kids to entertain with Santa stories! Just kidding,
your children will be the highlight of your lives.

We haven't had an email from June in a while. Please give
her our love and tell her we miss her funny stories.

Love you both, Mom

THEY LOOKED AS IF they were mourners. Maybe a brother and sister who had just lost a parent. Ethan and June sat slightly separated on the couch in their apartment, their feet planted on the wooden floor. Ethan's hands were clasped between his knees and June's rested on her thighs. They both stared at the ground and the silence was as empty and desolate as the view out the window behind them.

June raised her thumb to her mouth and began to tug at a hangnail. The almost inaudible sound of her teeth grating against her nail was enough to fill the room and caused Ethan to look up. His eyes were rimmed with red. "Junie. Don't chew."

"I know." June was wearing a UCLA football jersey and fuzzy socks on her feet. After a second of staring longingly at the hangnail, she sat on the hand and began rubbing one big toe back and forth across the top of the other foot, scratching. She looked past Ethan into the white glare coming from the window. "It's funny," she said. "Even with all the snow, it doesn't feel like the holidays."

"We're used to a warm, rainy Christmas in Los Angeles."

"And being together for the holidays."

"It's definitely strange."

"Very weird."

Ethan walked to the window and leaned against the wall, looking out. He crossed his arms and kept his back to June.

"How long is this going to last?" she asked finally.

"The snow?"

"You know what I'm talking about."

"What?"

June sighed. "I can't take this anymore. Let's stop this."

"Stop what?"

"This. Whatever this is. What are we doing?"

"Talking, I guess."

"We're talking but not communicating. We should though."

"June, I'm tired. You are too. Let's not start this now."

"Just tell me one thing. Have you slept with her yet? You can tell me."

Ethan looked washed out in the harsh light. "You don't have the right to ask me that question. You forfeited your right to act like the wronged one."

"I have apologized and apologized and pleaded and pleaded and you know what? It hasn't gotten me anywhere. So you know what? Instead of crawling on my hands and knees to you time and again, I'm going to tell you what I really think."

"I can't wait."

"I think what I did was wrong but not *as wrong* as what you are doing, just sleeping with some poor naive Bulgarian girl to get back at me."

Ethan's face turned red. "Poor and naive? She is self-educated and she's worked her whole life to make what money she has—and by work I don't mean using a walkie talkie to order a cappuccino for a prima donna director."

"Oh God, you have slept with her!" June said, slumping back down onto the couch. "Just tell me. It's not the same anymore. It doesn't make any difference."

"Okay. I have."

June let her hair fall forward over her face. "I want to go home," she said, her voice catching. "I can't take this anymore. The cold and the depression and this gray dirty snow. I can't take the dirt. All this horrible fucking ugliness."

"June . . ."

Her hands were shaking and covering her eyes. "God, oh God, Ethan. I didn't know it would hurt this much. How can it hurt so much?"

Ethan wanted to put his arms around her but the winter had already hardened him. He swallowed and kept his voice steady. "You said it didn't make any difference."

"It does make a difference. It means there's no hope for us anymore."

"I don't know what to say. I care about Nevena and I care about you. You're my wife but you are also a person I never knew. You betrayed me."

June's head tilted back and her shoulders heaved with silent sobs. She didn't want to say anything back, she didn't want to fight. "You have to know, Ethan," she said finally, when she could talk. "You have to know that I always loved you. I don't know what happened that night. Something was missing."

"Nothing was missing for me."

"We're even now, right?" she said, looking up. "That's what you wanted. We can let it go now, can't we? We can go on? I'll do it. I'll forgive you if you forgive me. All you have to do is say it."

Ethan cracked his knuckles and looked at the floor.

"Ethan, please say it. Think about our trip to Lisbon, or the weekend you found out you got the Locke-Fields and we just jumped on a flight to New Orleans. What about the vineyard we were going to have in Healdsburg? Think about the pool at the Miracle Manor looking out over the desert and the way you made it better after Claire. We were never going to be alone. That's what you said. No one else will understand. Please!"

"There are tragedies in this world other than ours."

"But this is ours! *Ours*, Ethan."

Ethan closed his eyes and clenched his fists. He swayed on his long legs and a part of him wanted to fall into her lap. "I love you," he said.

June started to go to him, but he held out a hand. "But I can't say it. I can't forgive you. Not yet. And I'm meeting her tonight."

June took a deep breath, wiped her eyes, and nodded. "So it's over then. What I did really was unforgivable. You've always been so proud, Ethan. And I've always been so proud of you, even wishing I could be like you. So focused, such high expectations." She paused. "So militant and unforgiving and sanctimonious. You think I don't know where you were the night I had to have my appendix out? Maybe you didn't sleep with your assistant—I still don't know—but you certainly considered it and you did fool around with her. I found Moira's notes, responding to yours. And I forgave you, in my heart, because I thought we were worth saving. I don't want to be like you anymore. I couldn't bear to be so cold. You think you don't make mistakes, but you do. And this is your biggest one yet."

Ethan opened his mouth to respond but he could not find any words. His hand went to his unshaven jaw and moved awkwardly over his face, somehow trying to conceal himself from June's eyes. "You're wrong," he finally said. "It wasn't what you're thinking it was."

"No, it certainly wasn't," replied June. And then she left.

A WEEK LATER, after night after night of imagining Ethan making love to a girl ten years younger, June knew what she had to do. She was packed and ready to go—but not back to Los Angeles. She would not give up so easily. If she didn't leave the apartment where his suits hung and his papers were stacked, however, she would go crazy—and she wanted to stay sane, if only in hopes that Ethan's punishment would eventually end. She made herself a cup of tea and took one last bath in her special tub. Then she sat on her suitcase, bounced up and down a couple of times until it finally latched, and called Chavdar. He agreed to meet her at his friend's apartment later in the afternoon to let her in, take the rent, and hand over the keys.

JUNE LOOKED AROUND before walking out the door. This place had never seemed like a home. She and Ethan had never lit the candles at dinner, never sat close to each other in the tiny breakfast nook, and rarely made love on the foldout couch, giggling at the squeak of the springs. Even when they had, it had been two bodies in motion, two sets of eyes staring away from the other, two minds remembering what it could be like—what it once was like. Two people wishing to recapture that feeling, but not sure it could be done. Maybe a few years back they could have found enough bohemian glamour in the miserable little dwelling to fill it with pillows and paintings and incense and love. Maybe after a separation. Maybe never.

June took the number two tram into the city, passed Journalist Circle, and got off at Popa Plaza. Following Chavdar's instructions, she walked up Graf Ignatiev to Shishman Street. It was narrow, charming, and laid with cobblestones. She passed a basement bakery and saw a little girl carrying out a see-through plastic bag of fresh croissants. The girl had pigtails and knee-high white socks and suddenly June felt like she was in a different part of the world. The neighborhood was not only breathtaking compared to the Socialist projects in the suburbs, but would have been considered lovely in any part of Europe.

June looked up from the child. Chavdar was waiting a block down the lane, holding a dozen roses. He stood next to a street lamp and was wearing a dark gray suit. It was like a black-and-white film from the twenties. A train should have been hurtling past on her left-hand side, her hair ought to have been swept up in a chignon, and instead of clutching a battered green Samsonite with bitten fingernails, she should have been clutching a mysterious little brown suitcase in her dainty, manicured white hand.

"Hello," he said warmly, touching her shoulder and brushing both of her cheeks with brief kisses. "I'm pleased you decided to take the apartment."

"Believe me, so am I."

Chavdar pulled the keys from his pocket. "Let's go up, shall we?"

The building's foyer was made of aged marble, and the lift had an old-fashioned metal collapsing door. June and Chavdar were forced to stand very close together as they rode the lift to the fifth floor. His aftershave was the same he had worn the night they'd met. "Do you like the way I smell, June?"

June was thankful for the lurching halt of the elevator's upward progress. "Mmm hmm," she said, wrenching open the collapsible grill and stepping out into the hall. "But if you weren't doing me such a nice favor, I might have a slightly more sarcastic answer to such a question."

"I guess I deserved that. It's number eight," he said, pointing to the door on their right. "I told you Konstantin had it remodeled and furnished. I've seen it and I think it is in good shape. You will probably need . . . what do you call them? Knickknacks?"

"I don't know. I'm not much of a knickknack girl."

Chavdar laughed as he motioned her inside. "I hope you like it, June."

June pulled off her shoes and entered the apartment. The living room was as big as the entire Darvenitsa apartment, and glass doors opened onto a veranda that looked out over a small park with tall trees and benches. Lace curtains framed the view and were tied back with blue rope that matched the pattern in the largest carpet. Adjacent was the kitchen. Light and modern, it was equipped with a full-sized refrigerator and a built-in stove. A breakfast table dominated the room. "It might make a nice working space," said Chavdar. "For writing stories or screenplays. Novels. Love poems. Whatever your heart desires."

"It's perfect," June said, imagining her laptop and papers spread across the hand-embroidered tablecloth.

The bedroom was separated from the living room by blue silk curtains. Inside was a wooden frame bed, an antique trunk, a polished wardrobe, and a matching mirror. A rose-colored old-fashioned glass lamp hung above the bed, making the room look even more like it belonged in a fairy tale, with its soft cranberry-colored glow.

"Without the furniture it could be Marlon Brando's apartment in *Last Tango in Paris,* couldn't it?" Chavdar asked.

"It doesn't have the sadness of that apartment," June answered, fingering the curtains. "I won't let this be a tragic place."

"But that apartment was also the site of love and lust. Of wild passion."

"Of alcoholism, violence, and disillusionment."

"Later. In the beginning it was wonderful between them."

"But I'm looking for happy endings now."

"How American of you. Anyway, I brought a little house-warming gift." He checked his watch, as if he had somewhere to be. "I think it would be a good time for you to open it."

"Tell me you didn't do any more than you already have. I mean, you've been so nice and generous. You've done so much—"

"Shh," Chavdar said, putting his finger up to his lips. "I want to do more for you than anyone else."

"But—"

"No," he said. "Really. You know, in my business I constantly must do things that I don't like. Please allow me to indulge you, June, because it is the only thing at the moment that I enjoy." Chavdar led her into the kitchen, holding her hand. "Open the refrigerator."

June did as she was told. Inside was a bottle of champagne, a container of gray Iranian caviar, a variety of imported cheeses impossible to find in Bulgarian stores, and a bowl of strawberries. She took in the seduction spread and blushed. It was so obvious it was awful, but under the circumstances there was nothing she could say, except, "How did you do this on a Sunday, when all the shops are closed?"

"I am resourceful," he said, opening a drawer and withdrawing a loaf of bread.

After warming the Brie, they carried the food and champagne into the living room. Chavdar removed his jacket and tie and loosened his collar. He took two candles out of the china cabinet and set them on the coffee table. "Sit here on the couch with me."

The balcony faced south, so when the sun was completely gone, the darkness took them by surprise. Chavdar drank the champagne slowly, and ate the caviar straight from the tiny spoon. "I envy your experiences, June. If I had another life to live," he said, "I would want to make movies. It has always fascinated me. I have always loved cinema. When I was young, I traveled with my father to the West and he loved the cinema too. He would take me to Paris and Geneva. While he worked I would go to the movies, and in the evening we would go again together. It was a wonderful escape."

"Your father must have been a very powerful man. To have so many privileges."

Chavdar's face was now partly in shadow, and the darkness across his eyes made him look even more pensive than usual. "That is true," Chavdar said slowly. "He knew things, and his knowledge gave him power."

"What kinds of things?"

Chavdar smiled. "Things that would make a great movie."

"Entertain me, please."

"Well," Chavdar said, shifting into a more comfortable position that brought him closer to June, "I do remember one rather remarkable story. He didn't actually tell me, because it would have been dangerous for me to know, and he wanted to protect me. I was not a child anymore, but still young. I think I was in my third year of prep school and was home for the summer. One night I heard him talking with some friends on the patio at our house in Plovdiv. Ivan was there, your boss, and they were drinking and smoking and yet I remember it was a very serious atmosphere. Much too serious for a Saturday summer afternoon."

Chavdar closed his eyes for a second, thinking, transporting himself back in time. "My mother had just had the fountain put in the garden, and I was dating a girl named Antoanetta. It must have been 'seventy-nine, or maybe it was 'eighty. One of the men sitting on the patio with my father was a Gospodin Kalev. He controlled Kintex, the biggest Bulgarian import-export firm. State-owned, of course. And there were two Turkish men there. I was listening from my bedroom, because my window looked out over the garden. After a few minutes it became clear to me that the Turkish men were Mafia from Istanbul. There was talk about smuggling guns from Bulgaria into Turkey, and smuggling drugs from the East back out. Apparently, the national import-export firm had some sort of deal with these Turkish businessmen."

"Quite a conspiracy."

"Oh, you can't imagine. As I was listening to Kalev talking to the Turks, I realized that in exchange for allowing us to ship weapons to militant groups such as the neo-Nazi 'Gray Wolves' and the Marxist 'Turkish People's Liberation Army,' Kintex had agreed to smuggle heroin out. Sofia was the center of the operation. Then they began to talk about something else. Their voices grew very soft and my father stood up to close the door into the kitchen where my mother was grilling sudjuk."

"And then what?"

"Besides the Turks, Kalev, Ivan, and my father, there was another person present. He was Russian, and he was worried about the election of the Polish Pope. You can imagine how it must have scared the Soviets to think of the Polish people mobilizing for religious freedom behind a Pope from their homeland. I believe it had been earlier that year that Cardinal Karl Wojtyla of Krakow became Pope John Paul the Second. The Kremlin panicked. They needed to get rid of the rabble-rouser."

"You mean it was the KGB who tried to assassinate the Pope?"

"Yes. But they gave the job to the Bulgarians, who had the contacts to arrange for an obscure Middle Eastern assassin. His motive would be assumed to be Muslim extremism, and he would never be linked back to the masterminds in Moscow."

"It's so . . ." June paused, searching for the right word to humor him. "So Hollywood."

"Um hmm," Chavdar said, pleased. "But in this case it is true. Mehmet Ali Agja, a Turkish assassin, did in fact attempt to assassinate the Pope. And it was, indeed, just as I said. Only, my father knew about it as much as a year before it happened."

"Jeez," said June. She gave a low whistle while shaking her head. "That's really scary. Does it make you feel weird about your father?"

"About my father? Why?"

"Well, the obvious. He knew and didn't do anything."

Chavdar set down his glass. After a second he got up and crossed to the balcony window, where he stood silently, his arms crossed over his chest. Finally he looked over his shoulder at June. "We come from such different worlds, June. The answer to your question is no. That story doesn't make me feel, as you put it, 'weird' about my father. I realize that he made his choices for reasons that I don't have enough information to understand."

"I don't know the whole story, and I shouldn't say anything. I'm sure your father did what he had to. I am sure . . ." June hesitated. "I'm sure that in many ways he was a good man."

"A good man?" Chavdar said, silhouetted against the moonlight outside. "Where do you come up with these things? Just because you are from Hollywood, June, does not mean you have to be a cliché. Good man? What is a good man or a bad man? If a man believes with all his heart in something, does that make him a good man? And if what he believes in backfires and leads to suffering, does that make him a bad man? Or is he only a bad man if he goes along with something he doesn't fully believe in to provide for his family, to give them a decent life? Which is it, June? Where do you draw the line?"

June stood up. "Murder is something most people agree on. Unless you're a *psychopath* or something." Looking at Chavdar's furious face made her immediately regret her last words.

Chavdar took a step toward her and though it was dark, in the candlelight she could see that a vein throbbed in his forehead. "And if a man protects innocent people, does that make him right? And if at the same time he sometimes has to hurt others in order to ensure the protection of the innocent, does that make him wrong? My father and I then," he said, his fists clenched. "Are we wrong? *Bad* men?"

"Chavdar, look. Just because I talk about right and wrong doesn't mean I think it's easy. The truth is, I haven't been as good a person as I wanted to be either. I'm sorry. Okay?"

Some of the tension drained from his face, leaving him looking softer, almost as if he had been scolded. He touched June's cheek and let his hand slide back over her ear. "If I get angry, it's because I can't help but pay attention to you. How can I help but care when someone thinks I am a bad person? Someone whose opinion I respect? I hate that. I hate the shame. I wish I could rid myself of the tendency to feel shame."

"But it's not your fault."

"Yes," he said. He looked at the ceiling and June could sense the wheels turning in his mind. "That's true. It's *not* my fault. Thank you, June, for understanding." The pulsing vein slowly disappeared. Now his fingers opened at his sides, and he looked at his palms, red from the pressure of clenching his fists. He collapsed on the couch, his hand over his eyes. "You are a miracle, June. Really."

June sat down by his side and poured him the last of the champagne. "When I'm not sticking my foot in my mouth."

Chavdar let his head fall to the side. "You always seem to make me think," he said, reaching out a finger to touch the hollow of her neck. His dark eyes drifted halfway shut, and his voice changed. "You seem to bring out my passion. The bad kind . . . and the better kind."

Before she knew what was happening, Chavdar's hand was under her hair, against her neck, pulling her toward him. His lips covered hers and she felt an immediate reaction run throughout her entire body. Chavdar's lips parted and his other arm circled her back.

As Chavdar kissed her, June could feel one of his hands pushing away the pillow behind her, making room for them to lie down. June experienced a simultaneous rush of fear and guilt. Fear because Chavdar was, in many ways, terrifying and brutal. Guilt because of Ethan. These two taboo emotions, combined with the fact that her body hadn't been touched like this in so long, made her hips arch toward Chavdar while she clutched his lower back. She was at once sickened by her response to his attack, but at the same time she was in awe of how excited she was by the very same sickness. It was barbaric.

"Stop," she said, pushing him away.

"What?"

"I said stop."

He lunged for her again, burying his face in her neck.

This time she yelled. "Get off!"

"Why?"

"Is this the deal then?"

"What do you mean?"

"Caviar, champagne, strawberries, *Last Tango in Paris* bullshit. Do I like the way you smell, for Christ's sake? Get off!"

He finally backed away, wiping his mouth with the back of his hand. "It seemed you were enjoying yourself."

"I'm sleeping here tonight. Without you. And tomorrow I'm leaving. You promised me you wouldn't do this. You promised me you didn't expect anything."

"I don't expect anything. I'm sorry. I was having a nice time. You look beautiful. Maybe I drank too much champagne."

June felt her heart lurch. He seemed sincere. The words reminded her of James. Adorable Jimmy. She had fallen once before but never so far. "Just leave, Chavdar. Please."

Chavdar's eyes bored into hers, sizing her up, weighing her resolve. Finally he stood, grabbed his jacket, and walked silently to the door. It slammed behind him and June rolled over. She pushed her face into the pillow at the back of the sofa and drew her knees up into her stomach. She wrapped her arms around her middle and counted her breaths as she had done every night for so long after Claire died. Curled up this way, she hid in the darkness of the strange apartment and prayed to be delivered from these feelings. She had never been so lonely in her entire life. She missed her mother, her sister, Jimmy, Laney, Ethan—she was suddenly afraid of the dark. Her stomach hurt, her heart hurt, her hand needed to be held in a way that she had never known. "*Please make it go away,*" she whispered. "*Oh my God. Please make it go away.*"

A few moments later, she felt a soft touch on the back of her neck—and she was relieved that she would not have to bear the racking sobs all night or be alone, untethered, unprotected.

"June?" Chavdar said softly. "I can't leave you like this. I just can't."

June turned over to look up at him, and he went to wipe a tear from the corner of her eye. It was dry. "You're not crying?"

"I can't. I don't know what happened. I can't anymore."

"I'm sorry if I scared you." He pulled her hair away from her forehead and kissed her gently on the top of her head. Then he kissed her temple. Then he kissed her palm.

June sighed and allowed him to continue moving his lips down her wrist.

"Are you afraid?" he asked.

"Yes. But not of you."

He slowly began to unbutton her blouse, and June closed her eyes, hoping the affectionate hands on her breasts would somehow heal the hole in her heart.

JUNE STOOD IN her new bathroom. She was using it for the first time to wipe away the traces of Chavdar left on her body: his spit, his sperm, his smell. She was trembling as she wiped herself off, running her hands under the tap water again and again for lack of a washcloth. Her nipples were still erect, her skin still flushed, her lips still swollen. It was a disobedient body. It had proven to her that she would never control it. Never.

When she finally left the sanctuary of the bathroom to return to Chavdar's company, she felt more in control. She was showered, clean, and calm. Chavdar was relaxing on the sofa in the candlelight. Music was playing and he was smoking a cigarette. He wore his slacks but no shirt, and he looked satiated, like a big, sleek, powerful cat. June walked toward the reclining chair, but Chavdar patted the sofa beside him. "Where are you going? Come here."

June hesitated and then padded on bare feet over to where he was leaning back in the pillows. She sat down awkwardly and laced her fingers together to keep him from taking her hand. Chavdar's eyes moved back and forth across her face in a disconcerting way. After studying her for a minute in silence, he said, "Already you have regrets."

"It's not you."

Chavdar reached out his hand to touch her wet hair. He curled a lock around his finger and let the water make his hand wet. "What happened here tonight is no reason to be sad or ashamed. What happened here was beautiful."

"I'm married."

"You are separated."

"Not officially."

"You are living apart. You said he is already with another woman, physically and emotionally. Your love ended long ago. It was not me that did it. I interfered with nothing. Your marriage is only an official document, June. Paper. It carries no weight. I would think you would be happy. You are young and beautiful. You just drank champagne and ate caviar." His big hands began to massage her shoulders. "A man who adores you just satisfied you. Made you feel very, very good, and yet you are sorry for yourself. Why?"

"I'm mad at myself, not sorry. I'm a slave to my emotions. Helpless in the face of temptation. Weak when it comes to sins of the flesh. A Midwestern preacher could draft an entire sermon based on me."

Chavdar squeezed her upper arm. "You don't feel weak. That's a strong arm. Make a muscle."

June pulled her arm away from his teasing, but couldn't help but smile. "Stop teasing."

Chavdar grinned, and for the first time June saw dimples in his cheeks. "You don't want me to know how strong you are," he said. He lowered his voice and struck a body-building pose with his right arm. "American women are strong. Like in the *Terminator* movies—rock hard. From aerobics and fighting off the sexually harassing men in their workplaces."

"A woman's pain threshold is ten times that of a man. I read that somewhere."

"How was your pain threshold when you were getting that strange little tattoo on your behind?"

"You saw that?"

"How could I not see? What is it?"

June covered her face and laughed. "It's a toadstool. A mushroom."

"Uh-huh. And . . . why did you have a mushroom tattooed on your behind?"

"I didn't especially choose what I wanted to have tattooed. I did it just to make my mom mad. I did it just so that I wouldn't have to wear bikinis on stages anymore. I was really dumb and young. I did it when I was like, fourteen."

"And did it hurt?"

"I don't remember."

"See? You are strong."

"Oh, stop it."

"I bet you could beat me up."

"I doubt that."

"Try."

June looked at him for a second and then pounced. She immediately twisted his arm up behind his back and kept him from retaliating by pinning the other arm to his side with her thighs. Chavdar strained against her, his face pushed in the pillow. June couldn't help giggling at the sight of him so helpless. "Say mercy," she said.

"Say what?" he asked, his voice muffled.

"Mercy," she repeated, fighting to keep her thighs clenched against his arms.

Suddenly his arm broke free and curled around her back, drawing her down into the pillows with him. "What was that word? What does it mean?" He held her body close against his.

"Mercy," she whispered. "When you say it, you're asking someone to show compassion. To be gentle and kind."

"Mercy then," he said softly, placing his mouth over hers. With his lips barely brushing hers, he trailed his hand down her spine. "Mercy... mercy... mercy."

18

Subject: Send more Anais Nin quotes
Date: Fri, 27 Dec 1996 02:36:14 -0800
From: June <jcarver@sof.cit>
To: Laney <laney@smnet.com>

Hi sweetheart—

I'm leaving for Greece with Chavdar, so I will be incommuni-
cado for a couple of weeks. I should feel great, heading off
on an adventure with a sexy man to an exotic island. But you
know what? I'd rather be sitting on the couch in my old little hole-in-the-wall apartment watching Ethan pick his nose
with the end of his pencil while he writes his dissertation.
But I can't just sit home waiting for him to get tired of
his new girlfriend and then welcome him into my loving arms,
can I? That kind of desperation and humiliation is nothing
but pathetic, right? Am I doing the right thing by telling
him I want him back, but that if he won't have me, I refuse
to sit and wait while he does whatever he wants? Two wrongs
don't make a right, I know. But now it's three wrongs, and
soon it will be four, and then five and will it ever end?
Laney, I'm afraid it will never never never end.

Love, June

*O*N NEW YEAR'S Eve, Ethan and Nevena rented a four-wheel-drive Jeep to take them down into the mountains. For less than two dollars apiece they stayed in a cellar converted into a guest room, in the home of an elderly couple. Their twin beds were covered with animal hides, and a gourd jug filled with mountain spring water sat on a small table between them.

They spent the evening in a tavern called Dyado Penyo after the proprietor, Grandfather Penyo. It was a fixed meal, and the granddaughters rushed around bringing all the guests shots of rakia and ceramic mugs of cloudy, warm, homemade red wine with cloves and cinnamon. Once the drinks were served, the girls started making the rounds with family-style platters heaped with mounds of many different cold vegetable and yogurt salads, slices of sausage and local cheese, fried potatoes, and hot rolls fresh from the brick oven.

Animal skulls and stuffed heads were mounted on the walls. A stuffed bobcat in the upper left-hand corner stared down at the diners, his mouth open in a death grimace that showed his fangs. The entire tavern had an earthy smell that struck Ethan as a mixture of mountain air and pungent decay. Nevena explained to him that the smell came from the shaggy, uncured animal hides hung on all the walls. They had never been tanned and so they would carry the scent of the animal until they rotted.

Several hours and many shots of rakia later, the dinner of pork chops and sauerkraut was served. While everyone was finishing off the main course, the broad wooden tavern door crashed open. Everyone began to applaud, and Ethan stood up to get a better look. The animal smell suddenly became very strong, and Ethan could see a group of people dressed head to toe in long goat and ox-hair robes, shaggy boots, and bone necklaces. Some of them sprouted sharp bone bulls' horns from their fur hats, and others had big black eye sockets painted onto leather hoods. They shook cowbells, waved tree branches, and screamed at the top of their lungs. A few of the teenagers jumped onto their chairs and howled with the men in their pagan costumes.

The door opened again, this time letting in more men in animal hides and a group of Gypsies playing folk music. As the songs started, the granddaughters rushed to remove dinner plates from the tables. All around the tavern people climbed up onto the tables and began to clap and whistle and dance. The granddaughters brought around glasses and bottles of champagne and when the New Year came in, Dyado Penyo emerged from the kitchen to ring a string of cowbells mounted on the ceiling. Everyone hugged and kissed, and then followed the Gypsy orchestra out into the snow. They were divided into sections, like an orchestra. Those playing the gaidas, or bagpipes, were in the center, flanked on one side by the kavals, or flutes, and on the other side by the string section, playing the gadulkas and tapans.

Several young women chanted slowly to the droning bagpipes, and Nevena pulled Ethan into the horo circle dance. They weaved like a snake through the snow, forming bigger and bigger circles until all the people from the tavern were linked in one ring. Their feet left a trampled pattern behind them, and the dark, winding, muddy trail stood out against the snow, which gleamed under the stars. Ethan felt his body surge with energy, he was so exhilarated by the freezing weather, the immense moon, the stench of death, and the dance of life. When the music slowed and people began to file back into the tavern for dessert, he was disappointed. He could have held Nevena's hand and danced under the stars to the primitive drumbeat all night. It was the best New Year's of his entire life.

IN THE EARLY morning of the first day of the year, out of the cold and naked underneath a pile of animal hides and blankets, Ethan drew Nevena's head onto his chest and whispered, "I think we must have woken the baba and dyado."

She looked up at the ceiling, which was the only barrier between them and the older couple. "Possible."

Ethan kissed the top of her head. "Isn't it amazing?" he asked, his whole hand cupping her forehead, his breath returning to normal. "That it can feel like that?"

Nevena was silent and Ethan propped himself up on his elbow to look down at her. "What?" he asked. "You don't feel the same way?"

"No, I do." Nevena stared at the ceiling and licked her lips. "But . . ." she said hesitantly. "It can't always be that way, can it?"

Ethan's eyes searched Nevena's. "You mean with June, was it? No, it was different." He kissed her cheek. "Has it ever been that way before for you?"

Nevena turned her head to the side. She focused on the wall. "No."

"Nevena," Ethan said, taking her chin in his fingers and trying to pull her back toward him. His voice was concerned and quiet. "Nevena, what's wrong? What did I say?"

She allowed him to turn her face toward his, and he saw her tears. "Please, Ethan. Please give me a second."

"I'll give you all the time you need, but I will still want you to talk to me. I don't want you to be sad. I want you to be as happy as I am."

"I am."

"You're crying, Nevena."

"Okay. Yes. Because I am angry," she said, her voice catching. "You know why I cry by now."

"Angry?" Ethan was shocked.

"Please, Ethan, don't look that way. I am not angry with you."

"Then what?"

"I just wanted to know if that is normal. For it to be so . . . beautiful. I asked my question and you answered. Now we can go to sleep."

"It's never been beautiful for you? Not at all?"

"No."

"Because of who you were with? Or because . . ." He paused. "Hadn't you ever before? You told me you've had boyfriends before, so I naturally assumed."

"No, no." Nevena wiped her tears away with the back of her hand. "You were not my first."

"Then what? You have to tell me if it's me."

"No," she said, closing her eyes. "It's not you. It . . . it was the soldiers the night my parents were murdered."

"What?" After a second his eyes widened. "No!" he said, gathering her body in his arms as if he were going to pick her up and carry her away. "Oh God, no. No."

Nevena's tears started coming faster and Ethan pressed her cheek into his shoulder and rocked her back and forth. One of his hands held her head, and with the other he stroked her hair over and over. "Oh God," he said again. "Oh my sweet little girl. I'm so sorry. I can't believe it. How could they do that to you? How could they?"

In between soft sobs, Ethan could hear Nevena mumbling. "Sshhh," he said. "It's okay. It's okay. What is it? What do you want to tell me?"

She looked up at him with her wide brown wet eyes. "I just said I am the one who is sorry."

"You should never be sorry," he said, placing his hands on either side of her face and staring into her eyes. "What they did to you was so wrong. Just please don't be sorry, I don't want you to be sorry ever again. I want to take care of you. If only I had known, I would have been more careful, I would have done everything differently."

"You did everything right," she said, wearily letting her head drop to the pillow. "Even now, even tonight, right this minute." She looked up at him and he could see how tired she was from her confession. "Thank you for not blaming me," she said softly. "In my parents' religion, a girl could be killed for allowing herself to be ruined."

"You are far from being ruined. You are new and perfect and beautiful and pure. Nevena, don't worry. Don't ever worry. I love you."

Nevena took a deep breath. He could see the relief on her face. "Oh, Ethan," she whispered. "I love you too. Thank you for saying that. Thank you for choosing just the right moment. I love you too." She smiled and tucked his hand against her heart. Then she closed her eyes for the night.

Ethan lay awake long after she had fallen asleep, thinking about the words that had slipped from his mouth. He did not want to take them back and yet he hadn't been ready to say them. He thought of what Nevena had gone through that night so long ago, and felt closer to her than to anyone else in the world. Like her, his life had been changed in a single instant. From now on, after just one night, nothing would ever be the same.

LIKE MOST businesses, IZTOK had officially shut down for the holidays. The regular employees were not coming in, but those higher up were using the time to discuss plans for the new year. The insurance agencies found themselves in a precarious position. Though the scandal in the fall had been averted by a timely assassination, it would not be long before someone else started pointing fingers and threatening to expose the crimes of the credit millionaires, Mafia parliament members, and other corrupt "pillars of society." It was a portentous time at IZTOK, and though they tried not to show it, even the men with their bodyguards, attack dogs, and villas in Simeonovo were beginning to feel uncomfortably vulnerable.

"YOU'RE GOING WHERE?" Rossen shouted, unable to conceal his frustration. Rossen was second-in-command to Stoyan in Chavdar's close-protection team. Now he paced back and forth in Chavdar's office.

"Mykonos," Chavdar said, arranging his desk. Rossen glared as Chavdar packed his briefcase with folders of work and his newest paperback, *Silita e v teb,* a translation of Louis Hay's American best-seller *The Strength Is Within You.*

"How can you go to Greece right now?" Rossen asked, shaking his hand in the air. "Taking a vacation now is not smart, Chavdar, and I know you are smart. Tell me why. Why are you doing this to me?"

"I need to get away from work for a while. June needs to get away too. The snow and the shortages are getting her down."

"You are being selfish at a bad time."

"I have a right to be selfish. You should read this book I just bought. You should see this new way of thinking. I have the right to do what is best for me. I am going away to build my strength for the battle. Look at it that way."

"To hell with your books that were written for people living in another world!"

"It is now one world. It can be our world." Chavdar paused and looked out the window. Down the alleyway a gray-haired woman had hung a carpet from her laundry line and was smacking it with a stick. Dust flew with each blow. The woman's bun was coming loose with each raging swing, and her old arms were shaking. Chavdar looked away. "Anyway. To tell you the truth, this city is getting me down too."

"Why Mykonos? Why not just go to the Black Sea for a few days, where we can reach you easily and where you can come back if you are needed?"

"You can reach me anywhere. And June has never been to Greece."

"Oh?" said Rossen. "That I did not know. Therefore you must go immediately! Waste no time in indulging the beauty queen."

"What do you have against June? She is a lovely girl."

"What did you have against Radka? She was lovely too."

Chavdar blinked. "I don't remember Radka."

"Zhendov's daughter. The ballet teacher."

"Hm," he said, rubbing his chin. "I guess the problem was that she wasn't memorable."

"And this American woman, she is so much better? Her polka-dot panties and loud laugh, they somehow make her worth a trip to Greece at such a crucial time?"

Chavdar looked up, finally perturbed. "Why does this upset you so much?"

"Chavdar, my parents' pensions don't even pay for their heat. My brother is selling books in Slaveikov square. I am the only one making money and even I don't have any anymore!"

"We're in a recession."

"No. We are in the worst depression imaginable, there are five new agencies competing with us, and there is a good chance that a currency board is going into effect soon."

"We haven't lost any business. No one has arrested us."

"We haven't gained any business, and the reason no one has arrested anyone is because they are compiling the evidence first so they can be sure to send us all away forever!"

"Don't be so melodramatic."

"Revolution is around the corner!"

"Stop it."

"I won't stop! You are the head of this office. We need to be more careful. We need to be more cunning. We need to make money! My parents need a new hot-water heater!"

"Buy them one. I'll pay for it. In fact, buy them not only a new boiler but a couple of electric heaters. I will take care of the bill. Consider it a bonus."

Rossen stared at Chavdar silently, his lips drawn into a thin line. Finally he breathed out of his nose and it sounded like a snort. "Okay. Fine." He put his hands on his hips and watched Chavdar close and lock his briefcase. "I hope you know what you're doing."

Chavdar walked past Rossen and patted him on his meaty shoulder. "Rossen, find the strength within you and hope for something better than that. It's Christmas."

19

Subject: IMPORTANT
Date: Thurs, 2 Jan 1997 19:51:48 -0800
From: Bob Summer <bsum@link.com>
To: June <jcarver@sof.cit>

June, your father called me very distraught after your last
email. I think the Mafia protests, rallies, and what-not
going on over there right now must seem very glamorous and
exciting, but the stakes for people in and out of power are
enormous. You will be sacrificed to their plans with no
thought whatsoever to what it means to you and your family
or your future. As a U.S. citizen in the Balkans you have
everything to lose and nothing to gain by being involved.
You may have already caused people to focus on you and how
you can be used (I am very serious about this) and it is all
the more reason you should come home and look at this situation from a better and bigger perspective. I have the background to say these things to you and know what I am talking
about. Stop seeing this Bulgarian man you wrote your sister
about and come home.

Love, Uncle Bob

*J*UNE SLIPPED IN the snow carrying her bags out to the street where Chavdar and his driver waited. She caught herself, but before she could pick her bag up out of the snow, Chavdar was at her side, one hand gripping her forearm, the other taking the suitcase. "Your knight to the rescue," he said.

She looked around and was surprised to see the streets so full of people. Dressed in winter coats, hats, shawls, and gloves, they were carrying pots and pans and candles. They were marching toward the city center. "What's going on?" she asked.

"A demonstration," he said. "Another one. This afternoon at the Parliament Square they will go and bang their pots and complain about the living conditions, the corruption, you know." Chavdar dismissed it with a click of his tongue. "They hate the Socialist Prime Minister. They want him to abdicate. They think if he leaves office, parliament will agree to new elections."

"They won't?"

"Never. Even if the Socialist parliament agrees to leave, and I don't think they will, they will simply replace themselves with more members of their own party. Why would they give the opposition a chance to win? The people are foolish. Nothing will change."

When they were both relaxed in the leather seats he leaned forward to speak to the driver. "Stop at the Vienna Cafe on the way out of the city so we can get some coffee, then head to the airport." Chavdar squeezed June's arm. "Would you like a cappuccino before we set off? I have to stay awake on the flight to finish some work."

"No thanks. I am more in need of a nap than caffeine. I like falling asleep on planes."

"Would you like a Valium to relax?"

"You have Valium?"

"Yes. They are like sleeping pills. Relaxation pills."

"I know what they are."

"I take them when I have too much work on my mind and can't fall asleep. They are harmless. Sold over the counter."

Claire had taken Valium. That was reason enough to refuse, but June had not been sleeping in the new apartment. Most nights she would sit by the window for hours on end alone, listening to the howling of wild dogs and the wailing of car alarms. "I have slept with her. Okay, I have." When Chavdar was with her, June still did not sleep, but went over and over the absurd events that led to this strange man being beside her in bed, and why it was that she allowed him to continue to come. Other nights it was a cat in heat in the courtyard or a child crying upstairs. *I have slept with her. Okay I have. I have. I have.* Hail hitting the balcony and a rat scuttling through the crawl space, her mother clapping in the audience and Ethan gunning his Mustang's motor below her dormitory window. She was so, so tired.

June squeezed Chavdar's hand. "Yes, please. I do want one."

Generous as ever, he gave her two.

THE CRESCENT-SHAPED BAY in Mykonos was dotted with brightly colored fishing boats. Whitewashed houses were stacked on top of one another, climbing the hill that rose from the sea. It was not tourist season, but the weather was unseasonably warm and the outdoor cafes were packed with beautiful Greeks away from the mainland for a weekend holiday. The women wore expensive sunglasses, and their hair was pulled back severely, making their elegant necks seem even longer, their bone structure even more regal. In loose linen suits and three-hundred-dollar sandals, they sat, drinking frappés with men who sipped ouzo and seemed to grow tanner and more gorgeous by the second.

While Chavdar checked them into their hotel, June removed her shoes and walked down to the small stretch of sandy beach. Fishermen were dumping barrels of shiny, silver fish out of their boats into troughs. Seaweed circulated in dark green patches in the otherwise clear water. June walked out to the edge of the beach, sat on a rock, and dangled her feet into the water. Attached to the rocks, just below the surface of the sea, June saw a reddish-orange starfish. She waded into the water, lifting her skirt, to get a closer look.

June had never seen a starfish before, and as she approached, it seemed to her that the strange animal was raising one of its fat, triangular arms to wave at her. She laughed out loud and bent down. The laugh died in her mouth. The starfish was sawing off its own arm against a sharp piece of the rocks. Slowly, back and forth, the animal twisted its body, pushing and pulling. The rock was like a dull razor, and soon the arm broke free. The wave carried the chubby red tentacle toward June, and she scrambled out of the water, cutting her own foot open in her haste. Her blood was the same color as the starfish arm.

"I saw a starfish trying to kill itself," she said to Chavdar when she joined him in the hotel lobby. The porter had just arrived to take their bags up to the room.

"What?"

"I said, I saw a starfish trying to kill itself."

"Why are you talking that way?"

"I don't know."

"Why are you limping?"

"I cut my foot. I cut my foot open when I saw the starfish trying to kill itself." She grabbed her foot, took off her shoe, and showed the two men her bare heel. "See?"

Chavdar made a face and took her elbow. "I think you need to lie down."

The porter shook his head. "It wasn't killing itself, miss. Don't worry. They just do that."

"It's normal?" asked June.

"It's nature," answered the porter. As June was limping away, the porter leaned toward Chavdar and whispered, "I'll send up a doctor."

THE FIRST FEW days in Mykonos passed pleasurably. Each afternoon came and went in a haze of fragrant floral aromas and distant laughter. June was at home, giddy, dizzy, feeling as if she had stepped out of Bulgaria into the Malibu beach print hanging on the wall of an Istanbul hotel. Out of stench into perfume, from pain into paradise. From one man to another. She had vague twinges of regret but the exhaustion was like amnesia. She slept twelve hours a day.

In the evenings, June and Chavdar would feast on seafood past midnight in the Greek taverns. They picked at enormous salads, overflowing with oily brown-skinned olives, sweet red peppers, and slices of feta cheese. They finger-fed each other from decorative platters of shellfish and toasted each other with bottle after bottle of wine.

After dinner, when the ouzo started to flow and the bands started to play, June would twirl onto the dance floor with the Greek women, and beckon to Chavdar. Sometimes he joined her and sometimes he watched. While the women swayed and swirled their arms and fingers to the music, the men would kneel around the edge of the dance floor, clapping their hands rhythmically to the song, paying homage to the dancers in an ancient tradition. When June grew clumsy, as she always did now at the end of the night, Chavdar would scoop her into his arms and carry her away. Sometimes she did not wake up and he would caress her lifeless body and put her to bed.

One night at an outdoor beach cafe, their waiter, a young handsome island boy, picked a handful of wildflowers from the courtyard. He took them to June, who was on the dance floor. June slipped the largest and most exotic flower behind her ear, and then continued to dance sleepily, the bouquet dangling from her right hand. The boy smiled at her, and she thanked him by blowing him a kiss. He blushed as if falling in love. Chavdar appreciated the sight of June drenched in flowers. While she was dancing with her eyes half-closed, he rose and walked toward the kitchen. June didn't even notice he was gone.

Chavdar found the waiter in the back, taking a pail of seafood shells to the garbage. The Greek boy looked up and smiled at Chavdar for a split second before the fist came crashing down into his face, again and again and again.

Back at the table, June saw a light splattering of red droplets across Chavdar's jaw. "What do you—" She stopped in mid-sentence while reaching out for his face.

"What?"

June covered her mouth with her hand and looked down.

"What's wrong?"

"Nothing."

"What is it, what do I have?"

"Something. Something on your cheek."

Chavdar touched one deep red speck. "Seafood sauce," he said, gesturing to the fried calamari platter on the table.

"Seafood sauce?" she asked, unsure.

"Of course."

"Of course," she repeated, and reached out to dab the boy's blood off Chavdar's jaw with her light blue napkin. She needed to believe him, but her hand shook violently.

Chavdar grabbed it and squeezed, harder and harder, until the shaking stopped.

ALONE IN THEIR hotel room that night, Chavdar turned the radio to traditional Greek music, and June danced just for him. Drinking scotch and smoking cigars, he sat and watched, clapping slowly to the beat like the Greeks, while she spun and sang and tripped over herself. After she shed her summer dress and jewelry, she continued to dance, closing her eyes and hugging herself. "Keep dancing," Chavdar whispered, when she began to look tired. His face was hidden in the shadows. "Don't stop until I tell you to. Don't stop until I'm ready for you. Come here. But don't stop."

She danced toward him, swinging her hips back and forth like a belly dancer. He grabbed her around the small of the back and used one hand to tilt her torso back. Then he poured a thin, cold trail of scotch down between her breasts. As he began to lick her from the belly button upward, he murmured against her stomach, "Don't stop moving. Keep moving. Keep dancing until I tell you to get in the bed."

Though it was June, it did not look like June, because she no longer wore her big, eager, and easy smile. Instead she looked entranced, drugged, on the verge of falling. When she began bumping into the table and strangely giggling at the floor, Chavdar stood up and pulled her into the bed.

When he had finished with her, he became tender again.

In such quiet moments before the sun came up, June could forget the way Chavdar looked when he was displeased. She would slip out the package of Valium he had given her and take two or three, depending on how much she'd had to drink. In the mind-numbing comfort of the tranquilizers, she could forget the way his voice became accusing and condescending within seconds. The Valium made her forget where her husband was, and with whom, as well as the words *Yankee Mafia bitch* and *I slapped my mom so goddamn hard.* It was a pleasant retreat, and she went there often. Far back inside this safe place, she closed her eyes and hummed old Abba songs from when she and her sister were girls. "Dancing Queen" drowned out the ringing of Chavdar's cell phone. She sang just loud enough to fill her own ears: *"Feel the beat of the tambourine, oh yeaahhhh."* This way, she did not have to hear his conversations with the agency—the ones that made her sick with an indescribable fear. She did not have to remember the light spray of blood splashed across his handsome, cruel jaw.

It was in this early morning state somewhere between waking and dreaming that June felt attached to Chavdar, grateful for his fingers tickling along her spine, flattered by his lust and lavish generosity. In the last moments before she succumbed to the sedatives, she felt a lovely contentment. Sofia seemed as far away as Los Angeles, Ethan less necessary to her than Chavdar, and James a figment of her imagination. It was easy to imagine that there was no reason at all for sadness. After all, every mother dies and divorce is common. She snuggled deeper into the cool sheets, imagining a brighter future. In Mykonos, that future was only as far away as the sunny afternoon awakening, and would consist of only more dancing, drinking, and drowning herself as pleasantly as possible.

DOWNSTAIRS THE GREEK music started to play as the family who ran the hotel began preparing for the breakfast crowd. Though the ocean was too cool for swimming, people would be getting up for walks along the shore. Kids would search for seashells and stomp on balls of seaweed. If they were alert, they might see a four-legged fire-colored starfish on the rocks, just starting to regrow its missing flesh.

The bed undulated beneath her like waves, and June thought with awe and horror about the reddish-orange starfish. It wrenched its own arm from its body, little by little, until the severed piece was free and floating away, dead. It floated through a pool of June's blood.

Dishes clanked downstairs, and the smell of baking bread permeated the room. Chavdar snored beside her, his heavy, hairy leg stretched across her pelvis. She was pinned, but she didn't dare move. Staring at the ceiling, June recognized her own approach to sleep by the drugged and incoherent repetition in her mind of swimming ocean images. A sea star was self-destructing but not dying, performing the amputation of its arm over and over. June lay perfectly still. Her green, half-closed eyes slowly traversed the ceiling, where she saw scarves floating in water, arms floating, the color red streaming from the cut on her foot, the color red streaming from the nose of a young and beautiful boy. It's nature, the porter had said. Barely awake, June contemplated the merits of evisceration while life went on in the kitchen below. She couldn't believe it was already a new day, and couldn't help wishing it were ending instead of starting. Ending and ending and ending. It was a comfortable thought to carry her away.

20

Subject: What?
Date: Wed, 8 Jan 1997 12:12:02 -0500 (EST)
From: Laney <laney@smnet.com>
To: June <jcarver@sof.cit>

June,

What is going on? I could not make heads nor tails out of
your last email. What exactly happened to your foot? Who is
this guy, anyway? You haven't had such a setback over your
mom in a long time. Please write me again, and this time not
at three in the morning after waking up from a nightmare,
okay? Why do you have to sneak around and write when he's
asleep? This does not sound good.

To catch you up on here—you know that the Goldmans are
suing O.J. for eight million dollars. Again, it's bloody
glove this, white Bronco that, mistresses, therapists,
houseguests, and day after day, nonstop analysis of Nicole's
dog's behavior and breed. The whole country is caught up in
the soap opera. Instead of ANYTHING on the crisis in the
Balkans you told me about, CNN is showing 'round the clock
OJ. I sincerely think that the U.S. is like a black hole. We
will soon collapse upon ourselves with shallowness and not
even a speck of intellect will be able to escape. Stupidity
is rampant.

Please take care of yourself!

Love you,

Laney

p.s. I hope you are not having any trouble over the
protests. I looked up the situation on the web today and
it sounds serious.

IN SOFIA, the dogs were growing thinner. Their ribs pushed through their matted fur, making deep indentations in their sides. With their tongues hanging out and their hot breath steaming into the air, they looked like striped jungle scavengers.

June raised her face toward a freezing sky, to look up at Raina's apartment. Every window was dim and frosty. If there were lights on inside, they were shrouded by curtains or an opaque layer of snow and ice.

There was a thin spatter of melting snow across the cement floor of the Block's entrance. Everything was dead and frozen. June turned the corner, ignoring the now familiar pile of refuse and graffiti. The lift was dark, and a hand-lettered sign taped to the door declared it out of order. June began taking the stairs as fast as she could, two steps at a time.

She paused for breath on the eighth-floor landing and could smell smoke from one of the apartments. It stung like a trash bonfire. She began running the stairs again. When she finally reached the twentieth floor, she had to bend over and put her head between her legs. "Raina!" she called, still slumped against the wall.

"Raina!" she yelled again, now heading for the door to the apartment. "Are you in there?" June pounded on the door and her cold fist stung with each blow.

After a long while, the door opened slowly, and a pale, sick white face appeared behind a locked chain. Raina's voice sounded as if she were speaking aloud in a dream. "June? Is that you?"

June breathed a sigh of relief and it was all she could do to keep from staggering into the apartment. "It's me."

"Hello, dear." Raina stepped back to let her in, and June's heart broke. She wore several heavy skirts over pants, layers of sweaters under a long, thick coat, and padded winter boots. Sadly out of place with the layers of mismatched hand-me-down clothes were the pink angora scarf and fuzzy pink hat that June had given her as presents. "I'm wearing the hat," she said, smoothing a sock-covered hand across the soft fur. "It's a beautiful hat, actually. I'm very fond of it. Don't you have a matching one? Where is your matching one?"

June threw her arms around Raina's stiff body. The older woman held still through the desperate hug, patting June's back with reserve. Finally, June pulled back and touched the pink hat. "Oh, Raina, look at you."

"What?" On her hands were two heavy wool socks. She glanced down, and then held them out shamefully. "I still have the matching gloves, you know," she said. "But these are warmer. I know they are ugly, but I thought no one would see me. I'm saving the gloves. I will wear the whole set out on a special occasion when it is safe to go outside."

"What happened?"

"What happened?" Raina seemed disoriented. "Nyama tok. I mean, no heat, no electricity. I would have called you, but as you know, for some time now I have had no phone. For some time now no heat. Now no electricity, no nothing. I ran out of money. For some time now . . ." She trailed off and trudged over to her couch. Rakia and a shot glass were placed on the coffee table.

"I would have gone for supplies, or help, or something. But the lift," Raina said, slurring. "And my arthritis is so bad." She coughed into the socks on her hands. "You know. So bad in the cold. I tried to get down the stairs but I couldn't."

"Have you had anything to eat?"

"Some crackers, tsa tsa, some of those little fish."

"We have to get you out of here."

"My dear," Raina said, suddenly sitting up straight, "there is nowhere to go." Her eyes couldn't focus and she stared drunkenly at the coffee table while she talked, her chin sagging. "It is not as if there are so many better places. This building is not the ghetto. It is full of teachers and economists. Working people and families."

"There are places that aren't on the twentieth floor. When are they fixing the lift?"

Raina gave an exaggerated shrug, almost falling over with the motion. "They say soon. Buh, buh, buh. The lift is on the five-year plan. Very soon, they say. Liberation Day."

June kneeled down next to Raina and looked up into her eyes. She was hit with the smell of someone who has been drinking steadily for a long time. "Listen," she said. "You need food. I am going to have to leave you for about a half an hour."

"Go on," Raina said, raising her hand and sticking her lower lip out in the way she always did. "Go on and get out then. Leave me!"

"Why didn't you use the money I left you to have the heat turned back on?"

Raina stared at the floor. Suddenly she looked up. "Get out of here, I said! I don't want you here anymore, Maria! Stay away, just like your father."

"It's June, Raina. And I'm coming back with food and coffee."

"Get out then!" she shouted, her voice hoarse. "Don't bother to visit either!"

"I'll be back in a half hour, Raina. I promise."

As she closed the door, June could hear Raina talking to herself. "Promises, they promise you, buh buh buh buh. Promises!"

RAINA WAS SLUMPED on the couch, staring straight ahead, when June returned. In her plump, sock-covered fist was an empty shot glass, the contents spilled all over her skirt. June entered the apartment with a cardboard box of takeout from the closest pastry stand. Inside she had two shots of hot espresso and four croissants.

"Wake up. I brought you something to eat. And someone's on the way over to help me get you down the stairs."

After finishing both shots of espresso and two of the croissants, Raina leaned back against the couch. "That's better," she said. "Feel much warmer now. Thank you."

"You're welcome," June said, wondering when the man Chavdar was sending over would arrive.

Raina opened her eyes, rubbed her face, and smacked her lips. "Be a dear and light me a cigarette, will you?"

"Oh Raina, are you sure you need one right now?"

She shook her head defiantly. "I don't need one, I want one."

June sighed and looked for Raina's cigarettes. There were none. All that was left were a few stale old butts, sitting next to her pipe. "Take what's left and unroll them," Raina said, motioning to the pipe. "Unroll them and shake the tobacco out and get the—"

"I know, Raina," June said gently. "Don't worry. I know how to do it."

RAINA WAS SMOKING her pipe peacefully when Petko arrived and pounded on the door. June rushed to let him in. "Zdraveite," she said. "Mnogo vi blugodariya da doida."

"Don't you remember me? From the bar? Taki shaks."

"Da. I remember."

"I speaking English."

"You speak English?"

"Yes, I said I speaking English."

"Well, okay. Thanks for coming."

Petko stood outside in a long, black trench coat. He was red in the face and wheezing from the climb. Nevertheless, he was finishing a cigarette. He dropped it at his feet on Raina's welcome mat. "Chavdar said someone have emergency."

"Yes," June said, ushering him in. "My friend Raina is sick. I need to get her downstairs and then drive her out to Darvenitsa."

Petko hacked into a handkerchief. "You tell me I just lose fucking lungs to climb up here and now I have to carry overfed cow down?"

June turned to face him.

"Hey," he said, seeing the expression on her face. "Sorry. Twenty flight stairs does not make me in best mood, okay?"

"Let's just get this over with."

"Fine. How we do this?"

June looked at Raina's lumpy figure on the couch. "I suppose you can't carry her?"

Petko put his hands on his hips and looked Raina over. "Not all fucking way down, I can't. Maybe one body part at time, you know?" His self-satisfied smile disappeared when he saw that June didn't appreciate his joke. He walked over to the couch. "Okay, baba," he said to Raina, as he slid his arms underneath her. "Gotova li si? Edno, dve, tri . . ."

Raina was surprisingly docile as Petko struggled to lift her from the couch. He held her in his arms for a second as if estimating her weight. Then he put her back down. "If you get some fucking clothes off, I can get it down. Might take while."

While Petko took one landing at a time with Raina in his arms, June packed her a bag full of warm clothes and toiletries. By the time June caught up with them at the seventh landing, Raina was throwing a fit. "Ostavime! Ostavi me na mira!"

Petko dumped her onto the ground.

With as much dignity as possible, Raina stood up and leaned against the wall. Pointing at Petko, she turned to June. "Where is he taking me?"

June couldn't help but smile. "Down to the bottom."

"He was hurting me."

Petko flung his arms out to his sides. "I hurting you! You was hurting me! You think so easy to carry down twenty flight stairs?"

Raina thrust her chin up at Petko. "I can walk. And I can speak *proper* English."

"Great," Petko said, looking sarcastically from June to Raina and then back to June. "She walk, I go home. See how far fucking proper English get her fat ass, eh?"

"She at least needs to lean on you. And we need a ride."

With Raina's weight distributed between the two of them, June and Petko managed to get her out of the Block and to Petko's waiting BMW. "Whose car is this?" Raina demanded, as June opened the door.

"My car," answered Petko.

"I'm not getting in this car," she said, bracing herself against the sides of the door. "You can't expect me to ride through the city in a Mafia car."

"Pretend you're being kidnapped," said June. "You're riding in this car against your will, so you aren't responsible. Okay?"

Raina jabbed her sock-covered fist in Petko's direction, and her pointed finger stretched the wool fabric. "Who is this thick-neck mutra? He's a mutra, I tell you!"

"He's a ride, Raina," answered June. Her voice was beseeching. "Won't you please get in the car?"

Raina narrowed her eyes. "I never thought I'd see the day," she mumbled, as she settled heavily into the backseat.

"Charming baba," Petko said, starting the car. "You *must* bring baba by club."

"That's funny. And you *must* learn that such a thing as an *article* exists in English."

"What?"

"Just drive."

"Not to give orders!"

"Okay then. May I *please* borrow your cell phone so I can call Chavdar and have him give you the same order?"

"Maika mu mrusna, shibina kuchka," Petko muttered through his teeth, shifting into gear.

In the back, Raina chuckled. She reached up and patted June on the shoulder. "Bravo, milichka. You've learned well. Braa-vo!"

☉

ETHAN HAD JUST FINISHED packing for another research trip to the provinces with Stan when Nevena arrived home from work.

"Hello, bebcho!" she said, entering. "What are you doing?"

"I just sat down to do a little work while I waited for you to get home. You're late."

"I know. I was afraid I might have missed you!"

Ethan glanced at his watch. "I'm supposed to be at Stan's shortly but I wanted to say good-bye."

"How sweet," she said. "I'm sorry I couldn't get here sooner. The trams were awful." As she began to cross the room to put down her bag of groceries and slip her arms around Ethan, the phone rang. She scooped it up with the hand that wasn't cupping the groceries to her chest. "Alo?" she said.

"Uh, Nevena?" The voice on the other end was hesitant, foreign and female.

"Da?"

"This is, uh, well, this is June."

Nevena stood silently, the phone pressed against her ear.

June cleared her throat. "Um, June Carver? You know, Ethan's uh . . ."

"Yes, yes, I know."

She set the phone down on the table and turned to Ethan, who was looking up from his work. When he saw her face, he stood. "What's wrong?"

Nevena felt the groceries slipping. She pointed to the phone. "It's . . ." She couldn't bring herself to say *your wife.* Instead she just pointed again, and said, "It's for you."

Ethan walked to the phone. "Hello?"

"I'm sorry for calling you there. I had to beg Roxanne for Nevena's number."

As soon as Ethan knew who it was, he raised his eyes apologetically to Nevena, but she was already in the kitchen, mechanically putting away the groceries. "What is it, June?"

"I need to talk to you about something important."

"Can't we find a better time?"

"I'm in the Darvenitsa apartment right now and—"

"What are you doing there? You moved out."

"It's just that it's kind of an emergency. Remember my tutor, Raina? Well, she's sick and the heat is off in her apartment and she lives on the twentieth floor and she has arthritis and couldn't get down." June took a deep breath.

"Slow down, June, I can hardly understand."

"I was afraid she was going to, you know."

"I can't hear you. Are you crying?"

"You know, I thought she was dead and she wasn't. But if I don't do something now maybe next time she will be and I'll be the one to find her. And the paramedics will come and all. I don't want that to happen and since you don't really live here either anymore, well . . . I mean, you've been spending all your time at Nevena's. And the apartment here has heat and it's only a couple of floors to the bottom, and Dimcho's mom has that little grocery stand right next to where the puppies used to be before that guy in apartment 67 killed them. I wanted to do this so that the *other thing* wouldn't happen. Not again. Please?"

"Please what? You're not making sense."

"Couldn't Raina live here until it's safe for her to go home?"

"Won't that be sometime in spring? Or never?"

"I don't know. But she needs help now." June stopped, and after a second of silence she plunged ahead. "And if you wanted you could put some stuff at my new place and if there was ever a problem with being at Nevena's you could always go there."

Ethan paced for a second. "Yeah, I mean, yeah. I'll have to talk to Nevena about it, obviously." He stopped walking back and forth and lowered his voice. "But I think it's okay. It's a good thing, what you're doing. We'll make it work."

"Thanks, Ethan."

AFTER THEY HUNG UP, Ethan walked slowly back into the kitchen. Nevena had her back to him and was straining yogurt to make snezhanka. He leaned against the door and crossed his arms. Nevena said nothing. "I'm sorry about that. It really was an emergency."

Nevena shook her head and continued with her work. "Um hmm."

"I wish you wouldn't get upset about this. Say something."

"Bread is up to three hundred leva. No more meat or milk."

"That's not what I was hoping for." Ethan uncrossed his arms and hooked his thumbs though the loopholes on his faded jeans. "Look. There's something we should discuss."

"What?"

"What's going on between us."

Suddenly Nevena dropped the plastic container of yogurt into the strainer and both items fell into the bowl of water. "Po diavolite!" she yelled, hitting the bowl and sending it clattering across the countertop and crashing into the sink. Yogurt flew everywhere.

"Nevena!" Ethan said, moving toward her.

"No!" she said, backing away. She had been trying so hard to be pleasant and easy, happy and confident—like an American woman. How many times had she bitten her lip and not said anything about his wife, how many times had she tried to tell herself theirs was a modern romance, like in the movies? But the Balkans was not a place of modern romances; it was a place where mistresses were habitually beaten, discarded, even traded. Nevena had seen it happen dozens of times. Ethan might be different, but he might not. What did she really know of Americans and their culture? Nothing except what he told her. And men lie. She had reached her breaking point. "I don't need to discuss what's going on between us. I know. I am with a married man. What else is there to say?"

"A lot!"

"Ethan, I don't know what you think we have to discuss, what you want to say about the future of our relationship. To me it's not a matter of discussion. In my language there is no word for share, only the word that means to divide. And if you are divided, like all these other men I know with a toothbrush here and a clean pair of socks there, then you are just pieces to me. And I don't want your pieces." She covered her eyes with her hand and leaned against the counter. "I love you but I don't want you. Not like this."

"We have to get past this."

"I can't get past this, not when there is a woman out there, in this very city, who has a claim on you. She has a right to call you in my own apartment because you belong to each other. In front of God and your families you made a promise, and how am I to know that you don't intend to keep that promise? And then where will I be?"

"Nevena," Ethan said, reaching out for her. "Come here, please."

Nevena didn't budge. "Can you tell me right now that you have no doubt, none whatsoever, that the two of you will never be back together?"

The question took Ethan by surprise. It seemed more logical for Nevena to ask him if he still loved June. That was the question he had been expecting and dreading. Instead she was asking him something more practical, something that required far more rational consideration. It was a Bulgarian question. Never? That was a strong word.

He realized he was taking too long to answer and sputtered, "I don't think so. I mean, no. I don't think we will ever be like we were."

Nevena sank into the chair by the table and rested her arm on Ethan's papers. "That is a weak answer, Ethan."

"It's the truth. I don't know what else to say except that I love you. You should know that."

"I do know it. And I am smart enough to know that love doesn't mean that we will end up together. Love doesn't mean that we will always be kind to each other. Love doesn't mean that we will never love someone else." Nevena looked up and met Ethan's eyes. "Don't you see? I have to protect myself. I have to."

"I'm not trying to hurt you, Nevena."

"I am not saying that is your intention, but things happen. Perhaps we have to do some thinking before we do the discussing. Perhaps I do, anyway."

"I don't want to lose you, Nevena."

She folded her hands in her lap and said simply, "From my perspective, you are the one with very little to lose."

"You don't understand me at all, then."

"It is possible."

"I don't like how cold you are being right now."

Nevena answered in a monotone. "I apologize if my coldness is unpleasant for you."

Ethan stared at her. Her face was impassive and tired. Disappointment and even a hint of disgust flickered in those dark eyes. He was reminded of June when she had said that this was his biggest mistake yet. He could not face any more disapproval, could not stand for one second longer Nevena's motionless hands in her lap, the neatly crossed legs, the pragmatic and unwavering assurance of her unblinking eyes.

He walked over to where she sat at the table, and her eyes followed him in a way that was unbearable. Instead of touching her arm or brushing her leg, he closed up his laptop, wound the chord slowly, and slipped it into his overnight bag. "Stan is expecting me."

"Yes, I know."

"We'll talk some more when I get back."

"If you come back."

Ethan hoisted the pack to his shoulder and walked to the door. He looked over his shoulder, but Nevena was staring at the floor. He stepped outside, paused, and said quietly, "I'll be back." He shut the door and was gone.

Nevena waited a moment, and then whispered to the table, to the wrapper from his chocolate bar, to his candy-smudged papers and empty coffee mug, "I'll be waiting."

ETHAN WALKED TOWARD Stan's apartment with his hands plunged in his pockets, and his face lowered against the cold. As he stared at the broken sidewalk, he imagined the sky whirling above him, fast and out of control. A change was coming, he could feel it. The life he had left behind in Los Angeles seemed farther away than ever. He was waving good-bye to a fading image that was about to fall off the horizon, like some forgotten dream that he might remember if he cared to, but didn't.

He felt like the pieces that Nevena didn't want. Part of him was here and now in Sofia, and part of him had departed from Los Angeles on a magic carpet with June, never planning on coming back to earth. There was even a little boy wandering around the world, through Haiti and Sri Lanka and Tunisia, still believing in his parents' Catholic priests, still believing that wishes could be granted by plugging quarters into fake light bulb candles inside a church. How had this feeling of incompleteness invaded his body and lodged itself there like a splinter? Had he left some hair behind on a brush when he was digging latrines in Panama? Had he clipped his toenails and dropped the moon-shaped cuttings onto different floors the summer he spent traveling and teaching English in Africa? Perhaps there was a trail of Ethan pieces all over the world, leaving him unwhole.

He raised his head when he heard hollering in the streets. He felt strange and wondered how he could have become so off-balance. A crowd was surging toward him from the top of Bulevard Vitosha, and they looked to him like a slowly flowing tidal wave of color coming to engulf him. He stood still and waited for them to take him over, and the closer they came the more he could hear. They were chanting and banging pots and pans and some of them wielded broken tree branches with deadly-looking splintered edges.

"Cherveni boklutsi!" they shouted, and Ethan felt his legs go numb. The crowd was chanting "red garbage" and they were headed for the parliament building. There had been protests and concerts and meetings before, but nothing like this. Tens of thousands of people were marching. This was extraordinary.

Ethan stepped into the crowd and marveled at the fact that he had stumbled unwittingly onto the start of something huge. Going along with them made as much sense as anything else, and Ethan felt a morbid desire to be swallowed whole by the marching masses. Stan would wait. Stan would not drive to Silistra, on the Romanian border, without him. There was time. Standing alone among many in the Parliament Square, he felt he had no real home, no real country, no responsibilities to anyone, nothing at all. Instead of worrying about who might be somewhere worrying about him, waiting for him, he became a part of everything. June, Nevena, Stan. It didn't matter. He was alone. He shouted at the sky. He clenched his fist and shook it at the moon.

21

Subject: Your long lost comrade
Date: Sat, 11 Jan 1997 07:51:32 -0700
From: June Carver <jcarver@sof.cit>
To: James <McKinnonJ@smnet.com>

Jimmy, hey!

I'm sorry for not writing in so long. I was confused and
didn't know what to say. I'm still confused, and I still
don't know what to say. Anyway, today I heard Easy Like Sunday Morning on the radio, and despite writers block pertain-
ing to you, I just had to write my (not so) easy Southern
boy back home.

Where are you, how are you, what are you doing? Here in Sofia
it's freezing and gray. Everything here is just DEAD. Trees,
dogs, cars, eyes, sky. I need to make some decisions soon.
Otherwise I will end up being a prescription drug addict and
never getting out of bed and will probably mysteriously ac-
quire about thirty cats to live with me in my spooky Bulgarian house with strange (and possibly illegal) weeds in the
yard and boards nailed over the windows.

In answer to your question about Ethan . . . it seems that it
is really over. He has a girlfriend. A serious one. I don't
know what to say, Jimmy. Just that it has been an awful
year. What doesn't kill you makes you stronger, though,
right? That is my new favorite saying. I use it all the
time. This time next year I will be able to bend steel bars
with my bare hands, and jump skyscrapers in a single bound.

So, please forgive me for being out of touch for so long and write me back, even just one cynical line to tell me you've gone from performing Hamlet in Austin to dressing as Indiana Jones at Universal Studios.

I miss you too. And in answer to your question, of course I care. Unlike you, I am not brilliant in the art of acting.

June

*I*T WAS NOON on Friday when Ploshtad Batenberg, with its yellow cobblestones and elegant buildings, began to look like a battleground. Men in stocking caps hung from trees, stood on roofs, and climbed on each other's shoulders in order to see the enemy. Beer bottles hurtled through the air and smoke bombs danced along the ground. A boy climbed the Tsar Osvoboditel monument to the "Liberator from Russia." A massive blackened statue depicting Alexander the Second on horseback arriving to free the Bulgarians from their Turkish oppressors, the monument towered above the parliament. The boy reached the top of the monument, straddled the horse, and, as if riding double in front of the Russian tsar, waved his Bulgarian flag. He shouted to his friends and father, proud of his unparalleled view of the city.

The Socialists were panicking. They did not want to give in to the crowd's demands, but neither did they want to incite their anger. They were both stubborn and scared. Outside, policemen climbed out of armored trucks, wearing uniforms with helmets and boots. They carried large bulletproof shields as well as bats, canisters of tear gas, and guns. They formed a complete circular barrier around the parliament building and forced the crowd to keep a ten-foot distance. Inside, the Socialists pushed couches and heavy tables against the doors, and nailed boards up over the windows. They loaded their personal firearms.

JUNE HAD NOT gone home to her apartment in the center the night before, after Petko helped Raina up to the Darvenitsa apartment. Instead, she put Raina to bed and slept in the kitchen, in case Raina got up in the night sick, or disoriented, or scared.

She needn't have worried. Raina burst into the kitchen when the sun was high in the sky, yelling, "June, wake up!"

June, who was sleeping upright in a chair, was the one who woke up in shock. "What? What is it?"

"With no electricity I haven't seen the news in days. I was just watching the set and, you won't believe. There are demonstrators in the streets, June. There is a protest at the parliament. We have to go immediately. I must see this. We must go, now, now."

June rubbed her eyes and stood up. "You can't go to a rally. You're not well."

"Look! Look at me!" Raina started jumping up and down, her bosom heaving over her round stomach. On the kitchen tiles her heavy socks made a muted pounding noise. "They are in the streets, they are jumping up and down, up and down! You have to see it!" She stopped and took a deep wheezing breath. "Let's go."

IT WAS COLD but sunny. Much of the snow had melted, washing away the slush and dirt, and Sofia looked different than it had during the previous months. The yellow bricks sparkled with patches of ice. Children bundled in winter parkas were perched on their parents' shoulders, and elderly men and women with canes pushed their way forward to get a good look through the metal barricades that had been erected around the parliament's perimeter.

A young man pushed his way through the crowd to the base of the Tsar Osvoboditel monument and yelled something up to the boy perched on top. The boy listened and then screamed out to the crowd, "They aren't making the decision today! We will have to wait!"

Infuriated expressions of disbelief erupted throughout the square, and then June was enveloped by chaos. People were running and colors swam in front of her eyes. She groped for Raina and latched onto her heavy coat. Everything seemed to be going so fast and yet she registered it all as if it were in slow motion.

"Look!" Raina said, pointing toward the left-hand side of the parliament building. A group of men had forced down the metal barricades and were fighting with the human wall of police. Bricks launched into the air and smashed through the upper windows of the building. A protester in a stocking cap, dressed in muted shades of blue, jumped up onto the window ledge. He punched a gloved hand through the lower window and began ripping out giant shards of glass to open up an entrance into the building.

"June! What are you doing here?"

June heard the sound of English and turned. There, carrying his camera and accompanied by another man and woman, was Kyril, the photographer. "I . . . I'm here with my friend," she stammered, half terrified that he would call her a Yankee mutressa again, and that the entire crowd would turn on her and attack.

Kyril glanced at Raina, who was swearing at the Socialists while she danced the horo with four other pensioners. "Come on, June! Come join!"

Kyril looked June up and down, thinking. Finally he said, "Be careful."

"I will."

He seemed about to say something else, when the woman pulled on his camera strap, urging him to follow. "Sega idvam," he said to her. Then he touched June's arm. A quick touch. "You should still watch yourself. But I'm glad you're here." Then he was swallowed by the crowd.

At the edge of the plaza the BMWs and Mercedeses belonging to the politicians were parked. People climbed onto the hoods and began smashing the windows with their feet. Two students opened one of the doors and swung it back and forth so violently that they broke it from its hinges. They flung the door toward the parliament building, knocking over guards. Everyone was yelling. "Y predi! Y sega! BSP e Mafia!"

June felt a brick whiz by her ear and ducked, pulling Raina down with her. "My God!" she said, moving toward the outer edges of the crowd. "What are they yelling now?"

"And before, and still now, the Socialists are Mafia." Raina waved her fist in the air. "Y predi! Y sega! BSP e Mafia!" More bricks were hurled and suddenly someone grabbed June's hand. Everyone was forming a human link to keep the arriving squads of policemen from getting to the front. June was just starting to feel a euphoric sense of invulnerability in the crowd when the first shots were fired and the tear gas was released. Her eyes started to sting, but before she could even react, she felt two strong arms around her waist, lifting her up. A thick-necked dark-haired stranger was dragging June out of the human barricade.

"Let her go!" Raina yelled, whacking him in the arm. "Let go of her, garbage!"

"The wrestler is hurting the girl!" someone yelled. "There's a mutra here!"

June struggled against his stronghold and found that she couldn't move at all. "Stop it!" she screamed, losing eye contact with Raina in the crowd.

"Shut up, June," Rossen said, and June felt herself go cold. She was so shocked at the sound of her name that she stopped struggling and let her arms hang down at her sides like a rag doll. He knew her. He had come for her, and she knew who had sent him.

THE ROOM THAT Chavdar's thug escorted June to was not unpleasant. The walls were the same tasteful stained wood as the rest of the private club, but here there were no elegant windows with sheer curtains. Along the back wall was a red couch, and on a small table was a pitcher of mineral water, some pretzel-and-peanut party mix, and a bowl of fruit.

Chavdar sat down heavily in the leather chair opposite June. His green-flecked eyes were bloodshot and he looked older than when they had met. He blinked and swallowed, and if she hadn't known better, June would have thought he was close to tears.

"June," he said softly. "This is a bad time for our country." Wearily he allowed his head to roll to the side. "This," he said, almost whispering, "is a day I prayed would never come."

"You can't do this, Chavdar," she said. "You can't treat me like this. You can't have your men drag me to your dungeon anytime you get the urge."

Chavdar loosened the top button of his dress shirt. Then he sighed. "I was trying to protect you. And if I had to do it all over again, I would do the same. Because obviously you are so naive that you still don't realize that you need protection."

"Well, if I do," June said, standing up, "it's only because I was stupid enough to get involved with you! But I can correct that right now! Let me out of here!"

"Sit down and stop talking nonsense."

"I'm not taking orders from you anymore!"

Chavdar stood up and grabbed June's arm so hard that she winced. "Really? Well then, instead of taking orders from me, maybe you'll take some advice. That street mob out there by the parliament is not slowing down. They are building fires, awaiting reinforcements, and preparing to stay the night. The police surrounding the building with their helmets and shields are bleeding. More people are going to get hurt, June. People from the opposition and people from the government. And when the fighting escalates, you will not blend into the background. Not in your Levi's and hundred-dollar shirt, with your shiny hair and clean white Western sports shoes. Your cute way of speaking our language will not charm the union of taxi drivers arriving from Kyustendil. They will see a rich bitch and you'll get a brick in the head. You will be a target. They are mad at people with money."

"They are mad at the Mafia."

"They will think you are Mafia. By the time they find out you are not even Bulgarian, you will be lying on the ground bleeding, unable to explain who you are or why you are here."

"You're just trying to scare me."

Chavdar leaned over and grabbed the back of June's head. He made a fist, wrapping her blond hair around and around, twisting and pulling, tighter and tighter. He pulled her head back so that her chin was pointing at his chest. His voice shook. "You should be scared."

June stared up at him, skin crawling, heart racing. She swallowed. "I'm sorry, Chavdar. I haven't been listening to you like I should. I'm listening now."

He studied her face and finally let go. "Okay. Good. Because what I am telling you is the truth, and it's going to get worse before it gets better."

June raised a tentative hand to touch the place at the back of her neck where he had pulled her hair. She wanted to keep him talking—talking and not touching her. "Why doesn't the parliament agree to hold elections?"

"Oh, June," Chavdar said, now showing a trace of exasperation. "Who are you quoting now? What do you know about these matters?"

"Nothing, Chavdar. Only what the people say. That the government is Mafia."

"And even if it is partly true, does that mean that there is no other side to the story, or that there are no honest men in the current government?"

June bit her lip and shook her head. "I don't know."

"Let me tell you another side of the story, hmm? Will you listen to another viewpoint? Have you ever heard of the MRL? The Movement for Rights and Liberties?"

"No."

"Well, they are a powerful political group in Bulgaria, and they are closely linked to the Union of Democratic Forces. The MRL has given support and money to the UDF for years, and they will soon unite as one. If the UDF is voted into power, they will be asked to keep their promises to the MRL, one of which is to give the Turkish and Muslim minority in Bulgaria their own state. They want an area in the Rhodope mountains to be given to the Muslims as a kind of homeland, as a municipality of Muslim leaders and citizens. Do you know what kinds of atrocities are committed in the Balkans to keep the Muslims from taking power? Look what is going on with the Bosnian Muslims! With the Albanians! If I put you in a car right now, in two hours we would be in a place where people are already killing each other over exactly this! Do you understand what something like that could mean?"

"Now I do."

"You better! If you hadn't noticed, June, the Balkan people bear no love for the Islamic infidels who kept our region in the darkness of slavery while the Renaissance cast its light across the rest of Europe. People here will kill to keep them from taking our land. People *have* killed. When that happens, you are not talking about some minor political unrest but rather a religious and ethnic clash fueled by fanatics. The hatred between Christians and Muslims in this country is as deeply rooted in history as it is with all our neighbors, and in the Middle East! The UDF does not realize that they are leading us down the road to a war. Unrest in the Balkans is contagious. The Macedonian border is only one hundred kilometers away, June, and the Slavs there are unhappy. Perhaps you haven't heard the rumors about what is going on in the Kosovo province of Serbia? The region—no, the world—is ready for a Christian-Muslim conflict and we are at a great risk. I would like to think we are more civilized than our Serbian neighbors. But we are all Balkan, after all."

June's eyes slid to the side, looking around the room as if for an escape. "Yes. You're all Balkan. I didn't think about these things before."

"Of course you didn't. You Westerners listen to your news reports and believe everything. You have been fed propaganda since you were born and you eat it up like candy. We too have been fed propaganda, but we are suspicious of everyone and everything, and we do our homework. We form our own opinions instead of letting CNN form them for us. And when we draw our own conclusions we must then formulate our own plans, our own means of retaliation. I want you to understand this, June, because in the following weeks you might see things in the paper. Things about my insurance company, possibly even things about me. And I want you to understand that what I have done, I have done out of loyalty to my government, love for my culture, love for my people and my country."

June looked back up. "What have you done?"

"I don't think it is in the best interest of the country to have the UDF and the MRL in power. I don't want war here. We are civilized people. If, in order to avoid war, we need martial law to keep the new Socialist cabinet in place, then so be it. If there is a bureaucratic necessity that a national state of emergency be declared before we can enlist the military in our efforts, then that is an obstacle that needs to be surmounted. And if the only way for a state of emergency to be declared is for people to die in violence, then that too is necessary."

"I think I understand what you are saying."

Chavdar put his thumb against June's lower lip and looked lovingly at her mouth. With the rest of his hand he caressed her pointed chin. "If not— you will."

June allowed her face to be handled. She sat quietly while Chavdar stroked her cheek and fondled the hair he had pulled a moment before. After a long, quiet caress he sat up, pulled off his shoes, and put his head in her lap. "That's nice," he said. "You need me, June. But I need you too."

"Mmmm."

"Tell me you need me. Tell me you understand that I protect you. That I want only to protect you and take care of you."

June closed her eyes, not wanting to answer. "I understand," she said. "I finally understand, Chavdar."

"That I take care of you."

"Yes."

His hand closed around her upper arm and squeezed tightly. "Am I your baby, June?"

June looked down at his face—the heavy brow, the sunken cheeks, the cleft chin. It was the gorgeous countenance of a murderer. His lips moved again. "Tell me. Am I your baby?" he whispered, his fingernails sinking into her skin. His eyes were closed.

"Yes," she answered, trying to pull her arm away. It was impossible.

"Dobre mi e taka. It's nice for me like this. I feel good with you. Tell me I'm your baby. Tell me you'll take care of me like I take care of you."

"I said yes."

"Say it. Say it all."

"You're my baby." Her fingers brushed the dark bangs away from his eyes, and combed wearily through his thick and tangled hair.

22

Subject: I am okay!
Date: Mon, 13 Jan 1997 03:21:13 -0800
From: June <jcarver@sof.cit>
To: Dad <Summer2@ncal.tech>, Lilly <org.beauty@ink.net>

Yes, yes, don't worry, I am fine. Thank you so much for writing so soon. It was scary for a couple of days but there is
nothing for you to worry about—I am being careful.

Friday afternoon I went down to the parliament with my
Bulgarian tutor to see what this new rally was all about.
Everyone had candles and signs and whistles and were shouting "cherveni boklutsi" which means red garbage, "izbori"
which means vote, and "ubiitsi" which means killers. Then
they started chanting "Vsichki pri Lukanov" which means
everyone go with Lukanov, the man who was assassinated. They
were tearing apart the Mercedeses and BMWs parked outside
and waving signs that said the BSP is Mafia.

At midnight the head of the UDF (Union of Democratic Forces)
gave a speech on the steps of the Nevski Cathedral. He explained what was going on. Basically the Communist/Social-
ists were "stepping down" but they were choosing their own
replacements, as they have the right to, according to the
Bulgarian constitution. They will refill the parliament with
more Communists/Socialists, so the people want it to be put
to a vote. Of course the Communists won't agree to that at
all. Then the new President from the UDF, Peter Stoyanov,
came up to speak. While he was talking some woman ran up and
started yelling that the police had started to beat people
and all of a sudden it got really scary with people running
around throwing bottles and tree limbs.

I've only been here six months and yet it was so cathartic
to see these beaten people rally. If it was a release for me
after such a short time, I can't imagine what it must feel
like for the Bulgarians. The next morning there were more
marches, and people are now flooding the streets into the
city coming from as far as Varna and Plovdiv and Kyustendil,
waving blue banners out of their cars. People are even taking their kids to the rallies and sitting them on their
shoulders and telling them that this is history. I can't
believe I'm here to see it. I gotta go find a friend with a
television to watch more of the coverage.

Love, June

JUNE FINISHED HER breakfast of hot tea and a tranquilizer, and checked the clock. It was after nine. Raina would be awake.

The uprising had crippled Sofia's public transport. Streets were blocked, taxis were on strike, and neither the buses nor the trams were running. People who couldn't walk or drive to work stayed home—and most of those who could walk or drive stayed home anyway. June knew only one person with access to a car, and Chavdar wasn't likely to approve of her decision to return to the Darvenitsa apartment to be with Raina—as well as to get away from him. Until the time she could manage a move, June had to settle for calling Raina every day.

Dimcho, the thirteen-year-old son of June's Darvenitsa neighbor, had ridden his bicycle an hour and a half through the snow and slush to the center to get money from June, and they made an agreement for him to help Raina get her groceries and run errands. June compensated him well. With forty dollars hard American currency, he was making more money than his mother and father together.

"ALO!" RAINA YELLED into the phone.

"Alo!" June yelled back, equally loud. Per usual, the connection was bad.

"June?" asked Raina. "That you, June?"

"It's me! Did Dimcho come by yet?"

"He was here yesterday. I have everything I need, don't worry!"

"I gave him extra money. He should be there every day. Now, when you see him—"

"June!" Raina interrupted.

"What?"

"You didn't even say good morning. You didn't even say good morning, Raina, how are you today. Stop worrying so much! I am fine."

"You have plenty of food?"

"June!"

"Okay, okay. By the way, good morning, Raina, how are you today?"

"I'm lousy, thanks for asking! I wish this city would get the goddamned buses running again so I could get my pupil back."

"Have Dimcho get you some juice. Please? It's better for you than rakia and soda water all the time."

"Yes, yes. Okay. Ciao milichka!"

"Good-bye, Raina."

JUNE BUNDLED UP in her fluffy orange winter ensemble—in which she no longer felt ridiculous but rather sort of quirkily cute—and walked through the center, past the park, to Roxanne's. She paused on the porch before crossing the threshold. "Before I come in, is you-know-who around?"

"No," Roxanne said, waving June inside. "Besides, you shouldn't care. You're the wife, honey. She's just the gold-digging concubine."

While June sat in the living room and looked out at the enclosed garden, Roxanne mixed Bloody Marys in the kitchen. June listened to Roxanne humming a distantly familiar love song, while outside the cold wind blew the occasional snowflake against the warm window. Finally, Roxanne sashayed in, her long robe swirling around pedicured feet, carrying a tray with a pitcher, two glasses, and a bouquet of celery.

June coughed after the first sip. "What, did you put a whole jar of Tabasco in these?"

"Just about. And a load of pepper and a dash of my own secret ingredient. I take pride in my Bloody Marys. I got the secret tip from a former cultural attaché to Thailand, and believe me, he knew how to make it hot."

"Why do I get the feeling that there's a quite intentional innuendo in that statement?"

"Because your mind is stuck in the gutter alongside mine. Speaking of hot, how's my favorite glamour boy? What scandalous adventures has he dragged you into recently?"

The celery stick in her Bloody Mary was pointing up at her like a twisted finger. June fished it out of the glass and bit off the accusing end. "I don't feel like talking about him, you know?" She crossed her legs in the plush chair. "I've got all this stuff going on in my head, and . . ." June trailed off, and began stripping the celery with her teeth in the same way that she had started stripping the skin from the sides of her fingernails.

"That's all right," Roxanne said with a throaty laugh. "We don't have to talk about him. There's plenty of conversation opportunities revolving around my eternal favorite subject . . . me. Glorious, needy me. I need someone to bounce some new ideas off of about an article I'm writing—"

June interrupted suddenly. "What did you mean by calling Nevena a gold digger?"

"Ah, everyone tires so easily of my favorite subject. Don't tell me you're unfamiliar with the term?"

"No. Of course not. But what made you say that?"

"The fact that it's true."

"You're telling me that metaphorically, Nevena is gold-digging in Ethan's mine?"

"Absolutely."

"I don't believe it."

"Open your eyes, June."

June bit on her thumbnail while she thought. "No. She must make him happy."

Roxanne laughed. "No one's better at making a man happy than a gold-digging Third World whore, June. Because no one tries as hard as they do. And believe me, Nevena is probably pulling out all the stops. She told me last summer that she was applying to the visa lottery. Little dreamer thought she was going to go to Colorado, of all places, get hired as a secretary by some skirt-chaser, and live happily ever after with a rich husband in a ski villa on the slopes. You should have seen her eyes when I told her that even if she won, she couldn't go to the States without a high-school education and giant nest egg in the bank. She switched gears faster than I switch lovers, and now she's on plan B." Roxanne pulled out her cigarettes. "And plan B, honey, is your husband."

"Ethan's a grown man, and a smart one at that. He's not falling for an act. He's . . ." June's voice caught and she took a deep breath. "He's in love."

"Maybe he is, or maybe he's just under the spell of a desperate girl. Don't get me wrong. I like Nevena, always have. She's been good help, honest, punctual, sometimes she was even fun to be around. But despite all that, the fact remains that she is desperate. I think she knew that I have a good relationship with the vice consul, and she thought I might be able to help her. It's always been her goal, June, to get out of this country. And, the truth is, I was going to help her—sooner or later. The reason I haven't already is because good help is so hard to find. But I'm not a witch. Nevena worked hard for me, she wanted out, and I was going to give her what she wanted eventually. But instead she attached herself to your husband like a tick."

"That's awful. I mean, I have my own obvious reasons for wanting to throw a glass of wine in her bony little kisser, but a tick? A tick, for Christ sake?"

Roxanne was quiet while she lit a cigarette. "Well," she said finally, "I'm a bit biased about girls like her. I told you that my second husband was a diplomat. That's how I got addicted to this kind of life. And I told you that he cheated on me and we divorced. But what I didn't tell you is that he ended up back in the States with a Thai wife."

"You're kidding."

"No. And I'm also not kidding when I say that I really loved the old motherfucker. Potbelly, skinny legs, snoring, and all."

"I'm sorry."

"It was a pretty friendly split, actually. But what was really terrible was when the twenty-two-year-old love of his new life ran off with a member of a Thai gang in San Francisco and Bob killed himself because he thought he was too stupid to live. That," she said, pointing at June with her cigarette, "was the hard part. Midlife crisis, scared of dying, Asian fetish, whatever, you name it. There's lots of ways to explain why he did what he did. But even if he was just a horny old toad with a weakness for beautiful young girls, he was still a good-hearted man. And he didn't deserve it."

"God, I'm sorry," June said, pulling her feet under the warmth of the quilt. She wondered how much of the story was true and how much was Roxanne's trademark fictional embellishment. If she'd had to guess, she would have erred on the side of exaggerated intrigue. "Did she seem like a normal girl in the beginning?"

"Normal! What do you mean?" asked Roxanne. "She was a normal girl! That's just it! Personally I think it would have been *abnormal* for a twenty-two-year-old girl who had spent her whole life working in the rice paddies of

Thailand not to go hog-wild over the chance for a new life in the States. I think it would have been abnormal if she had given all of her youth to Bill when he was getting old and decrepit. Do you see what I'm saying? Sure, you can blame her all you want. You can call her a little lying whore and a man-eater. I've certainly called her worse. But really, if I had been in her position, I probably would have done the same thing. Really, I'm just angry that it happened the way that it did. I wouldn't want to see it happen again."

"Well, whatever. I hate talking about this. Everything has gone so wrong."

"Oh, don't be so mopey and serious, June! You cheated, he cheated. Now you're even with just about every other married couple on earth. Personally I think you're better off with a man who will spoil you, but if you're sentimentally stuck on your husband, then fight."

"That's what I came to this country for in the first place," June said, looking up. "I wanted to fight to make everything work, but then I was just too weak. I was too weak to stop him when he started with Nevena, and I was too weak to be alone when he had someone. Now I just feel like giving up again."

Roxanne leaned over and wrapped her smooth dry hand around June's sweaty one. "If you love him, really love him, as you say, then you owe it to him to keep him away from a conniving and thieving Gypsy who'll laugh as she walks away with half his money and a green card. I've seen it happen before, right here in Sofia, to marriages that were more airtight than yours. The poor little match girl moves in with pheromones spilling out between her legs, the wife is on a plane home, and the sucker, or suckee, as is more often the case, doesn't even know that he is being conned until he's been divorced twice in the wink of an eye."

June stared at Roxanne's serious face and laughed out loud. Now Roxanne's imagination had spiraled out of control. It was all too ugly, too absurd, too Balkan to be taken seriously. June couldn't stop. She laughed so hard that her drink spilled onto her shirt, leaving a bloody splotch over her heart. June laughed until she thought her insides would spill out of her mouth, covering her completely in a mess of pills, wine, and something black that would smell like guilt. Suddenly she jumped up and ran to the bathroom.

Roxanne followed and found June heaving into the toilet. Nothing was coming out but Bloody Mary. "Oh God," she said, between gasps, "I need to lie down."

"What's wrong?"

"Maybe it's the Valium."

"Valium! You shouldn't be drinking! Are you crazy?"

"I know, I just thought it might help and not really hurt."

"Have you been eating? When was the last time you ate?"

"I just wanted to rest from thinking about Ethan and Chavdar. I just wanted to rest. All I wanted was a little break. Is that what she wanted?"

"Who?"

Then everything went black.

NOW THE PHONE WAS just a decoration. Nevena sat in her wooden chair in the cold kitchen, wishing it would ring, knowing that it wouldn't. It couldn't. Even though it had taken her two years as well as Roxanne's money and help to get the phone hooked up, Nevena had canceled it. The price of phone service had increased in the last few days by an unbelievable five hundred percent, and it would have been impossible to keep. Impossible, just like heating, which had gone up three hundred percent.

Scratchy music was playing, and Nevena stood. The false spring had passed, leaving behind another wave of bitter cold, and she needed to move around to keep warm. On the couch, folded neatly, was the blanket she and Ethan usually snuggled underneath. Nevena picked it up, wrapped it around her shoulders, and tried to dance to the static from the radio. The blanket dragged across the wooden floor, and Nevena dragged too. She had no energy or desire to dance, but she did it anyway. Ethan had not come home as promised. He had said he would be back on Monday, and it was now Wednesday. Nevena was not surprised, just heartbroken. Heartbroken yet hard, as she had been raised to be. She hummed in her misery, and swayed with graceful movements of despair.

EARLIER THAT DAY the lev had lost ground again. This time, however, it didn't drop a little, causing housewives to reevaluate how many cartons of yogurt they could get for the change in their hand. Instead, it spiraled out of control. Workers at the change bureaus stepped uncertainly out into the street early in the morning to update the buying and selling rates on their signs. With stoic expressions that couldn't quite hide their own disbelief, they removed the column that read "eight hundred leva to the dollar." As they changed the numbers, the people in line to change money assumed there must be a mistake. But there wasn't. The American dollar could now buy two thousand five hundred leva. It was a staggering overnight blow. The leva the Bulgarians clutched in their hands had just been turned into nothing but pretty paper. Now, it was not a matter of eating the stale bread they had once fed to the dogs, or of using tea bags over and over until they failed to give water even a hint of color. Now it was a matter of life and death. At the new exchange rate, the majority of Bulgarians couldn't buy anything at all with their savings.

Before the winter, Nevena had earned, in leva, the equivalent of almost one hundred fifty dollars a month for cleaning homes. It had been enough to help out her brother and sister and still have enough left over for the bills, food, and an occasional movie or snack at a cafe. Now, that same salary in leva had devaluated to almost nothing.

With the blanket draped over her shoulders, Nevena shuffled over to the kitchen. She had shut off her heat and canceled her phone, knowing there was no money to pay the bills. She opened the pantry, moved aside an empty box of powdered milk, and reached toward the back. She dug her fingers into a panel in the wood and pulled it away. Behind it was a jar that had once contained marinated red peppers. It now served as Nevena's own personal jar bank. She took it out and wiped a cobweb from the lid. A dead, dry spider fell off as she shook the contents onto the counter. My pantry cannot even sustain a spider, she thought, smiling a little.

Like everyone else, she had saved in hard currency: dollars and Deutsche marks. After counting it, she figured that all in all her savings amounted to about fifty-five dollars. If she was careful and tried to live off the food she was able to pop in her mouth while cooking for the expats, she could make it through this hard time and still be able to give something to her family. Thanks to Ethan, Georgi was now employed by a foreign company and was relatively safe. But Boryana? Nevena looked at the crumpled bills on the kitchen table and knew what a difference they could make to her sister . . . if Boryana were still alive.

Nevena's stomach growled and she pressed a fist into it to make it quiet. If Ethan had been here she would not have been hungry. Nevertheless, she did not long for his presence. She did not wish for his heroic salvation. Instead she squeezed her eyes shut, prayed for the well-being of her little sister, and reminded herself that she had survived worse things than the inevitable desertion of a married American man.

NEVENA WOKE SUDDENLY, her heart pounding. Was she still dreaming, or was that Ethan's voice? She jumped up from the couch and went to the window, taking her hair down from its haphazard knot as she went.

The window was warped and didn't latch completely shut, allowing in cold air as well as the sounds from the street. Nevena wrenched it open to lean out, and the freezing air hit her face. Ethan was below, squatting on the sidewalk, holding out food to a mongrel wagging its tail. "Ethan!" she called.

He looked up and waved. "I lost my key! I was just on my way to ring the bell!"

Nevena put a finger to her lips. "Ssh, it's late. I'll come down and let you in."

Before running down the sloping staircase, Nevena pulled on a sweater over the long underwear she had worn to bed. Down in the street, the dog was finishing off Ethan's falafel. Nevena watched as the dog choked down the last bit of the sandwich, not bothering with the pink, pickled onions that escaped through his chomping teeth. The stray had eaten better than she had that night. Nevena held the door open with one hand. "It's cold, Ethan. Hurry."

Ethan started up the stairs after Nevena. He stumbled on the rotting wood and laughed loud enough to wake the neighbors. Nevena remained silent and serious. Inside the apartment she turned on him with accusing eyes. "Are you drunk?"

"A little. Maybe. I was with Stan."

"More than a little, I think."

"Don't," he said, dropping to his knees. "Don't be that way."

"What way, Ethan? Scared and alone?"

"Baby, I tried to call you. What's wrong with the phone?"

"I had to have it canceled. The inflation is too much. I can't pay the next bill."

"Sweetheart, you know I would have paid it."

"You were not here to ask."

"Listen. We got a flat tire in Silistra and had to have the car towed to Russe to get it fixed. How could I have known about the phone? I called you five times."

Nevena tilted her head to the side, looked at him intently, and finally smiled. "Okay. I guess I just became worried. You know, because of what we talked about right before you left."

"I'm sorry about that. I should not have left the way that I did. You didn't deserve that."

Nevena lunged forward and hugged him. She dug her fingers into his hair and spoke against the side of his neck. "I am sorry too. I want to tell you that I am sorry for being cold . . . and for being demanding. We've had a short love affair, compared to what you have had with . . ." Nevena swallowed, and tried to say the words *your wife*. She couldn't. "What you had with her. You deserve more time and I will give it to you."

"I don't need it. I have an answer for you. They may not be the perfect words, but at least they are true. It's as truthful as I can be after seeing so many of the things I believed in turn out to be wrong. I promise you, Nevena, I swear that as long as you love me and are sincere and truthful with me, June and I won't ever be together again."

"Thank you, Ethan," she said, kissing him. His breath was musty with beer and whiskey but she didn't mind. She breathed him in and let the sharp taste of his tongue fill her mouth. "Ethan, come. Let's take out the sofa."

Side by side they pulled out the couch and then lay the length of it. Ethan did just as she had anticipated. He rubbed her feet with his own and covered her and caressed her with hot hands. He kissed her cheeks and neck, and as he worked his way lower, Nevena smiled at the ceiling. "This is what I wanted. This is heaven. It's too perfect that I have you here. If I knew also that Boryana was safe, then I would know for sure that I had never woken and this is all a dream."

With his mouth pressed against her shoulder, Ethan whispered, "You can be perfectly happy. I am here and Boryana is safe." He lifted his face to look into Nevena's eyes. His smile showed his pleasure at being able to give her such happy news. "Your sister is fine. I promise."

His lips parted to bring Nevena into a deeper kiss, but she pulled away. "How can you promise me that?"

"I can," he answered simply.

"What is this ridiculous talk?" she asked.

"Don't be that way. It's good to know she's safe, isn't it?"

"Who do you think you are? To know more about my sister than me? What do you know?"

The moment had been ruined and he rolled onto his back. "God, I must be drunker than I thought. I shouldn't have opened my mouth. I wasn't supposed to say anything."

"You're keeping secrets from me? About my own sister? I have worried about her day and night since she left. I dream about her always. I imagine her dead or starving—"

"Well, she's not doing any of those things."

"Ethan, she is my sister. She is nothing to you! How dare you be so smug with your secret. I love her! I have cared for her like a mother and you lie there as if your secret were more important than the fact that I am your lover! Who is your greater confidant? Me, or this person to whom you have sworn secrecy? What have they done with her? Who has threatened you so that you would not talk?"

"Oh, God," Ethan said, rubbing his eyes and starting to feel the headache of sobriety. "It's nothing like that. It was your sister who made me promise."

"What? You don't even know my sister."

"I met her."

"Where?"

"She dances at Tango and didn't want you to know. She thought you'd be ashamed."

Nevena remained propped up on her elbows, but was shocked into silence. She looked straight ahead. All this time, while she had been worrying for Boryana's safety and imagining the worst, her sister had been just a few city blocks away. Many nights Nevena had woken, terrified by the image of Boryana's face printed in black and white on a sheet of paper, with Ethan sleeping soundly beside her, guarding his secret. While Nevena had moved her lips in silent prayer, Boryana had been undressing for foreign men and Mafia. Suddenly Nevena burst into tears.

Ethan tried to put his arm around her but she pushed him away and got up from the bed. Ethan groaned. "Come on, Nevena, come back. Let me hold you."

After pulling her sweater on, she turned and pointed at him, shaking and still crying. "I have only once ever been this angry!"

Ethan sat up. "That's why she didn't want me to tell you. She knew you would be upset about her stripping and—"

"Stop!" Nevena yelled, no longer worried about waking the neighbors. "It's not with Boryana that I am angry. She is just a baby, just a young girl! What does she know? I had to be a mother to her. I had to punish and scold her, and she isn't old enough to know the real me. She doesn't know that I would understand! Her deception is understandable. But you! You have seen inside of me and you know everything that is there. Did you really think I would turn against my sister just because she is showing her skin for money?

Am I not humiliating myself for money as well? Scrubbing bathtubs filthy from rich foreigners?"

Ethan was shocked by her vehemence. She was still crying, the tears streaming from her eyes into her mouth. She pointed at him again, and even her finger was shaking. "I cried in my sleep for her safety, and you never told me! How dare you come here and tell me that if I am true with you then you will be true with me, and that we will love each other always? You have not been true with me! You lied to me, the worst kind of lie, from the very start!"

"I didn't know about Boryana until recently."

"It does not make any difference. You knew."

"If you give me a chance, I can explain why I didn't tell you—"

"Now I realize that we cannot talk," she said, backing away into the kitchen. "You say one thing and I hear another. I say something and you take it a different way. We are from different worlds. You may live in my country for a year to write your paper, but you know what? It will never be more than paper." She laughed through her tears and picked up a one-dollar bill from the counter where she had left the jar of money. She waved it in front of his face. "What you know about us will always be this thin!"

"Okay, stop with the Balkan melodrama."

"I am Bulgarian! What you call melodrama, for me it is real!" She held the jar out toward him. "You don't understand anything, do you? Of course you don't understand my melodrama. Write whatever paper you want, but you will never know what it is like to dig through the garbage because someone rich like you threw away a perfectly good glass jar! You have never scrubbed other people's floors or taken your clothes off for money, and neither has your perfect wife. You feed dogs when children are hungry, and you keep secrets, not even realizing that they are not yours to keep. Your trueness means nothing to me because it is a worthless meaning of true!"

Ethan climbed out from under the warmth of the blanket. He sat hunched over on the edge of the foldout bed, looking worn out and fed up. "I made a mistake, obviously, but I did it because I promised her. I would think that by keeping that promise I would have shown you I could be trusted. I can't win. And to tell you the truth, I am tired of trying to win. I'm tired of trying at all."

He stood up and took his coat from where it was draped over the kitchen chair. He pulled two crumpled twenty-dollar bills from the pocket and tossed them on the counter with the rest of Nevena's money. "That's so I don't have to worry about you every night."

Nevena picked up the bills and ran after him to the door of the apartment. "Don't leave me money as if I am one of the prostitutes you went looking for at Tango!"

"That's why you're so angry!"

"It is not. Fuck you! Fuck you and your prostitutes!"

"Is that what you think? You're right then! We don't know each other at all!"

"Take your filthy money back," Nevena said, her voice breaking. She tried to smash the twenties into his palm. "I don't want it."

Ethan stepped into the hall and his face fell into darkness. He kept his fist clenched and refused to take the money. "You don't want it? Now who's not telling the truth?"

"I spit on it! I spit on your stupid money!" Nevena yelled as he started walking down the stairs. She held the twenties out in front of her and spat on them with a hissing noise. She felt the childishness of her words and actions but couldn't stop. "I spit on them!" she yelled again, even though she could no longer see Ethan descending.

When she heard the sound of the front door open and then click closed, she wiped her eyes and squeezed the bills in her fist, as if she could wring the spit from them, or magically make them drip blood. "Luzhetz!" she said, bringing her hand down on the rickety stair rail and trying to control her spasmodic breathing. "Luzhetz!"

After he had been gone a full minute or two, Nevena's fingers relaxed and her hand opened slowly. Her eyes stung as she looked at the fortune in her fist. She spread the twenties out and wiped them against the side of her sweater until they were dry and clean. Before going to bed, Nevena wrapped the new twenties up with her jar-bank savings and tied the small wad together with a piece of string. She put the jar back in its hiding place in the pantry and made sure the secret wood panel was secure. Now that Ethan was gone she felt the pain of his absence more acutely than the pit of hunger in her empty stomach.

I was wrong, she thought. But he was wrong too. She went to the refrigerator and took out the stale piece of bread she'd been saving for breakfast in the morning and wolfed it down in two bites, crying silently as she ate. At least now, with the extra money in her jar bank, the pain in her stomach was one she could do something about.

23

Subject: Third quarter report
Date: Wed, 12 Mar 1997 09:55:24 -0800
From: Ethan Carver <ecarver@sof.cit>
To: The Locke-Fields Scholar Commission
<grant.schol@acad.com>

Dear Commission,

Per your request regarding demonstrations here in Sofia, I
am sending an update on my progress and well-being. As you
know, throughout January, the parliament refused to compro-
mise. The protests continued, with the opposition demanding
immediate elections and settling for nothing else. The city
effectively shut down throughout January and most of Febru-
ary. The main boulevards were closed off, public transpor-
tation was discontinued, taxis were on strike, and the
temperature outside for the walking citizens of Sofia was
subzero. As you can imagine, progress on my dissertation
slowed considerably during this very trying time in
Bulgaria. By the time the lev devaluated to 1,850, there was
full revolt. Around the country universities shut down,
workers went on strike, and main trade routes were cut off
with farm equipment. In Sofia, benches and newspaper stands
were overturned in the streets to block off areas for
protest. Bonfires burned all over the city. It was no longer
possible for the Socialists to ignore the opposition demand
for a response.

In the end, Dobrev agreed to early elections. If he had refused, the country might now be in civil war. Elections are
set for April. The country is calm and focused on the economic problems. Stores are closed, everything is scarce,
there are lines for all staple items, and the pharmacies
have no medicine. There is a political group here called the
MRL (Movement for Rights and Liberties) which supports the
Islamic movement in the Bosnian war. They have a close rela-

tionship with the UDF. If the UDF controls parliament, the
MRL will attempt to advance their interests. Tension between
Orthodox Christians and Muslims here could mean problems
yet. The currency has continued to devalue, and is now at a
staggering 2,750 leva to the dollar. A currency board may
be the only way to save the country. Progress on my paper
continues to be somewhat hindered by hardships, and yet I
know that the thesis will ultimately benefit from these
experiences.

Best regards,

Ethan Carver

*I*N THE BALKANS it snowed the first day of spring. The wind swept in
from over the Adriatic Sea, across Albania, on to Macedonia, Serbia, and Bulgaria, chilling the four countries, which on a map looked as if they were all
curled up together trying to stay warm. In the poor and beaten country of
Albania the cold marched slowly, in time with the civilian soldiers and their
hijacked tanks. Chavdar had been right. Unrest was contagious in the
Balkans, and the Albanians, clad in tattered coats, heavy socks, and boots
with holes, broke into warehouses full of Cold War arms half-forgotten under dusty brown tarps. They went north with their weapons to overthrow
the regime that had stolen their money and lives in a banking scandal similar
to the one in Bulgaria. Unshaven, cloudy-eyed from lack of sleep, and with
joints stiff from the unbearable weather, the offensive approached Tirana
with drunk drivers commandeering stolen tanks.

Macedonia, wedged between Albania and Bulgaria, slowly hardened.
The peak of Mount Vodno was white and clouded, looming over the capital
city of Skopje. Down below, the city's shallow River Vardar froze underneath the crumbling stone footbridge that linked—or rather marked the separation between—the Christian and Muslim neighborhoods. Children played
on either side of the icy path that cut between banks of the trash-strewn
trench. A group of Macedonian boys and girls dragged a sled behind them to
the south, and to the north Albanian boys flung snowballs and shouted.
There was an uneasy acceptance of the segregation in the city. It was too cold

for the men to make good on the threats they voiced at home around the coffee table and black-and-white television. It was not yet time to initiate the war they suspected was inevitable. On separate sides of the river, the Christians and Muslims stayed in and quietly, cruelly complained to others "like themselves" about the enemies on the other side of the city.

IN SOFIA, the uprising was over, but without a celebration. Nevena watched the uninspired news broadcast on Bulgarian Channel One with Boryana, who she had finally gone to see at Tango.

Boryana had answered Nevena's knock on the dressing room door holding a robe tightly around her body. She looked incredibly tall, and Nevena noted the thigh-high platform boots with towering, pointed metal stiletto heels. Her eyes were smudged with dark makeup, and her hair was piled haphazardly on top of her head. She looked like she had aged ten years.

Nevena hesitated. The girl who stood in front of her now looked radically different from the one who had disappeared, running, from the steps of the National Library almost a year before.

Boryana crossed her arms over her chest, pulling the robe even tighter, and wordlessly looked at the ground. "I knew you would find me," she said. Her lower lip trembled and suddenly she was the little sister again.

Nevena was overwhelmed. "Oh, Boryana," she said, stepping forward and hugging her. "I've missed you so much."

It took Boryana a few seconds of shocked silence before she raised her own arms to return the embrace. Then, pressed against each other, they swayed side to side. Wiping her eyes, Boryana stepped back. "I thought you would be angry. You were always so conservative."

"No," said Nevena. "I am just happy you're okay. Oh, Boryana, milichka, what is new with you? You must tell me everything. It's been so long."

"You can see how things are with me. I am fine. I have a boyfriend."

"Is he nice to you?"

"He's very generous."

"Have you stopped studying?"

"Secretary school, yes, I've stopped. But I am still taking English."

"That's good."

"And with you? Something new?"

"I went to Vodenicharsko. I saw Baba Safi."

Boryana cleared her throat. "I don't want to talk about home. Let's sit down." She motioned to the chaise lounge against the wall, and they sat side by side, knees touching.

"We don't have to talk about home if you don't want to," said Nevena. "We can talk about whatever you like."

"Who is the American?"

"He's a friend. A new, very good friend."

"He told you where to find me?"

"Yes."

"I knew he would. I thought perhaps I could trust him, but it was obvious he is in love with you. I knew he would have to tell you eventually."

"I think he kept the secret as long as he could."

"I am happy for you. He seemed nice."

Nevena looked down and played with the bracelet Ethan had given her. "He is." After a second, she slipped her hand around Boryana's. "You know, you didn't have to worry about me finding you, Boryana. If you are dancing, that is one thing. But if you are . . . if you are doing other things for even more money, then I would be much more worried."

"I'm not," said Boryana. "Not all of the girls do that."

"I am sure you will call me old-fashioned and say that I always overreact, but what about . . ." Nevena dropped her voice to a whisper. "What about the Mafia? If you are making as much money as it looks, then it is obvious what is going on."

"I know what you think, Nevena. But this club is a legitimate business. Just because it is profitable doesn't mean it's wrong. Assen is a good boss. He doesn't force us to do anything. He is not like the real mutras."

"But it is precisely because it is profitable that it is not safe. You have to be careful."

Boryana swung her leg back and forth nervously. "I'm careful," she answered, but without much conviction.

"Really, how much do you know about these men?"

"All I need to know is how much they pay me."

"That's not being careful, that's being naive!"

"Don't call me naive, Nevena! I'm not innocent, and I am not stupid, but I told you, I am careful. Okay? Just stop it. Just stop acting like you are responsible for me. I'm an adult now. I can take care of myself."

Nevena regarded her sister silently. Then, when she could hold it no longer, she burst. "I wish you wouldn't do this! Just come back and live with me!"

Boryana stood up and pointed at her sister. "I knew you would do this!

You can't support me any longer! We both have to live our lives, rather than you living yours just for me! I need the money."

"But no amount of money is worth the danger!"

Boryana began to pace and she covered her eyes with one hand. She was terribly skinny and with the spiked heels and short robe on, she looked like a girl playing dress-up. "So what am I supposed to do? Give up the money because of a few threats?"

"What threats?"

Boryana looked at the ceiling and sighed.

"What threats? Tell me!"

"It's nothing. Really. Just some mutra from IZTOK that wants to buy the club. Assen doesn't want to sell it. There is a little problem."

"There are no little problems with these men!"

"I know. I am just waiting to see if Assen will sell the club, or if they will take it from him somehow. If he doesn't sell it and they don't kill him, then I will stay. If not, I will leave. Maybe they would make me go, anyway. But I won't work for those other men. I know what they would expect. I won't do what the other girls do."

"Promise me, Boryana. You have to promise me, please."

"I do promise. I'll look out for myself. You should know very well that I would not allow myself to be hurt again."

Nevena gave her sister a long, serious look. Finally she nodded. "Okay. As long as I have your promise, I won't worry."

In the end, they did what Bulgarian women do and changed the topic. Boryana smoked a cigarette, and after a while they poured a couple of orange Fantas, opened a bag of pretzels, and went into Assen's office to watch the nine-o'clock news.

The Socialists' capitulation to hold elections was greeted with suspicion and wintry dejection from all the people, not just the Petkova sisters. *An election can end either way,* they said. *Nothing yet has changed.* Instead of marching and singing, the citizens of Sofia watched uninspiring speeches on black-and-white televisions at the local bars, through a collective mist of frozen breath. No one commented. It was too soon and too stupid to have hope.

*H*ELPLESS AGAINST the unfortunate fact that their own cycles were out of sync with those of nature, pregnant dogs gave birth in abandoned sheds and cellars. The malnourished mothers had no milk, and the cries of starving pups could be heard all around the city throughout the night. People left the animals where they died, curled up with their noses pressed into their hind legs. They would not be moved until the thaw, when the corpses started to smell.

When the Socialists had caved in to demands for early elections, the Union of Democratic Forces called on all members of the opposition around the country to tear down the barricades and go back to work. The intersections in Sofia were now free for unfettered travel, but there were hardly any cars on the road. A new fuel shortage had gripped the country, and buses and trams were few and far between. The ones that did function were more run-down than ever and still packed with people. No one could ride without being pressed against other passengers with rotting teeth, tumors, body odor, and wasting skin diseases.

IT WAS A BLEAK Wednesday morning when June called Raina to say that she wanted to at least *try* to come out to visit, maybe even bring an overnight bag for a slumber party to further the process of edging out from under Chavdar's control. The phone rang and no one answered. June hung up and tried again. It was not unusual for the first attempt to fail. Often it took three or four times for the phone lines to connect. June tried again. And again. She is asleep, thought June. She's drunk or in the bathroom. She went downstairs, she went out for a walk. "There's no reason to worry," she whispered to herself, but suddenly her stomach hurt so badly she could barely walk. "No reason to worry," she repeated.

June pulled on her warmest clothes and waited and waited at the tram stop. Finally, after two hours, the one broken-down tram that was running between the city and Darvenitsa emerged from the woods and ground to a shaky halt. Doors banged open and June forced her way up the steps and into the impassable crowd. She looked so exhausted and worried that a teenage boy stood up and gave her his seat. It was noon when she got off the tram at the second to last stop and crossed the tracks to the big square of apartments that had once been her home. Kids from school were running toward the Blocks for lunch, their scarves flying out behind them.

With her head lowered against the cold, June headed for the front door. Before climbing the stairs, she ducked into the grocery store in the garage on the ground floor. Dimcho's mother was cutting hunks of cheese and pork and wrapping them in thick white paper for two elderly women. She saw June enter and raised a hand in acknowledgment. Her forehead was permanently creased with worry lines, and her thin lips were pressed together in a perpetual frown. She handed the women the packages, the paper damp from meat drippings and moist cheese. The two women slipped their purchases into their plastic market bags and then left the shop.

Dimcho's mother spoke no English, so June struggled through all of their conversations in Bulgarian. "Good afternoon, Gospozha Dimitrova."

"It was not Dimcho's fault," his mother said. She wiped her hands on a towel and then came around from behind the counter. "She was an alcoholic, and she told him what to do. You can't blame my son."

"Blame your son for what?" June asked, though what had happened was written on the mother's face, in the red-rimmed eyes, the unwashed hair, the pale skin.

"You don't know?" Mrs. Dimitrova asked, looking uncomfortable. "They came for her yesterday. Dimcho said he was going to call you."

"Where did they take her?"

"I don't know. Wherever they take them."

JUNE OPENED THE door to her old apartment and felt the stillness. It was colder in the apartment than in the hall. She took a tentative step into the living room, where Raina had slept. Whoever had taken her away had not moved things around much. Unrolled cigarette butts and traces of tobacco littered the coffee table next to Raina's pipe, and a glass with the sticky remains of rakia sat on the floor. The sofa bed was unmade, and crumpled at the base were all the blankets June had given her, as well as Raina's heavy coat and a towel from the bathroom. The fluffy pink hat was lying next to the pillow. It was turned halfway inside out, as if someone had peeled it away from Raina's head. Not far from it, bunched in a ball, was the matching scarf.

On the bed there was no sign of Raina's death. June had expected a smell and there was none . . . except for the faint scent of alcohol and the staleness of old smoke. She closed her eyes and took a deep breath. Suddenly she had a vision of Raina under all the blankets, throwing on a coat, wrapping the towel around her feet. By the head of the bed was an empty bottle of rakia and a coffee mug.

Slowly June pulled off her gloves. She laid her bare hands against the central heating unit and felt the cold metal against her palms. The giant, built-in coils of the radiator were freezing to the touch. "Raina," she said, her voice shaking. "What did you do? God, Raina, what did you do?"

She ran out and down the stairs. With wild eyes, she pounded on Dimcho's door. "How did the heat get turned off?" she yelled, slapping the wood with her hands. "Open up and answer me, Dimcho! How the hell did the heat get turned off?"

The door didn't budge, but after a while, a small, scared voice came from the other side. "She didn't pay for it!"

"What do you mean, she didn't pay it? I pay it! I gave you the money to pay the heating bill!" The boy had only to drop the money off at a cashier's window down the street.

"But she asked for the money instead!" Dimcho was crying and stuttering now, his words mangled by hiccups. June could barely hear him through the door. "She said that, that . . . the money was for her, and that, that, that rakia would keep her warmer than that no g-g-good radiator."

"You bought her rakia instead of paying the heating bill?" June wanted to kick the door down, and kick Dimcho for being such a kid, and then Raina for being such a lush, and then finally she would beat up herself for failing at the one good thing she had tried to do.

"She said that spring was c-c-coming and that she didn't need the heat. Every day she complained that she didn't have enough money for cigarettes. When she asked me to get the rakia and cigarettes she said it w-w-was for a party! Please, Mrs. Carver, I didn't know, I didn't know!"

June was still facing the apartment with one hand on the door when Dimcho's mother appeared on the landing with a couple of bottles from the family store. June was crying and slapping the door over and over, but not as hard she had been before. "I thought you said you weren't going to bother him!" yelled Mrs. Dimitrova.

"The heat was turned off!" June screamed in English, though the woman couldn't understand. "You must have known she was freezing! Dimcho knew the heat was off! How could you let this happen? How?"

"Get away from here," Mrs. Dimitrova hissed, as she fumbled to open the door that Dimcho was holding shut.

June stopped yelling, and inside the apartment she could hear Dimcho crying. June collected herself and breathed heavily after her tirade. Dimcho's mother finally got the door open. "Listen. Tell him I'm sorry. I don't mean to blame him."

Mrs. Dimitrova closed the door on the last of June's words.

June covered her face. "Oh Jesus, Jesus. Oh fuck. How could you let this happen?" she asked again. "How could you, how could you?" This time she was talking to herself.

RAINA DIDN'T HAVE many personal possessions in June's apartment: a couple of books, a candleholder, and a deck of playing cards. Stacked on the bookshelf were all her notebooks for the classes that she no longer taught, and next to them was a photo of Maria, her daughter, who lived in Berlin and rarely wrote. In the drawer in the kitchen was a lighter she liked—an imitation silver Zippo with a palm tree painted on the side. There was nothing in the apartment to indicate that Raina had ever been involved in a tragic marriage and divorce, that she had ever been beautiful, that she had ever been an intelligent, rebellious college student, or that in a few months she had been about to become a grandmother. There was no photo album filled with snapshots from her youth, no heirlooms left to her from the parents who had been banished to the countryside, no drawers of cherished letters with German stamps. Instead there was a moldy loaf of bread in the kitchen, a dozen empty bottles lined up on the balcony, and a pot of congealed white bean soup on the stove.

June gathered Raina's possessions together and arranged them on the bed. She had spoken with her two days before, and Raina had said everything was fine. Now she was gone. June picked up the pipe. After a second she laughed out loud, thinking about tough old Raina sitting and smoking her leftover tobacco in a man's pipe while wearing the furry pink hat. Of course a woman like that wouldn't have called when it got too cold. She herself had turned off the heat, and she was too proud to ask for help. If the ceiling had caved in and a snow avalanche had fallen on her head in the middle of the night, Raina would have pulled another blanket over her body and opened another bottle. She was stubborn, waiting for the spring and for the sun . . . and for the elections. She had been so excited about the prospect of those damn elections. So excited she probably needed a few drinks to calm down.

June felt very tired and decided to lie down on the couch. It was comfortable. With the blankets over her body and her nose pressed into the smoke-scented collar of Raina's coat, June focused on the view outside, and saw her mother's face, Raina's face, and then her own reflection. Vitosha was visible, both treacherous and gorgeous, and behind it was a spectacular array of clouds, ranging from white to blackest black. Maybe Raina had been looking at the mountain when she let go.

June reached out and touched the soft scarf, and saw that the gloves were there as well. All winter Raina had worn heavy wool socks over her hands, saying that she would save the matching gloves for a special occasion. Raina had told Dimcho that the rakia and cigarettes were for a party. June closed her eyes and pushed it away. Two weeks more, and Raina would have lived to toast the elections, thought June. Instead, she had celebrated alone.

24

Subject: Huh?
Date: Mon, 10 Mar 1997 08:55:12 -0800
From: June <jcarver@sof.cit>
To: Lilly <org.beauty@ink.net>

You know about my silences? You know about my withdrawals?
You are living in your own melodrama in which you are the
amateur psychoanalyst who miraculously cures her psychotic
sister. If you are going to play my therapist then I will
have you know that Raina died, can you believe it? She DIED
and was buried somewhere, and they wouldn't even tell me
where. I am still here and it's another day in the fucking
bell jar. Psychoanalyze my attitude in this email, read into
me, predict my despair, do whatever you want, but quit harp-
ing about what a positive place California is. People suffer
there too. Everywhere. Get over it.

I love you even if you did too much acid in the seventies.
You are my sister, but sometimes you are just an annoying
hippie. And in answer to a question from a few mails back:
no I am not okay. Big deal, who is?

Love,

June

ONCE AGAIN, JUNE was packing her bags. Chaotically, neurotically, she rushed around the downtown apartment, throwing things at the bed, swigging from the wine bottle, turning up the music. She had been drinking pretty steadily since Raina died—most heavily after finding out there would be no funeral, no ceremony of any kind. The daughter was not coming back, the ex-husband couldn't be found, and June had not been notified of the cremation because, "Who was she anyway?"

Stumbling out of the surreal asylumlike corridors of Piragov Hospital into the freezing night air, June suddenly felt sober. *When someone close to you dies, you take a second look at life. It is inevitable you will change.* She repeated Raina's words over and over in her head as she hurried back to the apartment, knowing she could not spend another night under Chavdar's control.

The phone had been ringing all day. A car with tinted windows was parked across the street. She was drunk and afraid and sad and nearly hysterical. All she wanted was to get her things to the Darvenitsa apartment, turn out the lights, lock the door, and curl up on the couch where Raina died and lie still in the silence forever.

The downstairs buzzer went off twice in a row. June pulled the curtain aside, just a sliver, and peeked out the window. Chavdar was below, looking up, scowling. The buzzer went off again. She could see his finger on the button and the angry insistence in his eyes. He whipped off his red scarf, leaned in, and pressed again, this time not letting up. The ringer went off endlessly. There was nothing June could do. She hid the suitcase under the bed, shut off the stereo, and buzzed him in.

June cracked the apartment door and stood back, waiting. Chavdar's footsteps were heavy coming up the stairs. He pushed open the door and didn't even say hello. Instead he walked past her to the bedroom, looked around, and then returned to the kitchen. He opened the refrigerator. "Why is it empty?"

"I haven't been shopping."

"Get me something to drink."

June poured him a glass of wine and watched as he downed it in one gulp. She poured him another. "What's wrong?"

"What's wrong? What's wrong? Everything. Where the hell have you been?"

"Raina died."

He froze in the midst of raising the glass to his mouth. "How?"

June looked at the floor. She did not want to talk to him about pensions and poverty. "She turned off her heat. I don't know. I gave her money but she spent it on rakia. She was old."

Chavdar's expression changed and he walked slowly to June and embraced her. Into her hair he whispered, "It is a bad time for both of us."

"What happened with you?"

"I just came from a meeting with the IZTOK board members. Our chief executive officer is worried that people are going to start leaving the country. He said that to everyone, and Nestor Patskov replied, 'My plan is not to run away like a coward. My plan is to go home, pack my things, collect my wife, and quite leisurely head for the airport in my car. I'll fly to my apartment in Geneva, where I will comfortably watch the news about Sofia until I feel it is safe to come back. It is precisely because I do not want to slink out of the country with my tail between my legs that I propose leaving now rather than later.'"

"Maybe you should leave too."

"Eh! Nestor said the same thing. And I said, if we all do that, Nestor, who would look after business? Do you know what he answered?"

"What?"

"That there are many people here who are capable of running the business who are not on the list to be investigated. That our company will be of no use to us if we are all behind bars, or exiled to the provinces under house arrest."

"Are you on the list?"

Chavdar laughed and lit a cigarette. "At the top, June. At the top. But I am not ready to accept that the only solution left to us is to give up. We are in the process of acquiring a number of nightclubs, casinos, restaurants, even a computer software company. Every one of these self-righteous thieving bastards has his price. It can be done. I have worked too hard to see my business stolen. We fought before, and we will fight now. These new officials, do you really think they care about cleaning up the shadow economy, making the streets safe? No! If they wanted the streets to be safe they would let our agency do its job and protect the people, as has always been our first and foremost goal! They want money and power, the same as everyone else. They want to take it from us and keep it for themselves. They have challenged us, and like the hypocrites that they are, they have tried to turn this into a war between good and evil. The truth is they are no different than us! But, if they beat us, then they will be the survivors, and to the survivors go the spoils. We must not be afraid to fight. In the words of the renowned American best-seller Louis Hay, 'The strength is within us.' "

June laughed into her hand.

"What? What is funny?"

"Nothing. I've been drinking."

"Really." Chavdar stared at her where she stood, keeping her distance, in the shadows across the room. He could not see her eyes, but he could see that her arms were crossed defiantly over her chest.

After a second he sighed and lay down on the couch. He was in no mood to argue. At the meeting he had been fiery and passionate and inspirational, shouting about fighting and triumph. In fact, he had felt like a child masquerading as an orator. He was over six feet tall but he could be crushed like a bug; he was a full-grown man but he wanted to rest his cheek against a perfumed breast. He didn't want to lose everything but he didn't know how to save it either. Chavdar wasn't sure where he had found all those zealous words. Perhaps he had been impersonating the maniacal fervor of his father, repeating motivational speeches that had once been delivered for his own benefit. Chavdar didn't want to fight any more now than he had back in his school days on the playground, when he was forced by his stature to play the bully.

Chavdar had not lain down and cried since he was a boy, on his bed, after discovering disturbing facts about his father. What was he scared of most? He wondered about the answer to this question, while lying with his cheek pressed against damp leather. The only answer he could come up with was that he was scared not to believe in his own words. What he feared more than anything else was shame. The only way to avoid shame and disgrace was to continue to believe, just as his father had.

"June, come here."

"I am busy in the bedroom."

"I said come here."

After a second she walked over and stood above him. He reached out and took her hand. "I am going to make this work. Tonight I'm buying a new club, and tomorrow I am buying an advertising agency. I am not giving up."

"I'm not surprised."

"Don't you understand how hard this is for me? The IMF and the UDF misunderstand the insurance agencies. They don't see how necessary we are for the protection of the people. If the Democratic cabinet is elected, their first agenda is to fight the 'shadow economy,' and that means us. If the IMF comes in with a currency board, they will want to close down everything that they deem to be corrupt. And that means us. But what will they know? They are businessmen from another part of the globe. They will loan Bulgaria money from their big world banks, these Germans and Swiss and Americans, and then they will usurp all the power in our country, saying that they must protect their investment. What do they know about business in the darkest corner of Europe? They will lead our country like blind men. And because they don't understand us, they will kill us. I am telling you, June, they will kill us."

They will not kill us, she thought. *They will kill you just like you killed Raina. And I will dance on your grave.*

"I have heard it said that the Party members in Bulgaria are dinosaurs. Many times I laughed at that, but now I feel like a dinosaur. Not just slow and old, but close to extinction. I need you right now, June. I feel like resting my head in your lap. May I?"

"Chavdar . . ." She wanted to say no. Instead she sat down stonily. "Yes, go ahead."

He wiggled his head into her lap to find the softest, most comfortable position. "There, that's perfect. Now I am your baby again." Looking up into her face, he raised a hand and stroked her cheek. "Lean down and kiss me."

June kissed her fingertips and touched them to his lips.

"No. I want a real kiss. Iskam da te izyam, June. I want to eat you, devour you. Come closer." He tugged hard on her hair.

"Chavdar!"

"Come on, a real kiss."

June leaned down to lightly brush his mouth with hers, but his hands pulled her closer, and his hot breath invaded her mouth.

They kissed for a long while, and when he finally let her go, he sat up. "I want to take you into the bedroom."

June stiffened. There had to be a way out. She could think of only one— the truth. She was terrified of his reaction, but she was even more terrified of having to spend even one more night sleeping next to him. "Chavdar, I have to tell you something."

Then he continued. "But I can't. I have to go. We're making the down payment on the Tango, a nightclub out in Ovcha Kopel. It is an important meeting. The owner does not want to sell, and only I can convince him. I have to be there."

Maybe there would be no need for a confrontation. June nodded. "I understand."

"Thank you." He narrowed his eyes and studied her expressionless face. "You have been very understanding lately."

"Have I?"

"Yes. It is somewhat unusual for you."

"I'm just trying to be nice."

Chavdar looked at her suspiciously as he rose. "Nice?" he said. "All right then. I can play nice too." He kissed her lightly on the tip of the nose, while gripping her chin between his fingers. He squeezed. "Be good."

A SOFT LIGHT SPILLED out of the window of the otherwise darkened library at the Center for the Study of Democracy, and Nevena could imagine Ethan there alone, hunched over his computer. He was probably squinting at the screen rather than wearing the spectacles he hated, and he was probably drinking even though it made his typing sloppy.

That same soft light was visible through the cracks in the closed library door. It was not bright; a lamp rather than the huge fluorescent bulbs running the length of the ceiling. She could hear the soft tap-tapping of fingers on a computer keyboard. A cough, and then the clearing of a throat. Nevena pushed open the door without knocking.

Ethan didn't hear her enter. As she had imagined, his shoulders were hunched over his work, and a few large green bottles of Zagorka beer were arranged like bowling pins on the table. He paused and leaned back, rubbing his eyes with his fists.

"Ethan," she said softly.

He turned around in his chair. She stood by the doorway, her hand still on the knob, as if she shouldn't close it, as if he might send her away. Nevena wore the same sheepskin coat she had worn the first day he had met her, the old familiar clunky black shoes, and possibly even the same stockings. Her hair was in the exact same ponytail with a few strands loose, and yet she looked different to Ethan. Stunning even though he had never thought her classically beautiful, radiant though she had always projected inward rather than out.

"Hi," she said, faltering. "I hope you don't mind my . . ." She trailed off. The way he was staring at her was unsettling.

Ethan pushed back his chair from the table. He stood and Nevena loved the look of his long body unfolding, reaching its full height, walking toward her. He never took his eyes off her, and when he reached her he said nothing. Simply and with great feeling, he slipped his arms around her, closed his eyes, and savored the miraculous gift of her arrival.

She laughed. "So I guess you are not still mad at me?"

He pulled back just enough to look in her eyes. "No. Are you still mad at me?"

"I am here, am I not?"

"Nev, I'm so sorry about the money, and about your sister."

"No. Don't say anything about that. I just came back from seeing her, and we talked about you. I understand now."

"You do? I've been like a zombie. Just floating around this city feeling like a Gypsy, watching everything and thinking too much and trying to figure things out. All I did was walk and look and think, and every night I found myself coming to your block, looking at your window, wanting to be sure you were okay. I wanted to come home but I didn't know if you would forgive me, and I felt awful about the things I'd said. I know I was insensitive. But please, you have to understand; I thought I was looking out for you. I thought I was doing the right thing by protecting your sister's secret, and then even more by letting you know she was safe. At the time I thought it was right to give you the money, and I swear I was watching over you even when I didn't know if I should come home. I saw you pass the window last night and two nights before that. One night you didn't come home and I couldn't sleep. I just wandered the neighborhood until the morning—"

"I spent the night at Georgi's," she said, knowing he was telling the truth.

"And in the morning you came home," he finished. "And I didn't know if you had been with another man but I was so happy just to see you from a distance. I knew you were all right, and that was all that mattered. I have been crazy, Nevena. I was going to come talk to you. I just needed some time. I was only trying to do the right things . . ."

"Shhh," she said. "I know. It's okay. It is all over now."

THE FIRST CAR, driven by Damyan, slowly approached the turnaround at the entrance of the Tango. It stopped and Sasho stepped out of the passenger-side door, looked around, and drew out his walkie-talkie. "Looks fine," he said. "Bring him in."

A moment later, the second car with the last three bodyguards and Chavdar pulled up behind. Stoyan got out from one rear door, walked around the back, and opened the opposite rear door for Chavdar. Petko and Rossen emerged simultaneously from the two front doors. Chavdar slung his long legs out and stood up, adjusting his tie. Petko carried the briefcase with the money.

Sasho stayed with the cars, and the other four bodyguards flanked Chavdar as they entered the club. The doorman waved them in, and there was an awkward shuffle of men angling for position inside the door when Assen, the owner, approached, surrounded by his own protection team. All the enormous men avoided eyes and cleared their throats like two petulant football teams that did not want to shake hands after the game.

Assen was clearly in over his head. He looked more like the crew of bodyguards than a businessman about to meet with one of the heads of IZTOK. Chavdar towered over Assen as they shook hands, and smiled down at the greasy-headed strip-club owner as if he were nothing much at all. "Thanks for meeting with me," said Chavdar.

Assen shrugged. "It's nothing."

Stoyan and Rossen patted down Assen, and one of Assen's men patted down Chavdar. It all seemed like some bizarre part of the handshake, of the meeting ritual. Satisfied that neither of the negotiators was packing, the bodyguards stepped back.

Assen cleared his throat nervously. "Let me take you to the VIP lounge where we can talk."

Chavdar nodded at Damyan, who positioned himself by the door, arms crossed over his chest. Petko stayed by Chavdar's side, carrying the briefcase. Stoyan and Rossen walked a few steps behind the group, looking this way and that. It was not a bad place to have a meeting. Up on the stage, several girls in varying stages of undress were dancing.

Damyan, standing in the back, clicked on his walkie-talkie and said, "I like the one in the middle."

Petko and Rossen laughed and looked. Dancing center stage was Boryana, wearing thigh-high leather boots, red hot pants, and sequined nipple tassels. She smiled out at the audience as she writhed and played with her long streaked hair. Another girl danced close to Boryana, and the two girls caressed each other without much enthusiasm. "This is going to be bad," Boryana whispered to the other girl.

"I know."

Damyan watched the girls' routine and raised his radio again. "Op-paaah," he said. "Check her out now."

Stoyan brought his own walkie-talkie to his mouth. "Stay focused, man."

"Right," Damyan answered, chuckling.

Assen led the men to an enclosed booth on the upper tier of the club. He was trying to hold his own with the bigger mutras but was clearly uncomfortable. The seating situation was a debacle, everyone vying for position. In the end, Petko sat in the center with the briefcase on the table underneath his folded hands. Chavdar sat to his right. Next to Petko was Assen's bodyguard, and after Assen slid into the seat, a long-legged escort in a push-up bra and miniskirt perched on the edge of the booth, her arm draped around Assen's shoulder. Stoyan and Rossen stood by the railing that separated the booth from the rest of the club. It was a tense party.

Assen noticed Stoyan looking at Boryana, who continued to gyrate on the dance floor. "See something you like?" he called.

"No," Stoyan answered, inserting a sunflower seed between his teeth.

"Right." Assen smiled, revealing a dark rotten place on his incisor. He patted the escort's ass. "Go get Boryana and have her bring the drink cart, eh?"

The escort smiled and adjusted her miniskirt to expose the back of her thong panties before traipsing off toward the dance floor.

Assen turned back to Chavdar and took in the powerful man's manicured nails, aloof expression, and slightly relaxed posture. Arrogant asshole. Assen folded his hands and leaned forward. "So, to what do I owe the pleasure of this meeting, Kozhuharov?"

Chavdar tapped a long finger on the top of the briefcase. "I am buying your club."

"It's not for sale."

"Of course it is. Everything is for sale."

"I built this place. I handpicked the girls. My family works in the kitchen and behind the bar. It's my life."

"Your new life is in this briefcase."

"I'm not selling the club."

Chavdar smiled. His teeth were gleaming and white. Perfect, compared to Assen's cavity-ridden mouth and bad breath. "You haven't even asked about the money."

"I don't need to know about the money. It's a personal issue. Not a financial one. I know you need to legitimize and fast. But not here, not with me, and not with my girls. You think you can do anything you want, but you know what? Everyone is saying your time is up. What do you have, really? Besides a bunch of thugs that go around extorting money from people with nothing, or strong-arming legitimate businessmen into giving you their property? Nothing. What do you produce? What do you sell? What do you provide? Everyone says you are finished, and I'm not going to help keep you afloat by just handing over my business so you can fix your fucking books. This place is mine and it will remain mine."

Chavdar nodded and drummed his fingers on the tabletop. "I am offended." He turned to Petko. "Do you think I should be offended?"

"Yes," replied Petko.

Assen laughed, and when he threw his head back you could see the tufts of wiry hair springing from the throat of his sweater and the dark silver fillings in his back molars. His greasy hair shone under the flashing neon lights. "I'm not trying to give you attitude. I'm just trying to tell you where I stand. Let me be a good host and show you there's no hard feelings." He snapped his fingers and another escort appeared. "Darling," he said, "these are our special guests. Show them a good time. I don't want them to go home completely disappointed."

The dark-haired girl sauntered over to Chavdar, who disinterestedly used one hand to shove her away. She tripped in her heels and almost fell.

"That's not any way to treat a lady," said Assen.

"I have a lady, thanks," said Chavdar. "I don't need a whore."

Assen lit a cigarette. "I've heard about your lady. I heard an American bitch has you wrapped around her little finger."

Petko cleared his throat.

The original blond escort showed up again and resumed her position, nearly on Assen's lap. "Boryana is bringing the drinks," she said.

"Good girl." Assen's hand slipped inside the back of the girl's miniskirt.

Chavdar was staring at Assen as if he might leap across the table and strangle him. "Clearly," said Chavdar, "you don't know the difference between a bitch and a lady. I wouldn't expect you to, considering the low-class whores you pay to surround you."

"If you think my place is full of low-class whores, then why do you want to buy it?"

Chavdar leaned forward and smiled. "I came here with a respectable offer. Things have gotten off track. I don't want to trade insults with you. I just want to make a down payment to buy the establishment and finish our nego-tiations. Petko, please show him what we are offering."

Petko unlocked the briefcase and opened it. Thick, neat bundles of U.S. currency filled the case. Petko angled it so Assen could see.

"Two hundred thousand U.S. dollars. More than a respectable down payment," said Chavdar.

Boryana arrived, pushing a drink cart on wheels, laden with food, myriad bottles, a bucket of ice, and glasses. The wheels squeaked and clattered. As soon as she entered the VIP area she sensed the tension and slowed down. She saw the open briefcase of money and caught her breath. The drink-cart wheels caught on a seam in the carpet and a bottle of Jack Daniel's nearly pitched off the front. She awkwardly replaced the bottle and began inconspicuously un-loading napkins and dishes of nuts, chips, sausage, and cheese onto the table. All was silent. She was ignored.

Assen looked at the money, drew a handkerchief from his pants pocket, and blew his nose. "You don't have any fucking idea what this business is worth," he said. "You clearly don't have any idea about real value." Again he caressed the behind of the escort beside him. "You're a poser who runs around with American bitches and thinks he can have anything he wants. You're wrong. You can't buy my club."

"Eh," Chavdar said, as if forgetting the whole thing. "Okay! Actually, I'm not sure I want to buy it anymore."

"Good," Assen said, leaning forward to stare down Chavdar. "You fi-nally got the picture that I'm not selling."

"No," said Chavdar. "I wanted to buy it before I met you, when I was still extending you the respect of a fellow businessman. Now that I know you're an arrogant fool, I may just take it."

Petko pulled his gun from his holster and placed it on top of the briefcase.

Assen glared at Chavdar for a long time. Finally he cleared his throat and said, "What are you drinking?"

"Scotch."

Assen didn't move a muscle or divert his eyes from Chavdar. "Boryana, pour the pussy-whipped mutra a Scotch."

Boryana flinched as she saw the big man's bodyguard—the one with the briefcase—close his fingers around his gun.

Assen was faster. He pulled his own hidden gun from where it was tucked in the back of the escort's miniskirt, aimed, and fired at Petko. The

232 ❧ ANNIE WARD

shot hit the back of the open briefcase, sent it tumbling, ripped on through, and lodged in Petko's shoulder. He howled.

Stoyan and Rossen came running from their positions at the end of the separating railing. Boryana and the escort both hit the floor, crawling for cover under the table.

Chavdar, equipped with five bodyguards but with no weapon of his own, like any respectable businessman, stood and stared at Assen. "Shoot me and know that you are a dead man ten seconds from now. My men will literally rip your body apart."

Assen held his gun steadily, trained on Chavdar's face. Stoyan and Rossen were behind Assen, ready to shoot should he make a move.

Boryana and the escort were curled up under the table, surrounded by packs of red-splattered money. Petko's leg was twitching, and a bloodstained napkin slipped from his lap to the floor. Boryana closed her eyes and blinked back tears as she listened to the men posturing above them with their guns and egos.

"Lower your gun!" yelled Stoyan.

"Fuck you," Assen yelled back over his shoulder, holding a steady aim on Chavdar.

Assen's bodyguard made a slight move and Rossen shouted, "Reach for your weapon and you're dead!"

"I told you, Assen," Chavdar said calmly, "what was going to happen here. You were going to accept our respectable offer or die refusing. And that is still what is going to happen. You know very well that killing me is suicide."

"If I don't kill you, I lose my business. It's another kind of suicide. What do I care? What do I have to lose? You motherfucker!" Assen's finger twitched on the trigger. "Your time is over! No one is going to kiss your ass anymore!"

Under the table, Boryana pulled her legs up and curled into a ball. She was wrapped around wads of money.

Chavdar looked up and met eyes with Stoyan. Immediately the head bodyguard pumped a round into Assen's back. Assen's gun fired and hit Petko again, this time in the arm. The music in the front of the club suddenly came to a stop. The only sound was that of men screaming in pain. Assen fell to the ground and rolled back and forth, moaning.

Underneath the table, Petko's legs were kicking. Assen was twitching and appeared to be dying. His bodyguard at the table used the diversion to pull his own gun on Chavdar and began yelling at the top of his lungs.

Boryana covered her ears and was tempted to close her eyes and hum out loud. "Put the gun down!" yelled Rossen.

Assen's hysterical bodyguard continued shouting nonsense at Chavdar, whose only response was to look placidly around at the chaos. His lips moved as he counted men.

Underneath the table, the escort began to scream and cry. Boryana couldn't take it. She started to edge out from under the table, back toward the drink cart. She knew that the rest of Assen's men would be heading in from the back of the club any second. It was likely to be an even bigger bloodbath. As she crawled out, her hands dragged between clusters of rubber-banded bills. Her boss was dying, the club had been taken over, and she was more desperate than she had ever been. Like Assen, she had nothing to lose. The escort was clinging to Assen's leg, kissing his stubbly cheek and begging him not to die, and Boryana was alone under the table with piles of money. She grabbed the napkin soaked with Petko's blood, looped it into a small satchel, and began scooping the money in toward her body. She shoved wads of cash into her thigh-high boots and down the front of her little shorts.

Within seconds, Damyan and Sasho joined Rossen and closed in around the VIP area, trading insults and threats with the last of Assen's bodyguards. Stoyan grabbed Chavdar and covered him, trying to maneuver him out of the club.

With deranged eyes and shaking hands, Boryana hauled the bloody napkin bundle onto the lower tier of the drink cart. "Please let me out!" she yelled to the gang of bodyguards. Her voice caught with sobs and fear. "Please let me go, I'm begging you!"

"Get the girl the fuck out of here!" yelled Damyan, his gun trained on one of Assen's men. "Move your ass, bitch!"

Boryana used the drink cart for cover. She wheeled it out of the VIP booth while crouching behind. She cried and begged to be let alone as she made her way through the melee of shouting men.

When she stood up at the end of the walkway, she looked around the club. The clients had already run for the door. The girls on the stage were flattened against the lighted dance floor with their heads down, and the wait staff was hiding behind the bar. Up in the VIP area, the bodyguards were still facing each other down and shouting insults at each other's mothers, even while Assen was dead and Chavdar had been hustled outside and into the waiting car. It was over.

Boryana leaned down and gathered up the soiled napkin against her groin and the hot pants that bulged with wads of cash. She ran bent over—as if in terror of being shot—toward the back of the club.

She ducked into her dressing room, where she quickly emptied her shorts and boots and dumped out the contents of the bloody napkin. She rammed the seventy thousand dollars into the dress bag in the closet, threw it over her shoulder, and fled stumbling—still in her hot pants, nipple tassels, and stiletto leather boots, out into the dark city streets.

☾

JUNE WAS PACKED and ready. The only last issue to be resolved was the returning of the keys. With a note, it would give symbolic and nonviolent closure to a relationship that could have ended with fireworks and condemnation. June was not stupid—she knew what Chavdar was capable of, and had born the brunt of his temper more than once. To continue to see him was unthinkable, but to break up with him face-to-face would be suicide. There was no better way. The note she wrapped around the key said: *Chavdar, I can't see you for a while. Things have gotten too serious too quickly, and I need some time to think. I will be going home to my family soon. Please try to understand and forgive me, and please just let me go. June.*

She flagged down a taxi and directed it to the house Chavdar kept in the city, at the edge of the park. He would still be at his meeting, and his night guard, Hristo, would take the package she delivered and give it to him when he returned home.

The house was impressive for the neighborhood, with gnarled trees looming over the high stone wall. June had not spent much time at the house because she found it stuffy and sterile. Chavdar's mother had helped him decorate it with drab paintings and yellowing lace over functional antiques.

The Doberman's name was Fella and now he was jumping against the gate, snarling and showing his teeth. June didn't need to ring the buzzer. Hristo was walking up the sidewalk with a flashlight in one hand. The other hand was inside the waistband of his jogging suit sweatpants. "Koi e? Who is it?" His hidden hand was curling around a gun.

"Az sum! June sum!" she called.

He came closer and blinded her with the flashlight. When he saw the sheen of her hair, he let go of his gun and smiled weakly. "June. We weren't expecting you tonight."

"Sorry—"

"No, no," he said, walking forward. He was older than the usual mutras, and looked a bit odd in his matching jogging pants and jacket. "No problem. It's just been a bad night. We had uninvited guests earlier."

"Who was it?" she asked, slipping inside the gate.

"The police. Idiots. Part of that new Operation Mosquito they've been writing about in the papers."

"I thought they were pulling over nice cars and checking to see if the serial numbers had been scratched off."

"Now they're starting phase two. Bothering everyone with a big house. They showed up here tonight being very rude. I think they actually expected Gospodin Kozhuharov to be able to present documents to prove that he had paid taxes on the income he used to buy this house and his cars. No one has such documents lying around. Can you imagine the audacity?"

"Unbelievable," June said, mentally giving thanks for the fact that she would no longer have to engage in such false conversations. "He's not home now, is he?"

"You're in luck. He just arrived. Something went wrong at his meeting and it finished early. Perhaps you can cheer him up."

It was not supposed to happen this way. Suddenly she was nauseous.

Hristo put a hand against her shoulder. "Are you okay?"

"Sure," she said. "Thanks, Hristo. I'm fine."

"Go on up."

"Right." June turned toward the stained-glass panels bordering the heavy front door, illuminated with the glow from the chandelier in the foyer. She sighed and stared as if she were facing the gateway to hell. She walked slowly, as if to the gallows.

The doorbell reverberated through the home with a deep gong. June hated everything about the elegant home. It was the worst kind of lie.

Andranika, Chavdar's housekeeper, answered the door. She held up a hand that meant for June to wait and, in her short skirt, climbed the stairs to Chavdar's bedroom. After a second she appeared at the top of the landing and motioned for June to come up.

Chavdar's room was enormous, with elegant wooden carvings on the walls and ceiling. The craftsmanship dated back to the turn of the century, and the room was somber and worn, as if many people had lived and died inside. A few logs smoldered in the fireplace, and the bed was unmade. It looked like Chavdar had been napping. Now he stood between two green leather armchairs arranged around a small table strewn with magazines. Dressed in pajama slacks and a maroon robe open at the throat, he was pouring two nightcaps into cognac glasses. "What a nice surprise," he said. He spoke in a monotone. His movements were businesslike.

"You don't have to make me a drink," said June. "I'm not staying."

"You're not staying?" There was an unfocused look in his eyes, and suddenly June realized his robe was on inside out. Chavdar was meticulous about his appearance, showering sometimes three times a day. Now he looked as if he had been sweating, and he had thick black stubble on his jaw.

"No. I really only came to give you something. It has to do with what I wanted to talk to you about earlier."

Chavdar glanced at her, and his look was cold. "Fine. I'll drink them both. Talk about what?"

June hesitated, then took the envelope with the keys and the note out of her purse. She handed them over. As he read, she spoke nervously. "I needed to be alone to think about Raina and Ethan and you. Maybe I knew it all along and just didn't want to believe it. Or maybe I never understood, really understood . . ."

Chavdar crumpled her note in his hand and threw the key ring into the fireplace. When he turned back around he yelled, "Never understood what, you *stupid* bitch?"

June took a step backward and put her hand on the doorknob.

"You're not going anywhere!"

"I told you not to tell me what to do!"

"Finish your fucking sentence. Never understood what?"

"I didn't want to have this conversation!"

"Too goddamn bad!"

June straightened up and stared at him. If it had to go down like this, she was going to hold her own. "That you're the problem."

"What do you mean, I'm the problem?"

"With this place. With people like Raina, and Kyril, and everyone. It's all because of what you do, and I don't want to be a part of it anymore."

Chavdar set down his glass and walked toward her, very slowly. "You blame me for Raina's death? I didn't get drunk and turn off the fucking heat, did I?"

"It's because of you that no one has any money for heat."

"Uh-huh. You've heard more horrible things about us lately, haven't you? The people are not very happy with the agencies these days. They glare at us when we drive by, spit at us when we get out of our cars. I am sure you've heard all sorts of colorful names for us. And obviously you believe them. Do you want to hear the colorful names I have heard you called, June? Capitalist pig. Western trash. Arrogant bitch. American pussy."

June dragged a hand across her face, brushing away a tear. "I don't need you anymore."

"Without me, a disloyal slut like you would already be dead! Fucking kuchka!"

"How dare you call me that!" June slapped him as hard as she could and he stepped back, his face red.

He stared at her, his eyes glassy. She glared back, and then suddenly she was flying across the room, hitting the wall, crumpling to a heap on the floor. The edges of her vision went black. She was dizzy. When she looked down she saw that her white blouse was red. Blood streamed from her nose. From the Greek boy's nose. From her foot. Floating in seawater and blood. He was coming toward her and she couldn't move because everything was spinning and the little spots of light were blinding. Little spots of white light zipping and splashing like red flecks of blood between her and him, his jaw, his lips, his insane eyes.

"I'm sorry," he was saying. "My God, I'm so sorry. I have never hit a woman before. Everything is so bad right now. That wasn't me, that wasn't me . . ."

But it was him. It was exactly what she had feared and even expected. June grabbed the side of the chair with a bloodstained hand and tried to pull herself to a standing position. Her legs buckled beneath her.

Chavdar reached out a hand to help, which she ignored. "June, I'm sorry. I'll never do it again. June . . ."

Finally she was on her feet. The taste of blood was in her mouth, her nose and throat. It felt like she was choking. When she made a move toward the door, the room lurched sideways. The back of her head, where she had hit the wall, was throbbing. She focused on the door.

"No. No, you can't leave like this. We have to talk. June, I said I was sorry. Say something. Please say something."

June spit out a mouthful of blood and smiled at him with red teeth. "Say something? Okay, Chavdar. I know what you're afraid of. I see through you. And you know what? You *should* be ashamed of yourself."

She turned and walked out.

Chavdar stood there painfully still, his face growing white, his hands starting to shake. When he heard the front door downstairs close behind June, he looked up at the hand-carved wooden roof and howled. Then he fell to his knees, put his head in his hands, and collapsed on the floor. In his wildest and worst nightmares, he would never ever have dreamed that it could come to this—that he could be so thoroughly defeated.

PART THREE

"The Beginning of June"

[MAY 1997]

25

Subject: Commiseration . . .
Date: Tue, 6 May 1997 07:44:48 -0700
From: June <jcarver@sof.cit>
To: Laney <laney@smnet.com>

I felt bad reading your message, but I have to admit, horri-
bly, I found it somewhat comforting. I don't want to profit
from your pain, but at least I discovered I wasn't the only
one in the world feeling so goddamn confused!

The hardest thing in the world is to make big life
decisions. I am only now feeling that I might be able to
build myself into a new person who doesn't rely on the
approval of agents and producers, the love of actors and
artists, the friendship of the L.A. elite. Now, I am constantly wondering what I REALLY want to do—go back to L.A.
with a new awareness and resume my life, or travel the
world begging Ethan to take me back, or stay in Bulgaria
and marry a Balkan man and go blackberry picking on Vitosha
mountain with my blue-eyed babies? Maybe I should go somewhere new by myself and have an adventure, or devote my
life to charity, or disappear completely in a staged boat-
ing accident and re-create myself as some kind of international underworld spy with an intriguing new identity and a
suitcase of cash? (Okay okay—if I knew how to pull off that
last one I would have already done it by now, but you get
the point . . .)

Anyway, after all my mistakes, I sometimes lie on my bed
and know that I am not physically injured anywhere, yet
hurting so bad! It's just this aura of unbelievable pain
that surrounds you. But, it gets better, little by little—
if you just keep going. As my Uncle Bob says, if it turns

out that you have taken a wrong turn, go back. If you have
made a bad decision, try to correct it. And my own addendum
is: if you hurt someone, try to make amends. Even if it is
you yourself that you've hurt.

You will do the right thing.

Love,

June

*P*ASSPORT, PLANE TICKET, computer, hard copy of the dissertation,
disk copy of the dissertation. What am I missing?" Ethan was running frantically around Nevena's apartment, patting the pockets of his loose, faded jeans.

"What about clothes?" Nevena was seated on the couch with her legs
crossed underneath her. She rested her chin on her hand, enjoying the specta-
cle of his nervous energy. "What about money?"

"Yes," he said, snapping his fingers. "Yes, those are good things to have
too." As he crossed to the closet he kissed the top of her head. "What would
I do without you?"

"Go undressed and with no money in the streets of Los Angeles, I
suppose."

"Ah, but what's the fun of fitting in?"

Nevena laughed and leaned back with a dreamy expression. She crossed
her arms behind her head and sighed. "I wish I was going with you."

"So do I."

"Tell me what you're going to do while you're home," she said, closing her
eyes. "Home in America. Home in California. The Pacific. It sounds so romantic and exotic. I would do anything to go there. Do you think I'll ever see it?"

"Sure," he said, distracted. He held up a dress shirt that had once been
white but was now a dingy gray. "Do you think this shirt is too mangled to
wear to my interview?"

"When?" she asked, picking lint off the couch and avoiding his eyes.

"When? In the States, Nev. In a few days."

"No, I mean when do you think I'll see it? The Pacific."

"Nevena . . ." he said, dropping the shirt onto his bag. "You're really serious about wanting to go?" He walked over to stand above her, his hands on his hips.

"Yes."

"Look. I'm not sure I'll ever go back to live in the States permanently. Someday you will go there with me to visit. I can't say when though, Nev. You know that. Unless you can get a visa on your own, which I doubt, then we have to be married for you to go with me, and first there's my divorce. It's really complicated."

"I know. Everything has been so complicated, that is what I am afraid of. That you will never come back to this awful world and my complaints and complications. And what you call my melodrama."

"Of course I'm coming back."

"I will understand if you don't, of course. I am a realistic person."

"You're being a silly person."

"Perhaps you are the one who is being silly. Even naive. Things happen. Things and people change. You should know this well."

"Don't be such a pessimist."

Nevena shrugged, but after a second, she could not help but return his smile. "Do you know the Bulgarian joke about the pessimist and the optimist?"

"No."

"The pessimist says to the optimist, 'Our life is terrible. Things could not get worse.' And the optimist puts a hand on his shoulder and replies, 'No, my friend, I disagree. There is always the chance that things could get much much worse.'"

Ethan sat down on the couch and touched her nose. "I'm going to miss you."

"I should not have canceled my phone. Two weeks without your voice."

"But you have my parents' number, right? If something comes up, just call from the post office. And listen. Two weeks is hardly anything. I haven't been home in almost a year. My mom and dad would kill me if I went back and didn't go to see them."

"It would be interesting to me to meet them."

"I would take you with me if I could. I told you that."

"And what would they say when they see you are with a poor woman, a Balkan maid, from some Banana Republic–type place?"

"You're acting crazy, but I have an idea what might make you feel better."

"What?"

"Maybe . . ." Suddenly, like a magician, he pulled an envelope out from behind his back. "Maybe a surprise engagement trip to Istanbul?"

"What?" Nevena screamed, grabbing for the tickets.

She bounced up and down, reaching for them, but Ethan held them out of her reach. "Oh, I see you're not interested," he said. "I guess I'll just return them. I should have known you wouldn't want to go to Istanbul and the Aegean Coast for a week."

"Ethan, stop it!" she said. "Let me see!"

He handed over the envelope. Inside were two tickets to Istanbul on Balkan Air. "I am planning on starting my job there in August. At least that is what my dad's friend and I have talked about, and I need to go and take care of some administrative stuff. An interview here, a form to fill out there, and the rest of the time it's you and me in romantic cafes, touring huge mosques, eating grilled fish at a floating restaurant on the Bosporus."

Nevena turned her ticket over and looked at the back. Then she ran her finger across her name typed on the paper inside. "I have never been on a plane," she said softly, and then looked up. "I have never been out of this country."

Ethan took a strand of her hair between his fingers. "I know."

"Thank you so much."

"You're welcome."

"You are amazing. What can I say?"

Ethan checked his watch. "Good-bye. That's all we have time for now."

I AM DOING the right thing. I am doing the right thing. I am doing the right thing. I am doing the right thing. While Ethan sat on a plastic chair in the overcrowded lobby of the Sofia airport, June was leaving the ground. Her flight to Athens left an hour before his to Prague. As Ethan flipped through his dissertation in the airport, coughing from smoke and the scent of a sewage system gone wrong, June was gripping the sides of her seat and chanting in her head: I am doing the right thing, I am doing the right thing.

June sighed. She wasn't doing the right thing. She was doing the only thing. Happiness was hard to come by, and life was short. Chavdar was a killer, Ethan was in love with someone else, Raina was buried, and June was a wreck. This was behind her, and all of this was clear. The picture she had in her mind of the future was an abstract collage containing James with a dazzling smile and opaque black sunglasses, palm trees, wine goblets, clean stretches of sand, and glistening skyscrapers reaching with glass arms into a cloudless sky. There were no dogs in the street and no broken windows in the buildings. It was the world of her youth . . . and of eternal youth. No husbands but no mistresses, no thinking but no worries. There was no love but at least there was no loss.

∾

NEVENA WAS RETURNING home from work late, humming to herself as she took her keys to the apartment out of the deep pocket of her sheepskin coat. As she approached her landing, she saw something moving in the shadows. Someone was crouched by her front door. Nevena's hand dropped to the railing and she took a step backward. "Who is there?"

The figure in the corner scuffled about and then stood. Nevena hit the stairwell light and saw that it was a Gypsy boy. She couldn't tell his age because, though his body was small and wiry, his eyes were ageless and he wore a man's suit with the legs and sleeves rolled up.

He had a harelip and a skin disease that had eaten away part of his left ear. Nevena motioned for him to sit back down. "It's okay. You can sleep there. I will get you something to eat."

"You're supposed to come with me," he said, his speech impaired by the taughtly stretched skin of his upper lip. He slouched against the wall, his light eyes serious as he picked his nose with a dirty finger.

"I am, am I?" Nevena asked. "And why is that?"

" 'Cause a lady who looks like you paid me to come and get you. She is going to pay me again when I bring you to her."

The Central Train Station was north of the city, between the warehouse district and the worst of the city slums. Train tracks zigzagged through the buildings from all directions, passing through the mammoth, squat, concrete station. Taxis lined up outside, waiting for the continual outpour of travelers through the front doors. In a sedate voice, a woman announced the arriving and departing trains over a loudspeaker. The hollow, reverberating message echoed through the cold station and repeated itself every few minutes: "Vlaka za Skopje shte trugne v dvanaiset chasa ot peti kolova, vlaka ot Belgrade shte pristiga na treti kolova . . ."

Nevena turned to the boy. "Now where?"

The boy pointed into the darkness. "Down."

At the bottom of the stairs, there were two tunnels. One led north, underneath the station, toward the farthest boarding platforms. The other led south, underneath the city, toward a place Nevena had been warned about—a place of such reported horror that Nevena feared it without knowing exactly what it was.

The boy skipped into the darkness of the south tunnel. He picked up a piece of plywood off the floor and trailed it along the wall as they walked, and Nevena could hear him singing to himself. Thick, short, square pillars held up the concrete ceiling. They were everywhere, like stalagmites in an endless cavern.

At the outer edge of the concrete cave was a grimy public toilet. A stoop-shouldered woman was hosing down the floor, and sludge ran from the door out across the tunnel. Next to the toilet was a window with bars where squares of toilet paper were sold. Several men played cards inside. Behind them were two cots with pillows, and a wall papered with pornography. The stench was unbearable.

Behind the toilets, the underground room opened up and, like an amphitheater, went on for as far as the eye could see. Bare light bulbs hanging from wires illuminated plywood stands piled with used electronic equipment, jewelry, knives, cartons of cigarettes, and all kinds of clothes bundled with twine. Running down the center of the room from one end into the distance were food stands: glass windows displaying greasy rolls, raw sausages, hunks of wet cheese, fried dough with powdered sugar, Pleven beer, dirty plastic bottles of homemade rakia, espresso, and thick brown boza.

Beneath one of these windows, three boys huddled close together. They were passing back and forth a light blue plastic bag, inhaling glue fumes from inside. The first boy's eyes rolled up in the sockets, and then his head fell back against the food stand. While he slumped unconscious, the second boy grabbed the bag from his friend's lifeless hands to take his turn.

Limp bodies lay on the damp ground, and discarded needles glinted in the garbage heaped against the walls. Preadolescent and adolescent prostitutes roamed through the aisles, resting occasionally on plastic barrels of water to smoke and joke with the vendors.

The boy took Nevena's hand and she could feel his rough calluses and uncut nails. "Tuk e," he said, pulling her toward a casino with smeared and broken windows.

Nevena followed the boy inside and passed uncomfortably through the tables of shabbily dressed drinkers with shifty eyes. Their fingers were black contrasted against the white playing cards.

In the corner, seated drinking a beer, was Boryana. She stood up when she saw Nevena.

"Bobi!" Nevena said, walking over. "What are you doing here?"

"I tried to call you," said Boryana. "Did you turn off your phone?"

"Yes, I had to. What is going on?"

Boryana took some money from her purse and paid the boy. "Sit down, I'll tell you."

"Not here. This place is awful. Let's go to my place."

"I can't go anywhere."

"Why? What has happened?"

The two sisters sat down and Boryana grabbed Nevena's shoulder to pull her in close. "I did something that maybe I should not have done."

"What?"

"I don't know if I should tell you. I don't want you to know anything. I don't even want to involve you. It is just that I need help."

"You know I will do anything for you."

"Remember Assen? My boss who we watched the news with in his office?"

"Yes."

"Do you remember how I told you there were some mutras who wanted to take the club away from him?"

"Of course I remember what you said."

"I stole something from those men."

"Boryana!"

"I think someone saw me take it. One of the girls. An escort. I don't know if she would talk, but if they hurt her—"

"What did you take?"

"Money. There was a big fight at the club, and people were shot. The money fell on the floor, and it was all covered in blood. Everyone was screaming. It was chaos—awful. I didn't plan it. It just happened. I took some, Nev. I didn't think anyone knew it was me, but the day before yesterday I came home and saw a man picking my lock and going into my apartment."

"Give it back!"

"They would still kill me."

"What are you going to do?"

"I don't know. I did not have to work this weekend but when I don't go in tomorrow, they will know it was me. This is the only safe place I could think of to come. I would never go to you or Georgi, because they might come looking."

"Oh my God, Boryana, why did you do it?"

"How could I not do it? Look at us! Look at our lives! And look at those thick necks carting around enough money to support ten families for a year and not even needing it enough to watch it or protect it! It's wrong."

"What you did was wrong too."

"I don't think so. I really don't. They have stolen enough from us, haven't they? I hate those fucking mutras."

"They will find you."

"Eventually, yes. That is why I need help."

"But what can we do?"

"I don't know. Maybe it is hopeless, but maybe not."

There was nothing Nevena could say. The wrestlers weren't just above the law; they were the law. Nevena put one arm protectively around Boryana's shoulder and looked up at the ceiling that was under mounds of earth. The claustrophobia and smell were overpowering. It was as if she and her sister had been buried alive. Nevena had no idea what she could do. It was impossible. "It will be okay, Boryana," she said. "I will figure something out. I will take care of you."

26

Subject: Inspiration
Date: Wed, 7 May 1997 18:05:31 -0700
From: Laney Nathaniel <laney@smnet.com>
To: June Carver <jcarver@sof.cit>

Dearest Junie, thank you so much for your email of support.
I don't have time to write now because, as my first act of
putting my life together post-Eric, I am checking into a
clinic to get over this stupid bulimia once and for all.
Here is something I thought you would like . . .

"I ask the support of no one, neither to kill someone for
me, gather a bouquet, correct a proof, nor to go with me to
the theater. I go there on my own, as a man, by choice; and
when I want flowers, I go on foot, by myself, to the Alps."
—George Sand

More power to you. I'll talk to you when you are back from
Greece and I am out of the clinic.

Love,

Laney

*C*HILDREN PLAYED WITHOUT coats and scarves, and it seemed that the sound of their laughter had been as muffled all winter as their small bodies had been against the cold. Now they were loud and boisterous, screaming and chasing one another on the concrete plaza playgrounds enclosed by metal fences. Their voices were the sound of summer. In a girl's giggle from the playground, you could hear the delight of soft ice cream, Vitosha picnics, Black Sea sand castles, and splashes made from the high dive rising above the chemical-treated waters of the pool in the park. Teenage boys stayed out late in the warmth, drinking beer in the courtyards.

It was wrong. To Chavdar, it was incomprehensible that lovers walked arm in arm through NDK Park eating pink cotton candy. He had no one to hold his hand. He was in the darkest mood of his life on the sunniest day of the year. He looked around for the source of the irritatingly jovial folk music, and saw a bagpipe musician playing for tips on the sidewalk. Pensioners sat in big groups on sidewalks, clutching canes and staring at children on strange, newly imported Rollerblades. His eyes darted back and forth between poodles and beautiful women in short skirts. He suffered at these sights.

Chavdar walked along the rat-infested strip of trash-strewn bushes until he reached the center eyepiece of the park: a dark, monstrous sculpture that rose out of a deep pit. The massive modern sculpture was called the Thirteen Hundred Years Monument, and behind it, a group of skinheads had gathered to smoke marijuana and play hardcore music from a ghetto blaster. They danced in work boots around a rock covered with a red flag. A banner hanging from a tree declared "Red or Dead."

Chavdar slumped to a sitting position on a bench and stared at the anguished faces carved into the metal blocks of the monument. At the base were inscribed the words "We are in time and time is in us. We transform it and it transforms us."

Chavdar had never felt so transformed. Things had changed so quickly, and he, who had prided himself on his ability to adapt, had missed something. Who were those bald boys in jeans and work shirts, shouting and saluting their red flag? They had nothing in common with Chavdar's father. They had probably never read a word of Marx. Who were these children zipping around in Rollerblades and wearing New York Yankees ball caps? What great hand had suddenly descended from the sky, lowering a seven-meter-tall McDonald's logo onto the building opposite the monument? Chavdar scratched his chin. That great golden emblem had not loomed over the park the last time he'd walked across the plaza. Like the spring, it had taken over silently and quickly.

Time had transformed Bulgaria. The last four months had transformed the government, and nothing would ever again be the same. When the results of the April elections came out, the Union of Democratic Forces had won, and the new government intended to make good on its campaign promises. A four-pronged plan, they called it. The Democratic government's first and main missions were to carry out reforms in agreement with the World Bank, fight organized crime, open secret police files on public figures, and bring Bulgaria into the European Union and NATO.

Chavdar leaned forward on the bench and rested his elbows on his knees. His khaki slacks pulled up just a bit to reveal his dark socks, and with his crisp white shirt and sunglasses perched on his head, he looked invincible. Another irony, because for the first time in his life, he knew he was not. The news when he had entered the office that morning had been as staggering a blow as learning that it had been a ninety-pound stripper who had made off with seventy thousand dollars of his money. Like the Democrats winning the April election, the news was unbelievable.

Plamen had shouted the story at him over the phone. Rossen had waved the morning paper in his face. Their words echoed in his head: "Senior government officials dismissed on allegations of Mafia connections. The UDF has started a Central Service for Organized Crime Control, a Counterterrorism Commando, and together with the National Investigation Service, they are conducting covert operations throughout the country. The regional prosecutor of Kardzhali is behind bars. Local tax and municipal authorities are behind bars. Prosecutors in the National office and in the Armed Forces office are behind bars."

Chavdar had listened and blinked, and listened some more. "Bribery. Extortion. Counterfeiting. Embezzlement. Six illegal workshops for the production of black-market goods were closed down in Pleven and Sliven. Eight in Vidin and Pernik. The workshops were connected with two infamous insurance agencies. More arrests will soon be made."

Rossen had crumpled the paper in his fist. "This is us! This paper is talking about us, and this Counterterrorism Commando confiscated over a million dollars' worth of our machinery and supplies! We are going down and all you can talk about is how soon you can get on a flight to Greece to bring back a woman who doesn't want you!"

Chavdar's face had been ashen, his palms cold. He should have known about all this sooner, but his information chain had begun to break down. People were afraid. Chavdar didn't blame them. "I am going to take a walk."

"What?" Rossen asked, turning red. "You're going to? What? What?"

"Take a walk," Chavdar said. "To think."

"Oh! By all means! Take some time for yourself. Clear your head!" Rossen tugged at his collar with stubby fingers, and his bloodshot eyes blazed. "And in the meantime?"

"Try counting."

"Counting?"

"Just count in your head. Like in Elijah Winkler's best-seller *Me, Money and Meditation.* Count instead of thinking."

NOW CHAVDAR WAS sitting in the park watching a clown twist balloons into funny shapes. He was counting the number of dogs chasing one another around the plaza, the number of birds in the sky. One, two, three. He was a skipping record: June, June, June.

He had lost June, he had lost his business, he had lost his self-respect, he had lost his power, and he had lost the line somewhere. Where to cross, how far to go over, when to come back. After sending June flying across his bedroom it had felt quite natural to tell his men to kill the girl who had stolen the money when they found her. Now, he had in his pocket a ticket to Greece. He and one of his bodyguards would leave that evening to go find June, and to find whoever was staying with her in the double room at Sunset Villas. He hated June because it was her stubbornness that had forced him to do things he had not wanted to do, things that went against his nature, things that had contributed to the changing of his nature.

The changing of his nature, thought Chavdar. Put it that way and it sounded like just another part of life. As the monument read: "Time transforms us." Better if it said: "Time takes away our dreams, time opens our eyes to ugliness, time causes our bodies to wrinkle and sag, time kills us, but first it kills everything that was ever good in us." Chavdar was now capable of things he would not have considered before. In the past, everything had gone so well! His father had introduced him to all the important people and then died at a convenient time for Chavdar to take over. Doors had swung open, proposals had come pouring in, and money was made in bushels. There had never been much need for savagery. Chavdar's rites of passage now seemed so easy! A stolen car there, a broken leg here, burglary, arson. It was not until recently that he had become involved in such filth, and why? Because it was not until recently that he had been challenged. Challenged by June, by the law, and by his country.

So, yes. Time was passing and he was changing, and the sky was blue and people drank iced coffee under Coca-Cola umbrellas and kissed under the golden arches. More change and more violence hovered just over the horizon, preparing to wing its way into his world. Tonight he would see her. That was the only thought that made life possible. To see her, to ask her to forgive him, to hold her, to hate her. He did hate her.

Chavdar stood up and began to stroll, back and forth, up and down, following the sidewalks. An hour later he was back where he had started, unsure of where he had actually gone. Aimlessly, he continued, staring down at the bricks. He was counting cracks.

Ω

THE SUN WAS setting behind the white hull of the ferry, and James McKinnon waited on the dock, his pack resting at his feet. When June spotted him, he had all the colors of the sunset at his back. "Jimmy," she yelled, waving from the taxi. "Here I am!"

James walked over and opened the door of the taxi. June stepped out, wearing a long pale blue sundress, wooden sandals, and a straw hat. "Damn, girl!" he said, smiling and picking her up. "You look like you did at my sister's wedding."

"Sweet sixteen?"

"Just the same. Back when you were still tame, before the Goth girl phase. What happened to your bell-bottoms and platform shoes?"

"We're not in Los Angeles anymore."

James took her hand and led her toward the ferry. Greeks on holiday drank champagne and kissed, waiting for the boat to leave port. Music played and children leaned over the deck railings with holiday sparklers. "No, darlin'," he said. "We're not."

June felt the heaviness lift. It was just as she had imagined. The happiness of her past had arrived at the happiest place she knew in the present. "It's good to see you, Jimmy."

"Likewise."

When they were seated on the deck, James took out a gift bag overflowing with tissue. "Lilly made me promise to give you this right away."

"*Teach Yourself Yoga,*" June said, laughing, before she had even reached for the bag.

"How did you know? Sisterly telepathy?"

June opened the bag and it was just as she thought—the book Lilly had been promising to send and a vanilla face mask for the eczema that had actually disappeared months before. "I knew."

"Do you know what I brought you?"

"You didn't need to bring anything."

"I missed a birthday somewhere during your long absence, didn't I?"

"James—"

"Open it," he said, handing her a small box.

It was the size of a cigarette carton. "You know I quit smoking," June said.

"Just open it."

Inside was a night-light, shaped like a palm tree. At the top, the cheap plastic was inscribed with the word *Endless* in black cursive script. At the bottom it said *Summer.*

"Where did you find it?" whispered June. It was the same night-light Claire had given her when she was nine and scared of sleeping alone in her new room in the house in Sherman Oaks.

"I was with your mom when she bought it," said James. "The summer I spent with your family when my dad was in rehab. I remembered the souvenir shop on Hollywood Boulevard, because we went there right after she took me to the wax museum."

"Claire took you a . . . a . . . *wax museum?*"

"Yeah. And then we went to buy you a present. And that night I got to sleep in the twin bed across from you. And all night long, the night-light glowed and said 'Endless Summer,' and I prayed that I would be able to stay with you and not get sent back to Texas. I wanted my Endless Summer."

"Claire never took me to a museum," June said. "I didn't think she knew where any museums were."

"I tried to find the same store," James said. "But they didn't have night-lights, just T-shirts and pagers. So I went to a million other tourist-trap places on Hollywood Boulevard, but no one had it anymore."

"How did you find this one?"

"I didn't. I had yours cleaned up and fixed. You can't imagine what it's like to try to find someone who will undertake a loving restoration of a dime-store night-light from 1975. Must be as difficult as . . ." He smiled. "Trying to get a stamp at the post office in Sofia."

"You mean this one is—"

"It's the same one your mom gave you. It was in our toy box, the one in your Grandma Penny's attic, underneath the magic carpet. Along with a photo of you in your tiara, winning Miss Ventura."

"Really? I haven't thought of that in ages. I thought I threw it away when I left for college."

"I brought it. You can look at it when we unpack. Okay?"

"Okay." June lay down on the chaise beach chair and looked up at the moon—the size of a princess's fingernail, as Claire used to say. She closed her eyes and pictured Claire locking *Endless Summer* and her beauty queen daughter away in a wooden trunk underneath a magic carpet in her alcoholic mother's attic sometime before she decided it was time to leave the moving picture. Claire had lived and died in Los Angeles, in a soap-opera world of her own creation. June had fought with her mother at the kitchen table over calories, back-to-school clothes, and the quality and quantity of her friends, but late at night when June was asleep, Claire had slipped silently into the room and kissed her daughter's forehead like Prince Charming adoring Sleeping Beauty in the forest. Claire may have been melodramatic and demanding, but she had been able to cherish, been able to feel pride and admiration. She had saved a plastic night-light out of love. She had rescued a scratched and faded photo that June had thrown into the trash. Those items, as girlish and cheap and superficial as they appeared, were Claire's treasures—a shrine to a child whom she had clearly loved regardless of the way she bowed out of the mother-daughter drama.

June whispered, "Thank you," and James squeezed her hand. She was not talking to him, but he was there, and he understood.

27

Subject: Idle film talk
Date: Sun, 18 May 1997 13:59:43 -0700
From: June Carver <jcarver@sof.cit>
To: Benny <bgatwick@asb.com>

I am supposed to be on vacation but I've still got the computer plugged in. Here's a quick story I thought you might dig. It's a science fiction movie set circa 1975 I heard pitched by a Bulgarian photographer named Kyril who used to hate me but now wants me to come work with him.

Here's the story: This Bulgarian man has been applying for his visa to go to America for twenty years. Finally, as an old man, he wins the lottery and gets to go. He is called into a gray room where he is met with a committee of Russians. They explain to him that America never existed. It is a myth, simply a fairy tale for children, like Santa Claus. It was an idea conjured up by Moscow Studios, the greatest movie studio in the world, and they have made all the great American movies, to give people something to dream about and hope for while they toil away in the misery of Bulgaria. Moscow Studios has come up with the most effective propaganda imaginable: a heaven without religion that you can work for and apply to and hope to enter on earth. Now that the Bulgarian man has been selected to go to America, he will actually be sent to Siberia, and the KGB will send wonderful pictures and letters home to his family while he is a slave in the winter wasteland work camps. So everyone that gets to go to heaven is really going to hell.

I think I am ready to let go of the dream.

Love you,

June

ANSWERING MACHINES WERE a new arrival in Bulgaria, and only the elite owned them. Nevena herself had left a total of three such messages in her life: all calls to foreign employers to say she would be late to work. In each case, Nevena had found it humiliating to speak when no one was listening. She was embarrassed that someone would have a recording of her speaking English so poorly, expressing herself so awkwardly, and worst of all, giving away with her frequent hesitations and shaking voice that she was *scared* of the machine.

That morning she had gone to the central post office, waited in line for forty minutes, and finally paid to have the operator place her international call. Nevena knew Ethan wouldn't be in northern California yet, but she had hoped to pass along the message that there was an emergency in Sofia. Instead of reaching one of his parents, however, she had been greeted with the recording of a woman's syrupy voice, lilting and soothing and rather awful. "Hello there!" Ellen sang with melodic cheer. "You have reached the Carvers, but I'm sorry! We're not at home just now. Leave your name, number, and a brief message, and either George or I will get back to you juuuuust as quick as we can. Have a lovely day. Now here's the beep!"

Nevena's mouth had opened to respond, but nothing came out. How could she keep it brief? How could she respond to the sporty challenge offered in such a self-satisfied way? The recorded message told Nevena that at the Carver residence, life was good and the garden was blooming. Ellen's greeting told Nevena not to intrude on their blue-sky suburban life with her timid "I'm the other woman" voice and her scandalous underworld emergency. She hung up in a sudden panic and the next person moved in to use the phone. By then the wait to place international calls was an hour. Too many people had given up their home phones. Nevena picked up her bag, sighed, and walked to work at Roxanne's.

AFTER ENTERING THE house, Nevena looked up at the ceiling. Someone was thumping around upstairs, and she heard Roxanne giggle.

She walked quickly to the kitchen, hoping that whoever had spent the night would leave soon. Money was what Nevena needed to talk about, and Roxanne was the only person she thought might listen.

As if on cue, Roxanne appeared in the doorway of the guest bathroom where the laundry machines were kept. "Morning," she said, resting her arm against the doorjamb.

"Hi," Nevena said, standing up. "I am glad you are up because I was wondering if we could talk about something important?"

"Of course," Roxanne answered gaily, waving her hand toward the kitchen. "Let's get some juice and chat."

Nevena followed the smell of cigarettes and the diaphanous trail of Roxanne's filmy robe into the kitchen. Roxanne took a pitcher out of the refrigerator and poured each of them a glass of tomato juice. "Vodka?"

Nevena wiped her hands on her skirt. She was nervous. "Please."

"Well! A taker for once, how nice. Let's just sit at the kitchen table. It's too early for me to even look at my office."

Nevena sat down, her knees together primly, her feet tucked underneath the chair. Roxanne chewed on a bite of celery. "I know what this serious subject of yours is. Ethan is finished here, isn't he? Got that great, investment-tycoon-type job waiting for him in Istanbul, right? He's moving on, and you want to move on with him?"

"Not exactly . . ."

"Listen, I know. I *know*." She put a hand on Nevena's arm. "You want to get out of here. I don't blame you. I think I've just about had enough myself. Now, I realize that I haven't always been that nice to you, but I always appreciated you, Nevena. Always. And in my defense, the only time I was ever really awful was when you started up this ridiculous business with Ethan."

"Roxanne—"

"Listen. June is my friend. You are my friend. Ethan is my friend. I like to see my friends get what they want. I believe in scratching backs. I know you've always wanted to go to America, honey! Don't you think I know that? When I'm out of town you creep around like a little burglar, going through my things. You're just a daydreamer, and I understand! But you listen here. Ethan may be a ticket to the States, but honey, he's the slow boat to China. By the time you set foot in the land of opportunity, you'll be long past the age when it still comes a knocking on the door. Do you hear me?"

"I don't think you understand."

"Oh, *au contraire*. I understand better than you think. It appears the time has come for us to part ways, and I want to give you a good-bye gift." Roxanne got unsteadily to her feet and went to the drawer underneath the radio.

"But the problem I have now is much more—"

Roxanne turned to Nevena, holding out a thick white envelope. "It's cash."

"Oh? Oh God." Nevena took her first swig of the Bloody Mary.

Roxanne smiled as she set the envelope down in front of Nevena. "It's really not that much. If you had worked for me in the States I would have had to pay a hundred times this much to have someone as good as you stay with me all this time."

"Roxanne!"

"I got the better end of the deal, honey, believe me. And you know what?" Roxanne leaned down and put her hands on Nevena's shoulders. Her watery red eyes moved back and forth over Nevena's big brown ones. Her breath was stale. "You know, Nevena, that right there? That wad of hundred-dollar bills? It isn't even the best part. Leonard!" Roxanne turned toward the doorway, cupped her hand over her mouth, and shouted again. "Leonard!"

A second later a man in a terry-cloth robe entered the kitchen. He was bald and skinny, with bony knees and hairy feet. He saw Nevena and took a step backward. "Ho ho!" he said. "Didn't know she was here yet."

Nevena averted her eyes from his outward-pointing feet. She recognized him as one of the boyfriends who spent the night on occasion.

"Yes, she's here," Roxanne said fondly, sounding like an indulgent parent. "This is Nevena, Leonard. Nevena, this is the nice man from the consulate who is giving you a visa."

Nevena looked up at the two of them in wide-eyed shock. She stared at Roxanne, then at Leonard, and finally, completely overcome, down at Leonard's feet. Her hand, holding the envelope of money, was shaking so much that she dropped it. Her voice was barely a whisper. "I don't know what to say."

"Don't say anything yet," Roxanne answered, kneeling down beside Nevena's chair. Her smile was wet, and Nevena saw that red lipstick was smeared lightly across her chin. "That's right, honey. If something sounds too good to be true, then it probably is! It's an old American proverb. Don't you say a word until you hear the catch."

❧

THE MOON WAS high in the sky, drawing a long, pale trail across the sea toward the mainland. June sat alone on the rocks on the western edge of the island. She wore jeans, and had removed her shoes.

Behind her, in the winding streets of Santorini, ecstasy was unfolding. Mazes of cobblestone alleyways led to white flights of stairs, which led to beautiful blue curtains and ambient music. Psychedelic-colored clothes glowed in the windows of the boutiques, and fruit-topped cocktails were being delivered to outdoor tables surrounded by flowers. As they sipped their ten-dollar whiskey and Cokes, the men occasionally patted their jackets, where their cell phones were snugly encased. The women smoked thin cigarettes and dripped with fine silver bracelets.

Inside one of the white-painted cafes, June imagined James charming the locals with card tricks, James Dean monologues, and Marlon Brando impersonations. She had told him to go have fun without her. On the island with Christmas lights in the trees, music afloat on the air, and youth and beauty parading through the soft white pillowy streets, June had wanted to be alone. She had not yet opened the envelope guarding the portrait of the old June, the ultimate symbol of her former self.

James had put the photo in a folder; an ordinary one, like a high-school student's. June took it from the envelope and slipped out the headshot. It was black and white, eight inches by eleven, with a white border. June's teeth gleamed. It was an enormous smile, so big and infectious that it would cause anyone who looked at it to smile too. Her hair was feathered, her eyes sparkled, and the rhinestone tiara cast stars of light across the beads in her dress and the gloss on her lips. At first she did not recognize herself—the image was so different from the one she had recently seen staring back at her from the mirror in her tiny bathroom, and from the mirrors behind the bars of the Balkan taverns. The photo was from her second to last contest, when she was fourteen and a dancing queen.

June nodded as she looked at the photo, suddenly remembering the decision to place it in the plastic trash bag with the used notebooks, mangled T-shirts, and old magazines, back when she had been clearing out her room before heading off to UCLA. Despite the bright smile, June could now see there was no triumph in the eyes. Rather, they seemed to be searching the crowd. Now, after so much time, June recognized the glint of resentment. She knew who she had been trying to find. The memory of her mother, standing and applauding, hit her like a fist in the stomach. Why had she not blown Claire a kiss? Why had she not waved to her, acknowledged her, mouthed the loving words Claire had wanted so much to hear?

"Oh God," she whispered. "I'm sorry." She turned the photo over, needing the white and blameless back, anything not to look at the expression in her own eyes, that she suddenly understood and regretted.

But the back of the photo was not clean and empty. Black cursive script scrawled diagonally up into the right-hand corner. It was her mother's hand. Claire had written: "All I ever wanted was for you to be happy. I'm sorry if what I wanted for you was not what you wanted for yourself. Go for it, my darling. Go above and beyond what I ever did, and what I ever pushed you towards—and go for it in your own way. That is how you will continue to make me proud. I love you, June. Claire."

June smashed a small corner of the photo in her hand as she clutched it, clung to it. She shook with relief and tears and finally splashed seawater on her face. Claire had not been disappointed. Maybe then it was not her failure to be who Claire wanted her to be, that had made Claire do what she did. June looked upward and thanked her mother and said good-bye to her, as well as to Ethan. "Good-bye. I love you."

She hugged herself and admitted what was true. Being with James, or anyone else, could not complete her. Not yet. In Los Angeles, in an effort to both appease and please Claire, June had looked for herself in the mirrors of the posh reception areas at the movie studios, in the reflections of the pools at the premiere parties, and in the crystal glasses of the afternoon whiskies-on-the-rocks she brought to so many of her bosses. The images she saw were distorted. Later she sought to complete herself by adding to herself—making herself part of something bigger and stronger and sure. In the end she had not been sure or strong at all—not until now. The eternity with Ethan she had needed to believe in would have been an eternity of doubt. It was not enough.

For a very short time Chavdar had given her what she needed. He had made her feel valued. In his world worth was simple. It was money, and he had definitely given it to her, in the form of gifts—trips, jewelry, luxury, pills. That hadn't worked either, and June had left to look some more, trying to backtrack, to pick up whatever trail had seemed to lead the furthest. Marriage, work, sex, success, power, love. As Raina would have put it, buh buh

buh, buh buh buh. In the end, June had searched for worth using what she had *mistakenly* thought were Claire's criteria. That search had turned up nothing worthwhile. So here she was, on a rock in Greece, doing the math, figuring it all out. At long last she was confident enough to believe in her own answer.

28

Subject: Good for you!
Date: Thurs, 29 May 1997 22:41:23 -0400 (EDT)
From: Lilly <org.beauty@ink.net>
To: June <jcarver@sof.cit>

Hermana mía, tu alma está libre, no? I asked Joaquín how to
say "Your soul is free." Now that I hear your old voice
speaking from the computer screen in these emails I am less
inclined to urge you to come home. As I said, the require-
ments for development are devotion, concentration and direction. You have identified the problem and now you can
begin to make reparations. Don't torture yourself about the
past. Enjoy your freedom and look inside. Take it one day
at a time.

By the way, I am in love. *Yo estoy enamorada de Joaquín.* Dad
is not exactly thrilled, but I think he is beginning to
mellow in his retirement. Despite (or because of?) what
happened with Mom, he is recognizing that human union is
mysterious and problematic and that his daughters should do
whatever they must to be happy.

Te amo,

Lilly

*I*T WAS AN imperfect plan. Unfortunately, it was the only plan they had. Nevena had been sick to her stomach ever since agreeing to Roxanne's proposal, but whenever the crisis of conscience hit, she forced herself to imagine what would become of Boryana if she remained in the country and was found.

In the consulate office, Nevena had not been able to meet Leonard's eyes as he asked her questions and filled out her papers. When he gave her the visa and stamped her passport, he'd said, "Congratulations!" He was so congenial and comfortable that it seemed he doled out visas to uneducated, penniless immigrants all the time.

He didn't know that she was lying to him and to Roxanne. Rather than blame Leonard or Roxanne for unethical behavior, Nevena condemned only herself. She had taken the money and the visa on conditions she was going to flagrantly ignore. But, she reminded herself, the deception was only temporary. When Ethan got back, he would reimburse Roxanne for her provisional gift. As for the visa, perhaps Leonard would revoke it. But by then, Boryana would be somewhere in the States, with a new life, far away from the people who would want to take her life.

Roxanne's conditions had been simple. Leave now, and leave no explanation. That was it. Nevena knew what Roxanne was thinking. If she accepted the deal, then it was proof that she had never wanted anything other than a ticket to the States. In that case it was better for Ethan to be rid of her, and Roxanne had done everyone a favor, including June. If she had refused to accept the deal, then it would have proven her love for Ethan.

There was no heart-warming display of loyalty, however. Nevena had walked out of Roxanne's house with a wad of money and an appointment at the American Consulate. She had walked out and left her pride behind. All the way home, Nevena had cringed at the thought of Roxanne's bitter, knowing smile when she'd given them the answer: "Okay. I'll do it."

Now, Nevena was waiting anxiously on the corner outside her apartment. Every taxi that pulled up her street made her palms sweat as she thought, *It is time.* Each taxi that passed her doorway on its way to other destinations made her worry that something had gone wrong. She checked her watch. Air France flight 2122 would leave the Sofia airport in less than two hours. It would stop once in Paris before continuing service to New York, and when it touched down in the States, Boryana would be on it. Or so Nevena prayed.

Nevena unsnapped her handbag and double-checked to make sure that her passport was inside. She opened it, ran her finger across the official stamp of the American visa, and then flipped to the photo. Taken several years before, it was black and white and not at all flattering. Every mole stood out. The rings under her eyes were gray, and her hair looked oily at the roots. She shut the passport and put it back in her bag. Better not to compare the photo to Boryana's similar but hardened face.

This time tomorrow Nevena might be relieved and relaxed, envisioning her sister arriving safely in America. She might also be in a holding cell, seated on a plastic chair, answering the questions of chain-smoking police officers. If that happened, if she and her sister were caught, it would not be long before Boryana would receive whatever punishment the mutras saw fit. Once again, she and her sister's world and reality were going to change overnight— for better or for worse.

Finally, a taxi pulled to a stop next to Nevena. She opened the door and climbed into the front seat, next to the driver. Georgi was white and silent, and Boryana looked nauseous. Nevena reached over the seat and took her sister's hand.

None of them spoke during the fifteen-minute ride to the airport. When they approached the turnaround in front of the small, dismal terminal, the usual assortment of taxis and police vehicles were parked outside. Georgi instructed the driver to let them off on the sidewalk down the street, out of the way of the crowd that was congregated by the front doors. The driver got out, stepped on his cigarette, and opened the trunk. Inside was a battered brown suitcase and a red Marlboro duffel bag with a worn strap that had faded to light pink. Boryana took the duffel bag, and Georgi carried the suitcase over to the sidewalk.

"So," Nevena finally said. "Here's the passport."

Georgi reached for it. "It doesn't look like her."

"I know it doesn't," said Boryana. "This is crazy. Why are we doing this?"

"It is the best way to get you as far away as possible. And the picture does look like you," said Nevena. "If Ethan thought you were me, then an airport employee will believe you are me. As long as you aren't shaking and sweating and looking guilty."

"Nevena," said Boryana, "I hate letting you do this. You could be going instead."

"I would not be going. This would not be happening. Don't give it a second thought."

Georgi handed the passport to Boryana. "Do it," he said. "Just go in there and do it."

Boryana checked her watch. "Oh God."

"Come here," said Nevena. She took a compact out of her purse and powdered the nervous sweat from Boryana's forehead. "It's going to be fine."

Boryana took a deep breath. "Sure it will. Of course it will."

Nevena bit her lip and tried to smile. "You're all set. You should be thrilled."

"I might never see either of you again," Boryana said, wiping her nose and ruining all the work Nevena had done with the powder.

Nevena kissed her cheek. "Go. You better just go."

The duffel bag was still slung over her shoulder. Boryana opened it up and took out a gift-wrapped package. "It is something small," she said. "A good-bye present."

Nevena started to tug on the bow.

"No, no," said Boryana. "There is no time, and I am too embarrassed to watch. Open it when I'm gone." She picked up the suitcase and tried to give them a courageous face. Instead, she appeared to be fighting tears when she waved. "Sbogom," she said, using the word for good-bye that means "Go with God." It was rarely used and Boryana had never said it before. It was reserved for good-byes of the eternal kind.

"Sbogom," Georgi whispered.

Nevena would not use the word. "Ciao. Have a good trip. I love you."

Boryana started to walk away and Nevena nudged Georgi, who was always so reticent with affection. "I love you too," he said, looking up with red eyes. "Very much."

"She'll be okay, Georgi," Nevena whispered, as Boryana walked away. "She deserves some luck."

INSIDE THE AIRPORT, Boryana was getting what she deserved. Passport control waved her by with a perfunctory glance, and she checked the brown suitcase without a problem. She passed through security with the duffel bag untouched and no questions asked. Within the hour she was on a bus being driven out to the tarmac where the airplane waited. Lucky, lucky, lucky. When the plane took off, Boryana braced herself and left the ground for the first time in her life. The sensation was wonderful. She felt free and safe and . . . rich. When the stewardess came around with the duty-free cart,

Boryana asked for a carton of Marlboros, a bottle of Poison perfume, and the best American whiskey money could buy. She could afford it. In the duffel bag, wrapped inside panties and rolled inside socks, was forty thousand stolen dollars.

In a taxi headed back to the city, Nevena and Georgi didn't know whether to laugh or cry. They hugged each other and hid what was in their hands from the driver. The note in the gift package from Boryana read: *Fifteen thousand for each of you. I took forty. Please forgive me, but America is more expensive. I love you. Boryana.*

WHILE CHAVDAR SHOWERED in the hotel, Stoyan went for cigarettes and a snack. It wasn't as easy to find sunflower seeds in Santorini as it was in Sofia, but Stoyan managed. He looked very out of place among Europe's rich and beautiful, spitting his shells out on the sidewalk and glowering at paradise. The opulence and openness of the island irritated him. Faggots were out walking arm in arm in pastel pants, and what people were spending on drinks in one sitting could have supported his parents for an entire month. In his black jeans and black leather jacket, Stoyan was hot and damp. He stomped heavily through the streets, nearly spanning the breadth of the alleys. When his dark eyes fell on cafe tables surrounded by spoiled-looking women or girlish men, he spit seeds in their direction. Their language sounded as frivolous as the upbeat Greek disco music pumping away incessantly from speakers in the palms. People in this foreign country did not show Stoyan the proper respect. He preferred to stay in Sofia, where, as the Bulgarian saying went, he was "the rock with weight."

Stoyan had been looking for a nice dark tavern where he could have a few beers with a big dinner of sausage and chips. He could not find any place at all to suit his mood. Rather than dark, smoky taverns, Stoyan saw only bright sunny gardens and vine-draped patios filled with pretty people eating salads, grilled fish, and fruit. In each of these places he entered, spat sunflower shells, and exited with a thudding slam of the brightly painted door.

In the end, Stoyan bought a couple of large beers, a toasted ham and cheese sandwich, and a pack of dark Greek cigarettes. He took his meal to the park across from June's hotel and ate morosely on a bench under bougainvillea hanging from a verdant tree. After draining the first beer, he tossed the bottle onto the lawn by his feet. When he'd finished the sandwich, he crumpled the greasy paper wrapper and dropped it beside him on the bench. To top off the snack, he lit one of the country's strongest cigarettes and hacked in a cloud of smoke for five minutes until he thought his lungs would explode. Surrounded by his own trash and with the taste of smoke in his throat, he felt at ease.

He pulled out his cell phone and dialed Chavdar. "Eh. I'm outside her hotel. Okay. I'll call you when she comes home."

THE MOSQUITOES WERE out in Northern California, but the Carvers were impervious. The wooden deck was encased in a light screen, and by the dog door was a bug zapper plugged into an outdoor electrical socket. In the background of Ethan's conversation with his younger sister and parents was the soft repetitive sound of bugs dying. "Who wants more chicken?" Zap. "I do, pass it." Zap. "Take some saffron sauce. That's what it's for." Zap.

The four of them were seated around a table covered with afternoon picnic items of an unusual variety. George had barbecued a chicken, Ellen had cooked saffron sauce, rice with pomegranate seeds, and a Tunisian eggplant dish. Ethan had contributed a Bulgarian shopska salad, topped with feta.

"Ellen," said George, "I don't know why you're acting like you didn't see this coming. You always said June was a little flighty."

"George, I did not! For heaven's sakes, what a thing to say!" Ellen looked apologetically at Ethan, shaking her head. "I *adored* June."

"She wasn't flighty," said Carrie. "She was just a little original. God forbid anyone be original, Dad."

"I think I said her sister was flighty," continued Ellen, "not June."

George turned to Ethan and pointed at Carrie. "You know what her idea of original is? It's getting a dolphin tattooed on her ankle. She's twenty-five years old and she's still acting like a goddamned teenager."

"June has a tattoo," Carrie said, arching an eyebrow. She looked pleased with herself.

Ethan dropped his fork onto his plate. "How would you know?"

"She does, doesn't she?"

"I repeat, how would you know?"

"She showed it to me."

Ellen took a drink of her beer. "I can't believe these young girls today."

"June showed you her tattoo?" Ethan looked horrified.

"God, Ethan. It's not like I've never seen someone else's butt before."

"Carrie!" exclaimed Ellen.

George coughed into his napkin. "That's enough. I mean it. Ellen, go get the champagne."

Ellen got up and gave Carrie a look before going into the house. Carrie flipped her hair and slouched in her seat. "June was the only one around here who was ever any fun." After a second, she stood up and followed her mother into the kitchen.

Ethan rubbed his temples. He had no idea how to bring up the subject of Nevena.

George leaned toward Ethan, glanced toward the screen door going into the house, and whispered, "What's it of?"

"What's what?"

"June's heinie tattoo. What's it of?" His father looked fascinated and Ethan gave up. He'd break the news about Nevena some other time.

THREE CUTE TEENAGE GIRLS in surf shorts, sandals, and bikini tops whispered to one another as James and June walked past a high-school hangout on their way back from a late dinner. June looked over at James, gorgeous in simple faded blue jeans and a button-down shirt. He blushed. "What?"

"Those femme-bots certainly gave you the once-over. You big stud."

"No they didn't," he said, but you could tell he had seen it too.

"It was obvious. So obvious they must think I'm your mother or something."

"Rather than my—?" he asked, raising an eyebrow.

"Your *contemporary*," she answered laughing. "Nice try."

"Oh. Uh-huh." James leaned his head back to look at the moon. "You won't give an inch, will you?"

"James—"

He suddenly grabbed her hand and pulled her off the sidewalk, into the courtyard of a restaurant with a terraced roof covered in flowers and vines. Inside, a Greek band played a love ballad, and James twirled June once, twice, until she fell into the crook of his arm. "You won't talk about us. You never did much, but even less now."

"I'm just glad you're here. That is enough to make me feel better. I don't need to talk about everything. Sometimes that just makes it worse."

"As long as you're okay. I guess that's why I brought you the night-light and not a book or a CD or a pair of earrings. I brought it because I don't want you to be frightened or lonely, like you were when we were little. It sounded from your e-mails like you might be again."

June wrapped her arms around James and rested her head on his chest. "You know me so well, and I feel like I don't know you well enough. James, is there someone special in Los Angeles now?"

"There is a woman. Someone I'm dating, sure. But darlin', I never considered not coming to be with you. I'm part of the reason your life got so messed up, and I wanted to be here to apologize. And to make it better, if possible. Anyway, it's not that serious with Marnie. She's an entertainment lawyer."

"An entertainment lawyer?" June asked, looking up.

James took the opportunity to catch her chin between his thumb and forefinger. "She's not you."

He started to lower his face toward hers, and June quickly stood on her tiptoes to kiss his cheek. "I can't," she said. "I'm sorry."

"Well, I can't either," he answered.

"Really?"

"Not now. Not with the way things are. Maybe someday when you don't live thousands of miles away from me. Maybe someday when we want the same thing."

"I love you."

"I know you do, but for now the only thing left to do is have a slumber party. We'll go back to the hotel, plug in *Endless Summer,* get drunk, and write poems on the bottoms of each other's feet."

"Did I tell you I love you?"

"Yes."

STOYAN WATCHED as James and June approached the hotel. His arm was around her waist, and she was pointing to something up in a tree. James looked up, clapped his hands, did a dance step, and then a spin. June bent over at the waist, and when she stood up and flung her hair back, the street-light hit the tears of laughter under her eyes. James was laughing too, loud enough for Stoyan to hear. They sounded so happy. He dialed Chavdar. "She's back. What do you want me to do?"

Stoyan paused. "Are you sure? I think I should come with you. You don't know how to handle things like this. No, no. If you want to go alone I'll just stay here. Call me after—after whatever happens."

IN THE SMALL reception area of the hotel, June tugged on James's shirttail. "I'll go get the wine now, and you set up the slumber party."
"Okay. White."
"Red."
"White."
"A bottle of both."
"See you in ten."

JUNE HUMMED a Greek pop song, lyrics unknown and unneeded really, as she walked down the narrow alleyway to the hotel. She was balanced—in one hand, a plastic bag with a bottle of white Greek retsina, and in the other, a plastic bag with red Spanish wine. *Little Jimmy better be a big drinker tonight,* she thought. For the first time in a long time, she was okay, oblivious to all else but the comfort of her recent realization and impending contentment.

The dim light in the hotel doorway flickered down the way, casting angled shadows across the pillowed, whitewashed walls of the old town. It was illuminating. June felt overwhelmed by the beauty of it all, grateful for the way the loveliness was able to touch her, happy for small things and big, all things lost and gained.

When a dark form stepped out from an alleyway between her and her destination, it presented itself first as only an obstacle between her and what lay beyond. Then she recognized the strong shoulders, the narrow hips, and the long legs planted far apart to keep her from passing. It seemed like another lifetime, that day when she had encountered this same man, expecting her on another stone-paved street, holding flowers, waiting to gently take her elbow and steer her up the stairs.

Now, that once-hopeful lover glared at her with hatred and the hope of seeing her cower.

A part of her wondered if she could be imagining this, if it were yet another nightmare, like the ones that had plagued her since she had returned the keys to the apartment and he'd sent her flying across the room. This was the moment she had been dreading, and yet this moment had serendipitously arrived exactly when she felt capable of the confrontation. *Life is strange that way,* she thought, *strange and benevolent, providing you with what you need, reminding you that things do happen for a reason.*

Something had shifted inside. She had not forgiven herself for falling into this affair—for the time she had lost to it and for where it had left her—but she was ready to deal with the consequences. She had known for a long time who he was and what he was about—the bribes and bombs, the surveillance, restraints, and manipulation. All this had paralyzed her, but she was suddenly determined not to live in this powerless place anymore. She could no longer stand to wonder when and where he would find her and what he might do when he did. It was better to be done with it. Either she would move on with her life or he would leave her with no life at all. Either way, it was better than this constant preoccupation with the unknown, the recurring visions of capture and control that had begun to rule her life. This was going to end now, one way or another. June braced herself. "Look who's here," she said lightly. There was a hint of denial, even subdued shock, in her casual greeting.

Chavdar blinked, confusion flashing briefly across his face. This was, perhaps, the only response he had not expected.

"I was wondering when I'd see you again," she said, lowering the bags of wine to the ground. She walked toward him slowly, cocking her head to the side. "I didn't think it would be quite so soon, but it's okay. I'm ready."

"Well, you must have known that I would not allow you to run off like this. You knew I would not let you disappear forever without giving me the respect of an explanation."

"Yes," she said, pausing a few feet away. He towered over her, and she tilted her face up toward his. "I did know that, but I thought you'd send one of your thugs, like usual. I thought you'd give an order and let one of them carry it out. I've been expecting to turn the corner and find Stoyan, or Petko, ready to drag me away and bring me to you. Does this mean—?"

She paused, noting the outline of a gun through the fabric of his shirt. She was surprised, but careful to conceal it. The gun was not right. He wore it wrong and she doubted his competence. This doubt, and a flicker of contempt, was what he saw when she looked back up into his eyes. "Does this mean you've decided at last to do your own dirty work?"

"What I decided is that you and I are going to talk. You are going to tell me if you are here with someone. If that is true, you are going to tell me who he is. Then I am going to tell you a few things."

June's eyes traveled over him, noting the dark rings beneath his eyes, and the stubble on the jaw of a bloodless face that had lost its Greek holiday tan. There was something unhinged in the desperate way he stared. What he had lost was visible, even in the scuffed shoes and sagging waistline of his tailored pants. "Really," she said.

"Yes."

June stepped closer and extended her chin over his shoulder, to whisper in his ear. "I don't believe that you just came to talk." The voice was suggestive, and the languid movements inviting. Her hand closed around his bicep, and then fell lower, down the length of his jacket, until it came to rest on his waist, opposite the outline of the gun.

She kept her mouth close to his ear as she tugged at the hem of his shirt. "Am I right?"

He inhaled sharply. "June . . ." Her name, whispered with such emotion, was evidence of his hope for reconciliation.

She pulled on the edge of his shirt, and the gun was suddenly exposed. June reached for it, but Chavdar's left hand caught hers with a familiar pressure. She stepped back, but he didn't let go.

"See?" she said. "You didn't come just to talk, but in the end, talking is all you're going to do."

"You should not be so sure."

"Really Chavdar, what are you going to do with that gun?"

"What do you think I'm going to do with it?"

"I think you're going to hurt yourself."

Chavdar clenched his teeth and clamped down on her hand simultaneously. June cried out as her bones cracked. "You bitch," he whispered. He squeezed tighter, and she suddenly felt faint. She saw blood sprayed against olive skin, and pink angora gloves over frozen tobacco-stained fingers.

Absurdly, she laughed. "Do you remember the first night we made love?"

He closed his eyes, visibly softening, waiting for and wanting more of such words.

"You saw my tattoo, and I told you that a woman's threshold for pain is ten times that of a man's." She glanced at her hand breaking inside his. "Mine's even higher now."

A vein throbbed in his forehead, and he had to press his lips together to keep from shouting. He continued to tighten his fist. His whole arm was shaking with anger and the effort of increasing the pressure. Ever since he'd met her, he had wanted her to submit—he had been sure she would. He felt crippled by the desire to crush her, and by his continued inability to do so.

A tear slipped out of the corner of her eye, but she didn't look away or lose the hint of her knowing smile.

"Tell me if you are here with someone," he said, fighting to control his voice. "Tell me who is up there, in that room."

She stared defiantly back at him. "It's not your concern. *I am* not your concern anymore."

"You are *completely* mistaken."

"No, you are. And you know it."

With that, he realized she would not give in, she would not say *mercy*— that magical word that she had taught him, and that he so much needed to hear. There was only one way left to hurt her, and he could not help himself. He finished with the soft hand. Her bones snapped and collapsed. She gasped, and her legs buckled. First one knee dropped, and then the other, until she was on the ground before him, her breath shallow and hitching.

"I should shoot you!" he said, pulling out the gun. He had wanted to see her crumple, but not like this. He felt powerless rather than victorious. "Everyone told me you are nothing but an arrogant American bitch!"

"Do it then," she said, swaying, and fighting the blackness closing in at the edges of her vision. "Everyone told me you are nothing but a coward and a criminal. Prove to everyone that you are what they say you are. I would love for you to prove them right."

"I will do it," he said, even though he could suddenly see how this was going to end—with a look of triumph on her insolent face. He pushed this thought away and took a shaky aim. "I will do this one thing right." His finger twitched on the trigger, but he did not pull it back.

James suddenly appeared on the sidewalk, barefoot, a cigarette in one hand. He took in the scene, dropped the smoke, and stared. "What the hell is going on?"

June looked up. "James, go away!"

Chavdar turned with wild eyes and a flailing arm. He saw James, with his American blue jeans, white T-shirt, and tanned arms. He swallowed, convulsed as if sick, and fired spastically. James, a second after emerging from the dim doorway, took the botched shot in the ankle. He fell to the ground, clutching his leg.

Chavdar breathed heavily as his eyes rose from James's slumped figure to June, facing him. He aimed at her forehead, and his finger curled again around the trigger, again preparing to shoot. Sweat rolled into his glassy eyes, and he needed to bring up his other hand to hold the gun steady. James was crawling for the door to get help, leaving a black, bloody trail across gray cobblestones. June remained on her knees, almost like a girl awaiting communion. Chavdar towered unsteadily over the pitiful scene, cloaked in a disarray of dark, sweat-soaked clothes, malevolence, and indecision.

"Do it," she challenged, spreading her arms out to the sides. The broken fingers hung unnaturally. She was oblivious to the pain. She focused on him with a stoic shine in her green eyes.

Her provocation was obscene, the indifference maddening. Chavdar shivered, feeling there was something whorish about her readiness for what he was offering. Then he accepted it. What she said was true. He could not hurt her. She didn't care what he did to her anymore, and she didn't care about him. His world suffered a final and inarguable alteration.

"Do it," she said again. "Show me who you are. I know who I am. Show me who you are. *Do it.*"

He shielded his eyes from the sight of her and—perhaps more important—hid his own collapse. He turned on a shaky heel, stumbled, and sheathed the gun in his pants. With his head lowered and his gait awkward, he retreated into the labyrinth of the town. June watched him growing smaller—more dark and awkward, more slow and slouching—as he disappeared. She watched until he was nothing but a vague form in the distance, turning a corner, vanishing completely.

Still on her knees, June was dizzy and disoriented. She felt as if she were waking from one of her nightmares, traumatized by his words, his accusing eyes, and the guilt of *ever* having cared for such a man. James, bleeding behind her, asking the concierge to call an ambulance, brought her back to reality.

She went to him, folded down into a cross-legged position, and pulled his head into her lap.

"What was that, Junie?" he whispered. "What happened?"

The strong words that she had found moments before would not come. Her best friends's blood was spread in a semicircle around them, and she felt responsible, guilty, hollow. She had climbed to the edge of the cliff, stared down, and dived off. Now she found herself choking and crashing at the bottom. "I'm so sorry," she whispered. "That was something I thought I had to do. It was something I thought I had to finish."

"He almost killed you. Are you crazy?"

"Yes. I was crazy. I was out of my mind." Only now did she realize that she had been thinking only of herself—how it had to come to this, and how it could not go any further. Chavdar could have killed James. "I'm so sorry," she said. "Please forgive me."

At that moment, she began to sob. She had not meant to put James at risk. She had been consumed by a tragedy of her own creation, and for this she was ashamed. *I'm not all morbid and depressed and thinking it's glamorous.* She remembered these words, said to Raina on the first afternoon they had met. *It's circumstantial, really.* Circumstances had leveled her, and she had been forced to rise. Chavdar had lived his life among people who had fallen, people he had believed would never stand. Raina would have loved this performance, would have applauded June's Balkan pragmatism and resolve—her cold-blooded treatment of a killer. But June was foreign to this place, and her heart came rising up. She was reminded of the fragile nature of her own life, and of those she loved. *Stupid zhena,* she thought, *stupid for risking someone else, stupid for not finally being beyond these tears. Buh, buh, buh.*

"I never meant for you to get hurt. What I did was terrible. I'm so sorry."

"It was not terrible," he said, extending a hand up to touch her cheek. For the first time, he had a glimpse of what she had gone through, and what had just happened made perfect sense. "What you did was amazing."

It was somehow right, comfortable, and real that she was speechless. After apologizing to James, she had nothing more to say, explain, defend, convince, retract, or refute. It was just this, how she felt, and it was spiraling and unending. As she cradled James in her arms, she welcomed the rush of indefinable emotions. Raina had been hard but not unfeeling, and neither was she. She was part of what she had been before, and part of what she had recently experienced. Despite what had happened over the past year, she had not been left with a deficit in her capacity for love. June looked down at James, and down at her own bent fingers and swollen palm. His wound was seeping and soaking her stockings. It was not fair to him, and she was at fault. Yet she heard Raina saying, "Stop this American foolishness about fair, fair, fair. This is life." Such a thing would never have occurred to her before. Even James, with his expression of pained admiration and beatific acceptance, was an affirmation. June was assured.

She and James were stained with blood and marked with bruises. *"Buh, buh buh,"* she said, under her breath.

"What?" whispered James.

"Nothing. I'm so sorry," she said again, stroking his forehead, "but it's going to be okay. Believe me, sweetheart, when I tell you that all of this hurt will eventually heal."

29

Subject: From Dad
Date: Sun, 1 June 1997 22:41:23 -0400 (EDT)
From: Dad <Summer2@ncal.tech>
To: June <jcarver@sof.cit>

Dear June,

I am fine and Adelaide is too. I was concerned that you had
been sick. I hope you are okay now. You probably need to
gain some weight so that you will be strong and can go for a
few days without eating. Lately I have been forgetting where
I parked the Nomad, so I got a battery powered key chain
which has a light and a place to record messages so that you
can tell it where you parked. I don't like to do that to a
classic car, but I am getting older.

Last weekend Adelaide and I went to Palm Springs and spent
the weekend with Lilly and a Mexican she is seeing. I don't
think it is serious. We did a little shopping and saw a
movie, In and Out, which was a comedy about homosexuals. It
had gotten good reviews but I didn't think it was that
great. The Horse Whisperer is coming out. It is directed by
Robert Redford. Well, that's it from the movie critic. I
haven't heard much about the political stuff in Bulgaria.
Are things getting any better under the new Prime Minister?
You know June, I once told you that marriage is a contract
and you should not break it. I don't know what is going on
over there, but I want to tell you that I think it would not
be the end of the world if you were having some problems and
needed out. Your sister and I had a talk. I hope this is
clear. I may not say it often, but you know how I feel about
you. I am your father.

Best,

Dad

*N*EVENA WAS STRETCHED out on the couch with a book in her hand but she wasn't reading. Instead, the book rested on her chest, and her eyes were focused on the ceiling. Flies were buzzing around and the smell of meat frying was heavy in the air from a nearby apartment. Nevena was picturing Boryana in New York, walking through Times Square, taking the elevator up to the top of the Empire State Building, meeting interesting people, and drinking coffee with friends. Nevena could also see Boryana wandering the city looking for work, filling out applications, and being turned away from diners and shops. Her money would not last long. New York was expensive, and Boryana had no skills. Even her English was pretty bad.

Nevena was just getting up to make some tea when the doorbell rang. At last. She crossed the room and began to unlock the dead bolt while saying, "Georgi? Is it you?"

Suddenly the doorknob twisted in her hand, and the door burst inward with a thrust. The chain snapped and broke, and Nevena was pushed so hard backward that she nearly fell. Damyan stepped inside, drew his gun, and the first words out of his mouth were, "Don't yell or you're dead."

Nevena stood in the middle of her room in a long T-shirt. Her hair was in a knot on her head and knitted slipper socks covered her skinny calves.

Damyan thought for a second that he had found the girl who had stolen the money. Milena, one of Assen's girls whom he had interrogated, had said she'd seen the skinny stripper in the red hot pants with a wad of cash in her hand—the one Damyan had especially liked. What luck. The girl was staying at her sister's and here she was, right in front of his eyes. Then he took another look and realized that this one was a little older and not quite so pretty. Less makeup and less attitude. "Are you Nevena Petkova?" he asked, one eye lazily rolling downward.

"Yes," answered Nevena.

"You have a sister named Boryana?"

"Yes."

"When and where did you see her last?"

Before Boryana had left, Nevena had gone over with her several times all the signs that would give her away as a liar to passport control. Now Nevena was being careful to stand very still, not cross her arms defensively, and to look the man in the eye. "I heard she was working as an exotic dancer. I went to see her at this awful club, to tell her how angry I was. We got in a fight and I haven't heard from her since. That was more than a month ago."

"She hasn't contacted you since then?"

"No. What has happened to her?"

"Shut up. Give me the names of all your relatives."

Nevena shifted her weight and took a step backward. "Our parents died when we were girls. We were the only children."

"Friends then."

Nevena took a second to think. She didn't want to give him any names that he didn't already have. "She had a boyfriend who worked at the club. And one of the dancers. A girl named Svetlana. Her friends were people from the club. I don't know anyone else."

"Maika ti," said Damyan. "That's too bad for you. Your sister is a thief and she's in a lot of trouble. She stole a lot of money, and I'm holding you responsible for her debt. Do you understand me?"

"Boryana has always been trouble. I don't want anything to do with her."

"Too bad." He grabbed Nevena's chin and jerked her face upward. "You start looking for your sister. I'm giving you until tomorrow to find her. If you don't, then you're going to pay off her debt or take her punishment. And don't try to pull the same disappearing act. I gave the police your name, and no matter where you go, they'll bring you to me."

"If I find her, will you promise not to hurt me? If I can tell you where she's at, will you promise to leave me alone forever? I don't want any of her trouble."

Damyan smiled. This girl was going to make it easy. "You're a smart girl. Yes. If you can tell me where she's hiding, you're off the hook. I'll never pay you a visit again. You have my guarantee."

"Thank you," Nevena whispered, looking respectfully downward. "Sir."

She certainly was a nice girl. And prettier than he had first thought. A tear slid down her cheek, and Damyan couldn't help but reach out and catch it on his finger. He decided he would pay her a visit one way or another.

GEORGI FINALLY SHOWED up an hour later. He and Nevena locked all the doors, turned off all the lights, and sat close to each other on the couch, whispering questions back and forth. How long would it take the man to find out Nevena had lied and that Boryana also had a brother? Not long. What would they do to them when they couldn't find Boryana? Anything they wanted.

What should their next step be? None of the answers was easy. Wait to see how serious the mutras were, and wind up dead? Hide in a small town somewhere, terrified that the local police would pick them up and take them in? Ask for help, and hope that whoever they asked wasn't on the mutra payroll?

It was almost morning when Nevena and Georgi narrowed it down to a single solution. They had been through this thought process before, when Boryana was the only one in trouble, and now the answer was no different. They would not be safe as long as they could be found. The only thing to do was to leave the country. The only reason this was now a feasible solution was because, for the first time in their entire lives, they had enough money to make it happen.

"BUT GEORGI," NEVENA SAID, suddenly covering her mouth with her hand. "Oh my God. I gave Boryana my passport."

"Damn her," Georgi said, standing up. "How could she do this to us?"

"Come on, Georgi. She gave us more money than we ever dreamed of having."

"All right. Then this is what we do. I will explain everything to Stan. He can get me a visa to travel to Turkey on Center of Democracy business with him, and he has a car. He will drive us to Istanbul, and when we cross the border you will get in the trunk. The Turks barely ever give trouble to Americans."

"Georgi! In the trunk?"

"You come up with something better! You haven't got a passport! You're supposed to be in America! They have a record of you leaving the country!"

Nevena put her head in her hands. The sun was coming up and the sky was starting to pale. "Do you think Stan will do it?"

Georgi put his hands on his hips. "If he doesn't, he will be the one who must tell Ethan what has happened to you when he returns. That's what I will say."

☾

HOW MANY TIMES IN his life had he packed up his things to leave? Too many to count. Ethan never planned ahead for it, so he always did it in a hurry. The rush was part of the ritual. If he gave himself too much time, he knew he would linger over his belongings, and manufacture decisions and

choices when there really were none. Ethan didn't want to have time to look
through his piles of photos and wonder which ones to bring. He didn't want
to discover shoe boxes full of old love letters, or reminisce about the hikes
he'd taken in a certain weathered pair of boots. He'd had enough of that type
of thing. As a boy, he had been through way too many drawn-out good-byes.

Ethan was in his room at his parents' house, and it hadn't changed much
in the last ten years. Nothing in the room seemed real. The model airplanes
and the *Sports Illustrated* calendar seemed as if they had belonged to someone else, not to Dr. Ethan Carver. Now he collected war medals, rare coins,
and his calendar was a collection of paintings by Gauguin.

His stereo still sat in the corner, and on top of it, neatly stacked, were
tons of cassette tapes of old bands he had liked in the eighties. Lining the
shelves were mainly college textbooks he'd never bothered to sell back. A set
of keys on a blue-and-gold Bruin key chain gathered dust next to an old prescription bottle. He thought the prescription might have been tetracycline
for his acne, but as for the keys, he had no idea what locks they would fit. He
would never know again.

His arthritic dog was barking in the backyard, and he could hear his parents putting dishes away in the kitchen downstairs. He felt like he was back
in college, leaving to drive down to L.A. to his dorm after a weekend at home.
Everything contributed to the time warp. There was even a photo of June
tacked to the corkboard.

It had always been his favorite photo. She was crewing on a student film,
and was dressed in jeans and a white T-shirt with the sleeves rolled up. The
shoot was at Vasquez Rocks, and June was seated on a boulder next to a pile
of props. She had a notebook on her lap, a pencil tucked behind her ear, and
a clove cigarette smoldering between her fingers. Ethan smiled. The clove
phase had passed and been replaced by some trendy Indian brand, which finally gave way to old-fashioned Marlboro Lights. She'd quit completely a
few years back, and her kisses had stopped tasting of spices and smoke. He
reached out a hand and was about to touch the photo—

"Honey!" yelled his mother.

Ethan jumped. "What?"

"Do you want to stop by Sal's for churros and chocolate on the way to
the airport?"

"I'm coming! Be right down."

"All right! Your father is going to pull out the car!"

Ethan took one last look around his room, knowing he was forgetting something. It didn't matter. He had learned that he didn't miss the things he left behind. He flipped off the light. Afternoon shadows settled over his high school debate trophy, crumpled shopping lists for long-forgotten barbecues, address books filled with unknown names, and flyers for parties that had ended years ago. He closed the door, sending in a gust that raised the dust on the shelves. The photo of June fluttered and grew still. The desert sunrise behind her was muted by a thin layer of dirt. In Ethan's old room, June smiled at shadows and memories. Downstairs the phone rang, but the Carvers were already gone.

30

Subject: Important message for Ethan
Date: Tue, 17 June 1997 12:33:29 -0400 (EDT)
From: Georgi Petkov <CDSCC@sof.cit>
To: Ethan <M&Dcarver@tech.com>

Hello to Mr. and Mrs. Carver, can you please to give this
message to Ethan? I am sorry to write you at home, but it is
more easy for me to write than leave message on the message
machine when no one answer. Ethan, imam gulyam problem i
vednaga triabva da napusna stranata. Stan shte mi pomogne.
Shte te chakam v Turtsia, v nashiat hotel po predvaritelnia
plan. Lipsvash mi mnogo. Obicham te. N*

Subject: RE: Important message for Ethan
Date: Thur, 19 June 1997 12:33:29 -0400 (EDT)
From: Ellen <M&Dcarver@tech.com>
To: Georgi Petkov <CDSCC@sof.cit>

Mr. Petkov—We received a message from you here for our son,
Ethan. He has no permanent address or email for the next
few months until he relocates to Istanbul. If it is an
emergency you might try to contact his wife June there in
Sofia at 980-0140.

Best, Ellen Carver

*Translation: Ethan, I have a huge problem and I have to leave the country
immediately. Stan is helping me. I will wait for you at our hotel according
to our plan. I miss you so much. I love you. N

GEORGI, I DON'T THINK this is a good idea." Stan wiped his hand over the top of his nearly bald head and smoothed the few sweaty hairs above his ears.

Nevena walked out of Stan's apartment building. "Still no answer at Ethan's parents'."

"I'm telling you two," said Stan, "I just don't know about this."

"I don't either," she said, crossing her arms. "But what can we do? Stay?"

"Crap, crap, crap," Stan said, watching as Georgi loaded luggage into the trunk of his beloved Opel. "No, you shouldn't stay. Crap, I don't know."

Nevena stood quietly beside Stan, and together they watched as Georgi arranged the bags in the trunk. He had put a blanket underneath them. When they got close to the border, Nevena would get under the blanket and the bags would go back on top. Quietly she said, "Stan, I don't want to make you do something against your will."

Stan turned to her. His wire-rim glasses were sliding down his nose on a path of perspiration. "I am a lawyer, Nevena. My life is the law."

"Georgi," she said. "Take the bags out of the car. This has gone far enough."

Georgi slammed the trunk shut and turned to look at them. "It could go a lot further. When they find us. Stan, what would you have us do?"

"Don't be that way, Georgi. If he doesn't feel right, we can't make him help us."

Stan swallowed and cracked his neck, first to the right, then to the left.

Georgi sighed and opened the trunk again. "Okay."

"Wait, wait," said Stan. "Don't take them out yet. Just let me think for a second."

"Stan." Georgi put his hand on his boss's shoulder. "I told you. If they find Nevena, I say that I packed the trunk for you, and you had no idea she was there. I take all the blame."

Stan nodded, his chin bobbing up and down like a bird's.

"But no one's going to find her. How many times have you driven to Istanbul?"

"Eight," said Stan. "No, six. Six because I flew to the last two tennis tournaments."

"And how many times have they asked you to open your trunk?"

"Never."

"So," continued Georgi, "why would they check this time?"

"Because this is the time that I have an illegal alien whose sister is wanted wrapped up in a blanket suffocating to death in my car trunk."

"She is not going to suffocate."

Nevena had listened enough. "That's it. I'm dead tired and I—"

She stopped talking and watched as a sleek, long, black Mercedes turned down the street. Immediately Georgi and Stan looked up in that direction. "Jesus," whispered Georgi, stepping onto the curb. The car rolled down the street toward them, and Stan reached out a hand to steady himself against the wall of the building. The car, with its tinted windows and shiny chrome accents, glided past them without a noise. The black tail turned the corner and was gone.

Nevena cleared her throat. "I guess we're all a little nervous."

Georgi looked like he was about to collapse. He was nearing the frantic edge of hysteria. "That could have been them. That might as well have been them. If it had been them at least it would be over and there would be no more of this waiting for them to find us. No more waiting for them to do to Nevena whatever it is they planned to do to Boryana."

Stan reached out and took the keys from Georgi. "Crap," he said. "Let's just go before I start acting like a lawyer again."

THEY MADE GOOD time to Plovdiv, where the road narrowed and wound through increasingly barren farmland. They passed donkey cart after donkey cart, and a caravan of Gypsies waved at them as the Opel whizzed past their painted wagons with plastic tarp roofs. Two hours later, they reached the last Bulgarian roadside stop outside Svilengrad. Lining the narrow highway were stands selling fruit, liquor, cheese, and ice cream. Cars were pulled off to the side, and people milled around the grills where kiofte cooked in clouds of smoke.

They turned off the main road onto a dirt trail that seemed to lead nowhere. A goat shepherd was grazing his small herd in the field, while he rested under a tree. He watched, expressionless, as the expensive car stopped in the middle of the field and a girl climbed out of the backseat. Two men helped her into the trunk, covered her with suitcases, and then carefully closed the hatch. After a few seconds the car spun its wheels in the dirt, bounced over a few rocks, and then turned around to head back out to the highway. The shepherd waved some flies away from his face, took a swig of rakia, and began to snooze.

Stan and Georgi rode in silence toward the border. Stan looked out the window at the guard towers, painted black for night camouflage, sectioned off from the road by barbed wire. "Back before the Change, they shot people from those towers, huh?"

"Yes," answered Georgi.

"People trying to escape, huh?"

"Please. Let's not talk about this."

From a distance, the first stage of the crossing looked like a tollbooth. Stan blasted the air-conditioning for a second as they slowly approached, trying to cool down his face and stop the steady trickle of sweat from the top of his bald head. As they pulled up to the first window, Georgi whispered, "Turn off the air."

The Bulgarian guard stepped forward. "Do you speak Bulgarian?"

"I do," said Georgi. "But he doesn't."

The guard shook his head and asked for passports. He glanced at Stan's, but spent a long time looking at Georgi's. He inspected the visa, leaned down for a better look at Georgi, and then began inspecting the visa again. "Where are you headed?"

"Istanbul," Stan answered, too eagerly.

"I'm talking to him," said the guard.

"To Istanbul," Georgi replied. "On business with my boss."

"Not for pleasure?" asked the guard.

Georgi glanced at Stan, and then leaned forward to address the guard. He gave him a conspiratorial smile and spoke in rapid Bulgarian that only a native could understand. "How pleasurable could it be with this idiot for a boss?"

The guard chuckled, stamped the passports, and handed them back. "Pull forward."

At the next booth, Stan was asked to present the papers for his car. Two men passed the documents back and forth, mumbling and pointing. "Green card?" they finally asked.

Stan looked confused for a second, and then said, "Oh yes. For the car, yes." He handed them an additional document that proved he had the right to take the car out of the country. They looked it over, handed it back, and waved the car on with a disinterested air.

"Okay," said Georgi. "Customs number one."

Stan pulled slowly forward, and a man stepped out of a kiosk to wave him down with a red stick. "Crap, crap, crap."

Stan pulled the car over to the Bulgarian customs officer. He leaned in the window and there were bits of bread stuck in his mustache. They had caught him snacking. "Americans?"

"He is," answered Georgi. "I am Bulgarian."

"Where are you headed?"

"Istanbul," answered Georgi. "On business."

"What are you taking with you?"

"Clothes. Documents. Personal items."

"Okay. You're cleared."

ON THE SHORT drive across no-man's-land, Stan mopped his brow and put the air-conditioning on high again. "One down, one to go," said Georgi.

"Don't talk," said Stan. "Not yet."

A dip in the road was filled with chemicals, and they pulled the car through slowly, disinfecting the tires. At the other end, they again showed the papers for the car, and then pulled forward to the Turkish entry passport control. Stan had to park the car and walk to the cashier to purchase his visa to enter the country. Georgi's, the more complicated visa, had been acquired at the Turkish embassy that morning. After returning to the car, they drove forward, presented their passports, and were stamped without problems. "Now," said the Turkish guard to Georgi, "pull forward to customs. Park, open your doors and trunk, and stand next to your car."

"What did he say?" asked Stan.

Georgi looked pale. "Park right up there."

"But what did he say?"

"Park up there. We are going to get out of the car and open the doors and the trunk."

"Fuck!"

"Just do it. Do it and don't look at me like that. They are watching us."

Stan put the car in gear and lurched forward, staring ahead with a dazed, vacant expression. He parked and handed the keys to Georgi. He didn't trust himself to get the trunk open. He didn't trust himself to stand without buckling.

Georgi took the keys, got briskly out of the car, and opened up the trunk. While the Turkish customs officer strode toward them, Georgi whispered downward, "Be still."

At first Nevena welcomed the rush of light and air. She thought that they were across the border and was about to squirm when she heard her brother's warning. At the sound of his voice she froze, and it seemed that the pounding of her heart was wild enough to rock the car.

Stan finally managed to get out of the car and opened up both the back doors. He leaned against the hood and kept his hands in his pockets so no one could see them shaking.

"Passports!" demanded the Turkish officer.

Georgi had both of them and handed them over again. The Turkish officer lingered over Georgi's. "Petrol?" he asked, pointing to the open trunk.

"No," answered Georgi. "No petrol."

The officer bent down and sniffed the trunk. He placed his nose so close to the blanket that he could smell Nevena's shampoo. He took a deep breath, glanced over at Georgi, and said, "Okay. Close it." Then he poked his head in the front, took another whiff, and motioned that they could move on.

"My God," said Stan, when he was back in the driver's seat. "What was that about?"

"They don't want us smuggling in cheap Bulgarian fuel," answered Georgi. "They were sniffing for gas. We're free."

THEY ATE TOGETHER that night at a Kumkapi fish house in Istanbul. Tiny lights were strung over their heads, threading through vines. Littered across the table were half-eaten plates of fried calamari, mussels, octopus, grilled sea bass, and assorted stuffed vegetables and rice. A strolling band played at the side of their table, and Stan and Georgi were drunk on Turkish raki and water.

"Why are you so quiet, Nevena?" asked Stan, who had been boisterously humming along to the music, though too drunk to follow the tune.

She was thinking what a perfect night it would be if Ethan were with them. In a short time he would be, and together they could come back for romantic music, raki, and dinner under the heavenly lights. "I am thinking of Ethan."

"Yes," Stan said when the strolling musicians eventually moved on to another table. "Just in case, let me be sure I know the hotel where Ethan is supposed to meet you."

"Well, I will meet him at the Four Seasons, but before then, I will be at the Hotel Sede," Nevena answered, leaning forward. "It is less expensive, just south of the Blue Mosque, by the Four Seasons. Just tell him to follow the plan, and I'll meet him at our room the day he arrives."

"But you'll also call him yourself, right?"

"He has already left the States. I'll have to call you to find out where he is in Sofia, now that he can't stay at my apartment."

"He'll stay with me."

"So I'll call you. Or you can have him call me at the Hotel Sede."

Stan smiled and slipped the napkin in his pocket. "That's it then. Everything's taken care of." He raised his glass of raki and clinked it first against Georgi's, then against Nevena's. "Cheers. Here's to having your problems behind you."

31

Subject: Coming to be with James
Date: Thur, 19 June 1997 12:33:29 -0400 (EDT)
From: June <jcarver@sof.cit>
To: Audra McKinnon <audram16@nettx.com>

Hi Audra—

I bought my ticket and will be arriving in Austin just after
the holiday. I'm not surprised at all that James is being
such a good sport about everything—your brother is truly an
amazing person. Before he left he told me the whole thing
was a blessing in disguise because now his performance in
Cat on a Hot Tin Roof would have inarguable authenticity.

I'm looking forward to seeing you, Audra—it's been four
years—since Lilly's thirtieth birthday when you and I got
locked in the walk-in freezer at that rock-n-roll sushi
place in North Hollywood!

Thanks for passing along Shelly's invitation to Production
Manage their new project. So, they're shooting in Prague?
Should be fun! I can't do it, though. At the moment I am
collaborating with a Bulgarian filmmaker on a documentary
about the corruption here, and the uprising against it that
occurred last winter. The George Soros Foundation is giving
us a nice grant to complete the project. I'm very excited
about it—otherwise I wouldn't dream of passing up the great
offer. If you talk to Shelly again soon, please tell her I
said hello, good luck with CRASH and yes, I will keep my
fingers crossed that they get Brad Pitt for the lead. Thanks
again for looking out for me.

Please kiss and hug James for me, and tell him that I'm
proud of him and will be there soon.

Love to all,

June

As THE SUN ROSE over Nevena's hotel in Istanbul, it was just starting to lighten the eastern edge of the sky in Sofia. Ethan bounded up the steps to her apartment, pulled his keys out, and bent down by the door to open it. They didn't work. He rang the bell several times, with no answer. Then he knocked loudly and heard someone stir inside. "Who is it?" It was the voice of an old, tired woman.

Ethan looked around suddenly, to make sure he was on the right landing. After a second he leaned close to the door. "Nevena?" he called, perplexed. It was possible she had company. Maybe Baba Safi from Vodenicharsko.

"Nyama ya! She doesn't live here anymore!"

Ethan's hand slapped the door and he couldn't help but shout. "Molya?"

"Go away! Do you know what time it is?"

He pounded on the door. "I'm not going away. I know Nevena lives here!"

The door opened a crack, and a woman with wild purplish-gray hair peeked out. Underneath her eyes were red welts. She looked like she hadn't slept in years. "She does not. I am the landlady."

"What happened?"

"I moved in until I find a new tenant."

"I mean what happened to Nevena?"

"She moved out. That is all I know."

"Where did she go? What did she say? I'm her fiancé."

"She moved out. I told you, that's all I know. Dovishdane." With that, the old woman shut the door. Ethan could hear her shuffling away in her house slippers and settling heavily down onto the creaking springs of the foldout couch.

Ethan stared at the floor. Where was she? Too tired to deal with searching for a vacant room in a pension, Ethan flagged a cab and directed it toward Darvenitsa. June wasn't scheduled to return from Greece for another few days, and he still had his key. It had been a shock to find Nevena's apartment vacated, but there had to be an explanation. In Darvenitsa at least, he was sure, there would be no surprises.

Ethan's keys still worked in the lock to the Darvenitsa apartment. By the time he pushed the door open and stumbled across the threshold, he was already half asleep. He set his bags down in the hallway, pulled the door shut behind him, and shuffled toward the studio. He turned the corner into the room and was knocked sideways by a blow to his head. Everything went black, and he crumpled to the floor.

June knelt down at his side. In her left hand, she still held the frying pan that she had whacked down on his head. Her right hand was wrapped in a white bandage. "Ethan! I'm sorry. I thought you were one of Chavdar's thugs. Ethan?"

He looked groggily from one side to the other. Slowly June came into focus, wearing a pajama tank top, an old pair of his boxer shorts, and faded house slippers. She was peering at his face, stroking his cheek, and her mouth was moving. "Ethan? Ethan?"

"Whaaat?" he asked, finally sitting up. "What happened?" For a second he thought that he was in college and had had too much to drink. There had been many mornings when he had awoken to June's swimming face and worried caresses.

"I hit you over the head. I had this pan beside me in case Chavdar sent someone over to look for me. Here. Sit up. Let me help you onto the couch."

Ethan blinked and his sight cleared. He touched his head and felt a sore spot. It was already starting to swell. June grabbed his hand and he let her haul him to his feet.

"Right here," she said, patting the couch. "Park it. I'll make you a cup of coffee."

"No coffee," he said, rubbing his head. "I just want to go to sleep."

"Are you sure?" June asked, bending over and touching the bump. "It's not supposed to be good for people with head injuries to go to sleep. You could slip into a coma or something."

Ethan smacked her hand away. "I am not going into a coma. Leave me alone."

"Fine," June said, backing up. "Sorry for being concerned."

"Why aren't you in Greece, anyway?"

"There was a problem—an accident—and I came back earlier than I thought."

"Are you okay?"

"Yes. Thanks for asking."

"Look. It's just been a bad morning."

June sat down beside him. She bit her lip, and then tentatively touched his arm. "You found out about Nevena?"

"What?" he asked, his chin jerking up. "What about Nevena?"

"Oh," she said, taking her hand back. "I'm sorry. I shouldn't be the one to tell you."

☙

STAN WAS ENJOYING HIS drive back to Bulgaria. The border was a breeze, and now that he was alone, he slipped in a country-western tape and cranked it up. Shania Twain was belting out the story of her brave boyfriend and a barroom brawl, and Stan was singing along. He was feeling frisky because he had done a good deed. Stan, the macho wanna-be who had always been the law student in spectacles, had taken a big risk and come out on top. The law abider had challenged authority. Stan the man, Stan the savior. Stan, a one-man underground railroad for fugitives from the Bulgarian Mafia. It sounded great. Great enough to be the subject of a country-western song.

He relished the thought of relating his heroics to Ethan. "I saved your girlfriend, buddy. You weren't here, so I had to take charge. Nevena, I said, I have a solution. It may be dangerous, but it's the only way. She and Georgi didn't want to go along with it, but I knew it was their only hope. I just had to convince them to take the chance."

Stan was hollering to the music and had moved on to imagining how he would embellish the story for his law-school friends at home. The rebel savior! What a selfless act of courage! Ah, it was nothing. He was so engrossed in his knight-in-shining-armor daydream and in the raspy voice of a country-western woman that he didn't notice the car coming toward him, flashing its brights. With his foot on the gas, he topped the next hill and was exhilarated to feel the wheels lift slightly off the ground. Stan the race-car man.

He plowed over the hill and there in front of him was a KAT station and a police barricade. The wheel slipped in his hand as he fumbled for the stick. His foot came down on the brake but he was too late. When he skidded to a slow just before the orange cones, the smell of burning rubber was everywhere. He didn't even need to look up at the officer to know that he was busted. It was okay, it was no problem. He'd had plenty of speeding tickets before, and his wallet was full of cash. His biggest worries had been safely deposited in Istanbul. In comparison, this was a minor inconvenience.

The barricade was set up thirty kilometers out of downtown Plovdiv on the highway to Sofia. Stan had been flagged down about ten minutes north of the sugar factory, Stoyan's old neighborhood. The Mafia witch-hunts had started in Sofia and had not yet made a dent in the armor of the security firms in Plovdiv. Not much had changed in the sugar factory—except that now they were angrier than ever.

A heavyset officer with a bulging stomach motioned for Stan to step out of the car. He shouted something, pointed inside the car, and held out his hand.

Stan's Bulgarian was pathetic. "Ne razbiram," he said. "I don't understand."

The officer narrowed his eyes and barked again. He pointed at the car's dashboard for the second time and waved his hand menacingly in the air.

The one-man underground railroad was no longer feeling so high and mighty. "Please speak more slowly. I don't speak Bulgarian very well." Then he paused, and reached for his wallet. This was how these run-ins were usually solved. "What is the fine?"

The officer stared at Stan's fingers dipping invitingly into the wallet. He looked back up at Stan's hopeful, expectant face. "Come with me."

The officer grabbed Stan by the arm and began marching him toward the KAT station. His shirttail came untucked, revealing his chubby stomach. "What is the fine?" Stan pleaded over his shoulder. "Just tell me the fine!"

Stan was pushed into a small office. The whole room was painted a sickening shade of phlegm. Another officer was seated beside a manual typewriter, and on the desk behind him were several unopened bottles of rakia and a few cartons of cigarettes. These signs of bribes gave Stan hope, and he clutched his wallet tighter.

The officer with his fingers squeezed around Stan's upper arm said something to the other officer. The colleague acknowledged them with a wave of his hand, but continued to type. Stan was shoved down in a folding chair, to wait while listening to the click click of typewriter keys.

Finally the second officer finished with his document and turned to face them. "Da?"

The heavyset man let go of Stan's arm. "We need a translator."

The second officer was dressed differently from his colleague. He wore a rumpled suit and a cap at a rackish angle. "What do you speak, sir? German? English?"

"English."

"Are you a tourist?"

"A terrorist! No, for Christ's sake! Do I look like a terrorist?"

"A *tourist*, sir. Relax."

"No, I am not a *tourist*. I work in Sofia."

"Really?" The officer said something quickly to his partner and then turned back to Stan. "May I have your passport please, sir?"

He handed it over and the officer perused it at length. "What is your work, sir?"

Stan sat up straighter in his chair. "I am an attorney."

"But not a diplomat?"

"Almost a diplomat. Practically a diplomat."

"Almost. That means almost nothing, doesn't it?" The officer smiled, took out a pen, and began to doodle. "And what kind of work are you doing in Bulgaria?"

"Updating legislature. For CEELI, the Central and Eastern European Law Initiative."

"Ah. Rewriting our laws. I see." He spoke again to the other officer, who now left the room. When he and Stan were alone, the second officer took off his cap. Underneath, his hair was plastered to his head. He ran a hand over it and leaned back in his battered office chair. "Please excuse me for my inquiries. Sometimes we have to wonder what an American attorney is doing in Bulgaria. When there is so much money to be made practicing law in your own country."

"As I said, I work with CEELI. Specifically, I'm with a program that works in coordination with the University of Des Moines. That's Iowa."

"Uh-huh. And what is the American interest in rewriting Bulgarian laws? Sir?"

Stan was getting perturbed. "To help the Bulgarians. Sir. What is going on here? May I pay my fine and be on my way? This is ridiculous. I don't even know why you're questioning me like this. Did you ever tell me what I'm being charged with?"

"Not yet. In fact, I don't have to, in order to hold you."

"No, no, of course not. If you did, that would imply some sort of logic. Some sort of reasoning or infrastructure. Things that don't exist in this absurd backwards-ass country!"

"You were driving very fast. Recklessly fast."

"And I am sure you know exactly what the fine is for reckless driving. If you will tell me, I'll pay and we can both get on with it."

"Get on with it? Sir, a law has been broken. As an attorney, surely you realize that we are completely within our rights to question you. You might have been drunk or drugged."

"Yes, yes. Now I know how this goes. I've been through it before." Stan put his wallet on the table. "If you'd be kind enough to tell me the fine? I have a lot of work to do."

"More legislature to update?"

"Yes, exactly."

"You do know about the new law that says we have the right to pull over luxury cars and ask the owners to show us proof that they paid income tax on such possessions?"

"Oh, for Christ's sake!"

"It's a very new law. Perhaps you even helped write it yourself? Operation . . ." He made a buzzing noise. "How do you call that annoying blood-sucking insect?"

"Mosquito. It's called Operation Mosquito. But now listen here—"

"No, you listen to me." The officer flipped open Stan's passport and glanced inside. "Mr. Nordford. You can't expect to help pass new laws in a country where you reside and not expect them to apply to you. Do you have proof in your glove compartment that you paid income tax on the money you used to purchase your car?"

Stan let out an enormous breath and set his hands on his knees. "No. No I don't."

"And if we check under the hood to look at the serial number, what will we find? Anything out of order?"

Stan put his wallet back in his pants. "Crap," he said. "Crap, crap, crap."

CLOTHES WERE THROWN EVERYWHERE, both lamps were knocked over, and there was the indentation of a boot in the wall. June sat among the remains of the rampage, quietly looking out the window of the apartment.

"You!" Ethan had screamed, pointing his finger at her. He had crossed from one end of the apartment to the other, destroying everything. With a sweeping motion, he had sent all of her makeup flying from the dresser. Bottles of liquid hit the wall and trickled down slowly like seeping wounds. He pushed over the table in the kitchen and sent her printer clattering to the floor. With both hands he ripped down a painting she had brought back from Greece and smashed it over a chair. Then he kicked the same chair and sent it crashing into the window by the balcony.

Then he had returned to the living room, where June sat in the corner, her knees tucked up to her chest. She didn't yell back or throw objects at his face. "You did it!" he shouted, tears streaming down his blotchy face. "You couldn't stand for me to be happy!"

"You're wrong."

"How could you? How could you?" Ethan looked up at the ceiling and made a choking noise. Then he whirled around and kicked the wall, breaking the plaster.

"I didn't."

"Don't lie to me! You turned her against me! You bought her!"

"No I didn't. Roxanne is some kind of drama queen always causing trouble and the whole thing was her doing. I had nothing to do with it. I didn't know until after she was gone."

"You're sick, you know that?"

June stared up at him from the floor. "Ethan, I am sorry Roxanne did what she did, but I had nothing to do with it. You can't be mad at me for Nevena's actions."

When June said this, Ethan lost it completely. "*Her* actions? I could kill you!" He pulled down the bookcase. "Don't talk about her like that. Don't talk about her at all!"

She wished she could hold him, but that would never happen again. Nothing she could say would affect the way he felt about her. Silence was the only thing that would help. She would do as Ethan had ordered and not talk about Nevena. She would not talk at all.

Finally, Ethan's rage seemed to die. He blinked, rubbed his face, and looked around at the ruined room as if he had suddenly awoken from a long sleep. He staggered to the door. Without another word he walked out into the hall. June could hear each of his heavy steps on the stairs. It was taking him forever to go down. He had left the door standing open, but a gust through the broken window slammed it shut. Then June could no longer hear his descent.

Finally, it was over. Somehow she knew she would never see him again. June had lost everything and she was free. Free! There was something liberating about having nothing and no one. A few weeks before, she had promised herself not to be a weepy girl. Instead, to be a drunk girl, a sarcastic girl, a rambling girl. Dangerous or just in danger. It was time to make good on that promise.

June had written to everyone in her family, held James's hand until the very final second when they wheeled him onto the airplane, and had laid eyes on her husband for the last time. Now, this was the best thing she could do for James, and for Raina, and for herself. If something went wrong, she was ready to deal with the consequences. June picked up the phone and called the secret, unofficial office used by Kyril and his colleagues. "Alo?" she said. "Kyril, molya? Kyril, it's June. I am ready. I will call you again when I'm finished."

☙

STAN WAS IN TROUBLE. Deep shit, as he tried to explain to his boss when the Plovdiv police finally allowed him to make a phone call from their decrepit office rotary phone. "Bill!" he yelled into the old-fashioned receiver. He could hear static, high-pitched beeps, and the faint murmur of someone else's conversation. "Bill! Can you hear me?"

"Stan? That you?"

"It's me, Bill! I'm in deep shit. I'm in Plovdiv—"

"Stan? That you?"

"Yeah! Yeah, Bill, it's me. I got pulled over by the police and it turns out there is a problem with the papers for my car. See, it belonged to a diplomat in Romania, but it was stolen and ended up in Bulgaria, and that's why the serial number is gone. I swear I thought—"

"Stan, we've got a bad connection here. We have crossed lines. Call me right back."

"No! No! Don't hang up! Bill? Bill?" The line went dead.

Stan dejectedly handed the phone back to the desk sergeant. "I know one of you has a cell phone I could use," he said, using hand gestures to try to get his point across. "Cell phone? Come on, I'll pay for it! Pay? I'll pay extra for it. Come on!"

"Later." The desk sergeant pressed a button on his intercom, and another officer arrived to escort Stan back to the cell he was sharing with a glue-sniffing petty thief.

Stan's head drooped as they walked. The English-speaking officer passed by them and stopped to tap Stan on the arm. "You were given your phone call, correct?"

"The phone didn't work!" Stan's face was red. He hated the whining sound of his voice, but he couldn't help it. He wanted to wave his fist, shouting, "No fair! No fair!"

"I'm very sorry about that. It is always difficult to put up with such inconveniences. Perhaps tomorrow you will have better luck."

"I can't wait until tomorrow!"

"Be patient, Mr. Nordford. You realize that in this country, these things take time."

"Are you trying to tell me that tomorrow that antique rotary piece of crap phone in there is going to work better than it did just now?"

"The connections are unpredictable. It worked well an hour ago when I used it to speak with my colleague in Sofia about you. According to him, your blue passport was revoked and you haven't registered with the police in six months. He also says that you have a large home in Simeonovo. You know, luxury homes are the target of the second round of Operation Mosquito."

Stan gritted his teeth and couldn't help but strain against his cuffs. "This is harassment. This is police harassment."

"Unfortunately, I don't think anyone has gotten around to updating legislature in that department. Have they, Mr. Nordford?"

CHAVDAR SAT in his office, staring into space, inwardly dealing with the sudden awareness that he was suffering a meltdown. He tried to maintain control. He counted. Edno, dve, tri. Edno, dve, tri. Count and don't think.

Numbers were important. The number of leva you earned per year. The numbers in the accounting ledgers. The number of arrests, the number of seats in parliament, the number of employees who had given notice. The growing number of dead businessmen, the number of agencies that had lost licenses, the number corresponding to the amount of money lost during the confiscations. Edno, dve, tri. One, two, three. Hit it, roll camera. Chavdar laughed, and then caught himself. He cleared his throat and kept his composure.

While he leaned back in his chair and pondered the demise of the firm, he spat on his hand and rubbed it against his pant leg distractedly. Strange, he thought, how the days seemed to be running together. He began to count the last few days, the days he could remember.

The week had sped by, and soon it would be over. For Valezhkov it was over. In the firm's hierarchy, Valezhkov was equal in status to Chavdar. He ran the Levski office. Or, he *had* run the Levski office. The day before, Valezhkov's wife had discovered him floating facedown in their swimming pool. Accidental, Chavdar had heard. He wondered if the days had begun to run together for Valezhkov as well. Had he also begun to count his pens, count the number of times his mistress did not return his calls, count the growing number of legitimate police cars in the street?

The one thing that stood out from the pressing matter of counting and tallying was his new idea of starting over in Prague. Chavdar smiled as he thought of working on films in the Gothic city. Chavdar the head, Chavdar the Chief, would become Chavdar the movie producer; still the moneyman, but one with creative input and good ideas. Oh, the stories he could tell! He spat on his palm and began wiping it against the side of his pants again. After a second he picked up the phone and called his secretary. "Please go to the newsstand and bring me every movie magazine on the rack. All of them. But at least four. No less than four."

"Did you say movie magazines, Gospodin Kozhuharov?"

"Yes. And some popcorn from the corner. And one cola, and one candy bar." Cola and candy, the comforting things that he had shared with his father in pleasantly cool movie theaters long before everything had gone wrong.

"Right away, Gospodin Kozhuharov."

"And don't forget the bag of popcorn. A medium bag."

After a second, the secretary replied hesitantly, "Of course."

As he waited for his delivery of magazines and snacks, Chavdar put his feet up on the table. His cell phone rang, and he was pleased to have the opportunity to consider another number. He picked up the phone and looked at the screen. It was June's number in Darvenitsa. Chavdar suddenly felt sick to his stomach. He stared at the phone as it rang in his hand. He was too shocked to react. It continued to ring. Finally he pressed answer.

"Alo?"

"It's me."

"I know, I know. June, I didn't think I would ever hear from you again."

"I didn't think so either." Silence. After a long pause, June continued. "How are you? I was worried about you after what happened. You were clearly not yourself."

Chavdar sat up straight. "Yes! Exactly, I was not myself. June, I am so sorry. Can you ever ever forgive me?"

"Honestly, I'm not sure. I was terrified, and you hurt my friend."

"He was just a friend?"

"Yes. Someone from the past, someone from my childhood."

"I was crazy. You are right. We both were. But June, we only act so passionate, so insane, because of how we feel about each other."

"I think we should see each other. Just to talk things over."

"Of course! Let me take you to dinner tonight. I'll make reservations at—"

"I really need to see you now. I don't think I can wait until tonight. I have been so upset."

"Me too. Yes, now is perfect. Where should we meet?"

"You can come to my place if you want. But, Chavdar, please leave the bodyguards at home. This is just about you and me. They scare me and I am tired of being scared. I want us to be together like a normal couple. Can you come alone?"

"Yes. I'll come right now."

"Okay. I'll be waiting."

Chavdar hung up and his eyes darted back and forth. Her forgiveness was the only thing that could penetrate his madness and depression. He could be there in fifteen minutes. Fourteen or fifteen. He wouldn't bother even to call a driver. Time was wasting. Tick, tick, tick.

Chavdar pulled on his sports jacket. He slipped out without notifying Rossen and Sasho, and made a break for the elevator. Inside, he stood transfixed as the floors went by. Down, down, one after another. With each passing level, he wiped his hand against his pants.

He walked out into the sunshine and pulled his sunglasses down over his eyes. He turned the corner and saw his car. Something about it looked different. It took him a few seconds to remember what had happened that morning. Or was it yesterday morning?

He and Svetoslav, his new driver, had been flagged down by a police barricade on the way to the office. Svetoslav had rolled down the window. "What's the problem?"

The officer pointed to the IZTOK security sticker in the back window of the car. "Take that off. They're no good anymore."

"But," Svetoslav said, glancing into the backseat toward Chavdar. "But that's our insurance company. That's our proof of insurance."

"Those stickers are illegal now. Take it off or I'll have to detain you."

Chavdar had listened to all of this quietly in the backseat, his long legs crossed, his hands folded in his lap.

"I can't do that," Svetoslav said, looking first at the officer and then at Chavdar.

"Do as the officer says, Svetlio."

"Are you sure, Gospodin Kozhuharov?"

"Yes," he answered, looking absentmindedly out the window. "Actually, no. Never mind. I'll do it myself." He leaned back and picked at the edge of the sticker until it loosened. Then he peeled it off and held it up to the light.

"I'll take that," said the officer.

"By all means," Chavdar answered, handing it up to Svetoslav. "By all means take it away."

Now Chavdar could see the outline where the sticker had been. Not only had the sticker protected the car from theft, but it had protected the glass underneath from dirt and scratches. The spot where the insurance logo had been was clear, round, and see-through. It looked like a hole.

Chavdar pointed the key ring toward the car. He pressed down on the button twice to deactivate the alarm. One, two. He unlocked the front door, began to sit down, and suddenly there was a gun barrel pressed against the back of his head.

"Give me your gun and get in the car. Do it. You've got no one backing you up and I have nothing to lose by shooting you right here and now."

Chavdar handed over his gun and slid behind the wheel. The man unlocked the rear door and climbed in behind Chavdar, never moving the gun from its position at the back of his head. "Drive out of the city."

"Where are we going?"

"Take the road to Simeonovo and shut up."

"How did you know I would be alone?"

"None of your business, you mutra fucking assassin piece of shit."

"It was June."

"What?"

"She said to come alone."

"I don't know any June. Drive up the mountain. We've got some questions for you. Just be calm. Just questions."

"Of course," he said. "Of course it was her. A beautiful act. Pretending. Playing it out. I should have known." He smiled incredulously, with a kind of detached appreciation.

Chavdar was driving his own limo out of the city, with a man in a face mask holding a gun against the base of his neck. It felt appropriate, to not know where he was going. It was nowhere, anyway, after all. His knuckles were white where he gripped the stick, and he shifted into a higher gear. He was in a hurry to get to his destination, and he didn't even think to glance in the rearview mirror. He counted cars that passed him, heading the other way. Counting saved him. In front of him was the mountain, and as he drove out of the city he saw the sky was a giant, black, circular lens, collapsing and closing. Snapping, recording. So this was his exit, and in the end she had played a part in its direction. It was fitting. He would remember her for it forever, or for the next few hours, however long he lasted.

Chavdar was brave, even stoic—not a cowardly criminal, per her accusation. He turned to his kidnapper and said, "Nice day for it, really." June would love that line. If only she could be there to see the finale to her own drama.

WOMEN. BACK-STABBING, LYING, gold-digging, cheating women. Ethan was alone, as he now felt he was destined to be. The room at the Serdika Hotel was smelly. The walls were brown, the bedspread was brown, and the carpet was brown. The room suited his mood. Music thumped beneath him, coming from the Tequila Bar. Students from the university were down there, laughing and waiting for the band to start. They were flirting and falling in love. Assholes.

Ethan hadn't taken June's word for it. He was smarter than that, but as it turned out, he wasn't so smart after all. In fact, he was the world's biggest buffoon. A fool. A sucker. Roxanne confirmed it. The embassy confirmed it. Fuck, he had even bribed the bitch at the Air France office and she had confirmed it. Nevena Petkova had checked in and left Bulgaria on Air France flight 2122 to New York. Her apartment had been vacated, her brother was on a business trip with Stan, and Boryana was nowhere to be found.

The hotel had provided Ethan with a single dirty glass. He'd washed it out with brown water from the tap, and then began filling it over and over with rakia. No chaser. In the room there was no television or radio, so Ethan drank in silence, watching the erratic progress of the cockroaches across the carpet. Each time he topped off his glass, he toasted himself in the grimy mirror. "Here's to you, idiot!" Later, he pointed his finger at his reflection and winked. "Way to pick 'em, old boy!" Finally, when the room was spinning and he couldn't feel a thing, he stood and swayed. "This one . . . this one . . . Here's to true love."

Then he flopped backward onto the bed, covered his face, and groaned. How could he have been so stupid? The second time he'd met her she had been trying on Roxanne's clothes, reading *Cosmo* and *Glamour*, drinking pop, and watching MTV. She was just a kid. She had revealed her intentions a million times, and he'd ignored it all, choosing to believe that she wanted to be with him more than she wanted to be in America.

Suddenly he smacked his head with his hand. He remembered the conversation they'd had before he'd left. "When do you think I'll see the Pacific?" she had asked.

Instead of answering, "Maybe someday," he could have answered, "Soon." How would his life be different right now if he had told her what she wanted to hear?

"No," he said, sitting up. "Nope." He didn't want to think that way. There should be no thoughts about how he could have saved it, when it was something that shouldn't have been saved. Why should he want Nevena here with him right now if she had never cared for him? Why should he blame himself for losing her when he had never had her at all? Why should he ever give her another thought for the rest of his life, except to remind himself of what a fool he had been? Because he loved her God he loved her he loved her so goddamned much he wanted to die.

He would have given anything to be freed from his train of thoughts: it was all a lie, she had never loved him, she had planned it from the beginning, she was laughing at him even now. In passing he had even entertained the wild fantasy of killing himself. A man like him, with such a weakness for undesirable mates, should give up and let the rest of the world go about the obviously superior business of lying and cheating and screwing and leaving. Apparently, the romantic was a dying breed. Survival of the fittest.

Of course, Ethan knew he would never kill himself. For one thing, the subject of suicide was one that he associated with June. It seemed like a Summer family thing to do. Besides that, after giving it some thought, he decided that it was too ridiculous. The most efficient and immediate means of circumventing his pathetic donation to the world's gene pool would be to hang himself. Right here, right now, with a belt over the Tequila Bar. The cockroaches would love it. The problem with that method, however, was Ethan's image of his own dangling body. The last thing he wanted from death was for it to attest to what he had been his entire life: a puppet that twitched and dangled and was easily manipulated.

It seemed to Ethan that the best revenge would be to live and learn. Eventually, perhaps, he could prove that he was not blind and not stupid. If he steeled himself, he was sure that he could get over his susceptibility to love. All these years he had been studying politics and sociology, and yet he knew nothing about people. Of what, exactly, was he a master? Of what importance was his doctorate if he was too naive to know when he was being used? He had called June a monster, but now he felt he had been mistaken. Nevena had been just as deceitful as June. Perhaps he was the monster. Perhaps he was the one who was defective without knowing it. Certainly there was nothing advantageous to this particular mutation. The capacity for caring was nothing more than the capacity to be hurt.

Lying on the brown quilt in his brown room, Ethan abused himself for studying all the wrong subjects. He knew now that what he needed was to be a student of life. In the past, he had left many things behind, and this year would be one of them. For a while at least, he was determined to forget his doctorate degree, the job waiting for him, his wife, and his lover.

Ethan got up and went to the bathroom. He cupped the rusty water from the sink in his hands and then splashed it against his face. He felt awake. Ready to take on the task of learning a new lesson. Nevena had gone to New York and as his first assignment he would force himself to go in the opposite direction. Part of him wanted to track her down and search for answers, but he killed it. He would be graded on indifference. Passing required a heart as gray and ugly as the bricks of which her city was built. Nevena had gone west and Ethan would not follow. In the morning he would catch a bus, leaving no word for June, his parents, his school, or his prospective employer. He would go east, and start in the city where he had meant to spend a lover's vacation. There he would be alone. Lesson one: feel no affection for places, no nostalgia for unfinished plans. In the morning he would leave to immerse himself in the anonymity of Istanbul.

THE MORNING OF THE long-awaited day, Nevena rose early. She washed her best outfit and undergarments and hung them out to dry on the roof. Alone, she drank a coffee at a cafe and daydreamed about making love to Ethan in a big, beautiful bed that night. On the way back to the pension, she stopped and splurged on some henna shampoo and hibiscus-scented body lotion. Before putting on her freshly laundered clothes, she showered, combed the henna through her hair, and moisturized her skin while it was still damp. Then she stood in front of the mirror and smiled. The sun was coming through the window, and it brought out the auburn glow from the henna. Her skin was soft and radiant. She looked like what she was: a beautiful young woman anticipating her lover.

She and Georgi had agreed that she would go to meet Ethan alone and explain everything that had happened. They would spend the night together, and the next day they would come for Georgi and discuss the future. As Nevena picked up her bag to leave, Georgi looked up from the book he was reading. "Have a nice time."

Nevena knew that her brother did not trust Ethan as she did. Even after Ethan's generosity and help, Georgi could not bring himself to approve of his sister's situation with a married man, a fickle American, and she was grateful for his effort. "Thank you. Jouro—have some faith."

AS NEVENA WALKED TOWARD the Four Seasons hotel in Istanbul looking for Ethan, Damyan was walking up the stairs of her old apartment building in Sofia, looking for her. His chin was glistening and orange from the kebapche sausage on stale bread that he had choked down moments before. He wanted a cigarette, but had decided to put it off until after he had dealt with the stripper's sweet and seemly older sister. He checked his watch. She might not be home, but that was no problem. He'd just let himself in, sit down, and fantasize about her arrival. If she didn't have any information or money, Chavdar had told him to just kill her.

Damyan reached the top landing and knocked loudly on Nevena's door. He waited a few minutes before picking the lock. There was a dirty dish on the coffee table. Someone had eaten a salad a short time before, and there was a pair of women's underwear hanging out to dry on the laundry line. They were still damp. They looked far too big and frumpy for the bony girl he remembered, but some girls just didn't know shit about lingerie.

Satisfied that she had not fled, Damyan went to the refrigerator. What luck . . . inside was a cold bottle of rakia and some lemon soda. He poured himself a shot. Then he walked around the apartment, looking for any signs of new wealth that would indicate that Nevena had profited from her sister's theft. It didn't take him long to case the entire place. It was virtually empty, except for a few ugly dresses in the closet, some old clothes in the drawers of the dresser, and a pile of tattered books on the shelf.

Damyan switched on the junky portable radio on the table next to the couch, turned it down very low, and sat down. He leaned his heavy head back and allowed it to rest on the back of the couch, so that he was staring at the ceiling. He imagined what a rush he would get when he heard her footsteps on the stairs, and the sound of her key sliding into the broken lock. By the time she knew what was going on, he would have yanked her from the hallway into the apartment.

Damyan shifted in the cushions, easing into a more comfortable position. He took the gun from his waistband and placed it on the pillow beside him. After a few tedious minutes of staring around at the dismal apartment, he began to hum along with the radio. He sighed, scratched himself, and checked his watch. Finally he slipped his hand inside the waist of his Adidas sweatpants. The girl was so little and scared with such big eyes. He bet she would cry and beg. He bet she would run and whimper and cower in the corner. His hand began to move inside his sweats, passing the time until the girl got what she had coming. He smiled at this thought, and his breath came faster. He closed his eyes.

Suddenly the front door banged inward, and Damyan's squinted eyes flew open. Filling the warped rectangle of a doorway was a sixty-five-year-old overweight baba in a baggy black dress with a ripped hem, carrying a container of yogurt. She stared at the mutra in sweatpants and gold jewelry masturbating on her couch, screamed, and dropped the yogurt. The plastic container exploded on the floor beneath her, sending milky white liquid splashing all over her bow-legged blue-veined legs.

Damyan pulled his hand out of his pants and fumbled for the gun to shut up the shrieking baba with her crazy purple hair and orange lipstick. Before he could close his hand around the weapon, the wild-eyed woman had already pulled her own handgun from her dirty white plastic purse. She aimed, took a quick breath, and fired a shot into his heart.

Damyan uttered a low *oooof.* He stood, clutching his chest, and took a few shuffling steps to the side. He swayed and flopped over the side of the couch. After teetering for a moment, he landed on the floor with a clunk that shook the entire apartment.

The baba stood over him, enormous breasts swinging, the runs in her recycled panty hose starting up her heavy legs from his eye level. She pointed the gun downward and fired again, using both hands. After the recoil, she stepped back and stared at the body—at the twitching fingers and convulsing leg. She waited a second, wild eyes blinking. Then she screamed again, swung her leg back, and kicked him in the gut with her dirty boot. The ripped sole flapped as she launched into him again and again. Blood leaked from his chest and along with the yogurt, trickled into the pattern of the dusty carpet. The landlady's slip sagged and shredded and her old heart sped but she kept kicking, shouting "stupid mutra" with each satisfying thud.

W*ITH HER SMALL PACK* slung over her shoulder, Nevena walked the several city blocks that separated her humble pension from the sprawling and sophisticated Four Seasons. She was intimidated as she passed through the garden to the revolving glass front doors. Upon entering, a bellboy moved to take her bag, and Nevena jumped. She snatched it back from him and then realized that he was only doing his job. Embarrassed, she walked away with her arms crossed defensively across her chest, and looked around for the front desk.

An elegant Turkish woman with shiny black hair in a chignon was working at a computer under the sign marked Reception. Even though her own clothes were clean, Nevena wished that her blue dress had not faded so much, and that her black shoes were not so scuffed and worn. Suddenly she felt self-conscious about her hair, and she twisted all its gleaming red highlights back into a knot. After a slight hesitation, she approached the desk. The woman looked up. "Iyi gunlair!" she said brightly.

"I don't speak Turkish." Nevena's voice was soft and apologetic.

"I speak English," the woman answered, spreading her perfectly lipsticked mouth into a welcoming smile. "What can I do for you?"

"I am checking in."

The woman turned to the computer and poised her hands over the keys. Her nail polish matched her lipstick. "You do have a reservation? We haven't a single vacancy."

"My fiancé made the reservation. His name is Ethan Carver. Has he arrived?"

"I don't think so," the woman said, tapping on the keys. Her gold earrings jiggled as she typed. "No . . . no."

"What do you mean, no? No, he hasn't arrived?"

"No, I don't see a reservation under that name."

Nevena swallowed and tried to think. She scrambled through her pockets and drew out the paper where she had written down the information. "Is this the Four Seasons?"

The woman looked at her strangely. "Of course."

"But you see, znam, znam che . . ." In her panic, Nevena was stumbling and switching back and forth between English and Bulgarian. "Izviniavaite! Iskam da kazha . . . I know this is the hotel. Sigurna sum. I know this is the date. I checked many times." She held up the paper with the scribbled note. "Vizhte. Tuk pishe Four Seasons, nali? Please, molya vi se, I know this—"

"It is all right, miss. It's all right." The woman cocked her head to one side sympathetically. The poor girl in front of her was literally shaking. "Perhaps there is a misunderstanding. Wait here."

On towering navy blue heels that matched her crisp suit, the woman strode over to another office. Through a glass window, Nevena could see her bent over a different computer.

After a few minutes, the woman began walking back, and Nevena felt the hairs rise on her arms. Her stomach clenched. The woman was smiling but Nevena was not comforted. "Yes, miss. We do have a record of that reservation."

"Oh!" Nevena let out a breath and slumped against the desk.

"Yes, but it has been canceled."

"I'm sorry?"

"Mr. Carver called to cancel that reservation."

"I'm sorry?"

"Apparently you and your fiancé will be staying elsewhere in Istanbul."

"I don't understand," said Nevena.

The woman pressed her lips together and then said very slowly, "The reservation was canceled, miss."

"But Ethan wouldn't do that."

"I am afraid he did. We had his credit card number for down payment, and he confirmed it with us when he canceled. Per policy."

"Is there a message for me?"

"No message."

"He is not coming then?" Nevena asked, turning away and speaking to no one in particular. She reached out to steady herself on the desk.

"It is a misunderstanding, miss, not the end of the world."

"Nishto ne znaesh," said Nevena flatly. *You know nothing.*

It is the end. She walked away from the reception desk toward the lobby, where she slumped on a couch facing the front door. Her bag dropped to the floor, and she left the strap sprawling across the carpet. For several hours she sat there like that, with her eyes fixed on the revolving doors as they spun inward and outward, inward and outward. Her lids drifted halfway shut but still she watched, hoping against hope that he would appear suddenly in front of her eyes, smiling and holding out his arms. As time ticked by, she began to feel as if she were waiting for a vision of a saint. It was then that she knew. "It's true. It's over."

He had gone home to the United States, and driven his pretty car up the shore to his family's home, where his perfect mother with the perfect telephone-answering-machine voice lived, and realized that he had been living a lie. The worst had happened. Ethan had gone home and decided not to return. Nevena had always dreaded this—after every fight, and with every attack of insecurity. What if he were to go back and find that the easiest way of getting rid of his relationship with a hot-tempered Bulgarian maid was just never to return?

Ethan had arrived in Sofia as a married man. Nevena had eased his pain and lust when he and his wife parted. Perhaps he really had thought he wanted her forever. Perhaps when he was in Bulgaria, surrounded by poverty, he had forgotten how good his life had been before. Now he was a doctor, and he had always been the son of a gentile, wealthy family. Ethan had gone home, and it had reminded him who he was. He was not the husband of an uneducated Bulgarian maid. That this would happen—this had been Nevena's secret fear. A lifetime of victimization, low self-esteem, and feelings of national inferiority could not be erased by nine months of flattery and attention. He had gone back to his world, and she had just left hers. This was her reality, this was her life. She was destined to be abandoned, always. That was what had been written in the cards for all Bulgarians. The people of her country knew that all hope would lead to disappointment. All happiness would lead to loss. There was nothing to be done about it.

Nevena's revelation coincided with the manager's approach to ask her what business she had slouching on a divan in the lobby of the most expensive hotel in Istanbul. Before the manager had a chance to launch into his interrogation, Nevena blinked, stood up, and reached down for her bag. She looked around at the grandeur of the vaulted lobby: first the lush flowers, then the stone fountain, and finally the many gilded mirrors in which she saw repeated reflections of a shabbily dressed servant-girl. There were more images than in Roxanne's walk-in closet, and they were all of a poor, lower-class, dirty, Turkish whore.

The expression on Nevena's face stopped the manager from speaking. Instead he looked down and cleared his throat. Nevena straightened her back, lifted her chin, and hoisted her bag up onto her shoulder. "Thank you," she said. "I am going now. Don't worry about me. I am gone."

32

Subject: Thanks Dad
Date: Mon, 30 June 1997 22:41:23 -0400 (EDT)
From: June <jcarver@sof.cit>
To: Dad <Summer2@ncal.tech>

Hi dad. Thank you for your last message. I want you to
know, honestly, that I am fine. I wasn't for a while, but I
am better. I just realized that I am free to do whatever I
want. I can go back to school to study Slavic languages or
psychology or I can apply to the Peace Corps or I can come
home and work with Lilly or I can go to Moscow and write a
new screenplay or I can go back to crewing on films, but in
Europe, or I can even stay here and work at this Bulgarian
American organization called Say No to the Fear which is
fighting the Mafia and human trafficking and investigating
ethnic cleansing crimes. They're making a documentary, and
have a newspaper, and are organizing a big film festival
right now. They could use me, and I need this. I am coming
back here for a while after visiting James. It's okay. I'm
happy, dad.

Much love,

June

*B*Y THE END OF JUNE, everyone was alone and the world had been turned upside down. The United States had sent soldiers to Bosnia and Serbia again, after the most recent Western news broadcast filled with images of ruined towns, mass graves, and violated women and children. Rumors were spreading about something horrible and unimaginable under way in Kosovo, three hundred kilometers from the Bulgarian border. Americans were being airlifted out of Albania in military helicopters. They were flown directly to Sofia, the closest sanctuary of relative security in the Balkans. Bulgaria . . . a place of refuge. The idea was enough to make anyone who knew better laugh—or cry.

THE RAINY SEASON had descended on Sofia with torrents, and Roxanne had recently stopped leaving her house. Part of the reason she was alone inside was that June had not been returning her calls. She knew that June disapproved of what she had done, rather than thanking her as she had hoped. It seemed Roxanne had lost her only friend. She had not hired a new housekeeper and the place was in shambles. Roxanne even missed Nevena; not the cleanliness, but rather the girl's quiet way of walking around the house, her whispered words of affection to the fat Persian cat, and her habit of turning all the radios in the house to a station that played Rhodope folk music. Ashtrays overflowed, empty vodka bottles were lined up by the door, and the furniture was damp because the windows had been left open during the storms. Everything was neglected.

Upstairs, Roxanne sat alone on her bed with an array of photos spread out around her. She wore a filmy negligee. In the gray light from the storm outside she smoked and fingered her photos as she hummed along with the radio. It was a lonely sound.

The photos formed a quilt of tragedy across her bed. There she was, in the arms of a handsome Asian man, much younger than she, standing before a backdrop of lush green mountains. And there, in that one, the young man was kissing her and bending her backward. She was laughing and her hair was hanging down in a beautiful black mass. She looked happy, like a different person.

So she had lied to June and said that her second husband, Bob, had killed himself over the loss of his young Thai wife. So what if she had been the stupid one, who left Bob for a twenty-eight-year-old with white teeth against brown skin and a laugh that made her feel ten years younger? So what if she had married him and brought him home to New Orleans only to have him disappear six months later? What did it really matter that she was the one who had tried to kill herself, and that she was the one who had spent the rest of her life broken-hearted, not Bob? The truth was it didn't make much difference. Roxanne held the photo of her young boyfriend against her silk-covered bosom, and the sound of her sobs was lost in the pounding of the rain. She had tried to stop it from happening again, but it was a tragedy anyway. After everything, it was the same story. More or less.

THE STORM THAT POUNDED against Roxanne's window also relentlessly attacked the white-capped waves of the coast. From Bulgaria's Black Sea, the contaminated waters touched those of the Bosporus Strait and flowed toward the Aegean, where they mingled in the turquoise Greek sea that had seemed so bloody in June's dreams. These same waters were connected to the Tyrrhenian and Ionian seas, spreading west to the Mediterranean. It was all connected. Flow was inevitable and pollution spread and dispersed. Eventually, these smaller bodies would join the oceans, and vice versa. Eventually, the same slick, oily water that pooled underneath the rotting rafters of the Santa Monica pier in Los Angeles would find its way to the eastern edge of the States, and surround the island of Manhattan.

THE DAY THAT Boryana arrived in New York had started out as the happiest of her life. She thought little of what she was leaving behind, but looked forward to the beginning of a bright, new, rich life. She disembarked the plane at John F. Kennedy International and was surprised to find herself inside a tube-shaped tunnel rather than descending a portable staircase to the tarmac. She had imagined stepping out of the huge silver plane into the bright sun and the breeze off the Atlantic Ocean, with glittering skyscrapers on the horizon. Inside the tunnel, she felt immediately claustrophobic, and held her duffel bag close against her body. The sound of foreign languages greeted her as she entered the airport. Not just English, but French, Spanish, Italian,

Chinese, Japanese, Spanish, and Russian. Recorded instructions boomed throughout the immense building in a jumble of incomprehensible words.

Walking toward passport control and customs, the underarms of Boryana's silk blouse were drenched. She tried to ignore it. Nevena had instructed her to draw no unnecessary attention. Boryana was to act normal and smile. Behave calmly and rationally. Meet people's eyes and do not stare at the floor. Display composure and confidence.

Immigration control stamped her passport after a cursory glance at her visa, and Boryana was once again able to breathe normally. Now, she had only to pass through customs with her bag stuffed with cash, and she would be free. After that, everything would be easy.

"Do you have anything to declare?" asked an overweight black woman in a monotone. The woman didn't even look at Boryana when she posed the question. Her eyes were on the wall clock in the corner.

"No," answered Boryana.

"Welcome to America."

"Thank you," Boryana answered, strangely touched. They welcome me. They are glad I am here. Elated, she walked out of the airport to look for a taxi. She knew vaguely where she wanted to go. Downtown. She had made no preparations, knew not one single person, and didn't have the name of a hotel. None of this mattered. Boryana had money.

The street was utter chaos. Boryana looked around in confusion. She put a hand out and wiggled her fingers at the taxis whizzing by. No response. She stepped out into the street and smiled imploringly. Still no response. She put on fresh lipstick and glanced around at the pushy people with indignation.

"Just arrive?"

Boryana turned to look at the man who had spoken. He had an accent, but Boryana couldn't tell. Dressed in a white suit, black shirt, black belt, and shiny black shoes, he looked like an actor from a 1970s sitcom. His polyester button-down shirt was open halfway, and he wore several heavy gold chains as well as a thick gold watch. Massive green-tinted sunglasses covered most of his face, so that his most prominent feature was a neatly trimmed thick brown mustache. "I said, you just arrive? You speak English?"

"Yes," answered Boryana. "And yes, I just arrive."

"I was here picking up a friend, but he missed his flight. You need a ride?"

Boryana glanced back at the intimidating crowd in line for taxis.

"I'm going downtown. I am leaving now. You want a ride or not?"

Parked in a loading zone was an old, white Chrysler LeBaron convertible with plush black seat covers. It was dented and the side molding had been ripped off, but Boryana saw only a Western sports car with no top. It would be like a dream, driving away from the airport toward downtown in a white convertible. Something out of a magazine or a movie. She looked back up at the man. Now he was wiping some sweat off his forehead and shifting back and forth. "What's the problem? You turning down a free ride? Fine. Take a taxi. Fifty bucks to downtown. I'm just being a gentleman, okay?"

"Yes," she said finally.

"Fine, whatever. Where you going? Where do I let you off?"

Boryana climbed into the passenger seat and leaned back into the plush seat cover. Her forehead wrinkled in thought.

"You got no place to stay? Your first time in America?"

She looked down and began to finger her new bracelet from duty-free. She was not feeling as confident as before. "I'm going to a nice hotel."

"I show you a place to stay, okay? Lots of nice girls there, okay? No problem?"

"It's a hotel? You know a nice hotel for me?"

"It's a kind of hotel. Sure it's nice for you. Sure. You'll like it. No problem. Lots of nice girls there. You are new in the country, you need friends. I'm a good person to know."

He smiled, and she could see that one of his teeth had been capped in gold. He had money, and he liked her, and she'd only been in New York five minutes. Boryana couldn't believe her good fortune. Anything was possible.

THERE HADN'T BEEN much hair on Stan's head to start with, but now there was even less. He was absolutely diminished. He'd lost almost ten pounds, partly from stress and partly from the prison diet of tripe soup and old toast. Never in his wildest dreams would he have thought that he would spend so much time in a back-country Bulgarian jail, stuck in a cell with a glue-addict car thief from Stara Zagora who was rarely conscious. He'd had no books, no papers, no television, and no cards. It didn't matter actually, because the glue addict had broken Stan's glasses (in an attempt to break his nose) the second day of their cohabitation. There had been nothing to do in that filthy jail cell but sit on his cot and dream of home. Des Moines—safe, normal, fair, sane Des Moines. When he was finally released, Stan was a shadow of his former self, obsessed with home. A national chauvinist. A xenophobic American patriot.

Back in Sofia, it took Stan a few days to deal with his rapidly accumulating legal problems. Then he set out to find Ethan in order to sort out the whole Nevena mess. Now, he considered it more of a mess than ever. Stan had practically forgotten that he had been speeding and singing country tunes at the top of his lungs when he'd been pulled over. Now he considered the "escape mission" to be the cause of his arrest and all his subsequent misery. Because of that insane plan to save Ethan's scrawny girlfriend, he'd been put in jail, he was going to trial, and he was going to lose his job. Exposing the fact that he had, in addition to falsifying taxes and dealing in stolen property, also helped a Bulgarian to illegally immigrate to Turkey, was not likely to bode well for his future as an attorney-at-law.

Stan's plan was to find Ethan, give him the lowdown, and swear him to secrecy. Unfortunately, Ethan was nowhere to be found. Stan made all the appropriate phone calls: to June, to the Carvers in Palo Alto, to Ethan's prospective employer in Istanbul. He told no one why he was trying to track down Ethan, because the explanation was, after all, about a clandestine plot with coconspirators and a variety of unimaginably horrible repercussions. No one knew where Ethan had gone, and no one knew when he would be coming back.

EVEN ETHAN HIMSELF didn't know where he was headed, or if and when he would come home. He didn't know and he didn't care. Taksim Square was the newer and more cosmopolitan part of Istanbul, and it was there that Ethan had found a hostel. He had stayed in Sultanamhet with June and had planned to stay there with Nevena, so it no longer suited him. He was happy in Taksim, where the headbanger bars were filled with students dressed in black, and drug addicts nodded out in the corners of the cafes. Ethan had become comfortable at one particular place just off the main drag. It had low tables, cushion-covered stools, only beer and raki, and like the Serdika hotel, plenty of cockroaches on the floor, walls, and tables.

Ethan sat there by himself, flipping through a small pile of travel books. India would be good, and so would Southeast Asia. The truth was he didn't care where he went. Wherever he traveled, he'd find a bar like this, sit down for a drink, and think about Nevena. Curse her. Attempt to hate her. And when it got late and he could no longer have any more drinks, he would stumble home thinking how stupid he was to have loved her; to love her still. That was what he had done since arriving in Istanbul. So far he had proved to be a poor student of life.

He put down his book, lighted a Turkish cigarette, and looked out the window. Across the street he could see a barber giving a haircut through the smudged window of his shop, and next door, an unidentifiable animal carcass hanging from a hook in the ceiling of a butcher store. Gypsy girls ran up and down the street selling packages of Kleenex, and trendy-looking girls in bell-bottoms walked arm in arm toward the bars in the back streets.

There, immersed in the crowd, was the small, retreating figure of a young woman who looked out of place among the rest. Ethan dragged on his cigarette and watched as the girl walked slowly away, down the busy street. She held her body something like Nevena, with her head up and her thin shoulders pulled back. Even the girl's blue dress and clunky shoes looked like something Nevena would wear. The only difference, perhaps, was the reddish, henna color of this girl's hair, and the fact that though her upper body was erect, her legs seemed to drag, as if she had no energy to go where she was headed. Ethan fought the urge to run after the girl and spin her around just to be sure, just for his peace of mind. He didn't. The girl disappeared down the street, lost forever, and Ethan felt only the slightest twinge of disappointment. He was learning.

LIKE HIS PREDECESSORS, Chavdar's disappearance made the papers. Not a big spread, but a small story. It said nothing about him as a man, except that he had so many enemies everywhere and so many reasons to flee the country, that his disappearance might never be solved. The article hinted that Chavdar would inevitably be discovered; not in Prague or Geneva, but rather lying in a shallow grave on the mountain. June read it at her desk in her new office, where she was working for local wages on the documentary. She had a pile of papers to sift through. In addition to cowriting the documentary, she was in charge of organizing a Central and Eastern European film festival that would attempt to heighten awareness of young former Block talent, as well as deglamorize the Mafia in developing countries. She was tired and over-worked and it felt good.

On the other side of the room, a girl named Gergana was cutting footage from the riots. Instead of working, June read the newspaper article over and over again, somehow expecting it to say more each time.

Kyril had refused to tell June what had happened up on the mountain the day they arranged for Chavdar's kidnapping. He said only that it was better for her not to know. June had been told that Chavdar would be threatened into confessing, and then arrested, but clearly that plan had failed. June didn't know what was worse: imagining Chavdar on his knees in the mud awaiting execution, or him breaking free and running through the woods at top speed to safety. She could easily picture him escaping first from a captor and then from the country. He might now be roaming the world in dark sunglasses and tailored suits. With a shiver of fear, she imagined him in Paris or Prague or Budapest, dining at the best restaurants, attending concerts, and bedding beautiful women. Perhaps he really would become a film producer. Maybe he really could re-create himself and start over—leaving behind the ruins of the darkest corner of Europe in search of adventure in the bigger, brighter cities of the world. Dead? June didn't think so, and had decided that she did not want to know. If anyone could get away with it, he could. Chavdar was a sur-vivor. She just hoped he would not come looking for her.

June looked out her window. Soon she would be back in America for a visit—but the thought of not returning was impossible. There were things to be done.

Down below, on the street, some kids were kicking a ball around. Every few seconds, the ball slammed into a car and an alarm would sound. Just as one wailing alarm died, another would go off. She sighed and bit on her pen-cil. Chavdar's disappearance had brought back memories of other disappear-ances . . . Claire, Raina, even Ethan. These people were gone, vanished, but they remained in her thoughts. It seemed every day her teacher Raina was be-side her, holding her arm, whispering with cigarette breath into June's ear: "When someone close to you goes, my dear, it is inevitable that you will change."

Subject: VERY IMPORTANT—URGENT NEWS
Date: Mon, 1 Dec 1997 05:43 -0400
From: June Summer <jcarver@sof.cit>
To: Ethan Carver <ecarver@smnet.com>

Dear Ethan,

I called your parents today and they said that you had finally surfaced and actually have an email address. What is life like in Djibouti? I hate to admit that I have never heard of it, but if you are there I am sure it must be exciting. I miss you and wish, after all this time, that we could be friends. Maybe what I have to tell you will make a difference.

Nevena's brother Georgi is here in Sofia after a long stay in Istanbul. I ran into him last week at a fund-raiser for the Center for the Study of Democracy. (My organization is now raising money for Kosovo—it's starting to look like the worst situation yet.) Ethan, there is something important you need to know. Nevena is in Istanbul. She is working there as a waitress. Georgi has her address and you can reach him at the Center. Apparently there was a huge misunderstanding and she never went to the States. It was all a mistake. I am not the right person to explain to you what happened, but let me just say that you should find her. You must find her. She loves you, Ethan. It was real.

I love you as well. Still. Please just understand that this is painful for me, and yet it is the one last, good thing I can do for you out of my love.

June

p.s. Laney has rubbed off on me and here I go sending you quotes. But this one I especially like.

"If this life be not a real fight, in which something is eternally gained for the universe by success, it is no better than a game of private theatricals from which one may withdraw at will."—William James

MY DEEPEST GRATITUDE TO . . .

My editor, Hillery Borton, and agent, Douglas Stewart, for their friendship, advice, expertise, and support, but most important, for believing.

The people of Penguin Putnam who became my closest confidants or respected mentors: Marilyn Ducksworth, Mih-Ho Cha, Michael Barson, Ken Siman, Robin Caine, Julia Fleischaker, Peter Hynes, and Wendy Patin.

The coconspirators in the Balkan adventure: Darren Fitzgerald, the love of my life who held my hand through the beginning; Amy Gorin and Lindsay Moran, the two most intelligent and inspiring women ever to dance on all the tabletops of Sofia and whose friendship I value more than words can express; Kamen Velkovsky for his steadfast loyalty and critiques; Bea and Kras Gorin, Chip Gulick, Steve Angel, Anthony Zarr, Loreen Vonnegut, Andrew Vonnegut, Michelle Stern, Chris Saunders, Kamen Kalev, Todor Todorov, Matthew Brunwasser, Ajani Williams, Vessela Apostolova, and Phillip Bay for bringing so many of us together at the "Balkan Summer Camp for Wayward Drifters."

My mentors: Carolyn See, Anna Roth (where would I be without you?), Lynn Roth, Nancy Sackett, and the exceptionally dedicated teachers of the Blue Valley School District in Stanley, Kansas, who told us anything was possible.

The enduring circle of support: Jennifer Niven, Martin Garner, Douglas Sadler, Bruce Mason, Shirin Ghotbi, and Gioia Parnell.

Finally, I want to thank my family: Laura, Wendy, and especially Russ—who actually read the original 750-page version and gave the story a happy ending. Mom and Dad, I am at a loss for words to describe your strength, goodness, perseverance, and influence. I could not have done any of it without you telling me my whole life to "Go for it."